# PRAISE FOR SUE MARGOLIS'S NOVELS

## BREAKFAST AT STEPHANIE'S

"With Stephanie, Margolis has produced yet another jazzy cousin to Bridget Jones." —*Publishers Weekly*

"A heartwarming, character-driven tale . . . a hilariously funny story." —*Romance Reviews Today*

"A comic, breezy winner." —*Booklist*

"Rife with female frivolity, punchy one-liners, and sex."
—*Kirkus Reviews*

## APOCALIPSTICK

"Sexy British romp . . . Margolis's characters have a candor and self-deprecation that lead to furiously funny moments. . . . A riotous, ribald escapade sure to leave readers chuckling to the very end of this saucy adventure." —*USA Today*

"Quick in pace and often very funny." —*Kirkus Reviews*

"Margolis combines lighthearted suspense with sharp English wit . . . entertaining read." —*Booklist*

# NEUROTICA

"Screamingly funny sex comedy . . . the perfect novel to take on holiday." —*USA Today*

"Cheeky comic novel—a kind of *Bridget Jones's Diary* for the matrimonial set . . . Wickedly funny." —*People* (Beach Book of the Week)

"Scenes that literally will make your chin drop with shock before you erupt with laughter . . . A fast and furiously funny read." —*Cleveland Plain Dealer*

"Taking up where *Bridget Jones's Diary* took off, this saucy British adventure redefines the lusty woman's search for erotic satisfaction. . . . Witty and sure . . . A taut and rambunctious tale exploring the perils and raptures of the pursuit of passion." —*Publishers Weekly*

"Splashy romp . . . giggles guaranteed." —*New York Daily News*

"A good book to take to the beach, *Neurotica* is fast paced and at times hilarious." —*Boston's Weekly Digest Magazine*

"This raunchy and racy British novel is great fun, and will delight fans of the television show *Absolutely Fabulous.*" —*Booklist*

# ALSO BY SUE MARGOLIS

# Original Cyn

Sue Margolis

DELTA TRADE PAPERBACKS

ORIGINAL CYN
A Delta Book/May 2005

Published by
Bantam Dell
A Division of Random House, Inc.
New York, New York

Book design by Glen Edelstein
Cover art © 2005 by Cindy Liu
Cover design by Lynn Andreozzi

Delta is a registered trademark of Random House, Inc., and
the colophon is a trademark of Random House, Inc.

Library of Congress Cataloging-in-Publication Data
Margolis, Sue.
Original Cyn/Sue Margolis
p.   cm.
ISBN 0-385-33734-5
1. Young women—Fiction.  2. Women in the advertising industry—Fiction.
3. Identity theft—Fiction.  4. Copy writers—Fiction.  5. Revenge—Fiction.
6. London (England)—Fiction.  I. Title.
PR6063.A635 O75 2005          2004056924
823/.914 22

Printed in the United States of America
Published simultaneously in Canada

10  9  8  7  6  5  4  3  2  1
BVG

This book is dedicated to the Scottish midwife who said to me, less than twelve hours after I had delivered a ten-pound baby boy:

"Och, Mrs. McGoolis, you have an enormous amount of stretch marks and flab to get rid of."

My only reply was stunned silence and a weak, apologetic smile. Twenty years later I still fantasize about how I might have handled the situation differently . . .

# Original
## Cyn

# Chapter 1

"Elizabeth Taylor died? Ah. Still, the old girl was getting a bit past it." As Cyn switched her mobile to the other ear she felt the taxi slow down and turn left. "Are you sure you're OK?" her mother asked tenderly. "I know how much she meant to you."

"I'm fine," Cyn said, rubbing at the condensation on the rain-speckled window and peering out. "I mean, it wasn't entirely unexpected."

"The vet did all he could," her mother was saying. Cyn's mind immediately conjured up a frantic scene in pet *ER*. She could hear the vet instructing everybody to "Stand clear" as he turns poor Elizabeth onto her shell and shocks her scaly chest with two tiny tortoise-sized resuscitation paddles. Half a dozen attempts later he wipes his brow and announces, "OK, I'm calling it. Time of death, ten after four." His face etched with failure, he snaps off his rubber gloves and throws them into the bin. Meanwhile, a tearful nurse sniffs and covers Elizabeth with a tiny white sheet.

"I remember the day I found her," Cyn's mother went on. "It was February 1981. The Canadian cousins were over and I'd gone to the garage to get some vol-au-vent cases out of the freezer. And there she was, hibernating inside a pile of sunlounger covers."

Elizabeth Taylor was by no means the only animal her mother, Barbara, had "rescued." In the years before and since the tortoise joined the Fishbein household, there were assorted stray cats, lost budgies and the odd hamster. There had even been an actual lame duck, which, having been attacked—probably by a fox—had somehow managed to waddle the half mile from the park pond to find sanctuary in the Fishbein kitchen. Barbara found homes for all the other animals. Even the duck was nursed back to health and eventually, with much ceremony, released "back into the wild" of the local park. She wasn't so lucky with the tortoise. Despite "tortoise found" notices stuck on virtually every lamppost in the neighborhood, nobody came to claim her. In the end the Fishbeins adopted her, but it was Cyn who loved her. It was Cyn who spoiled her with slices of tomato and painted ET Fishbein on her shell in Wite-Out, and it was Cyn who worried obsessively every winter about her not waking up from hibernation.

Back then it wasn't just tortoises and lame ducks Barbara had taken in. She also rescued people: best friends going through messy divorces came to stay for weeks on end—usually with several badly behaved, bed-wetting children. For a few years she did emergency short-term fostering for the local council. This meant that every couple of months an "at-risk" baby or toddler would be delivered by social workers and stay a few days. Barbara loved the babies as if they were her own, but they were never around long enough for Cyn or her brother, Jonny, to get jealous.

Not long after Elizabeth Taylor's arrival, the miners went on strike. Straightaway, thousands of them headed down to London for rallies and marches. Being on strike they couldn't afford accommodation. Barbara, whose father, Sid, had been a union shop steward all his working life and had raised her in the old-fashioned Labour Party tradition, which regarded the working man as nothing less than a hero, immediately phoned the Miners' Union HQ and offered to take in half a dozen. To her everlasting dismay, all the Hampstead and Highgate middle-class liberals had gotten there first and there weren't any to be had for love or money.

Sometimes when the crying babies or sleeping bags all over the living room floor got too much for Cyn's father, Mal, he would escape to his shed. Cyn would find him with his feet up on the workbench playing his John Lennon LPs or listening to the cricket on his old Roberts radio, muttering about how the house was turning into "the blinkin' *Inn of the Sixth Happiness*." But he never asked Barbara to put a stop to her rescue missions. Cyn knew that deep down he loved and admired her far too much.

Barbara's mother, Grandma Faye, had accused her of having a Mother Teresa complex. Barbara just shrugged and said, "Call it what you like. I'm just doing my small bit to make the world a better place."

Barbara was in her sixties now, and although she still took in the odd stray cat and wrote the occasional outraged letter to the *Guardian* about cuts in education and the health service, there hadn't been any friends, babies or oppressed workers needing a bed for years.

"You and your brother named her Shelley," Barbara said about the tortoise. "Then she kept getting ill. The vet brought her back from the brink so many times that Grandma Faye started calling her Elizabeth Taylor." The name stuck, despite the vet having informed Barbara on at least five occasions that Elizabeth Taylor was a boy.

Cyn carried on looking out the window, vaguely aware of her mother chortling to herself. She was pretty sure the car showroom was about half a mile farther down on the right. Her heart rate started to pick up. Her very own shiny, freshly minted, brand-spanking-new Smart Car was sitting there, waiting for her to claim it. What's more—and this was the truly amazingly fabulous bit—she was getting it for free.

Cyn was a junior copywriter at a cutting-edge and very much on the up advertising agency, Price Chandler Witty. Occasionally, companies whose accounts they handled would, after a particularly successful campaign, express additional gratitude and appreciation by offering the agency a car for an employee to have on long-term loan. The "long-term" bit was fairly ambiguous, but it pretty much meant that unless the recipient left the agency, nobody would ask for it back. The deal was that the car would carry advertising for whatever it was the donor company manufactured. Of course nobody at the agency minded, since it was generally thought that driving around advertising a sleek PalmPilot, digital camera or laptop was a pretty fair exchange for a new car.

Whenever a car came up—usually once or twice a year—the names of all the agency staff, from the directors to the cleaners, were put into a hat. The draw always took place in the function room at the Bishop's Finger across the road and afterward there would be a bit of a party. Last week there had been a couple of cars up for grabs. Although they were from different companies, both happened to be Smart Cars.

Cyn took no more than a passing interest in cars. It was partly that like many women she found the subject less than fascinating and partly that taking a proper interest would have led to yearnings, and yearnings ended up costing money. She had just bought her first flat. What with the mortgage payments and the loan on her new Ikea kitchen, she couldn't even contemplate replacing her old Peugeot. Nevertheless she adored the Smart Car. Its tiny, almost cartoonishly cute wedge shape made her laugh. She liked the way its straight back gave the impression that it was in fact the front end of a much larger, longer vehicle from which it had somehow been severed. Even though it looked like the transport of choice of a circus clown, there was no doubt that the Smart Car had style. She was aware, of course, since it was the coolest, most must-have two seater on the market, that everybody who drove one looked like a fashion victim; but that night, as she'd sat in the pub drinking with her little gang from the office, Cyn had decided that if she were ever lucky enough to own one, she would find a way to live with the shame.

Until last Friday Cyn had never won anything in her life, apart from the Yardley lavender bath soap selection box, which didn't count because she'd secured it in the school fete raffle when she was nine.

The first name out of the hat was Chelsea Roggenfelder. Chelsea was from New York and another junior copywriter at PCW. Since she had only been with the agency six months, it was spectacularly good luck. Chelsea managed to look utterly bowled over. A few meaningful looks were exchanged among PCW employees. Everybody knew she was loaded and that deep down she probably wasn't feeling much more than mild amusement. The truth was that had she the inclination, Chelsea could have afforded to go out and buy a dozen Smart Cars. Chelsea's father was Sargent Roggenfelder, the Madison Avenue tycoon who had been behind the advertising for a successful presidential campaign and several gubernatorial contests. Although she never said as much, it was perfectly clear that he paid the rent on her Sloane Street flat and had bought her the BMW Z4, the perfect zipping-down-to-the-country accessory.

Her face on full beam, Chelsea stood up and pulled at the cuffs of her exquisitely tailored black jacket. With a flick of her Nicky Clarke highlights, she sashayed over to the tiny podium where Graham Chandler, one of the CEOs, was standing at the mike waiting to present her with her car key. On her way she stopped for a few seconds to smile and wave at everybody. One of the blokes sitting next to Cyn mumbled something about Chelsea's performance reminding him of Catherine Zeta-Jones dispensing largesse at the Oscars.

The applause was trailing off when Cyn heard her mobile ringing. She rushed outside where she could hear, only to discover it was somebody flogging plastic window frames. As she walked back into the pub she was met by loud cheering. It was a few seconds before she realized it was being directed at her. She frowned and looked questioningly at one of the temps from the office, who happened to be standing next to her. "It's you! You've won the other car!"

"Geddout."

"No, really." Then she saw Graham Chandler nodding and laughing.

After Graham had kissed her on both cheeks and handed her the car key, and Natalie, one of the PAs, had come rushing up to her, thrown her arms around her and made her do that jumpy up-and-down thing like kids in the playground, she went back to her table and just sat there with a daft grin on her face, completely overwhelmed. She was suddenly aware of how good news can be as much of a shock as bad news. Chelsea, on the other hand, was swanning around doing her best to convince people how stunned and delighted she was and that she simply couldn't believe her luck. "This is just too perfect," she simpered to Cyn, at one point. "Now I can keep the Z4 for driving to the country on the weekend and use the Smart Car in the city."

"Lucky old you," Cyn said, with just a hint of sarcasm.

"Yes. Lucky old you." The slurred Welsh accent belonged to Keith Geary, another copywriter. Keith, who was lanky and awkward, with jutting-out hips and shoulder blades, had been brought up in a small mining town. He liked to think of himself as a Marxist and was forever taking the piss out of what he described as Chelsea's Saks and the City lifestyle, particularly after he'd had a few, like now. Chelsea always gave as good as she got, though. "You know, Keith," she said, making use of her elegant nose, which had been perfectly engineered for looking down, "in you, I really do see a face unclouded by thought." Her tone made Camille Paglia sound affectionate.

"And on you, Chelsea," he said, "I see a head so big that your ears have separate zip codes."

Ouch, Cyn thought, suppressing a giggle. For once Chelsea was lost for words. Her mouth opened and closed a few times, goldfish-style. Then she turned on her long, spiky-toed Kurt Geiger heels and walked away.

"That showed her," Keith snorted, digging Cyn in the ribs. Then he staggered off, back to the bar.

Chelsea had come to advertising relatively late in life. She never talked much about herself, but a couple of people had found out that after university, she'd spent ten years in L.A., trying and failing to make it as a screenwriter. Finally, she decided to make a fresh start in London. There was no doubt that she had found her niche at Price Chandler Witty. Even though this was her first job in advertising, she was creating a considerable reputation for herself among PCW's clients. When it came to thinking up advertising slogans or designing campaigns, witty, razor-sharp ideas seemed to spill out of her like jackpots from a slot machine. It was quite obvious that she had inherited her father's talent.

Chelsea refused to be intimidated by the fact that nearly all the bosses at PCW, all the people she had to pitch ideas to, were men. From the off, she had never been scared to go into meetings and argue her corner. She was highly competitive and absolutely refused to be cowed. Fear simply wasn't part of her vocabulary. "You know, Graham," she would say, insisting on pronouncing Graham like most Americans do, as Grahm, to rhyme with ham, "I think we really need to start thinking outside the box here. I mean, it seems to me that you guys just haven't considered the click-through rate on this thing. And have you calculated the cost per click? . . . I figured not. Well, I have some preliminary data here which I've printed out and would like to pass round." The way it usually worked was that everybody would sit there examining her figures and come to the conclusion that she had a point.

While she wasn't exactly easy to warm to, women forgave her because they were in awe of her New York hey-mister-don't-bullshit-me feistiness. A few women—Cyn included—made no secret of wishing they had her balls. Some of the men felt the same. Mostly though, with the exception of Messrs. Price, Chandler and Witty, from whom she commanded considerable respect, the blokes referred to Chelsea behind her back as "the Terminator."

Cyn's relationship with Chelsea hadn't gotten off to a good start. Before she was taken on by PCW, Chelsea had three interviews over a four-week period. During that time the coffee machine kept going on the blink and Cyn, along with everybody else, took her turn at doing a coffee run to the sandwich bar over the road. By pure chance, each time Chelsea arrived for an interview, Cyn was handing out cups of coffee. On the day she started work, Graham Chandler took Chelsea round the office and introduced her to everybody. "And this is Cyn, another of our junior copywriters."

"Ah, yes, I've seen you getting the coffee. Be a sweetie, would you, and fetch me a skinny cappuccino, hold the chocolate." Had Graham not introduced Cyn as another copywriter it might just have been reasonable for Chelsea to assume she was one of the office juniors, but even then, her puffed-up, snooty manner was inexcusable. What made the whole thing worse was Graham standing there and saying, "I know it's not really your job, Cyn, but maybe you wouldn't mind."

"Of course not." Cyn smiled thinly, realizing she had no option but to go and get Chelsea her coffee.

As the weeks went by, though, Chelsea's manner changed where Cyn was concerned. It never became warm, exactly, but she seemed to be making a real effort to be more friendly. Cyn put it down to guilt over the coffee incident. Soon Chelsea was inviting her out to lunch, and Cyn decided it would be churlish to refuse. She had even got round to apologizing over the coffee incident, claiming she didn't realize at the time that Cyn was a fellow creative. "You know, I'm perfectly aware of how the men at PCW see me," she said on one occasion, referring to the "Terminator" epithet, "but the fact remains that women still aren't getting the opportunities they deserve in this business. The only way for us to push through the glass ceiling is to fight. You are clever and talented, Cyn. Women like us need to stick together—to keep faith with the sisterhood. Say, if you ever want to brainstorm some ideas with me or have me give you my opinion on something, feel free."

"That's so kind of you," Cyn said. "I really appreciate that. And if you have any thoughts or ideas you'd like my opinion on, don't hesitate to come to me."

"Oh, how absolutely darling of you," Chelsea simpered, smiling at Cyn over the slitty black-framed glasses she'd taken to wearing. Cyn couldn't work out why she felt as if she'd just offered Nancy Reagan a joint.

Then a few weeks ago, Chelsea had said something to Cyn that made her feel even more uncomfortable and took her right back to the coffee episode. It was the day all three agency directors were taking Cyn out to lunch to say thank you for the work she had done helping secure a big shampoo account. Most people in the office had patted her on the back and said well done. Chelsea, on the other hand, had come striding over, all radiant smiles, her arms wide open. She wrapped Cyn in a huge bear hug and kissed her on both cheeks. The expression on her face seemed to convey genuine delight. "Well done, *you*," she cooed. Cyn returned the smile and thanked her, but there was something about Chelsea's emphasis on the word *you* that had felt not so much congratulatory as patronizing and condescending. It was as if Cyn was the class dunce, who had despite all the odds somehow managed to win a house point.

Later on, when she thought about it, Cyn told herself she was just being ridiculously oversensitive. When did she become so paranoid that she was starting to judge people purely on the emphasis they put on one word?

On the other hand, Cyn was no fool and she knew there was a strong likelihood that Chelsea was being bitchy because she saw her as a rival. One of the senior copywriters was leaving PCW and it was common knowledge that Cyn and Chelsea were both being considered for the job. Normally the agency wouldn't have considered promoting somebody who had been there for as short a time as Chelsea, but since she was so talented the directors knew that if they didn't promote her, they risked losing her. Cyn knew she wasn't without talent—she'd won the Aqua Elite shampoo account after all—but since then, her professional life seemed to have taken a bit of a downturn.

First there was the stupid joke she'd made to Keith Geary. He'd been taking a conference call with a Japanese electronics company launching some new, very powerful loudspeakers, and she was sitting in. "Keith," she giggled at one point, "tell them they could always say 'The XL2000 speakers. The loudest you've ever heard. From the people who brought you

Pearl Harbor.'" Of course they were on speakerphone and the Japanese heard everything. PCW lost the account.

Then a few weeks ago she came up with a pretty innocuous, fairly average slogan to promote Secure roll-on deodorant: "No more embarrassing underarm stains." How was she supposed to know the deodorant people were going to market it in Nigeria where the slogan translated in one of the local languages as "Secure roll on—no more pregnant tadpoles in your armpit"?

In both cases, Graham Chandler had been gracious enough to see the funny side and told her not to worry, but she could tell he was cross, particularly about losing the Japanese account.

There was no doubt in her mind that Chelsea would get the senior copywriter job. Surely Chelsea knew that, too. How could she not?

"Anyway, I dug a hole and buried her in the garden."

"Who?" Cyn said, suddenly coming back to earth.

"Elizabeth Taylor," her mother said. "You OK? You sound like you're miles away."

"Sorry. Look, Mum, I don't mean to be rude, but I have to go. I'm almost at the car showroom. I'm picking up my new car."

"Oh, yes, the Smart Car. Funny-looking thing, if you ask me. Shame they didn't offer you a nice Renault Clio or a Fiesta. So much prettier."

Deciding she wasn't about to be addressed on style by a woman whose kitchen possessed an Alpine-style breakfast nook, Cyn said, "Look, I'll phone you later when I've got more time to chat. Love you. Say hi to Dad for me." Cyn flipped her phone shut just as the taxi was pulling up outside the car showroom. Casting thoughts of Elizabeth Taylor from her mind, she concentrated on the utter joy she was going to feel in a few minutes as she climbed into her new car and slid the key into the ignition.

Inside, the showroom smelled of rubber, TurtleWax and new car interior. She breathed in. She decided the smell was right up there with her other nonbottled favorites: her mum's roast chicken, coal smoke and skin of bloke on a bitterly cold day. Of course the bloke had to be one she was seeing rather than blokes in general. Cyn looked down at her watch. It was ten past six. She and Chelsea had arranged to meet at the showroom at six. Chelsea had suggested a few days ago that it would be "such fun" for them to pick up their cars together. "Then we can go off and celebrate with champagne." Although Cyn was aware that Chelsea probably felt threatened by her, the champagne gesture suggested she had a warmer side and that it would be a mistake to write her off.

Cyn glanced around the showroom. Behind the reception desk a woman with a caramel tan and matching hair was on the phone. At the back, a lad was fixing a plastic price sticker across a car windscreen. There was no sign of Chelsea, who had the day off work and was coming from home. Cyn was wondering what was holding her up when a stout, fifty-something chap—clearly one of the car salesmen judging by the gray-green double-breasted suit and chunky gold bracelet—came ambling toward her, smiling a greeting. Cyn explained that she was here to pick up her new Smart Car.

"Ah, Miss Fishbone. I've been expecting you."

"Actually, it's bine not bone."

"Miss Bine."

"No. Fishbein. As opposed to Fishbone."

"Oh, right. Gotcha. So, you're the lucky lady who's won the Smart Car. You'll love the power steering. It's wonderful for all you girlies who need a space the size of Wembley Stadium to park in."

She smiled. He seemed harmless enough. She decided not to take offense. "I'm meeting my friend here." She explained about Chelsea winning the other car.

"Oh, yes, Miss Romanfelter."

"That's Roggenfelder."

"Really? I was sure it was Romanfelter. Anyway, she collected hers last night."

Cyn frowned. "Are you sure? She didn't say anything to me." It occurred to Cyn that Chelsea had probably left a message on her answer machine. She'd been out until late last night and had forgotten to check her messages this morning. "Oh, OK," she shrugged. "No problem."

"Your car's over there," he said, nodding toward the back of the showroom. They weaved their way past a row of gleaming, new and very long Mercedes. As they reached the minuscule Smart Car, she noticed how the corners of the narrow metal grill under the hood turned up in a half smile. Ooh, it was Tiffany blue. Fab. She stood there feeling like all her birthdays had come at once. She ran her hand over the smooth, shiny hood.

"Now, you know about the corporate advertising on the side?" the salesman asked her. Cyn nodded. Chelsea had told her that both cars had come from drug companies. Since she didn't handle their accounts, Cyn couldn't remember the names. "Well, I have to hand it to you," the salesman chuckled, "you've certainly got balls, if you take my meaning."

"Don't see why." Cyn shrugged, still stroking the hood and making no effort to walk around to the side of the car to look at the ad. "God, it's gorgeous. Really gorgeous. So, can I drive it off?"

"Absolutely. She's all yours." He said he would get one of the lads to move the car onto the forecourt.

It was only then, as she moved round to the side of her precious Smart Car, that she saw it. Shock seemed to render her temporarily dyslexic and it took a few moments for the three syllables to register simultaneously on her brain. First she read *sol*. That was Spanish for sun, wasn't it? Hmm, maybe she'd gotten it all wrong. She hadn't been listening that carefully when Chelsea told her who was giving them the cars. Perhaps this one had come from a company that made fruit juice. The next thing to hit her was the image of the giant tube. Toothpaste? Sunny, fruity toothpaste? Then she saw it. The twelve-inch-high lettering seemed to flash at her in brilliant neon: *Anus*. Her stomach flipped and she felt sick. She stepped back and read the words in front of her: "Anusol—shrinks piles, soothes itching." Panic rose up inside her, and although she knew it was utterly stupid and futile, she couldn't prevent herself rubbing at the words to see if they would come off.

"What the . . . ? I can't. I mean people will see and . . ."

"Bloody hell, you didn't know, did you?" the salesman said, barely concealing his amusement. She shook her head. By now she was completely lost for words. Her heart was pounding and beads of sweat were bursting through her foundation. She felt like Blanche DuBois going through menopause. She swallowed hard and turned to the salesman. "My friend, Ms. Roggenfelder, just as a matter of interest, could you tell me what her car was advertising?"

"I think it was Stella McCartney," he said. "Bit of luck her getting here last night, eh?"

"Yes," Cyn said. "Wasn't it just?"

# Chapter 2

Huge—aka the Honorable Hugh Thorpe Duff—was one of Cyn's oldest and closest friends. Once or twice a week, if they were both at a loose end, he would pop round bearing takeout and a video. Usually he phoned first, to check if she was "at home to callers." Tonight he hadn't. He happened to pull up as Cyn was getting out of the Smart Car. Of course she had parked it directly under a streetlamp and he noticed the Anusol ad straightaway. He cracked up.

She gave a weak smile. She was doing her best to see the funny side, but it didn't help that on the way home she'd stopped at traffic lights and a couple of drivers had started pointing at the side of her car and sniggering. She would phone the company tomorrow and see if they would agree to change the ad to something a bit more discreet.

"Blimey, it's the Butt-Mobile. And two seats—one for Butt-man and one for Rub-in."

"Yeah, yeah, very witty."

He seemed to have noticed her rather pinched expression and was now doing his level best to contain his laughter. "Fab car, though. Great color," he said, trying to keep a straight face and failing miserably. His eyes were practically watering with mirth. "But, the ad. I mean, God, what a pain in the arse." His lips were twitching now. "So . . . um . . . I bet you were itching to drive it off." More stifled laughter. She shot him a come-on-give-me-a-break look and opened the main door to the building. He followed her upstairs to her flat.

Cyn adored her flat. It was a small one-bedder in a fairly unremarkable Edwardian building in Crouch End, but it was the first place she'd owned rather than rented and that alone made it special. More than once she'd caught herself wandering about the place, affectionately patting the walls.

She loved the white paintwork and mellow yellow stripped floors, her brand-new Ikea kitchen with its brushed aluminum cupboards and Smeg fridge. Most of all she loved her bedroom. It had a pretty cast-iron fireplace. Cyn had painted the wooden surround the palest mint green. When she moved in, Barbara and Mal had clubbed together with her brother, Jonny, and Grandma Faye to buy her the Art Nouveau glass vase she'd spotted in an antique shop and had been going on about for ages. It sat slender and fragile on the bedroom mantelpiece, its swollen base saturated in iridescent pinks and greens. Although she adored the simple minimalism of the rest of the flat, the vase, along with the fireplace and the seventies imitation Palace of Versailles telephone table in the living room, softened the atmosphere and made it feel more feminine. She hated those cold, functional, art installation houses where you walked in and felt like saying, "Excuse me, which way to X-ray?" She tried to keep the vase filled with freesias. That way, the first thing she noticed when she woke up was the scent of flowers.

"You know," she said to Hugh as she took a couple of beers out of the fridge, "it's really great of you to pop round with food. As it happens, I was going to get takeout, but the thing is, I'm going out. It's Tuesday. I've got group therapy at eight."

"God, of course you have," he said, pincering lint off his Dolce & Gabbana suit trousers. "My mind's been full of work stuff today. I totally forgot you were off to madness . . . So, what are you wearing?"

"What I've got on. Why?"

He looked her up and down. "Really? O . . . K."

"What do you mean, 'O . . . K'? What's wrong with how I look?"

"Nothing at all. I mean, it would be fine for anything apart from therapy."

"Sorry, Huge, I'm not with you."

"Well, if you take my advice, you'll lose the lip gloss. Too glam. They'll think you're attention seeking. And the skirt's gorgeous, but it's got to go. Far too smart and businesslike. You're running a serious risk of them thinking you're a control freak. Now, personally I think the fishnets are fab, but has it occurred to you that the group might just think they scream sex addict?"

She laughed and explained that dressing for her very first session in group therapy had been worse than getting ready for a first date. "You wear black, they think you're depressed. Red equals anger. Green says jealous. Now I've given up and I just go as I am." She handed him two bottles of Rolling Rock and picked up the pizza box and two plates. "Come on, let's eat in the living room. It's more comfortable on the sofa." It also meant they could get away from Morris. Morris was Keith Geary's mynah bird, which was sitting in its cage on Cyn's kitchen table. She was looking after him while Keith was away on a series of pitches in South Korea. Morris was no trouble except when he started talking. It wasn't just odd words he repeated incessantly, often waking her in the early hours, but entire sentences. He could also impersonate any human voice perfectly. After having Morris for a week she had gotten utterly fed up with hearing him at five in the morning doing his Keith Geary impersonation, complete with impeccable Welsh accent: "Fucking 'ell, I am so desperate for a shag. God, I haven't had a shag in three months."

Hugh stopped at Morris's cage to feed him a tiny bit of tomato off his pizza. "God, I'm desperate for a shag," Morris said by way of thanks.

"Morris, there's something you and I need to get straight," Hugh said. "I'm gay, which means I don't shag birds and that includes the feathered kind." He followed Cyn into the living room.

Almost as soon as they sat down, he started teasing her about the Smart Car again.

"So, which way did you come home," he said, crossing his legs to reveal a couple of inches of navy Paul Smith sock covered in tiny tennis rackets, "on the main road or up the back way?"

"Yeah, yeah, most amusing. Look, I know you find this whole thing hysterical, but . . ."

"No, no. Hang on, I've got one more. This is brilliant." He tore off a triangle of pizza and held it in midair. "Why are hemorrhoids called hemorrhoids? Surely they should be called *arseteroids*." He was laughing so much he had to put down the pizza slice.

"Huge. Please."

He wiped his eyes and looked at her with a meek little boy face. "OK, that's it."

"Good."

"I promise. Not another word."

"Excellent."

A beat. Then: "So, er . . ." He cleared his throat. "Did you, um, drive carefully? I mean, you were in such a state you could have caused a . . ." pause for dramatic effect, "a massive pileup?" He lay back on the sofa cushions, laughing and kicking his legs in the air like an expensively suited beetle stranded on its back. Cyn located a spare cushion and threw it at him.

"Oh, come on, gorgeous," Hugh said sitting up. "Give me a break. There's not a gay man in the world who doesn't like a good arse joke." He took a swig of beer.

It was then that she noticed three black olives bunched up in the center of her pizza. Usually she adored olives, but she found herself stabbing them with her fork and sliding them to the side of her plate.

"But I agree," he went on, gravely, "this whole thing is a total bummer." His laughter was so contagious that this time, try as she might, she couldn't stop herself from joining in.

"How is it that at the same time as annoying the hell out of me, you manage to cheer me up like nobody else I know? You know, Huge, I don't half love you."

He smiled and patted her knee. "Love you too, gorgeous."

She'd known Hugh since university. They were both at Leeds. She was doing history, Hugh was doing mechanical engineering, which he loathed. His father, a retired brigadier general, said it was either that or the army. He was determined his son should reach the age of twenty-one having acquired a "proper skill." When Hugh told him that he wanted to read English literature, his father said that was for "faggots and socialists." Since Hugh rarely rose before midday, after which he bathed and partook of toast, thinly spread marmalade and a cup of Lapsang Souchong, he couldn't quite see himself hacking it in the army. If he wanted his father's financial support, engineering was his only choice. He had told Cyn recently that he was certain his father had always suspected he was gay and forcing him to do something macho was his way of trying to knock it out of him.

Hugh had always been determined to become a writer.

In his first term at Leeds he started doing pieces for the student newspaper. Cyn, who was considering going into journalism after she graduated, was also writing for the paper. They met in the office one day and immediately hit it off. Since they were reasonably talented and enthusiastic—most people who got involved with the newspaper were neither— by the second year they were editing the thing.

Correction. Cyn edited it while Hugh sat on the office phone trying to con his way into getting interviews with his latest Hollywood crush. "Look, I'm sure if you explain to Mr. Cruise," he would say, in an accent that sounded like it had been minted during the Raj, "that the piece is for the London *Times*, he will agree to a brief interview." Of course nobody ever did.

Even though she knew perfectly well that Hugh was gay, it hadn't stopped her fancying him. He was just so tall, patrician and handsome. So ridiculously gentile. Sleeping with him would be like having a glass of milk and a bacon sandwich on Yom Kippur, only heaps more fun.

One night toward the end of that second year, the pair of them got very drunk and she persuaded him to let her try and "cure" him.

"Don't you think my father has already tried that by forcing me to do bloody engineering?"

"Yeah, but engineering is boring. This won't be." He laughed and agreed let her have her way with him—or at least try to. The scene that followed was an almost exact replica of the one in *Some Like It Hot*—which happened to be her favorite ever comedy film—where Marilyn Monroe tries to seduce Tony Curtis on the yacht. The only differences were that instead of being on a luxury yacht, Cyn and Hugh were in Cyn's room in a crummy flat in Meanwood, and Marilyn hadn't actually been going down on Tony.

For nearly two hours, Cyn worked away trying to effect

what Hugh insisted on referring to as a "froth in the groin department." "Ooh, hang on," she said at one stage, "I think I definitely felt something just then." He shook his head. "I'm sorry, my darling, there's nothing. Absolutely nothing," he said doing a perfect impression of Tony Curtis. Finally Cyn developed jaw ache and they decided to give up and just be mates.

When Hugh wasn't trying to intimidate L.A. film agents with his accent, he was busy penning his latest literary masterpiece. How he fitted in his academic work, she had no idea, but somehow he managed to come away with a bachelor's degree.

To date, Huge had penned thirteen literary masterpieces and half a dozen screenplays, all of which had been rejected. Cyn had only read a couple of the screenplays, but she'd plowed through almost all his novels. There was no doubt he was a gifted writer, but his incessant classical references, turgid, rambling sentences that could last an entire page, and the lapses into poetry somehow got in the way of the story. On top of all this, the subject matter was always unrelentingly bleak. She could never understand how somebody as funny and witty as Hugh could write such disheartening stuff. Each novel was a three-hundred-thousand-word tome of unrelenting darkness and misery—usually set in a Neolithic cave or a windswept, disease-raddled Viking settlement. By the time she was halfway through, she was practically reaching for the Prozac.

Even now, when a rejection letter arrived, Hugh would hibernate in his flat, marooned in a Strindbergian depression. He would sit there for days on end, putting venomous reader reviews on Amazon; his anger was aimed at any author to whom he considered himself superior, from Salman Rushdie to John Irving. Then, miraculously, he would manage to pull himself round and throw himself into a new project. "All literary geniuses have struggled," he would declare, convincing himself that this next oeuvre would have the publishers or film companies "coming in their pants."

To make ends meet (the Thorpe Duffs were penniless, having sold the family seat years ago to pay death duties on Hugh's grandfather's estate), Hugh worked at Selfridges as a surrogate boyfriend. The revolutionary scheme had been introduced a few months ago. His job was to escort women around the store and help them shop for clothes, while their boyfriends stayed in the boyfriend crèche playing video games and reading lad mags.

It should be said at this point that if male sexuality was represented on a continuum that began with Jack Nicholson and ended with Jack McFarland, Hugh came in round about Will Truman. He was straight looking, tall, with a great figure and boyish upper-class good looks—think a young Jeremy Irons—but with a style and elegance that few straight men either achieved or desired. Hugh happily described himself as a "fashion savant." "And since I am also endlessly enthusiastic, attentive and admiring, I am the perfect retail therapist. And it's not easy, particularly when you're trying to buy a frock for some brick of a woman with an arse like a mobile home." Hugh's mother, who knew her son was gay and had no problem with it, also knew what her son did for a living. His father had no idea and never asked.

The reason he pretty much lived for free was that the Thorpe Duffs' extensive circle of aristocratic friends were extremely mindful of the family's embarrassed financial position. Hugh's parents, who lived in a delightful but shabby Gloucestershire farmhouse, were always being offered villas for the summer. The same friends—desperate for a house sitter while they flitted off on six-month jaunts to their second and third homes—would offer Hugh their London flats and houses. For the last eight months he had been living in a majestic four-story house in Knightsbridge, which he was "keeping an eye on" for friends of his parents who were busy remodeling their house in Cape Town.

Tonight, Hugh was feeling particularly gung ho because he had just submitted a screenplay to Warner Bros. "Come on," Cyn said, "what's it about?"

"OK . . ."

As he stared off into the distance for dramatic effect, Cyn prepared herself for the rest of the sentence, which usually went: "Picture it: winter AD 900, a small Hebridean settlement. A lone, wounded rider emerges from the dawn mist . . ."

"I've made something of a historical departure," Hugh said. "It's set in the twentieth century for a change." Hmm, already an improvement, Cyn thought. "Picture it: 1940, a courtroom in South Carolina." He was leaning in toward her, his voice soft, but urgent. "It's summer. The air is like thick, hot soup. A ceiling fan is turning relentlessly. The camera pans round and stops at two men sitting next to their lawyer. He's short and overweight and wears rimless glasses and suspenders. The camera moves in for a close-up of the two men. It takes awhile for you to work out that there is something odd about them. They are identical, clearly twins. But not just ordinary twins. These men are Siamese twins, joined at the abdomen for the last forty-seven years."

"Blimey."

"See, it's already drawing you in, isn't it? Anyway . . ." By now Hugh was on his feet, pacing. "One of them has murdered this guy in a bar. If he's found guilty he faces the electric chair. His brother had no part in the murder and is completely innocent. What does the jury do?"

She sat there, speechless, half expecting him to say, "God, I really had you going there" and announce it was a joke. It was a few seconds before she realized he wasn't joking and that he actually believed somebody in Hollywood was going to take this seriously. "Wow, so what does the jury do?"

"I've brought you a copy of the screenplay," he said. The shoulder bag he'd been carrying when he arrived was sitting on the floor by the living room door. He went over and pulled out a thick manuscript. "I've called it *My Brother, My Blood, My Life*. You can read it and find out what happens. I see the whole thing as a philosophical allegory, a metaphor if you will, for the futility of human struggle." He sat back down next to her.

"O . . . K," she said slowly. "I can see that." In fact, she couldn't remotely see it.

"You'll be able to say more when you've read it, but what do you think in principle?"

"I . . . er. I think it's good." She saw his face collapse. "No, what am I saying? It's more than just good. It's sparkling, original and deep. Very deep. Deeply profound."

"Thanks, Cyn," he beamed. "God, you know I'm really excited about this one." She took the screenplay from him, kissed him on the forehead and said she hoped he made a million. Some hopes. A month from now the rejection would arrive and he would be sitting alone in a darkened room, sticking pins into effigies of the brothers Warner.

"So," he said, changing the subject, "how on earth *did* you end up getting a car that doubles as an ad for Anusol?"

She explained how there had been two cars on offer and that both were meant to be from drug companies. "But when Chelsea went to the garage last night, it turns out that one is from Stella McCartney. Not only that, but it arrived early."

Hugh raised an eyebrow. "How wonderfully convenient."

"Yes, I know. The thought had occurred to me."

"What's your relationship like with her? Do you get on?"

Cyn told him about the "well done, *you*" remark and

how she thought Chelsea saw her as a rival. "But I guess it is possible the whole car thing could be a coincidence."

"Yeah, right. And Elton John's hair is natural."

"But Chelsea is loaded, why would she be that bothered about getting one up on me?"

"You've just said it—she sees you as a rival. It's as simple as that. Look, I know you want to give her the benefit of the doubt, but I'm telling you, if you get any nicer you are in danger of growing big floppy ears and waking up one morning to find yourself starring in a Disney cartoon."

"Huge, you're missing the point. I don't have any evidence that she knew about the Anusol car and until I do, I'm not about to risk making false accusations."

It was then that she realized she hadn't checked her answer machine to see if Chelsea had left a message last night to say she wouldn't be able to meet her at the car showroom. She got up, went over to the phone. No messages were registered on her caller display.

"See," Hugh said, "she didn't even bother to make up an excuse. She just went ahead and did the dirty."

"We don't know that," Cyn insisted. "There could be an explanation." Hugh rolled his eyes as if to say "I give up."


Cyn's therapist, Veronica, was always telling her that she was "too damned nice." During a one-on-one session, Cyn had mentioned how hard it had been to chuck her last boyfriend, Mark.

He was gorgeous and the sex had been brilliant, the best she'd had. Ever. When Mark went down on her, the earth didn't merely move, it shifted on its axis. She wouldn't have been remotely surprised to have come round from one of her glorious orgasms to discover that winter had turned into spring.

The only problem was that Mark had very little conversation beyond his work. She wouldn't have minded so much if he had been a doctor or a lawyer or a journalist. She would have enjoyed listening to tales of who he'd cured or saved from a life sentence, or who Camilla Parker-Bowles was now shagging on the quiet. Dishy and sexually adept as he was, Mark was in public health. To be more specific, he was a restaurant inspector. "Did you know," he would say as they lay snuggled up in her bed basking in their postcoital glow, "that raw meat and poultry contaminated with fecal matter are among the most frequent causes of food-borne illness?"

She was forever trying to explain why, when one of her girlfriends invited them to dinner, it was less than tactful to discuss E. coli and ptomaine poisoning at the table. He would take the point and then at the next dinner party he would be off again, chatting away about mice droppings and European chopping board protocols.

It had taken her weeks to find the courage to end it. She hated hurting people and apart from his passion for food hygiene, Mark was one of the kindest, sweetest boyfriends she'd ever had.

"But at least you did it," Veronica had said, leaning forward in her chair, eyes gleaming. "That is real progress." According to Veronica, the reason Cyn was in therapy was to learn how to be bad.

For the record, Cyn was not a doormat. It was more complicated than that.

In 1982, when Cyn was nine, Barbara was diagnosed with breast cancer. The tumor was minute and successfully removed. After three months of chemotherapy she made a complete recovery. But during that time, nobody knew how it would turn out and the family was thrown into complete turmoil. Her dad was at his wit's end, and both Cyn and her brother were constantly being told by relatives to be on their best behavior so as not to worry their parents. Jonny, who was seven, responded by doing the very opposite. For a while he turned into an uncontrollable monster, desperate for parental attention. Cyn saw that this was only increasing the pressure on her mum and dad and became a model child. She never grew out of the habit.

Even when she was going through her brief punk phase, Cyn hadn't done anything really bad. OK, she'd smoked a bit of weed with Jude, her best friend from school, and once or twice the two of them had gotten severely drunk, but that was about as far as it went. Her rebellion was very much rebellion-lite. She never trashed her pink princess bedroom (which she'd had since she was nine), never hung out with the wrong crowd, never shoplifted (God forbid!) nor swallowed a tablet more potent than Tylenol. When she lost her virginity at seventeen, it was to Jason Lieberman, a nice Jewish architecture student from Stanmore. Admittedly, a couple of years later she tried to seduce an Aryan homosexual, but that was hardly a hanging offense.

Sin didn't sit easily with Cyn. It wasn't in her nature.

She was one of those women who find it hard to stick up for themselves, but have no problem rushing to somebody else's defense.

Ages after somebody had made a bitchy comment or insulted her, she would be lying in bed or relaxing in the bath and the perfect response would hit her. Then she would kick herself for not thinking of it at the time.

One night after a couple of glasses of wine, she thought up what she firmly believed was a wonderful riposte (albeit a month late) to a sleazy pickup line this bloke, Milo, had used on her. Since he was a friend of a friend she was able to get his number and, without thinking, phoned him. "Hi, Milo, it's Cyn, Lucy's friend. We met a few weeks ago at a do at Bar Med. You don't remember? OK, I was wearing a pink halter-neck top and new Paper Denim Cloth jeans. Anyway, what I wanted to say . . . What do I look like? OK, I'm five five, shoulder-length hair, brown hair with these subtle copper highlights. I'd just had it cut into soft layers. The hairdresser said they really frame my face and give me this sort of gamine look." God, why was she prattling on about her hair? Despite the wine, she supposed she was still a bit nervous. "But none of that matters," she went on. "The point is you came up to me, put your hand on my bum and asked me if I had any Irish in me. When I said no, you leered at me and suggested I might like some. At the time I was too taken aback by your boorish behavior to think of an appropriate reply, but I would just like to say in response to your suggestion . . ." Pause for maximum dramatic effect: "Yes, please. Mine's a Guinness." Huh, that would put this sexist jerk in his place, let him know she was a wit to be reckoned with. He wouldn't mess with her again in a hurry.

"Oh yeah, I remember you. Cyn—the woman with the fabulous tits. Look, if you fancy meeting up for a drink sometime . . ."

Yep, she'd really shown him. Yes, indeedy.


Cyn and Hugh had just finished eating when the door buzzer rang. Cyn went to answer it. Standing in the hallway, her faced etched with panic, was Cyn's other best friend, Harmony.

"God, wassup?" Cyn said.

"I think it's started." Harmony came in and began pulling off her coat.

"What's started?" Cyn took her coat and hung it on the coat stand.

"The perimenopause."

Harmony had hit forty last month. No matter how much people tried to convince her that forty was the new thirty, she remained convinced that she was tottering over the hill toward Crone City.

Not that she even looked forty. Harmony was stunning. People who met her for the first time always took her for a decade younger.

In her twenties she had been a lingerie model. Her photograph had appeared in practically every underwear catalogue in the Western world. "You want to know Victoria's Secrets?" she would joke. "Then I'm the girl to ask."

She should have been a catwalk model, but at five seven, she was way too short. Fashion photographers also turned up their noses because her look was more glam chick than heroin chic. But even now men (and women) did double takes when they saw her. It was partly her figure, but mainly it was her face. Her eyes were a true violet with a wide doelike quality. Her lips were full and sexy. Add to the mix lustrous chestnut hair and dark olive skin, and there was a woman who made most other women want to slash their wrists the moment they clapped eyes on her.

Since he was possessed of the most impeccable manners, Hugh rose to his feet the moment Harmony came into the living room. "Ah, the glorious Ms. Harmsworth McFarmsworth," he teased, arms outstretched. Then, noticing her strained expression he added: "As ever a symbol of unbridled bacchanalian delight." He gave her a hug and a kiss.

"Watcha, 'Ewge." Her accent, pure, unreconstructed working-class Liverpool, collided spectacularly with her Miu Miu minikilt and pointy Jimmy Choo boots. She turned to Cyn. "What's he on about?" she giggled. "Bacca what?"

"He's taking the piss," Cyn said.

"I think I got that much."

"Yes, but in a gentle, caring, sharing way," Hugh piped up, his face a picture of incorruptibility. "What's up, Harms?"

"She thinks she's got perimenopause," Cyn said.

"Isn't he that band leader from the sixties?" Hugh said, sitting back down. "Perry Menopause and his Tijuana Brass Band. Did *Little Spanish Flea*."

"You know full well that was Herb Alpert," Harmony replied, plonking herself down next to him and gently punching his arm. Although she pretended to get offended, she was used to Hugh's constant teasing. Like Cyn, she knew it was his way of showing affection.

"I do? OK, so what did Perry Menopause do, then?"

"Weddings and bar mitzvahs," Cyn said with a roll of her eyes.

"Really?"

"No. He didn't *do* anything. He isn't a person. He's an it. You get it. At least women of a certain age get it."

"It's when you start getting the first symptoms of the menopause," Harmony broke in as she rooted around in her bag for her fags. "I've looked it up on the Internet. Apparently they can begin ten years before everything packs up completely. Your periods become irregular, you bloat, you have sandpaper sex . . ."

"Urrgh, please. Too much information." Hugh's face contorted with distaste.

Harmony swiveled round to face Cyn, who was sitting in one of the armchairs. "The thing is," she said, drawing deeply on a Marlboro Light, "I'm three weeks late and there's no way I could be pregnant. Me and Justin haven't done it for two months. I told him ages ago, no sex until he agrees to take me up the aisle."

"You know, Harms," Hugh said, "some straight men do find that sort of thing a bit kinky."

" 'Ewge, behave. You know perfectly well what I mean."

She looked back at Cyn. "Three years we've been going out. I want to get married, but he won't even talk about it."

"This whole Justin thing has gotten to you," Cyn said. "It's stress. That's why your period's late."

"You reckon?"

"I'm certain. And you've probably been overdoing it at work."

These days Harmony was a hairdresser, but not any old hairdresser. After she retired from modeling, she trained at Vidal Sassoon. By the midnineties she was the top stylist at the South Molton Street Salon. One day Justin, a merchant banker, came in for a haircut. Instead of tipping her, he asked her out. Three years later they were still together. Justin was also her business partner. It was only because of his financial investment that she was able to set up her own salon off High Street Kensington. The business hadn't merely taken off, it had gone stratospheric. She was a regular on daytime TV doing hair makeovers and all the London department stores sold her hair-care products.

She and Cyn had met at the launch of another hair-care line—Victoria Beckham's Posh Locks. Price Chandler Witty had been handling the advertising. Naturally the launch at Harrods was a major media blitz and the place was packed with press, photographers and TV crews. At one point Cyn stepped back to make way for a waiter carrying a tray of drinks and managed to collide heavily with the body behind her. There was a cry of "Bloody 'ell" in a thick Liverpool accent. Cyn swung round to see Harmony staring down at the spilled champagne, which was now soaking into her scarlet taffeta Vivienne Westwood dress. Cyn recognized her at once. "Oh, God. I am so sorry. What can I say? Please, you must send me the dry cleaning bill."

"Oh, don't be daft," Harmony said with surprising jollity. "It's only a frock. It's not the end of the world." Cyn said the least she could do was get her another glass of champagne. And that was it. For the next hour, the two women stood drinking champagne and chatting. Almost immediately, Harmony confessed that these events bored her rigid. "I only came," she whispered, "because Victoria used to be a client and she sent me an invite. Plus, I need to keep an eye on what the opposition's doing. Just between you, me and the gatepost, though, I'd much rather be at home with *Coronation Street* and a bottle of wine."

"God, me, too," Cyn said, realizing she had really taken to this un-starry, straight-talking woman. As the party began to break up, Harmony suggested they go out for Chinese. "I don't know about you, but I could murder some sweet-and-sour pork." Cyn said she would love to.

They loaded crispy aromatic duck onto pancakes and carried on yakking as if they'd known each other for years.

Harmony chain-smoked and talked about her family. "Me dad buggered off when I was seven and our mam raised five of us kids on her own in a crappy council flat on one of the worst estates in Liverpool." She drew deeply on her cigarette. "But since I opened the business I've been able to buy her a bungalow and a little car. It's just my way of saying thank you. And I help me brothers and sisters, too. I took 'em all to Florida last year. I'll never forget the look on our mam's face when I showed her the plane tickets. Totally made up, she was." For a few seconds she sat staring off into the distance. Cyn could see her eyes were filling up. "So," she said eventually, flicking ash into the ashtray, "how did you end up with a daft name like Cynthia? It's almost as bad as mine." This was typical Harmony. She never avoided saying what was on her mind. "You see," she went on, not giving Cyn a chance to reply, "I was named after the make of my dad's electric guitar. I was baby number two and our mam said it was his turn to choose the name. Apparently he was sitting strumming his guitar at the time and that was that. If he'd been holding a pint glass, I'd have probably ended up being called Special Brew. Special Brew Milhandra O'Farrell." She laughed a hoarse, throaty laugh and lit another fag.

Cyn explained that her name was also music related. Her father had been a mad Lennon fan since the sixties. When Barbara got pregnant, Mal insisted that if the baby was a boy, they should call it John. When a girl arrived, he considered naming her Yoko.

"Omigod!" Harmony roared. "Yoko Fishbein! I love it."

"Yeah, but my mum didn't, so they compromised on Cynthia. Then two years later my brother came along and they named him John, but we call him Jonny."

Harmony asked her if she liked her name. Cyn said the Fishbein bit had never bothered her, even though half the family had changed it to Fisher. "Anyway, there were loads of other Jewish kids at school with far weirder names. A boy called Benny Lipschitz took the heat off me by taking most of the flak." She said her first name hadn't bothered her either until she was about eight or nine. Then she'd started hating it. Even though she was too young to articulate it, at some primal, instinctive level she knew that Kate, Sophie and Amy represented sexy, while Cynthia equalled prissy, spinsterish, anally retentive librarian. It wasn't until she was sixteen that she realized Cyn—the name her friends always called her—had a certain raw, streetwise edginess to it. "So, I went off to Camden Market with my friend Jude from school and we became punks. I bought this ripped black leather jacket, got my eyebrow pierced and my hair spiked and sprayed Day-Glo pink. From then on I started hiding out in my frilly pink princess bedroom playing The Stranglers at full blast. Mum and Dad went mad."

They left the restaurant well after midnight, swapped phone numbers and that was it. They had been friends ever since.

Cyn hadn't been sure how Harmony would hit it off with Hugh, but there had been an instant spark. Hugh adored Harmony's ballsiness, that she said precisely what was on her mind and refused to be intimidated by his posh background. Within five minutes of meeting Hugh, she was accusing him of being a toffee-nosed, chinless toff. (In fact he had a perfectly well-formed chin.) He called her a chippy proletarian. The more they drank, the more they insulted each other, but Cyn could see they were loving it. Hugh didn't have a truly snobbish bone in his body and the working-class chip on Harmony's shoulder was an act more than anything else.

Hugh came back with a bottle of beer and handed it to Harmony. "Get this down you. You'll feel better."

"Ta, 'Ewge." Cyn said there was pizza left if she fancied some.

"God, no. I can't go eating pizza now. I can feel this whole lack of estrogen thing is already making me put on weight." She patted her nonexistent stomach.

"But you're as thin as a reed," Cyn said.

"Yeah, right. Oliver Reed."

Hugh looked thoughtful. "Look, I know I've been taking the piss, but seriously, Justin will come round, you know." Harmony shook her head. "We were up all last night, talking. The bank has offered him a job in Dubai. He said we could carry on as we are—you know, seeing each other two or three times a week—or he could take the job. I told him to take it."

"Do you really mean it?" Hugh asked. She said she did. "Deep down I knew it was never going to work. I mean he's

an earth sign. I'm a water sign. Together we just made mud."
She gave a soft laugh.

"What about his investment in the business?" Hugh said.

"My accountant says I can afford to buy him out."

Cyn and Hugh came and sat next to her on the sofa. Hugh put his head on her shoulder. Cyn squeezed her hand. "It'll be all right," Cyn said. "You've got us." "Thanks, guys," she said. Then she perked up and said she wanted to talk about something less depressing. Hugh changed the subject back to Chelsea.

"Whadda cow," Harmony said after she'd heard the story. "You know, where I come from, if a woman does the dirty on you, you make blinkin' sure she gets what's coming to her."

"Hmm, that would be one approach," Hugh came back, "though not one I would necessarily endorse. Holloway Prison isn't really at its best this time of year."

"Er, hello," Cyn butted in, "can I say something here? Look, I don't know yet if she even did it on purpose. I can't go blasting in, accusing her. I will talk to her, though."

"You just make sure you get to the *bottom* of it," Harmony giggled.

"Oh, God, no more arse jokes, please," Cyn groaned.

"Well, you have to admit," Harmony said, "it is quite funny."

As Cyn cleared away the plates and pizza remains, Harmony noticed Hugh's screenplay lying on the coffee table.

"*My Brother, My Blood, My Life* by Hugh Thorpe Duff," she read aloud. "Wow, hev-ee." Hugh gave her an outline of the plot.

"You're kidding me," Harmony said with a confused, slightly nervous laugh. She was looking at Cyn, who was standing by the door violently shaking her head and motioning her to shut up. "This is a windup, right?"

"I'm absolutely serious," he said, looking exceedingly put-out. "*My Brother, My Blood, My Life* is a classic example of film noir." He looked over at Cyn. "And Cyn loves it—don't you, Cyn?"

"I think it's very powerful," Cyn said diplomatically.

"I'm sorry," Harmony said, putting an affectionate hand on Hugh's knee. "Look, maybe it was daft trying it out on me. What do I know? We didn't have too many art house cinemas where I grew up. We didn't even have TV until I was ten. If we wanted to watch something we went to visit our washing at the Laundromat."

Cyn took the plates out to the kitchen and put them in the dishwasher. When she came back Hugh was trying to educate Harmony in the loftier aspects of film noir.

"But I just find it so depressing and boring. No offense, 'Ewge, but it isn't me. I'm more of a chick-flick girl." She jumped up, went over to Cyn's video shelf and ran her finger along the line of boxes. "Wow, I didn't know you had this," she said pulling out a copy of *Working Girl*. "It's my all-time favorite film. Why don't we put it on? I love the way Melanie Griffith kicks that Sigourney Weaver's tight little arse after she steals her idea."

Hugh let out a sigh. "Christ, I've seen it a thousand times."

Cyn looked at her watch and realized she was due at her group in twenty minutes. "OK, guys, I've got to go. Stay and watch a vid if you want to."

"You sure?" Harmony said.

"No problem. There's more beer in the fridge. See ya." As she stood in the hall putting on her coat, she could hear them still discussing the film.

"Oh, come on, 'Ewge," Harmony was pleading, "I know it's a bit plebeian and not some black-and-white Japanese thing with subtitles, but can't we just chill out for a bit?"

"I'm perfectly happy to chill out," he replied evenly. "I like a bit of escapism as much as the next person. But chick flicks are just so tedious and idiotic."

"But you're gay. Gay blokes are supposed to love chick flicks."

"You're right," Hugh said, his sarcasm rising, "and we can watch it with me in a tank top, giving myself a leg, chest and back wax while at the same time whipping up a pomegranate mousse and arranging a vase of calla lilies. Ooh, why not go the whole hog and have a Judy Garland CD playing in the background?"

"Oh, for Chrissake, 'Ewge, get down from your blinkin' high horse, will you? You know I didn't mean anything."

"I'm not remotely on my high horse."

"Yes, you are. In fact your horse is so high I'm surprised you haven't got altitude sickness. Anyway, I want to watch the film."

"Well, I don't." Hugh's arms were folded in childish defiance.

"OK," Harmony said, "there's only one way to settle this. Arm wrestling. Whoever wins gets their way."

"Right, you're on."

As Cyn opened the front door, she could hear an occasional deep, primal grunt coming from the living room.

# Chapter 3

Since the drive to therapy would take about twenty minutes, Cyn decided to phone her mum back as she'd promised. Of course now Barbara couldn't remember the other thing she'd wanted to talk to Cyn about.

"There was definitely another reason I called. Now what was it? Oh, yes, I was talking to your cousin Miriam, you know—who got married last year while you were away. Anyway, she just had a baby boy. So sensible to get married and have a baby while you're still in your twenties."

Gawd. Cyn could practically read the sign. Welcome to Lectureville. Population: you.

"Mum, please. I'm thirty-two. Hardly any of my friends are married. I know you think my ovaries are shriveling as we speak, but I do have plenty of time." Cyn screwed up her face. She knew precisely what was coming and had started to mouth the next part of her mother's speech before she had even gotten going.

"OK, maybe at thirty-two your biological clock isn't exactly going tick-tock, but it's certainly going tick. And it's been ages since you finished with that nice Mark."

"No it hasn't, it's been three months." Actually it had been three months, two weeks and five days. Three and a half months since she'd last had sex. If she carried on like this, pretty soon she would be qualified to go to the Vatican and hold master classes in celibacy. Of course she wasn't about to admit to Barbara that she was missing having a man in her life. She and Grandma Faye would only get busy setting her up on blind dates with the grandsons and nephews of the women in Faye's bridge club.

"Like I said, ages. Anyway," Barbara went on, "it wasn't your biological clock I wanted to talk to you about."

"It wasn't?"

"No. I just wanted to ask you if you agree with me that it's in poor taste for Miriam to serve miniature frankfurters at the baby's circumcision."

Cyn giggled. "It's up to her."

"OK, I'll get straight on to her mother and suggest Miriam has a rethink."

"Mum, that's not what I said."

"Oh, by the way, I bumped into Sylvia Goldman the other day—you know, from the synagogue Ladies' Guild. Turns out her daughter is your age and not married. Anyway she's frozen some of her eggs. Sylvia promised she'd get her to ring you with the name of her gynecologist."

For a while Cyn had been wondering what she was going to bring up at her therapy session. Now she had something: why she seemed incapable of getting her mother off her case.

"So what are you doing tonight?" Barbara asked. Cyn had blurted it out before she had time to think. "I'm on my way to therapy."

"Darling, I really don't understand all this therapy nonsense. You're the sanest person I know. Why do you need therapy? I mean, it's not like you're mad. Not like your late

Aunty Millie, God rest her soul. Your dad took her to see a therapist once because she had suicidal tendencies."

"What happened?"

"I don't know, but I think the therapist made her pay in advance." She giggled at her joke. "Seriously, though, is it me? Is it something I've done? Or your dad? You hate us because we called you Cynthia, don't you? It was all your dad's fault. Never forget that it was me who saved you from being called Yoko."

"Mum, it's nothing to do with my name." One day she would discuss how Barbara's cancer affected her, but she wasn't ready yet. She didn't want to hurt her—after all, her mother had been the one with the illness, the one who thought she was going to die. And even though Barbara had been clear of the disease for over twenty years, Cyn didn't doubt that at the back of her mind, she still worried about the cancer returning. "I just find it hard to be assertive sometimes and therapy helps."

"Of course, you get that from me. I've always been a bit of a shrinking violet."

Cyn smiled to herself. Her mother was many things. Neither shrinking nor violet was among them.

The traffic was unusually heavy and Cyn arrived a few minutes late. There were no parking spaces outside Veronica's house, so Cyn was forced to park around the corner. This was no bad thing she decided because it meant that when everybody left after the session, nobody would notice the Anusol ad.

Veronica always left the front door on the latch on group therapy nights so that clients could let themselves in. Cyn stepped into the hall and opened the door to Veronica's large white office. There were four people plus Veronica sitting in a circle on hard black Ikea chairs. Cyn slipped in silently, hoping she looked sufficiently apologetic, and took the nearest empty seat. The woman who had been speaking broke off and looked up at Cyn. "Sorry I'm late," Cyn whispered. "Traffic. Please, carry on." The woman gave her a small smile. "I was just saying that sometimes I just don't know who I am. I'm still really struggling with this whole identity crisis thing."

"God, Jean," Cyn said, "that must be awful, constantly trying to work out who is the real you."

"My name is Jenny."

"Omigod. Jenny. Of course you're Jenny. I'm so sorry. You've been here for three months, how could I think you weren't Jenny?" Cyn sat there, feeling her cheeks burn with embarrassment. Jenny was looking down, now fiddling with her nails.

"It's all right, Cyn," she said. "Not to worry. I know I don't have very much impact on people. The thing is I just don't know what to do to change."

"I do." It was Clementine, a bossy, Sloaney sex addict who worked as a fashion assistant on *Vogue*. "You're forty-five. Losing the hair plait and calf-length florals might be a start." Clementine could be blunt to the point of cruelty. Cyn watched Jenny recoil in shock.

"You know, Clementine," Cyn came back. "I think that's a bit much. I wonder why you always feel the need to be so unkind."

"And I wonder," Veronica broke in quietly, smiling at Cyn, "why you find it so easy to stick up for other people, but not yourself. Maybe you would like to say a bit more about that."

Cyn shrugged. "I don't know," she said, feeling cross with Veronica because she had managed to cast aside her good intentions about Jenny. She knew she needed to stand up to Veronica and tell her she was angry with her—practicing saying stuff like that was the main reason she was in group therapy—but she let it go.

It was hard to judge, but Cyn suspected most people in the group found Veronica as intimidating as she did. The woman had this quiet, almost smug confidence about her. Throughout the weekly one-and-a-half-hour session, she said very little. Instead she sat feet together, hands neatly folded in her lap, eyes constantly roving around the circle, watching and waiting for reactions and feelings to reveal themselves. Her silence and the fact that nobody knew anything about her beyond her name, address, telephone number and what they saw was, of course, very powerful. She revealed nothing about herself, while the group revealed everything.

She was in her late fifties, heavyset with thick ankles and an auburn bob so straight and symmetrical that it looked like it had been cut with the aid of a set square. Clotheswise she favored soft, elegant, loose-fitting layers, set off by chunky amber jewelry—very much the uniform of choice for post-menopausal Hampstead Brahmins who had piled on a few pounds lately.

Since it was the end of the month and payday, everybody had slipped a neatly folded check under the box of tissues that sat on the glass coffee table. Cyn had often noted how Veronica never discussed her fee beyond the first session. It was so British, she thought. She imagined how different it would be if this were New York instead of London. She couldn't imagine a New York shrink having the same issues surrounding money. Quite the opposite, in fact: "OK, it's March and these are my spring specials: schizophrenics and passive-aggressives half price. If you book now, there's also a 20 percent reduction for hypochondriacs. This will include a complimentary MRI scan, a colonoscopy and a Barneys voucher. Also, look out for my twofer deals. Until April I'll be taking on two anorexics for the price of one overeater."

Just then, Ken, thirty-six, a deeply sensitive and earnest former Catholic priest who had left the priesthood three years ago and was still plucking up the courage to have sex (and whom Cyn was convinced had the hots for Clementine), turned toward Cyn. "I think Clementine was only trying to offer Jenny some constructive advice. I'm sure she meant no harm." Cyn didn't say anything. Instead she sat there wishing somebody would offer him some constructive advice along the lines of: "Ken, since you're not actually Amish, have you considered the possibility that a beard with no mustache is not a great look?"

"Clementine's right," Jenny said. "Maybe my appearance is something I need to think about. Perhaps I could do with a bit of a makeover. I've been thinking about it for a while." She turned to Clementine. "I want to thank you for having the courage to say what you did. It was important for me to hear it." Poor Jenny, Cyn thought, you could mug her and she would put it down to a "valuable learning experience."

Clementine offered Cyn a victorious smirk, then said she had something she would like to share with the group. "I finally managed to give up my car maintenance class." She had started the course, not because she had the remotest interest in learning about car engines, but because it was somewhere to pick up men. "I only slept with nine of the men." Cyn asked her how many there were in the course. Clementine stared down at her French manicure. "Eleven," she said without looking up.

"Oh, but you're getting there," Jenny trilled. "I mean, Rome wasn't built in a day and all that. You should be very proud of yourself."

"I wish I could be proud of myself," Sandra, a Jewish yo-yo dieter, was saying forlornly. "My mother says her postnatal depression began when I was born and won't end until I get married. How do you live with all that guilt?"

"Oh, for God's sake," Clementine snapped. "Can't you get her on Prozac?"

Sandra shook her head. "She tried it, but she says it interferes with her suffering."

"You know," Clementine said, "I think my insecurities stem back to when my mother used to come and meet me at school wearing a brown corduroy Donny Osmond cap. Before I came here, I spent ages trying to find the right support group."

The jokey, most probably apocryphal story was typical of Clementine. In the time that Cyn had been in the group, she'd never heard Clementine talk about her past—at least not in any significant way, in a way that might explain her sex addiction. Whatever happened to her while she was growing up, she still wasn't ready to go back and face it. Veronica would prompt her from time to time—try to encourage her to talk about her mother, who had apparently brought her up alone. Clementine would go silent for a while and lose herself in her thoughts. Occasionally her eyes would fill with tears, but after a minute or so she would come to, brush Veronica's prompting aside and make another joke or smart remark. It seemed that as long as she was making smart remarks, she felt safe.

"That must have caused you such unbearable pain," Ken said to Clementine about the Donny Osmond cap. His face etched with sympathy, he reached for the box of tissues and handed it to her.

By now, Jenny-with-the-identity-crisis was looking more distraught than ever. "I would like to know why Ken hands the tissues to Clementine when she's upset, but when I'm upset he just ignores me. I mean, am I really that invisible? Doesn't anybody recognize that I'm in pain, too?"

"Of course we do," Cyn replied gently. But nobody backed her up. Everybody sat in silence because the truth was that apart from Cyn everybody found Jenny a complete pain in the arse.

The silence seemed to go on forever. Long silences were common during group therapy, but Cyn had never gotten used to them. She always felt the need to take control and say something. Anything. Hey, how many psychotherapists does it take to change a lightbulb? Just one, but the lightbulb must want to change. Boom, boom.

Veronica had often made the point that Cyn wasn't responsible for the welfare of the group and that she needed to learn how to be comfortable with the silence. She tried, but it wasn't easy. Right now, she focused on the small vase of flowers on the mantelpiece. She liked the way Veronica always took the trouble to make sure there were flowers in the room. Then she started looking at the Mondrian prints hanging on the white walls, the shelves full of books on psychodynamic theory.

It was Sandra Yo-yo who broke the silence. "You know," she said morosely, pushing her dark curls behind her ears, "if I had to write my epitaph, it would read: Sandra—Eight Stone Three to Eleven Stone Six." Everybody giggled at this, even Veronica, who didn't laugh much as a rule.

"I'm sensing a great deal of repressed rage coming from you," Ken said to Sandra. "I mean, when you're overweight, there must be some kind of payoff."

"Ken, you sound like you've swallowed a bloody therapy textbook," Clementine said. "Veronica is the shrink, not you."

He sat there clearly grappling with the put-down. Before he could say anything Cyn spoke. She had noticed the empty chair next to Jenny.

"I thought we were getting a new member tonight," she said to Veronica.

"Yes. Jo is coming," Veronica said, touching her amber necklace. "I got a message on my answer machine just before we started. Apparently there's a burst water main along Camden Road." More silence. "So, Cyn. Maybe you could share your feelings with the group about not being able to stand up for yourself." Cyn thought for a moment. Her mind was a blank. She felt as if she had been put on the spot. It was a bit like being back at school and the French teacher asking her to conjugate an irregular verb she hadn't learned. Then her mind suddenly flew back to an incident that had happened a few years ago when she was working as a nanny for an English family in Hong Kong.

The job had only been meant to last a year, but she'd stayed five. It was the usual story: agency finds nanny a job with nightmare mega-rich couple. Nanny is desperate to leave but can't bear to abandon kids.

Tim and Mimi Clydesdale owned a vast colonial villa in Chung Hom Kok. When Barbara and Mal came to visit, Barbara took one look at the closets and said, "My God, you could sit twenty down to lunch in here."

Tim was a corporate lawyer who earned shed loads. Mimi was pretty, without an emotion to speak of and so thin that she practically disappeared when she turned sideways. She did squat all day apart from going out to lunch with her expatriate girlfriends and moving salad around her plate. In the afternoons she might partake of a little light antiquing. She spent practically no time with her children. The only things this woman had ever nursed was a vodka glass and her American Express platinum card.

Mimi may have been a rubbish mother, but she was a generous employer. Every Christmas she bought Cyn an expensive gift. One year it was a cashmere twin set.

"I put it on straightaway to please her," Cyn told the group. "She stood there scrutinizing me and said, 'Cyn, that looks just perfect on you.'" She could imitate Mimi's cold, haughty voice perfectly. "'But, you know, I'm just not sure about your breasts.' Anyway, I couldn't believe what I was hearing. I asked her what was wrong with my breasts and she said: 'Well, let's put it this way. You might want to rethink your choice of bra.'"

"So," Veronica said gently. "What did you say to her?"

Cyn could feel her eyes starting to water. "Nothing. I said nothing. My mind just went blank. I could feel the adrenaline pumping through me, but I didn't dare be rude in case she sacked me. That would have meant abandoning those poor children. I couldn't have done that. Anyway, I realized that Mimi was only jealous because she had two fried eggs on her chest instead of real breasts."

"I sense that you are really getting in touch with your anger," Veronica said approvingly.

"Too right I am. I mean, I have really nice breasts." By now she was getting quite carried away. "They're biggish, but they're really firm and perky. They're not remotely saggy. To hear Mimi go on, you'd have thought I was suckling sextuplets. All the men I've slept with have been extremely complimentary about them. You should see me in a Wonderbra." She failed to notice that Ken was shifting uncomfortably in his seat and practically drooling. "Although I say it myself," she went on, "I have a rather magnificent cleavage."

By now she was vaguely aware that she had lost the attention of the group. Her voice trailed off.

"Hello," the voice behind her said. "Sorry I'm late. I'm Joe."

Cyn swung round in her seat to face the door. Not Jo as in a woman, but Joe as in a man. An exceedingly cute and sexy man, who now knew all about her firm, perky, not re-motely saggy tits and magnificent cleavage.

For the second time that night, Cyn was crippled with embarrassment. One at a time, everybody stood up to shake Joe's hand. "I am so sorry about what happened just then," she said to him when her turn came. "I'm not usually like that. I mean, I'm not usually so in-your-face with my breasts . . ."

"That's OK, I understand." He was giving her the most delicious smile. "But do you think that maybe I could have my hand back now?"

"Oh, God. Yes." She released his hand from her grip and watched him flex his fingers as if he was trying to get the blood flowing again.

He took his seat between Jenny and Veronica. "Welcome to our little group," Clementine trilled, raking her fingers through her hair. Judging by his tight-lipped expression, Ken was watching Clementine's trilling and raking with mounting jealousy. "So, Joe, what do you do for a living?"

He said was a film and documentaries editor.

"Wow, that sounds so creative and glamorous," Clementine simpered.

"Not really," Joe said. "I just sit in front of a computer screen all day, cutting film, trying to make it tell a story."

Clementine soon established he wasn't married and had no children. What he did have, Cyn couldn't help noticing, was a broad, toned upper body and the softest, warmest brown eyes that were a perfect match for his short choppy hair. She was particularly taken with what he was wearing. His blokey, un-put-together look really appealed to her. Hugh would have recoiled at the battered suede jacket and jeans, but she liked it. She was less than keen on that magazine makeover look in women. In men, she positively loathed it.

"So what brings you to therapy?" Clementine asked him.

"You know, you really are giving this poor man the third degree," Ken said, although it was clear to Cyn that Ken didn't think Joe was remotely poor.

"That's all right," Joe replied with an easy smile. "OK, why am I here?" He leaned his head back while he thought. Camper boots, Cyn noted. Nice. "I think I have a problem with emotional intimacy. I tend to keep people at a distance. It's really affected my relationships with women. They've all been pretty casual. I tend to pick women who aren't looking for commitment."

Bugger, why was it that all the good-looking men were either gay or damaged? It was a couple of moments before she remembered that she was in therapy and not out on the pull and that everybody here was meant to have issues.

Cyn didn't say very much for the rest of the session, not that she would have gotten much chance since everybody was focusing on Jenny, who was wittering on about how threatened she felt when a new member joined the group because she felt her position—such as it was—was being usurped.


When Cyn got home, Hugh and Harmony had gone. She went into the kitchen to check on Morris Mynah. He had black feathers with flashes of white on his tail and yellow on his head. She thought he looked like a glitzed-up miniature crow. "Fuck, I need a shag," he said in a perfect imitation of Keith Geary. "It's been three months. Three sodding months since I last got my leg over." Cyn giggled. She'd heard this nonstop for a week. Even though it was starting to drive her seriously round the bend, there was no getting away from it—Morris's imitative ability was nothing short of genius. Even now he could still make her laugh. She was going to miss him when he went. Keith was due back at work tomorrow and they'd agreed (to be more precise, Keith had agreed) that the simplest thing (since it would save Keith having to make the twenty-minute drive to her flat) would be to do the handover at the office.

"Morris, you need a shag. I need a shag. Join the club. Instead, all I've got to look forward to tomorrow is the Pickersgill double-glazing people coming in to discuss their new advertising campaign. God, Cyril Pickersgill's a miserable, boring old duffer. He must be over seventy. I don't know why somebody hasn't had the sense to put him out to grass." She checked Morris had plenty of food pellets and water and put a towel over his cage. The dark tended to keep him quiet. "Night, night, Mo. Sleep tight."

Realizing she wasn't tired yet, she poured herself some wine and went into the living room. The video of *Working Girl* was lying on the coffee table. It needed rewinding, which meant Harmony must have won her arm-wrestling match with Hugh. She decided this was unlikely and that Hugh had let her win on purpose because she was feeling down.

She picked up the tape. Like Harmony, she adored the way the spunky Melanie Griffith character, Tess McGill, sticks two fingers up at fair play and uses guerrilla tactics to get revenge against her slimy, duplicitous boss.

Cyn wasn't about to go all L.A. flake and start having an epiphany based on a mindless piece of romantic Hollywood tosh. Nevertheless she couldn't help thinking that Tess McGill symbolized a missing piece of her emotional jigsaw—the disobedient wayward piece.

She slipped the video into the machine, pressed *rewind* and went to fetch a packet of Doritos and the wine bottle.

For the next hour and fifty-five minutes, apart from

drinking wine and dipping her hand into the Doritos bag, she barely moved. By the time it was over, the idea of doing something wicked and brave—for the most honorable and noble of reasons, of course—was beginning to hold a certain, almost irresistible, appeal.

# Chapter 4

Morris's cage was three feet by four and Cyn had quite a struggle getting it downstairs without tripping over or spilling his food. On top of that, Morris was frightened by the movement and refused to stop squawking and shouting about how much he needed a shag. Old Mr. Levinson, who lived with his wife on the floor below, was taking in the milk as Cyn and the cage went by. "Fuck, I need a shag. It's been three sodding months."

"Three months?" Mr. Levinson chuckled. He'd met Morris on the day he moved in and found him hugely entertaining. "That's nothing. You want to try living with Mrs. Levinson. It's been thirty years." He insisted on carrying the cage downstairs for Cyn and held on to it while she unlocked the car. Then he slid it onto the backseat. "Thanks, Mr. Levinson. I really appreciate it."

"No problem. Bye, Morris."

"I like a woman with a really big arse," Morris said.

"Really?" Mr. Levinson chuckled and looked at Cyn. "You know, on second thought, maybe Morris and Mrs. Levinson would hit it off."

Morris was no better on car journeys than he was at

being carried. Cyn covered his cage with the towel in an effort to calm him down.

She arrived at PCW just after nine. Two or three people saw her drive into the office car park. Of course they all noticed the ad, and the jokes started flying faster than you could say *anal fissure*.

A bit of her wished she could have left the car at home, but even if she hadn't had Morris's cage, she would still have needed to drive. Everybody at PCW drove to work because the office, a converted warehouse in Shoreditch, was a bleak fifteen-minute walk from the tube.

Inside, the place was more industrial workspace than traditional office. The rough brick walls had been painted white and covered with gigantic arty photographs and brightly colored abstracts. There were light wood floors and two metal and wire staircases that led to either end of a mezzanine floor where the directors had their offices. The twenty-foot-high ceiling was supported by a lattice of polished metal girders. Workstations were dotted about the perimeter.

In the middle of the space was an absurdly long, rustic wooden table that was used for meetings and conferences. If people needed to meet in private, they could adjourn to one of four small trailers that were parked as if they were in a campsite in the country. There was also a "thinking area"—a garden hammock on Astroturf—and a "play area" complete with pinball machines, snooker table and miniature trampoline.

The idea was that "creativity and vision" were exchanged in a fun, fluid, informal way. There were no doors and no partitions, and no appointments were needed to see the bosses. A few people like Chelsea insisted on wearing suits, but mostly people slouched around in jeans and Juicy Couture track bottoms.

The entire operation was, to say the least, self-consciously trendy. Most of the staff, Cyn included, saw the trendiness for the gimmick it was. The media was less cynical. Umpteen magazine and newspaper articles had raved about PCW's "egalitarian management style" and the fact that 10 percent of the agency's work was for charity, which it usually undertook pro bono. Stella McCartney had been their first big client. Soon, other young cutting-edge fashion designers, dot-com entrepreneurs and other corporates with a social conscience were following in her wake.

Cyn walked into the building and put Morris's cage down on the big conference table. "OK, now you sit there quietly. If you're good I'll bring you some apple later on." God, she was treating him like a person, as if he really understood. The table was in a major thoroughfare, which meant Morris would get lots of attention from people passing by. It was only when he got bored or frightened that he started his mad chatter. Of course everybody at PCW knew about Keith's mynah bird and nobody would have found Morris's perfect imitation of Keith moaning on about needing a shag anything other than hysterically funny. It was the fact that Morris tended to do his impersonations at the shout that eventually drove people mad.

Cyn was thirty when she joined PCW, so, like Chelsea, she was a fair bit older than the other junior copywriters. After university she did an internship at the *Daily Mail,* but quickly came to the conclusion that spending days stalking adulterous game show hosts wasn't for her.

When the *Mail* offered her a full-time job, she turned it down and spent four years nannying in Europe and Australia. Finally she got the nightmare job in Hong Kong.

By the time the two youngest Clydesdale children had

started school, Mimi was quite happy for Cyn to work part time for other families, as long as she was there to pick the children up from school.

It was around this time that Cyn's interest in advertising began. She had found some extra nanny work during school hours, but not enough to keep her occupied. With time on her hands she started reading. When she got fed up with books, she would flick through magazines. She realized that when she read magazines she always stopped to study the advertisements. It was the same when she watched TV. Instead of going out to make a cup of tea when they came on, she stayed to watch. She found herself analyzing bland soap powder or toothpaste commercials, trying to work out precisely why they were so successful. She found herself staring up at billboards, criticizing the slogans and thinking up ways they could be improved.

Eventually Cyn decided she wanted to come home and find a job in advertising. But she refused to leave the Clydesdales' children until she had found a replacement nanny. It wasn't hard. Marcia, an old friend of Barbara's whose husband had just left her, was desperate for "a fresh start" and was looking for a nanny-housekeeper job abroad. Marcia, who was in her late fifties, had raised four children of her own and was endlessly patient, loving and maternal. She flew out for an interview. Within five minutes the children were jumping all over her. The Clydesdales hired her on the spot. Cyn stayed on an extra month to help with the changeover, and the last she heard Marcia was still there and had no plans to come home.

Cyn's interview at Price Chandler Witty hadn't gotten off to a good start. It was a scorching hot day and she had decided to wear her new Monsoon flip-flops, which matched her pink skirt. Before she left, she had painted her nails and moisturized her legs and feet, which were tanned from having spent a week sunbathing in her parents' back garden. She'd bought the cream in Selfridges. A woman at one of the cosmetics counters had seen her looking at it and had then spent a solid ten minutes rubbing it into various bits of Cyn's person in order to demonstrate how richly nourishing and rehydrating it was. Of course by then, after all the trouble the woman had gone to, Cyn had felt compelled to buy it—even though she thought it had a rather tacky feel to it.

It was only on the long walk from the tube to the office that she realized that all the pavement dirt was sticking to her feet. When she arrived they were nearly black. There wasn't time to clean herself off in the ladies' room, so she spent the entire interview trying to hide her feet under the chair.

If that wasn't enough, Messrs. Price, Chandler and Witty—who were playing on one of the pinball machines when she arrived and greeted her with "we are so totally chilled out" mockney accents—suddenly seemed to sharpen up and made it clear they had their doubts about a candidate who had left it until she was thirty before deciding to make a career in advertising. Graham Chandler lay back in his chair, hands behind his spiky gelled head, and suggested that her outlook on life was less than focused. "You see, focus is what it's all about." Then Phil Witty started asking her what she knew about brand building (not a lot, really), balance theory (umm, something to do with equilibrium?). What about awareness-consideration-reaffirmation-confirmation-action-reinforcement theory? (Right. Well, you've sort of got me there.)

At this point Andy Price took off his narrow rimless specs, leaned forward and asked her if she knew there was such a thing as white salmon. She frowned, wondering where on earth this was leading, and said she didn't. "Well, there is. Now, this is a true story. In the twenties, a fish canning company in Alaska got landed with tons of salmon, which for some reason was white. Now, as you know, salmon is either pink or red, but they managed to shift all their white salmon in record time and make a huge profit, thanks to a brilliant advertising slogan. Can you guess what that slogan might have been?"

Jeez. How in the name of buggery was she supposed to know? "God, well . . . I mean . . . hmm." By now she realized the whole thing was hopeless and was on the point of getting up and leaving.

"It's not easy," Andy Price said, giving her a sympathetic smile. "Look, why don't I put you out of your misery?"

"No, hang on." An idea had come to her. In a flash—in one of those "Holy-Riddler-Robin-Gotham-City-is-saved-fetch-the-Batmobile" moments—she had it. "OK, it would have to be something about white salmon being superior to the pink or red . . . What about 'The salmon that doesn't turn pink in the tin'?"

Price, Chandler and Witty sat there stunned. Andy Price picked up a red rubber stress ball and kneaded it a couple of times. "Bloody hell. That's right," he said. "That was the exact slogan. Come on, you must have heard it somewhere."

She assured them she hadn't. The three men exchanged gobsmacked glances and said the job was hers if she wanted it. "The post is junior copywriter, the money's pretty crap, but we offer excellent opportunities for promotion."

"Yes, please," she said.


Her hope that people in the office would tire of the hemorrhoid one-liners after a couple of hours couldn't have been more in vain. Like Hugh, they immediately christened the

Smart Car the "Butt-Mobile" and not one of them got remotely fed up—even when the jokes became really infantile. All morning people kept trying to outdo each other by making more obscure pile references. Work was "really *piling*" up. Carpets had "a really soft *pile*." "Ooh, what's that terrible noise outside. Could it be a *pile* driver?"

Chelsea came in about twelve. She'd spent the morning visiting a client.

Cyn noticed her about fifteen minutes later, standing at the coffee machine. She decided there was no point going on the attack—at least not yet. First, she would listen to what Chelsea had to say.

"So," Cyn began lightly, "did you happen to notice my Smart Car in the car park?"

"God, sweetie, what can I say?" Chelsea said, raking her highlights. "Everybody's talking about it. I am so, so sorry. I was certain both cars were going to be carrying ads for painkillers or something. It was a complete shock when the guy at the showroom gave me the Stella McCartney car. I feel really bad. It's awful the way everybody's making fun of you. I'd give anything for it to be me. If it hadn't been for this excruciating abscess on my tooth, I would have waited until the next day to go to the showroom." She gave a sudden (rather theatrical, Cyn thought) wince and brought her hand to her jaw. Then she explained that the only appointment she could get at the dentist had been precisely when they were due to pick up their cars.

Hang on, Cyn thought, this didn't make sense. "But if you were in so much pain that night," she said, "how did you manage to go and pick up the car?"

"I was on extra-strength painkillers. I figured it was the lesser of two evils. The pain was bound to be worse the next morning. I talked to the people at the showroom at about four that afternoon and by pure chance one of the cars had already arrived. It just happened to be the Stella car. I'm so sorry I didn't phone you. I just forgot. I think it was probably the pills making me feel a bit weird. I don't know how I managed to drive home."

"But you're all right now?"

"Oh, you know," she said with another grimace, "the pain comes and goes." Then her face broke into what Hugh would no doubt have described as a martyred smile. "But I'm dealing with it." Cyn didn't know what to make of her story. She knew what Hugh and Harmony would think—that Chelsea was putting on an act and that she had taken the car on purpose.

"You know, I feel so guilty about this whole thing that I just phoned Stella's people to see if it would be OK for us to swap cars, but they said there would be a problem with the insurance. I didn't quite understand, but apparently . . ."

"That's OK," Cyn said. "Don't worry. I'm going to phone the Anusol people in a minute. I'm sure I'll get it sorted out."

"You sure? What can I say?"

"It's OK," Cyn said, "you don't have to say anything."

Cyn had been completely thrown by Chelsea's thought about wanting to swap cars. Now she didn't know what to think. She was still dithering, wondering whether to let the whole thing go or just come out with it and say, "Look, Chelsea, I'm not sure I buy any of this toothache nonsense. I think you have a problem with me and wangled it so that you got the Stella car," when Graham Chandler interrupted them.

"OK," he announced, "show-and-tell session in trailer one at two o'clock." He sounded a bit irritable, Cyn thought. No point mentioning the Anusol ad to him and seeing if he would phone the company to try and persuade them to tone the ad down a bit. He clearly had more urgent matters on his mind. She knew it wasn't just work pressure. He was also exhausted. Three months ago his wife had given birth to IVF triplets, and judging by the dark circles under his eyes, they still weren't sleeping. "Hang on," Cyn said to Graham, "I thought that meeting wasn't until the day after tomorrow." After a brainstorming session the previous week, Graham had sent everybody away to "think wild" about ways of promoting the new Droolin' Dream low-fat doughnut. It was agreed that those thoughts would be discussed at the next show-and-tell meeting.

"I know what I said," Graham said briskly, "but things have changed. I'm off to New York this evening. This Droolin' Dream account is worth a fortune. We need to get some ideas up and running before I go." Andy and Phil had been in New York for a couple of months setting up PCW NY. Apparently Andy had phoned a couple of hours ago to say things were going seriously wrong with the attorneys and Graham's presence was needed urgently.

It was only after Graham had gone that Cyn noticed that Chelsea was looking strained and rather pale. "You OK?" she said, thinking that maybe this tooth abscess was for real after all.

"It's OK, I'll be fine when the antibiotics kick in." But something about the expression on Chelsea's face left Cyn thinking that it wasn't just the tooth that was troubling her. Cyn was certain she was seeing something in Chelsea that she had never seen before. It was hovering about her eyes and looked remarkably like panic.

"So," Cyn said, "I bet you've got loads of ideas to take into this show-and-tell session."

"Oh, a few, maybe," Chelsea said, minus her usual smug smile. It occurred to Cyn that for once in her life, Chelsea was scared that her ideas would be found wanting. God alone knew why. They had never been found wanting in the past. Chelsea was clearly taking this promotion thing so seriously that it was starting to get to her. All that stood between her and it was winning the Droolin' Dream doughnut account. Of course there was always the possibility, Cyn thought, that she, Cyn, might win the account and then the promotion could be hers. Remote as the possibility was, Cyn still had some faith in herself.

She had never quite understood the way Chelsea's creative mind worked. At initial briefings when it was announced that a client was looking for a new advertising campaign and that PCW had been invited to pitch for it, Chelsea remained uncharacteristically quiet. While everybody else threw initial thoughts and ideas into the pot, she would simply listen. It was only days later—at the show-and-tell meetings—that Chelsea came into her own and stunned people with her brilliance. Like everybody else at PCW, Cyn assumed that Chelsea simply had one of those brains that worked best when she was alone and not under pressure.

"Anyway," Chelsea said, "I should get going. I've got some calls to make." With that she walked off, still looking distracted.

Cyn sat down at her desk and checked her e-mail. The first was from Keith Geary saying he was going to be in South Korea for at least a couple more weeks and he was sure she wouldn't mind hanging on to Morris. "Hmm, all the same if I do," she muttered, thinking about carting Morris all the way home and having him in her kitchen for another fortnight, yakking away at full volume about his lack of a sex life. She wrote a reply to Keith:

*No prob. Me and Morris great pals. Have you managed to get a shag yet? Morris says it's been three months. XXX Cyn.*

She giggled and pressed *send*.

Then she phoned Anusol. When she finally located the person she needed to speak to—a woman named Lisa Patterson—all she got was her voice mail. The message included her e-mail address. Cyn decided to bash out a quick e-mail. But try as she might, she just couldn't get the tone right. It was vital not to appear demanding or ungrateful because it could threaten PCW's relationship with the company. It took nearly an hour before she felt she'd hit the right note. Finally she let it go.

"*Pile* of mail for you." Luke, the office runner, was standing next to her holding a stack of letters, which he dumped on her desk.

"Cheers, Luke," she said with a smile, refusing to rise to his teasing. Realizing he wasn't going to get the reaction he wanted, he replaced his headphones, turned his Walkman back on and loped off. When she looked up a few moments later, he was moshing next to the water cooler.

As she started to open her mail, she noticed Chelsea was on the phone. She seemed quite frantic. Cyn thought maybe a client was giving her a hard time and decided to go over and offer to get her a cup of coffee.

"Charlie, please," Chelsea was saying, pressing her eyelids with her fingers. "I know I said it wasn't for another two days, but things have changed. I really need for you to do this. No, it can't wait. I'm desperate. Yes, I know it's the middle of the night in L.A. I'm sorry, but this is the last time. I promise . . . Please, Charlie—for me . . . What do you mean, you can't? Can't or won't? . . . Oh, all right then, screw you."

"You look as if you could do with a cuppa." Chelsea was red in the face. She jumped when she saw Cyn.

"No, I'm fine," she snapped. "Totally fine."

"You sure?"

"Perfectly. Why shouldn't I be?" Cyn was completely

mystified. She couldn't begin to work out what was going on. Chelsea was always so composed and in control. Cyn had never seen her so agitated. "If you say so." Cyn turned to go.

"OK, here's the thing," Chelsea came back sounding a bit calmer, clearly deciding Cyn deserved an explanation. "I'm running a bit short of cash—you know, too much month left at the end of the money. I asked my brother to loan me a couple of hundred dollars, but he said no."

It made no sense. Surely all Chelsea had to do if she was short of money was to ring her dad. Unless, of course, Chelsea's Harvey Nicks habit meant she had run up huge credit card debts. Maybe her father was doing the tough-love thing and refusing to bankroll her. Or maybe Sargent Roggenfelder paid her rent and her car expenses and that was it. Perhaps Chelsea was having to fend for herself more than anybody realized.

"Chelsea, look, if it's money you need I can always let you have a bit."

Chelsea's face softened. "God, no. I wouldn't dream of taking money from you. I'll be fine."

"OK, if you're sure."

"I'm sure," Chelsea said, offering Cyn a grateful smile.

Cyn went back to her desk to find an e-mail from Graham Chandler to say he was now catching an earlier flight to New York, the show-and-tell meeting was canceled and could everybody please write down their ideas for the Droolin' Dream doughnut TV spot. "No e-mails, please. I'd like hard copies on my desk in fifteen minutes."

Cyn got up the notes she'd made on the low-fat doughnuts. She'd had a few thoughts, but there was one idea in particular that she reckoned wasn't at all bad. In fact, although she said so herself, she thought it was rather brilliant. Nevertheless, she was sure it wouldn't compete with anything Chelsea had come up with. The idea had come to her in bed a couple of nights ago, just as she was dropping off.

She saw a commercial shot in black and white. Six plump sixties housewives are sitting around a Formica kitchen table drinking coffee, complaining about their weight and how boring diets are. Enter gorgeous Audrey Hepburn look-alike in a tiny suit and pillbox hat maybe. She is carrying a large box of Droolin' Dream doughnuts. She offers round the doughnuts, but of course the women all refuse them and are mad with envy that she can eat doughnuts and stay so slim. Audrey sits down, picks up a doughnut and lets them into her "little secret": "Girls, this is no ordinary doughnut. This is the new Low Nut from Droolin' Dream. Same delicious Droolin' Dream taste. Ninety percent less fat." The ad ends with a sixties-style harmonized jingle: "Do not doughnut, why not Low Nut?"

It took Cyn ten minutes to turn the notes into a proper proposal. She was just about to print it out when her phone rang. It was one of the girls on reception to say that the people from Pickersgill Double Glazing had arrived. Cyn felt panic rise inside her. "Oh, God, I completely lost track of time. Look, could you sit them down at the big conference table and offer them some coffee? I'll be two minutes."

Pickersgill Double Glazing was one of the agency's smaller, bread-and-butter clients that had first used PCW early on, when the company was just setting out and its fees were laughably low. Cyn was due to talk the Pickersgill people through her idea for a poster campaign. It was based on the twister scene in *The Wizard of Oz*. She envisaged a photograph of Dorothy, Aunty Em and Uncle Henry snuggled up in their cozy little shack in Kansas, unaware of the raging twister outside. The caption underneath would read: "There's no place like home—with Pickersgill Double Glazing."

She still needed to print the handout she'd written to accompany the presentation. Plus she needed to print out her proposal for Graham. She decided to do the proposal first.

She clicked on *print,* but nothing happened. "Come on, come on," she muttered, giving the printer an encouraging tap. "Work." Then she saw that it was calling for paper. "Anybody seen any printer paper lying about?" she called out to nobody in particular. Nobody had. She ran over to the stationery cupboard. Everything but. By the time she found a packet of paper—lying on the counter in the kitchen area—a full ten minutes had passed. She tore back to her desk.

As she ripped her Droolin' Dream proposal from the printer she saw Chelsea heading toward the stairs that led to Graham's office. "Hey, Chelsea," she called out, "I'm running late for a meeting, you couldn't hand in my proposal as well, too, could you?"

"Sure," Chelsea said easily, coming over. "No problem."

Cyn handed her the proposal and turned back to the printer, but it had clearly picked up her tension and now was refusing point-blank to print the handout she needed for the Pickersgill meeting. Her heart thumping because she was now fifteen minutes late, she decided she had no choice but to forget the handout. She would take her laptop to the meeting and refer to the notes on her screen.

She virtually ran over to the long meeting table. "Now, then," Cyril Pickersgill said gruffly as she stood in front of him, breathless, her hand extended, "what time do you call this, young lady?" He ignored her outstretched hand and began shoving tobacco into his pipe. "You trendy young advertising folk with your sun-dried tomatoes, stress balls and caged birds sitting on the table may not think it's important, but in Yorkshire where I come from punctuality is still the hallmark of a good businessman."

"I am so sorry, Mr. Pickersgill, but I've been having trouble with my printer. And the bird wouldn't normally be here. It's just temporary." She found herself praying that Morris would keep his beak shut for the next half hour or so.

"And what's wrong with old-fashioned pen and paper, if I might ask?"

"Dad, I'm sure Miss Fishbein's doing her best." Wayne, Mr. Pickersgill junior, was about thirty-five. He was wearing a black Hugo Boss suit, two chunky gold signet rings and brown shoes with rubber soles.

"Ay, I've no doubt she is." Cyril lit his pipe and began puffing. "And that's what makes the whole thing so pitiful."

"I'm really sorry, Mr. Pickersgill," Cyn said, "but this is a no-smoking office."

"Bloody 'ell, whole world's gone mad. I thought I were still in London—me own capital city, not flamin' California."

"Dad, please." Wayne Pickersgill shot Cyn an apologetic look.

Cyn suggested they sit down. She put her laptop down on the table. "Right, I think I should get to it. I've got all my notes on my laptop here."

"Don't patronize me, young lady. I do know what a laptop is. I may come from a different generation, but I still know how many beans make five."

"Dad!"

Cyn cleared her throat. "Right, am I'm correct in thinking you've both seen *The Wizard of Oz*?"

"Ay. And what, if I might ask, does that have to do wi' t' price of fish?"

"OK, let me explain . . ." She had been going no more than ten, maybe fifteen seconds when it happened.

"Fuck, I need a shag. I need a shag. It's been three months. Three sodding months since I got my leg over."

Cyril Pickersgill was practically choking on his pipe. "What the bloody 'ell . . . ?" Cyn could do nothing except smile a sheepish, inadequate smile. "It's a mynah bird. It belongs to one of my colleagues. It repeats everything it hears. I think I'll just move it so that we can have some quiet." She stood up and took hold of the cage handle. But it was too late: "God, that Cyril Pickersgill's a miserable, boring old duffer," Morris went on, doing a perfect imitation of Cyn. "Put him out to grass. Put him out to grass."

# *Chapter* 5

Three days later Cyn got an e-mail from Graham Chandler, who was still in New York, informing her that her idea for the Droolin' Dream TV commercial had come across as "rushed, ill-considered and lacking in wow factor." He went on to say that in his opinion, "there is no way this is going to fly with the client. Am concerned that lately you've not been performing to your usual standard. Let's talk when I get back."

Cyn could hardly believe what she was reading. Her "Do not doughnut, why not Low Nut?" slogan may not have been in quite the same league as "Go to work on an egg" or "They're grrreat," but she had been rather proud of it. She'd bounced it off Hugh, who could be exceedingly snotty about TV advertising, which he described as "brutalized low art," and even he had said it was brill.

Her confidence having taken a severe bashing, Cyn was finding it hard to be her usual upbeat self. The Pickersgills' furious walkout hadn't helped. Nobody apart from Cyn and the girls at reception had seen them leave, but when Graham came back and read the inevitable letter of outrage from

Cyril Pickersgill in which he would declare that he was taking his business elsewhere, she would be toast.

Whereas Cyn—along with two or three of the other copywriters who also thought they had come up with pretty good ideas—was feeling pretty miserable, Chelsea was ecstatic. It seemed that her Droolin' Dream idea had "flown with the client." Nobody was in any doubt that when he came back, Graham would tell Chelsea that the senior copywriter's job was hers.

Chelsea spent the rest of the week on the phone and e-mailing with the Droolin' Dream people in preparation for a big meeting with their marketing department in Slough.

Harmony had told Cyn not to worry if she got the sack. "You can always come and work at reception at the salon. You never know, one of my rich clients might ask you out. Nick Bruciano asked me out last week."

"God, I've seen him in the papers. He's gorgeous. Isn't he one of the richest men in the country?"

"Yeah, he's also married with three tiny kids."

"So, what did you say?"

"I told him I wanted to spend more time with my blender."

Unlike Cyn, Harmony was a veritable virtuoso of the put-down.

By the following Tuesday lunchtime Cyn was thinking seriously about handing in her resignation before she was asked to go. Suddenly, the idea of a low-stress life in the country held enormous appeal. Perhaps she would open a cutesy little teashop in the Yorkshire Dales. She could call it The Cake District.

Feeling like she really needed to escape from the office

for an hour or so, she decided to go to the gym. It was only round the corner and everybody at PCW had cut-price membership. Cyn had been three times since Christmas. It was now early March. Most people at the office were as bad and only a handful went regularly. This small group included Chelsea, who was there at half past seven every morning.

Today the place was almost empty apart from a few regulars Cyn recognized.

Sylvia and Pam waved to her from their treadmills. The pair worked for the modeling agency up the road. They were in their fifties, a size eight (between them), with wind-tunnel faces covered in so much makeup that if it had fallen off it would have killed the cat. There were a couple of muscle-bound gay guys—whose names she didn't know—in skin-tight tank tops. They were taking turns on one of the weight machines and, judging by the loud grunts, seemed to be giving themselves hernias.

Cyn was heading over to the StairMaster when she noticed Chelsea. She remembered her saying something about having a breakfast meeting that morning. She'd clearly missed her gym session and was catching up now. Cyn thought she ought to say hi, but since Chelsea was standing in front of the huge wall mirror doing yoga stretches with an otherworldly, transcendental look on her face, Cyn thought it best not to interrupt her. Instead she stood watching her for a while, taking in Chelsea's tiny Lycra shorts and crop top. Cyn suddenly felt self-conscious in her sweatpants and baggy "Firemen do it with a big hose" T-shirt.

Chelsea was lying on her front, now in the cobra position. Cyn couldn't believe a person could arch her back and neck to the extent Chelsea was arching hers. "God," Cyn thought, "some people just get all the ligaments." She watched her change into the lotus position. More ostentatious back stretching and neck lengthening. She watched as Chelsea closed her eyes and breathed in and out very slowly. Finally she opened her eyes and noticed Cyn. "Pranayama," she announced.

"Sorry?" Cyn said, blinking.

"These movements. They're known as Pranayama. It means stretching one's life force. You should try it." Chelsea stood up, stretched her arms above her head. Then she bent down from the waist and gripped her calves with her hands. As she did this her tight little butt was on full view. A couple of the young lads who worked at the gym stopped wiping floor mats and began staring. Cyn could practically see the drool.

"Think I'll just hit the StairMaster," Cyn said to Chelsea. "Oh, by the way, I haven't had a chance to say well done on getting the Droolin' Dream account."

"Oh, it was just a lucky break, really," Chelsea cooed, sitting down on the mat and starting to hook her foot around her head. "Don't worry, Cyn. I'm sure your moment in the sun will come. You just have to be patient, that's all."

"Yeah. I'm sure you're right." Cyn managed a small smile. She walked over to the StairMaster. Chelsea's foot was now fully behind her head, her Lycra covered crotch fully exposed. If the two young boys had been staring before, now they were positively ogling. The two gay guys were watching, too. "My God," Cyn heard one of them say, "what a contortionist. This woman could die in her own arms."

Cyn stepped onto the StairMaster. A few feet away a balding middle-aged chap in short shorts was doing sit-ups, his knees bent in front of him. Cyn tried diverting her eyes, but she was too late. She had seen up one of his short legs and gotten a magnificent close-up of his scrotum.

Feeling slightly queasy, she turned her attention to choosing an exercise program. She decided that since she hadn't done any exercise for ages, she would ease herself in gently.

She punched in level three on the touch pad. She was just wondering if she could manage fifteen minutes when somebody let out a shriek that actually sounded like it could curdle blood. Cyn's eyes shot to the mat. It was Chelsea. She was rolling around, clearly in the most appalling agony, her foot still behind her head.

"Omigod. Omigod. Please help me. Please." Chelsea's face was contorted in pain. "It's locked. I can't move."

Cyn and the two young gym hands went tearing over and knelt beside her. "OK, take it easy," one of the lads said. "I'm going to try and ease your leg down." He put his hands round her calf and tried to dislodge the leg. Chelsea cried out. "It's not just my leg. It's my back as well. I think I may have done something to my spine." One of the boys stood up and said he would call an ambulance. "It's all right, Chelsea," Cyn said. "Hang on in there. Can you get yourself vaguely comfortable?" In the end Cyn and the remaining lad managed to ease her onto her back.

It took fifteen minutes for the ambulance to arrive and all the time Chelsea just lay there with tears streaming down her cheeks. When the paramedics arrived they were too scared to move her leg in case they did any more damage. In the end it took four of them—the paramedics and the two lads, plus substantial amounts of oxygen mixed with painkiller—to ease her onto a stretcher.

"Don't worry, I'll come to the hospital with you," Cyn said, walking beside the stretcher.

"No, I'll be fine," Chelsea stuttered, lifting the gas- and air-mask off her face. "My mom's in town. I'll get the hospital to call her. I'd rather you went back to the office and phoned the Droolin' Dream people and explained I'm not going to be able to make our meeting this afternoon. Tell them I'll call as soon as I can." She insisted on giving Cyn the

Droolin' Dream phone number there and then. "Don't worry," Cyn said, "it won't take a minute to get it from Directory or from your computer files."

"No! Don't touch my files." She sounded almost hysterical.

"OK," Cyn soothed. "Don't worry. It's not a problem."

"It's just that there's personal stuff on my computer," Chelsea said, her voice softening. "My diary, stuff I wouldn't want anybody to see. Please, just take down the number." One of the paramedics passed Cyn a Bic and she wrote the number down on her hand. "Listen, Chelsea, are you sure you want me to go? At least let me stay with you until your mum arrives."

"Don't worry. I'll be OK." She screwed up her face against the pain, brought the mask back to her face and inhaled deeply.

Cyn watched Chelsea being loaded into the ambulance and gave her a tiny wave good-bye. Chelsea just about managed to lift her hand in response.

She collected her clothes and dashed back to the office without bothering to get changed. When she explained that Chelsea had hurt her back getting her foot behind her ear, most people grimaced in horror, but several blokes saw it as a cue to get down on the floor to see if they could get their legs behind their heads. The teasing, joshing and bet-taking must have gone on for a full twenty minutes and ended up with Luke the office runner managing to get both legs behind his head at the same time and winning twenty quid. Eventually somebody asked what would happen about Chelsea's Droolin' Dream meeting. Cyn explained that she was about to phone them.

She made her way over to her desk, sat down and picked

up the receiver. It was only when she opened her hand that she saw the number had disappeared. Stupidly she had written it down on her palm rather than on the back of her hand and she had sweated it off. A few faint bluish squiggles remained—nothing she could make out. She rang Directory. "Sorry, all of our operators are busy at present. Your call is being held in a queue and will be dealt with as soon as possible."

"Soddit," she muttered, irritably. She replaced the receiver. She knew she wouldn't have been made to hang on for more than half a minute or so, but she couldn't wait. After all the adrenaline that had been pumping through her veins today, her blood sugar had plummeted and she was ravenous. All she wanted to do was to make this call to the Droolin' Dream people and get some food inside her. She got up and walked briskly across the office toward Chelsea's desk. "Chelsea knows I don't gossip. Why would she think for one minute that I would be interested in reading her diary?"

She sat in front of Chelsea's open PowerBook and pressed the space bar. The screen saver—a picture of herself with Hillary Clinton—disappeared and was replaced by dozens of icons. She clicked on My Documents. The Droolin' Dream file was about halfway down the first column. She went into it. The phone number, e-mail address and contact names appeared at the top of the screen. She was just about to come out of the file when she noticed the heading: Droolin' Dream Proposal. Cyn simply couldn't resist finding out what it was that Graham and the doughnut company had gotten so excited about. She started reading. "Scene: early 1960s—a group of housewives are sitting in a kitchen at one of those old-fashioned blue Formica kitchen tables. They're all a bit plump and discussing how boring diets are . . ."

If Cyn's jaw had dropped any farther it would have made contact with the desk. "What the . . . ?" "In comes this

Audrey Hepburn look-alike in a tiny suit . . ." "Bitch. I don't believe it. You total, utter and complete bitch." She read on. "I suggest the end line: *Do not doughnut. Why not Low Nut?*"

Cyn put her head in her hands. Instead of taking her proposal to Graham Chandler the other day, Chelsea had copied it out, changed a few words around and put her own name to it. Presumably Cyn's name had gone on Chelsea's original proposal. But why? Why had she done it? Deep-seated insecurity, Cyn guessed. But Chelsea was so talented. Was it possible she could be so full of self-doubt? So insecure that she needed to steal an idea from a colleague? Apparently so. By now, any doubts that Chelsea hadn't done the dirty on her over the Smart Car had vanished. Tears of hurt and rage poured down Cyn's cheeks. Her hands formed fists so tight that her nails dug into her flesh. "She will pay for this. God, she will pay for this." Distressed as she was, Cyn couldn't help thinking how much like the end of a Scooby-Doo cartoon she sounded. Nor did it escape her how pleased Veronica, her therapist, would be to discover that she was not only getting in touch with her anger but contemplating vengeance.

Cyn came out of Chelsea's document file and walked back to her own desk. As she slumped into her chair she noticed a stress ball lying next to the phone. She picked it up and started to pummel it. Chelsea must have been completely round the bend to even think she would get away with it, Cyn thought. At the first meeting to discuss how the project was going, Cyn would have found out she'd pinched her idea. Then she remembered that Graham was in New York. It was possible that meeting would never have taken place and that Chelsea and Graham would simply have communicated by e-mail. But even that would only have delayed Cyn finding out. The truth would have come out eventually—after which Cyn would have told Graham what Chelsea had done and she would have been dismissed immediately.

Or would she? It suddenly struck her that if Chelsea was so scheming and manipulative, and apparently without any conscience, she might well deny stealing Cyn's idea. What if Graham believed her? Anything was possible. After all, Cyn's career had taken a bit of a downturn these last few weeks—culminating in the Pickersgill fiasco, which Graham still knew nothing about. Maybe when he got back, Chelsea would convince him that the stress of the job was getting to Cyn and that she was cracking up. Much as she wanted to punch Chelsea's lights out and promise to tell Graham precisely what had gone on, she decided against it.

Just then the phone rang. It was Lisa Patterson from Anusol. She said she had been off sick and apologized for taking so long to get back to Cyn. "I have to confess to being a bit perplexed about all this," she said, kindly. "I made a point of asking if the ad was going to cause problems. The woman I spoke to assured me it wouldn't."

"This woman," Cyn said, rubbing her forehead, "did you happen to get her name?"

"She didn't give a name, but she spoke with an American accent." Cyn dug her nails hard into the stress ball.

"Look, I understand that you're upset," Lisa Patterson went on. "I can't say I'd be particularly happy driving around in a car advertising Anusol and I work for the company. The thing is, I'm not sure there's much I can do about it now. I realize you would like something a bit more discreet, but it cost us rather a lot to get the ad done. I'm not sure we have the budget to take it off and replace it with something else. Of course you're perfectly welcome to return the car."

Cyn couldn't really think straight, but her head was clear enough to know that her Peugeot was on its last legs and virtually only fit for scrap. She would have to keep the Smart Car. Plus, apart from the ad, she absolutely loved it. Lisa was fairly junior at Anusol. Maybe when he got back Graham

Chandler would speak to one of the bosses and see if something could be done to change the ad. "No, that's OK," Cyn said. "I'll hang on to the car for the time being."

"Well, if you're sure. And once again I'm really sorry about the mix-up. Somebody at your end clearly got their wires crossed."

"Didn't they just," Cyn said bitterly. Then she thanked Lisa for calling.

Eventually she got up and went over to the coffee machine. A couple of people noticed her red eyes and asked if she was OK. She said she was fine and made up a pathetic excuse about having an eyelash in her eye.

She took the coffee back to her desk. As she sat down, her phone rang again. She thought about ignoring it. Then on about the eighth or ninth ring, she decided it might be something important and picked up. It was Hugh to say he had left his tie at her place the other night. "Oh, right, yeah," she said. "I found it on the coffee table."

"Gorgeous, you sound wretched. What on earth's the matter?"

Slowly, between sobs, she told him what had happened, ending with the call from Lisa Patterson. Hugh was rarely lost for words, but apart from the occasional "My God," he listened in stunned silence. "Screwing you over with the car is one thing," he said, when she'd finished telling the tale, "but to steal your idea . . . That's something else. It's in a different league. It simply beggars belief. It's so cruel. So evil."

"I keep trying to work out why she did it. I mean, was it insecurity, jealousy, an obsessive need for power and control?" She wiped her eyes with the heel of her hand.

"For chrissake, who cares why?" Hugh said. "You've been in therapy too long. You're the victim here, not Chelsea. It's not your job to start analyzing her and feeling sorry for her."

"I don't feel sorry for her. I hate her."

"Good. So, have you spoken to your boss?"

"Can't, he's away."

"You could e-mail him."

"I know, but I'm not sure he would believe me," she explained.

"Even when you've got the evidence on Chelsea's computer?"

"It proves nothing. Who's to say the idea wasn't hers?"

"But it's on your computer, too. Surely that looks suspicious?"

"Absolutely," Cyn said, "but in fact it gives Chelsea even more ammunition. She would twist things around and say that the moment she went into hospital I copied her Droolin' Dream document and transferred it to my computer."

"Why would you do that?"

"She would argue that it was because I was jealous of her and wanted to discredit her. I've no doubt that people in the office would believe my version of events, but Graham has a lot of time and respect for Chelsea."

Hugh went silent for a moment. "OK," he said, his voice rising in excitement, "call me a genius, but I think I've got an idea. Every document on a computer is time coded. If you go into the proposal she nicked from you, you'll find the time she started writing it, the time she finished it, the lot. If it's after the time that you wrote the proposal on your computer, then you can prove without doubt that you had the idea first. Do you know how to get up the properties of the document?"

She said she did.

"Right, why don't you go and take a look? I'll hang on."

Her heart thumping with anticipation, she raced back to Chelsea's computer and made a few clicks with the mouse. In a moment utter dismay had overtaken her again.

She went back to the phone. "Chelsea turned back the

time code and changed the date to make it look like she wrote it days before."

"God, she's nobody's fool. I don't know what to suggest . . . It's so ironic—me and Harmony watching *Working Girl* the other night."

She gave a small laugh. "Isn't it?"

"So, what are you going to do?"

"Not sure. I need some time to work things out."

"Look, if there's anything you need, I'm always here."

"I know. Thanks."

"Love you, gorgeous."

"Love you, too."

Sipping the hot coffee made her feel better. After a few minutes she started to think more clearly. She needed to convince Graham of the truth. How she was going to make that happen, she wasn't quite sure. But somehow she would prove to him that the idea had been hers all along and then he would have to give her the senior copywriter's job.

She turned her attention to the number she'd written down for Gary Rossiter, the head of marketing at Droolin' Dream. A thought was starting to take shape in her mind. It seemed so obvious. After all, the Droolin' Dream idea belonged to her, not Chelsea. What if she went to the meeting with the Droolin' Dream people instead of Chelsea? Of course she could hardly go in bleating about Chelsea having stolen her idea. It would look highly unprofessional. She would have to invent a reason why she was replacing her, but that shouldn't be hard. She took another sip of coffee. Maybe she would tell this Gary Rossiter that the Droolin' Dream commercial had originally been her idea but the whole thing had been passed over to Chelsea when . . . When what? OK, when her flat flooded? She would say she had taken some time off to get the flat sorted, but everything was fine now. She was back on the case and raring to go.

Deciding her excuse sounded perfectly feasible, Cyn picked up her work clothes, which were draped over the back of her chair, and went to the ladies' room to get changed. She'd made up her mind. She was off to Slough.

As she was touching up her makeup it occurred to her that she had done absolutely no preparation for this meeting. Suddenly she wasn't sure she could handle it. She had absolutely no idea what the Droolin' Dream people would want to know. "Course you do," she said to her reflection. "You've done these things a hundred times." She was right. Meetings like this were a formality more than anything. They would ask a few questions, but nothing she couldn't handle.

She came out of the ladies' room, picked up her bag and coat and went to find Brian Lockwood. He was one of the senior creatives and had been left in charge while Graham was away. She told him that she had an afternoon meeting and wouldn't be back today. Brian was a piss artist who, even when he was sober, only took in a quarter of what was said to him. Right now he had just got back from a boozy lunch at the Oxo Tower and was looking particularly bleary-eyed. "Right, fine, whatever," he said, barely bothering to look up.

# Chapter 6

The Droolin' Dream HQ was on one of those ominously depopulated, tinted-glass-and-metal industrial parks. As Cyn drove past the immaculate lawns, beds of daffodils and newly planted conifers, she half expected to see mad government scientists in white coats and wiry hair accompanying a group of freshly programmed Stepford Wives on their afternoon constitutional.

Cyn felt a sense of mild relief when the girl at the Droolin' Dream reception desk turned out to be a Britney Spears clone and couldn't have looked less ominous if she'd tried. When Cyn walked in, the girl's hair was draped over her face like Cousin Itt and she was busy examining the strands for split ends. At the same time she was yakking away on the phone. "So anyway, I'm like, 'Tell it to the hand' and she's like, 'You bitch.' Dah. I mean who's the bitch here? She slept with my boyfriend." At this point the girl noticed Cyn, made her excuses to whomever she was speaking to and put down the phone. She tossed back her hair. Cyn said she was there to see Gary Rossiter.

"Oh, right chyew are." She tapped out his extension with an impossibly long nail that had a tiny fake diamond stuck to its center. "Mr. Rotisserie, yer three o'clock's here." She looked up at Cyn. "Says he'll be down in a jiffy."

Cyn sat down on one of the imitation brown suede armchairs. The receptionist went back to her split ends. Several jiffies passed. After about ten minutes, a beaming chap in his midthirties came bounding toward her. He was short and chunky, rather like a small sofa, Cyn thought. He also had a smile full of crooked teeth.

"Chel! So, you found us all right." Chel? What was with the Chel? Talk about overfamiliar. Loathe Chelsea as she did, she couldn't help feeling indignant on her behalf.

"Yes. No problems." Cyn smiled, extending her hand toward him. But Gary Rossiter ignored the hand. Instead he leaned in toward her and kissed her on both cheeks. Strong whiff of coffee breath. "We don't stand on ceremony here at Droolin' Dream. Anyway, after all those e-mails I really feel like I know you."

"Ah, right. Well, actually, I should put you straight on that. You see there's been a change of . . ." But she could see he wasn't listening. Instead he was doing up the button on his shirt, which had burst open at the midsection of his paunch.

"So, not too much traffic on the M4, then? Nice one! I was just saying to our boys upstairs in sales that our roads must seem pretty pathetic to you. I mean, where you come from it's all six-lane highways. I was watching a helicopter police chase in Florida the other night. Amazing. And I mean amazing with a capital Wow. Do you get a lot of police chases where you come from?"

"No, Crouch End tends to be pretty quiet as a rule," Cyn said.

Gary cracked up. "Nice one! I like it. I like it. No, I meant, do you get a lot of police chases where you come from originally?"

"No. Not really," she said briskly, aware that if she didn't tell him who she was right now, the situation could spin out of control. "Look, Gary, before we go on, there's something I need to explain."

"Call me Gazza. Everybody does."

Gazza? Gawd. "Right. Gazza. Well, you see . . ."

"It's funny, your American accent is not as pronounced as it was on the phone . . . Oh, must get you a visitor's pass before we can let you go upstairs."

"Right." Bugger. Now he'd noticed her accent. Tell him. Tell him. But Gazza had walked off and was already standing in front of the reception desk. Cyn followed him. The It Girl was faffing around looking for a pen that worked. "By the way, Kelly," Cyn heard Gazza say to the receptionist in a taut whisper. "The name is Rossiter. Right? Not Rotisserie. Got that?"

"Right chyew are. Sorry." With the kind of slowness that would have driven even Pollyanna to eat her own head, the girl filled out a card and tucked it into a plastic pouch. Gary insisted on clipping it to the lapel of Cyn's jacket. "OK," he said, "your lift awaits. If you'd like to follow me."

"Fine. Lead on. Look, Gary . . ."

"Come on, now," he grinned, wagging a playful finger, "you promised you'd call me Gazza."

"Sorry. OK. The thing is, Gazza . . ."

The lift arrived and Gazza stood back to let her in. "You know, Chel," he said as the lift doors shut. "You don't mind me calling you Chel, do you?"

"No. I mean yes. Well, you see, actually . . ."

"Nice one. You know, Chel, I have to tell you from the get-go that all of us at DD were massively impressed with your concept. And I mean massively with a capital Huge."

"Wow. That's great, but there is something you should know."

"Of course our chairman is a bit of a—well, to be honest with you, he's a bit of a dinosaur—and he couldn't quite see where you were coming from artistically speaking. In fact he couldn't see it at all. Took some persuading from the rest of us, I can tell you. But when we mentioned your name his ears pricked up, I can tell you. 'If she's good enough for Procter and Gamble, then she's good enough for us,' he said. Until then he'd been thinking of giving the account to Saatchis, but it was your name that won him over."

"Really? I'm flattered."

"And so you should be. *Do not doughnut, why not Low Nut?* It's genius. And I mean genius with a capital Mastermind." Cyn's heart was pounding in her chest. God, what did she do now? If she told him she wasn't Chelsea Roggenfelder, PCW could lose the Droolin' Dream account. If she pretended to be Chelsea she would be committing a gargantuan act of deceit. Of course she knew what Tess McGill would have done, but this wasn't some daft Hollywood movie, it was real life and in real life people didn't go round imitating other people to get even with them—even when it could be argued that said imitation was utterly and completely justified. The lift bell pinged. The doors opened.

"You know, Chel," Gazza said as they stepped out, "your voice really does sound different from how I remember it on the phone. What happened to the accent?"

"My accent? Right, my accent . . ." OK, she either had to backtrack and reveal her true identity or pretend she was Chelsea and explain why she sounded so different. She could feel sick panic rising inside her.

Veronica said she needed to be in therapy to learn how to be bad, but not this bad. Cyn had been thinking more in terms of allowing herself to go overdrawn at the bank a couple of times a year or performing the occasional illegal U-turn. She had planned to give herself five years or so to reach this level of bravery. Now she had five seconds.

If she was going to commit the biggest sin of her entire

life—or to be more accurate, the first sin of her entire life—
there was no time to consider the morality of it all, no time
to think about the consequences, no time to phone Hugh
and Harmony so that they could reassure her she was doing
the right thing. If she was going to do it, she had to decide
now.

"Oh, right, of course, my accent. My American accent.
Yes, well, um. You see, the thing is . . ." Make a decision.
Make a decision. She could feel her heart pounding in her
chest. She inhaled deeply. "OK, the thing is that Graham
Chandler, our managing director, is very conscious of wanting PCW to come across as a very British company—you
know, Cool Britannia and all that, and he . . ." He what?
What? ". . . and he insisted I went on a course. That's it—a
course, to learn how to speak with a Bridish accent. I mean,
a Bri*tish* accent, there I go, nearly getting it all wrong again."
Omigod. She had done it. She was actually pretending to be
Chelsea Roggenfelder. She half expected to hear a thunder-
clap from on high.

"Well, it certainly worked," Gazza said. "You sound like a
native. And I mean native with a capital Brit."

"Yep, well, I do have a bit of a gift for these things. Apparently my mum's distantly related to Renée Zellweger." She
could not believe she had just said that. Like he was going to
believe her. She glanced over at the fire exit and thought
about making a run for it. "She says the talent for impersonating accents runs in the family. I learned to speak like this in
two days."

"Whoa. Gifted and beautiful," Gazza said, winking at her.
What? He had actually bought her daft story? Poor, gullible
Gazza really was a few fries short of a Happy Meal.

As they walked along the corridor, he seemed to sense
her tension. "No need to be nervous, Chel. You'll find all the
guys here at DD are really easygoing."

He ushered her into a conference room. A dozen or so people—a few women, but mainly men in suits—were sitting at a large oval table. In the center were two white plastic insulated coffeepots, a tray of cups and saucers, and a plate piled with doughnuts.

"OK, chaps and chap-esses," Gazza began with a single clap and rubbing of his chubby hands, "it gives me great pleasure, and I mean great with a capital Vast, to introduce the little lady who came up with the idea for the Low Nut ad. Without further ado, I'll hand the floor over to her."

"Thank you, Gazza." Cyn surveyed the chaps and chapesses and swallowed hard. She looked at the door. She didn't have to go through with this. There was still time to make a run for it. "Right, well, er . . . Hello, everybody. My name is Chelsea Roggenfelder." Christ. Now there was absolutely no going back. "And I would like to talk to you about my vision for the Droolin' Dream Low Nut campaign." On the drive over she'd defined the target market, how long it would be before she could organize a shoot, various actresses who might play the Audrey Hepburn character, whether or not there should be a poster and magazine campaign to accompany the TV ad.

"With *Do not doughnut, why not Low Nut?* I would like to think I have achieved a clear, objective, one-sentence focus statement . . ."

"I'll certainly second that," Gazza piped up.

She held everybody's attention for a good ten minutes. It was all going even more smoothly than she could have hoped. Then the chap sitting next to her started to ask her about cost. Of course the money was the only thing she hadn't had time to work on. "Right. Well, of course, over the last week or so, I have been working on a detailed strategic financial analysis . . ." To buy herself time to think about what she would say next, she stretched across to the plate of dough-nuts, picked one up and bit into it.

"Excellent," said the suit. "Admittedly, you've given us a ballpark figure, but we really need to know the bottom line." Of course, as a "creative" it wasn't strictly her job to work out the bottom line. That was left to their financial people to work out. No doubt Chelsea had already discussed it with them by e-mail and probably had a printout of all the costs. Of course Cyn hadn't thought to look for it in Chelsea's files. There was nothing for it but to bluff. "The bottom line. Yes. Well . . . sorry, I don't think I caught your name."

"That's because I didn't throw it," the chap said smugly, causing a ripple of male laughter. "But it's Dave."

"Well, Dave. Let me put it this way. I'm thinking that what with one thing and another and factoring in this and that based on our qualitative research methodology and bear-ing in mind that we need a greater synergy between product summarization and functional goal, I would say we are talk-ing somewhere in the region . . . ooh, I'd say . . ." She took a second bite of her doughnut. The next thing she knew, jam had spurted out onto Dave's trousers. His knee was covered in a patch of bright pink gloop the size of a ten-pence piece. He jumped up, muttered something about this being a brand-new suit and disappeared to the loo. Meanwhile Gazza said that he was sorry to cut things short, but he was overseeing a team-building exercise in a few minutes and that he was sure everybody had enough information to be getting on with. Cyn said she was disappointed they hadn't gotten round to discussing costs, but she would be sure to e-mail a detailed breakdown ASAP.

"Nice one." Gazza smiled.

He walked her back to the lift. "You were brilliant in there, Chel," he said. "You know, I have to confess that I find a woman talking about the synergy between product summarization and functional goal rather attractive."

"You do?" She was feeling distinctly uncomfortable now.

"Look, tell me to sling my hook, but I was wondering if you fancied going out sometime?"

Bloody hell. "That's very sweet of you, Gazza, but—" Just then Gazza sneezed. As he reached into his pocket for his handkerchief, his keys fell out and onto the floor. Cyn bent down and picked them up. Hanging off the key ring was a large red plastic nose with the words *Fart Detector* written across it. Suppressing the urge to roll her eyes, she handed him the key ring.

"Really works, you know," he said, taking hold of the nose. "Made in Korea. Here, listen." He pressed a tiny button on the side. "Fart detected. Fart detected." The mechanical voice sounded like an Amerasian Dalek.

"Brilliant," Gazza snorted. "Cracks me up every time. Do you want a go?"

"Not just now." Cyn smiled. "So, Gazza, about us going out . . ."

"You know, over the last week or so, I feel I've gotten to know you and I think there's a real chemistry between us. I'd like to get to know you better. So, I was thinking we could kick off with a couple of pints. I know this great sports bar. Then we could go for a curry and take in a late movie. Don't worry, I enjoy a good chick flick. I'm not one of those blokes who pretend we're going to see a film about orphans and it turns out to be ninety minutes of blowing stuff up. So, what do you reckon?"

There was no way she was going out with a man called Gazza. Particularly not one who said things like "amazing with a capital Wow," owned a fart detector and whose idea of a date involved beer, curry and a sports bar.

On the other hand she didn't dare jeopardize this deal. It

wasn't just that it was worth a fortune to PCW. To Cyn it was far more important that she got even with Chelsea. That meant seeing the project through and making a colossal success of it—colossal with a capital Gigantic. By refusing Gazza she was risking him turning against her and recommending to Droolin' Dream's chairman—with whom he clearly had influence—that the company take its business elsewhere. She decided to try and play for time.

"The thing is, Gazza," she said, "I'm very busy at the moment."

"Come on, you have to eat. I promise there'll be no strings. No pressure." She racked her brain, desperately trying to invent an excuse. "Actually, I'm off to the Brazilian rain forest the day after tomorrow to film a . . . a muesli commercial." Bugger, bugger, bugger. What on earth had possessed her to say muesli? "Won't be back for a week," she added.

"A commercial for muesli? In the Brazilian rain forest? Funny, I'd associate muesli with a more alpine setting."

"Yes, most people do, but I see this commercial as a deconstruction of neo-Bergmanesque, postexistential ennui." She hadn't the foggiest what that all meant—if anything—but it was the kind of intellectually impenetrable guff she'd heard Hugh spout when he was banging on about art-house films.

"Wow! I'm impressed. I just know we're not going to regret hiring you, Chel. OK, let's put our date on hold until you get back."

"Great," she said, massively relieved that she had been able to negotiate some breathing space.

"In the meantime, I'll e-mail you."

What? No. On no account could he be allowed to e-mail Chelsea. Posh private hospitals like the one Chelsea was in were bound to have Internet access. She could be checking her e-mail within hours. "Er, getting e-mails in the middle of the rain forest might be a problem. It'll be easier if you e-mail my assistant. Her name's Cyn. She's a lovely girl. She'll phone our hotel and pass on any messages." She gave him her e-mail address, which he wrote down on an immaculately folded Kleenex Man Size tissue. "Wicked. I'll be in touch."

"I'll look forward to that," she said.

As she headed out toward the M4, Cyn felt positively euphoric. It was partly the adrenaline still pumping through her, but it was primarily the realization that she was fulfilling her desire to do something bad and brave for the most honorable and noble of reasons. She pulled up at traffic lights, opened the window and started singing at the top of her lungs: "You know I'm Bad, I'm Bad, I'm Really, Really Bad . . ." A prim-looking woman in a red Metro alongside her gave a disgusted look. Whether this was in response to what Cyn was singing, the Anusol ad on the side of the car or both, Cyn had no idea. What was more, she didn't remotely care.

As she as she came onto the M4 slip road, she put her foot down and forced the Smart Car up to 70. Since the vehicle was so tiny, this felt more like 170. For a few minutes she flew along, the icy wind gusting through her hair, feeling as if she could take on the world.

She was still singing when her phone, which was lying on the passenger seat, started ringing. She wound up the window and picked up.

"Hey, Cyn, it's me, Chelsea." The shock of hearing Chelsea's voice instantly segued into fury. Bad back or no bad back, her instinct was to blast Chelsea with a character reading that would have her cowering under her hospital bed, begging for police protection. Almost at once her rage turned to panic. For some stupid reason, it hadn't occurred to her that Chelsea would phone to check up on the situation at

Droolin' Dream. She wasn't even remotely prepared. Did she have the wit and the nerve to fool Chelsea like she'd managed to fool Gazza? Heart thumping, she fought through her emotions, desperate to keep cool head.

"Chelsea, how *are* you?" She prayed she didn't sound suspiciously caring and upbeat.

"Pretty spacey from all the medication, but at least the pain's gone. The doctors say I'll be in the hospital for a few weeks. Apparently I've slipped three discs. Pretty major. Listen, Brian Lockwood told me you were off for the rest of the day. I just wanted to check that everything's OK with the guys at Droolin' Dream."

"Everything's fine," Cyn soothed, wondering how she was managing to sound so calm. "I've had a conversation with Gary Rossiter and he said he's happy to put everything on hold until you're back on your feet. He told me to tell you're not to worry about a thing and just concentrate on getting better."

"That is so darling, but I'll give him a call, just to reassure him."

What? No. She couldn't do that. It would blow the whole thing. Think, Cyn, think. "You can try calling him, but I don't think there's much point. He's on holiday for the next few weeks. I spoke to him a couple of hours ago. Your meeting was going to be his last appointment. Since you couldn't make it, he said it gave him the chance to leave early."

"That's strange. He never mentioned a vacation."

"Um. Hill walking in the Himalayas, apparently. Can't be reached."

"Funny, he didn't strike me as the hill-walking type. But you've definitely sorted everything out with him?"

"Definitely. It's all under control. You just take it easy."

"OK, I will. And thanks for calling him. It's really put my mind at ease."

"My pleasure," Cyn said, with a smile that would have done Snow White's stepmother proud.

Gradually, the traffic began to slow down. After a few minutes all three eastbound lanes were bumper-to-bumper. At the same time, Cyn's high gradually morphed into a not quite so high. Not only was she starting to think that impersonating Chelsea was immoral, she was imagining what might happen if she got found out. And she was bound to get found out. Did she really think she was going to pull this thing off? This wasn't a movie, it was real life. She saw herself in a few weeks having been sacked without a reference and effectively unemployable. Her thoughts were interrupted by her phone ringing again.

"Cyn, it's me, Harms. 'Ewge just told me what happened." Harmony was so outraged she was barely pausing for breath. "I-tell-you-if-I-got-hold-of-this-Chelsea-cow-I'd-bloody-swing-for-her." Cyn said that was a very sweet thought.

"Look," Harmony said, lowering her voice, "I know this bloke back in Liverpool. Petal, he's called—only don't be fooled, he's built like a brick shithouse. Ex-boxer. He does freelance jobs . . . on a contract basis, if you get my drift."

"Bloody hell! I'm not going to kill her!"

"No, I wasn't suggesting killing her. But maybe Petal could put the frighteners on her. You know, gently persuade her that it would be in her best interests to own up."

"*Put the frighteners on her?* Sorry, have we just stepped into a Philip Marlowe novel?"

"OK, it was just a thought."

"Look, Harms, I love it that you care, but I'm not sure violent intimidation is quite the way to go. Tell you what, let's agree to put it on the back burner and look at it again if my plan doesn't work out."

"Oh, right. I didn't know you had a plan."

Cyn explained.

"Omigod, just like in *Working Girl*. That's amazing. But do you think you can pull it off?"

"Dunno. That's the scary bit."

"You will. You will. I just know it. You just have to keep your nerve, that's all."

Harmony's encouragement boosted Cyn's mood, but not for long. As she hit the North Circular, she realized it was past six. Buggeration. She was desperate not be late for her therapy session two weeks running. Repeated lateness was something the group always seized on. They would question her commitment to the group, suggest she was late because subconsciously she had issues she didn't want to confront or that being late made her feel powerful and gave her a hold over the group. It would go on for hours.

In the end the traffic eased up just past Brent Cross and she arrived at Veronica's a few minutes early. The only person there was Joe, the exceedingly good-looking new chap in front of whom she had humiliated herself so thoroughly the previous week. He was looking slightly nervous and uneasy, she thought, but ever, ever so sexy.

"Bitter night," she said, taking in the gray V-neck sweater that he was wearing over a white T-shirt. Her eyes moved down. Same battered Levi's. Ah, but trendy new trainers— the Puma ones—which did up with those wrap-over strips. Umm. She really approved. "Sensible chap taking the seat near the fire."

The deal was that when the group wasn't in session, like now, conversation between members should be kept to the superficial and mundane. It tended to feel a bit false and awkward, but it made sense. Everybody agreed that the important stuff should be discussed in front of the whole group, when Veronica was present. On top of this, surnames were not revealed and Veronica asked them not to meet socially outside the group. The theory was that alliances would be formed that "might threaten the therapeutic process," in Veronica's words.

"If you're cold," Joe said, "please sit here. I'm fine." She hadn't noticed last week—probably because she was too taken up with her own embarrassment—but he spoke with a distinct Irish accent. He started to get up.

"Goodness, no, I wouldn't dream of it." She took a chair opposite him. OK, why opposite? Why not sit next to him? That would be the friendly, welcoming thing to do. But she knew why. She wouldn't have felt comfortable sitting next to him because she found him attractive. So, in order not to give him the wrong idea, she was sitting as far away from him as she could.

"So, you're Irish," she said, stating the stark staringly obvious.

"Yes. I'm from Dublin, but I've lived in London for the last five years."

"I've never been to Dublin. It's meant to be beautiful."

"It is," he said. His voice reminded her of Liam Neeson. He had the same inflection, the same deep but gentle tone. He asked her where she lived.

"Crouch End. Except tonight I drove from Slough. Work thing." She nodded because she couldn't think of anything else to say. He nodded, too, and they fell into silence for a few seconds. Then he said, "There's that famous John Betjeman poem about Slough, isn't there?"

"That's right," she smiled. " 'Come friendly bombs and fall on Slough' . . ."

" 'It isn't fit for humans now.' " They laughed softly. Another silence followed. She sat there thinking how sexy she found his Liam Neeson voice and wondering if his sweater was cashmere.

"I love that painting," he said, nodding toward the abstract print over the fireplace.

"Umm. Cashmere."

"Actually, I think you'll find it's Mondrian."

"Oh, God, sorry. The print. Of course it's Mondrian. Sorry, I was just admiring your sweater. Must keep you very warm."

"Yes, it does." His rather bemused smile began at his lips and moved to his eyes.

Just then, the rest of the group, including Veronica, began to trickle in. As everybody sat down and got comfortable, Cyn's mind went back to the Chelsea affair. She was just about to tell her story, when Sandra, the yo-yo dieter, announced: "I called in fat to work today."

Cyn burst out laughing. "That's really funny," she said. It was only when she saw Sandra's despondent expression that Cyn realized she hadn't been joking.

"Sorry," Cyn said, cringing inside.

Ken, the earnest ex-priest with the Amish beard and no mustache, shot Cyn a pitying look, which made her feel worse. Then he suggested to Sandra she must be in great pain and that maybe she would like to share with the group. Sandra shrugged.

"We're all here for you, Sandra," whining Jenny with the plait said in that sickly sweet, caring-sharing way of hers.

Clementine gave a loud snort and rolled her eyes. "Jenny, do you have to be so bloody compassionate all the time? It's so tedious."

"I'm sorry. It's a problem I have. I brought up my sister after our mother died. I suppose I've always seen myself in a mother role."

Veronica broke in at this point and, with a good deal of tenderness, asked Jenny why she felt the need to apologize for being herself. Jenny shrugged and said she didn't know.

"I think it's time," Veronica went on, "that you found the courage to stand up for yourself, don't you?"

"I know and I am trying," Jenny said.

Ken tried to bring the discussion back to Sandra's weight problem, but she had begun to get tearful and said she would rather not say anything for a bit.

It was Joe who spotted Cyn's faraway look. "Is there something you want to say?" he asked her. His expression was warm and encouraging. She found herself wishing that everybody else would disappear and that it was just the two of them on her sofa with a bottle of wine.

"I'm not sure," Cyn said, looking down at her hands and then back up at Joe. She was starting to feel the same emotions she had felt this afternoon when she discovered what Chelsea had done. Therapy was like that. You'd think you had your feelings under control and then bam, they came crashing down like a wrecker's ball. Her eyes were filling up and she was biting into her bottom lip.

"Come on, Cyn," Joe urged gently, "what is it?"

She took a deep breath. "OK, something absolutely dreadful happened to me today. I discovered that a woman I work with has been very cruel and deceitful. I don't think I have ever been so angry. I wanted to stick pins in her eyes."

It took her nearly ten minutes or so to tell the Chelsea story. She kept getting choked up and having to stop. Joe looked particularly concerned. When he passed her the box of tissues, she looked into his eyes and got goose pimples down her back.

"Anyway," Cyn went on, "to get even, I did something a bit wicked. Well, really wicked, actually. In fact, I think it's the first really wicked thing I've ever done and it felt great." She told the group how she had impersonated Chelsea. "It was as if I'd been trapped inside myself all my life—always having to do the right thing and finally I was free. I was actually singing in the car."

Veronica raised her eyebrows. "Ah-ha, Cyn has sinned at last," she declared with a glimpse of approving smile. "Finally, you are standing up for yourself and it feels good." Cyn said it had felt good and it still felt pretty good, but she wasn't sure about the morals of it all. "I mean, stealing somebody's identity is a pretty heavy thing to do. It's almost as bad as what she did to me."

Clementine said Cyn was just being a drip and that Chelsea was a total bitch who deserved everything she got. Ken, Sandra and Jenny sat shaking their heads, their faces furrowed with concern. Jenny wondered if Cyn had really sat down and considered the possible consequences of what she had done. "I mean, it could all go so terribly wrong. You could lose your job."

"Yes, of course, I have thought about it," she said. "But does that mean I shouldn't have done it?" As an ex-priest, Ken took this as his cue to start spouting religious ethics. He wasn't at all sure that she had done the right thing. "As Gandhi so rightly said: if we all adopted the 'eye for an eye' approach, the whole world would be blind."

"Gawd," Clementine said with another roll of her eyes. "Ken, do you always have to be so holier-than-thou?"

"I'm with Clementine on this one," Joe said evenly. Clementine started to blush—presumably because it was Joe agreeing with her. "I'm not sure Ken's Gandhi analogy applies in this case," he went on. Everybody turned to look at him. They were clearly taken aback. As a rule, new group members tended to be wary of challenging people so early on. Joe didn't seem to be remotely bothered. He looked at Cyn. "Look, this might be the worst move you could have made. You're risking being found out and you're risking losing your job. You also risk being seen as a bad person and if I understand you correctly that's the bit that worries you most."

Cyn nodded.

"The way I see it," Joe went on, "sometimes risks are necessary. In fact they're vital—even if you can't always defend them morally. I also think there are times when the end justifies the means. And just because you do something a bit bad, it doesn't make you a bad person." Cyn thanked him and said she really appreciated his support.

Veronica turned to face Joe, who was sitting to her left. "Joe, you say it's vital to take risks and yet you have never risked having a permanent relationship."

"Ah," he said with a self-conscious half-laugh, "I thought you might pick up on that." He spent the next few minutes bent forward in his chair, hands clasped between his knees, talking about how his parents had always been emotionally distant. "Then when I was eight my mother left my father for another man. Even I could see how devastatingly handsome he was. I think he just swept her off her feet. Anyway, he made it perfectly clear to her that he wasn't interested in being around another man's child. My dad was devastated by her going and didn't want me around either. I think it was because I reminded him so much of her. Since neither of them wanted me, they sent me to boarding school. I remember the day they packed me off. There I was, this lost little mite clutching his teddy and a *Dr. Who* annual."

"So what happened to you during the school holidays?" Jenny said, reaching for a tissue to wipe her eyes.

"My mum would have me for a week or so. Of course she was always careful to organize it so that lover boy was away on business. I'd get spoiled rotten with toys and then she would send me to stay with my gran. She's a dear old soul and we're still very close. My dad would visit and bring more toys, but I could see how hard it was for him. I knew it was because I looked so much like my mother. Before one of his visits I shaved off my eyebrows, thinking he would start to love me again because I didn't look like her anymore. Of course he just got angry and it didn't make the blindest bit of difference. Dad never got over her leaving. He went on the booze and died of a heart attack when I was sixteen."

He said that the legacy of his upbringing was fear of rejection—and not just in his relationships with women. Keeping people at an emotional distance meant never having to experience it again. "I sort of get my retaliation in first, if you like."

"Umm," Clementine purred, practically batting her eyelashes. "I am amazed some woman hasn't been able to pin you down. They clearly didn't have my kind of staying power."

Cyn couldn't help noticing how Joe had colored at the remark. It also hadn't been lost on Ken, who had taken on a look of complete despair. He was clearly jealous of the attention Clementine was paying Joe.

Veronica was holding Clementine in her steely gaze. "Clementine, may I remind you that this is group therapy."

"Now I feel really told off," Clementine said crossly.

"That's because you were being told off," Veronica came back with one of her superior smiles.

Feeling an overwhelming need to ease the tension, Cyn stepped in. "But I don't understand how you coped," she said to Joe. "There you were, this little boy desperate for his mummy and daddy to love him and they turned their backs on you. It's absolutely heartbreaking. You must have been devastated."

Joe gave an easy shrug. "In the beginning I can remember

feeling desperately lonely, but that's about it. Later on I stopped feeling anything. I suppose I was protecting myself. I just got on with it."

"And what about now?" Veronica said. "How do you feel now?"

"I still don't feel much really. I know I should be angry, but for some reason I'm not. Having said that, I hardly visit my mother. I see her at Christmas and that's about it. So I must be feeling some sort of bitterness."

Veronica asked him what he thought might happen if he allowed himself to get angry.

He thought for a moment. "Maybe there would be so much that it would overwhelm me and I wouldn't be able to stop it or control it."

"So," Veronica said, "why are you here? What do you want from therapy?"

"I think I want to find the courage to make closer relationships—especially with women. I'm thirty-six. A big part of me feels ready for a permanent commitment."

"What about the other parts?" Veronica asked.

He shrugged. "The rest of me wants to keep the world at a safe distance. It's what I've always done. It's the only way I know to protect myself." Veronica gave a slow, understanding nod.

Cyn's eyes were filling up. She was still thinking about his parents. How could a mother and father find it in their hearts to reject their child like that?

Joe said he was feeling uncomfortable being in the spotlight, particularly as he was so new and didn't know the group that well. Veronica tried to encourage him to say more, but he said he would rather hand the floor over to somebody else. When Clementine began talking about how she had spent Sunday afternoon hanging round the plumbing section at Homebase in order to pick up men, he visibly relaxed.

———

After the session, Cyn was getting into her car when Joe came up behind her. She gave a start. "Sorry, didn't mean to make you jump," he said. "I just wanted to say that I really meant that stuff about doing something bad not making you a bad person. I hope it all works out and you get your promotion. I'm sure you deserve it."

"That's really kind." Wow, sexy and caring. In Cyn's book this was a heady mix.

"I hope you manage to find what you're looking for, too," she said softly.

"Thank you."

He was looking slightly awkward now, as if he'd overstepped the mark, which, according to the group rules, he had. In fact, they both had. "Right, well, see you next week."

"Yeah. See you next week," she said.

He was about to go when she noticed him spot the Anusol ad on the side of her car. Amusement crossed his face, but he didn't say a word. There was no smart-aleck remark, nothing to embarrass her.

As he walked away, the pitiful image of him as a helpless, unloved little boy came back to her. She would have loved him. How could anybody not?

# Chapter 7

"You know what I reckon?" Harmony knelt down, picked the smeary, plaster-encrusted electric kettle up off the floorboards and began pouring boiling water into mugs.

"Nope," Cyn said, watching Harmony stir the coffee granules, "what do you reckon?"

"I reckon that some people drink at the fountain of knowledge, but you only gargle."

Cyn started to laugh. "How do you mean—I only gargle?" She picked up a carton of milk—presumably left by the builders—sniffed and immediately recoiled. "Urgh. This is so off." Harmony said she was sorry, but since she had no fridge yet, there wasn't a lot she could do. "We'll have to have it black." She stood up and handed Cyn a mug.

"So, go on," Cyn said. "How is it I only gargle at the fountain of knowledge?"

"What I'm trying to say is that thirty-two years on this planet seems to have taught you nothing about self-preservation. Keep away from this Joe bloke. He's in therapy. He's a head case."

Cyn blew on her coffee. "I'm in therapy," she said, taking a sip. "Does that make me a head case as well?"

Harmony grinned. "No, you're just thick because you haven't worked out that you don't need sodding therapy." Cyn told her she would take that as a compliment. "I mean, look at the way you've handled this whole Chelsea thing . . ."

"But most people would say only a complete loon would do what I'm doing. Let's not lose sight of the fact that I've done something pretty bloody dreadful. On top of that I'm scared stiff. I mean, I could lose my job if it all goes wrong. And they're hardly likely to give me a glowing reference."

"I agree it's a massive risk. Sometimes you just have to do these things. But as for this fella . . ."

"Look, I fancy him, that's all. I can't help that. But you're right, he does have problems."

"He'll hurt you. Saying he has problems with emotional intimacy is just a polite way of admitting that when the sex gets boring, he walks. I've been out with a few guys like that in my time and when it's over you feel so used."

"Don't worry," Cyn said, "I'm not about to do anything stupid. Plus it's against the rules to get friendly with people in the group. I promise you, nothing's going to happen."

"Good," Harmony said, taking a mouthful of coffee. She wiped her finger along the window ledge and rubbed the dust between her fingers. "You know, sometimes I don't think this place is ever going to be finished."

Harmony had closed on the Holland Park garden flat a couple of months ago. It was the bottom half of an exquisite cream-painted Victorian villa. On the outside there were wrought-iron balconies and black metal canopies over the windows. Inside, there were grand white marble fireplaces and original covings and cornice work. In the front living room where they were sitting, a ceiling-high bay window looked out onto a pretty square full of trees and flower beds.

The bad news was that the last time the flat had been decorated or updated, the workmen had probably been paid in groats. Simon, the smarmy estate agent who had shown Harmony around three months ago, had urged her to look past the "few superficial bits of work needed" and to "consider the truly vast potential." Harmony didn't need telling twice. It was love at first viewing. Cyn had come to see it a few days later. She had taken one look at the damp patches, the rotting window frames and prewar electric sockets and urged caution. She pleaded with Harmony to get some quotes for the building work before she committed herself to buying the flat, but Harmony said she wanted it so much, she didn't mind what the work cost. "I'll be in that flat forever. The only way they'll get me out is in a box."

She had reckoned on a bill heading toward six figures. What she hadn't bargained for was the chaos the work would cause. She had been forced to move out of her old place quickly because the people buying it were expecting a baby. So, for now, because the flat was nothing more than a rubble-and dust-filled shell, she was living at a chichi boutique hotel in Kensington, just round the corner from the salon. Cyn had said more than once that she was welcome to stay with her until the work was finished. Hugh had said the same, but Harmony knew she would only end up scrapping with Hugh, and that Cyn's place was too far from the salon.

Harmony had asked Cyn if they could meet at the flat that morning because she wanted some advice on decor. So here they were, sitting on the window ledge, drinking the builders' instant coffee out of smeary builders' mugs, trying to imagine the place done up. Since there were ceilings down, walls half plastered, and wires and copper pipes jutting out all over the place, it wasn't easy. Harmony said she was toying with a Chinese teahouse look. "I read about it in this interiors mag. It's grass-cloth wallpaper, stained black floorboards and loads of twisted metal." Cyn nodded tactfully and said it was definitely a thought, but maybe something more traditional might be easier to live with long-term. They had been tossing ideas around for more than an hour, but nothing seemed to have the "in yer face" factor Harmony was looking for. "You know," Harmony said eventually, "I think I'm going to get a designer in." Cyn agreed that might be her best bet.

They were still drinking their coffee when Harmony started rubbing her forehead with the back of her hand. "Blimey, is it me, or is it hot in here? I feel like I'm burning up." At this point panic set in. "Oh, crap, Cyn, it's happened, I'm having a hot flash. I know I am. It seems to be coming from my legs and working its way up through my entire body."

"Harms, calm down. You are not having a hot flash."

"How do you know?"

Cyn's face broke into a smile. "Look." She nodded her head toward the electric kettle. It was on the floor, still boiling away. The only thing heating up her legs was steam. "If you'd been standing any closer, you could have been burned," Cyn said. She bent down and pulled the plug from the wall. Then she took a look at the kettle. "I see what's happened. The automatic off switch has stopped working because it's clogged solid with tiny bits of plaster. It just needs a clean."

The color that had drained from Harmony's face started to return. "Oh, thank God for that." She slapped her hand to her chest just like Grandma Faye. "Right, I need a smoke. Where did I put me ciggies?" Cyn looked at her watch. It was past midday. "I'm going to have to shoot off in a bit," she said as Harmony rooted around among the builders' estimates and kitchen and bathroom catalogues, which were strewn over the window ledge. "Saturday lunch at Mum and Dad's."

"Oh, go on, stay for a bit. I thought you could help me go through some of these bathroom catalogues."

Cyn looked at her friend. Her expression had changed

from relief to troubled. "Hey, wassup?" Harmony made a thin smile and said nothing was up. "Yes, there is. I can see it in your face. You still haven't had your period, have you?"

Harmony put down her coffee cup. "No, but it's not that."

"What, then? It's the Justin thing, isn't it?"

"No. That's really over. It's something else."

"What?" Cyn said gently. "Come on."

"Dunno. Can't put a finger on it." She picked up her mug again and brought it to her lips. "I've got everything I could possibly want: the success, the flat, the fancy car, posh parties, fabulous holidays, expensive restaurants . . ."

"OK, no need to rub it in."

"Sorry. God, I'm going to sound like a spoiled princess, but there's something missing."

"OK, I admit a proposal of marriage from Colin Firth would round things off nicely, but a girl can't have everything."

"No, it's nothing like that." Harmony sat struggling with her thoughts. "OK, have you ever thought that life is like a holiday? You get up on the first morning and think, OK, today I'll just relax by the pool. Then suddenly it's day thirteen and you realize you've done nothing but relax by the pool. You've seen none of the sights. You've missed the glass-bottom boat trip, cycling round the countryside and all the little villages. Well, that's how I feel."

"What, that you've missed a trip in a glass-bottom boat?"

"Dah. You're being thick on purpose. The point is I've earned tons of cash, but I can't help feeling that I haven't done anything really worthwhile."

"Like what?"

She shrugged. "I wish I knew. All I know is I don't want to cut rich people's hair for the rest of my life. To make it worse, I have this sense of time running out."

"Which takes us back to the turning-forty thing."

"I guess. Did I tell you that I've started using Clairol's Loving Care. And I don't mean on my head." Cyn fell about laughing.

"OK, if you think that's funny, get this. I found this hair growing under my chin." Cyn made the point that everybody got the odd chin hair. "Not like this, they don't. It was over an inch long. And white. I just hadn't seen it. I must have been walking around with it for weeks. At first I thought it was a piece of thread. Then when I tugged it, I realized it was attached to me. God knows how many people must have noticed it and been too polite to say anything. Shit, Cyn, I'm turning into a blind, hairy, shriveled-up old crone."

"Come on," Cyn said, putting an arm round her. "You know full well you are young and beautiful and not remotely shriveled or cronelike. You're just knackered, that's all. Running the salon, ending it with Justin and all this building work has worn you out."

"Yeah, right. Tell that to the single mum who's working six days a week at the supermarket checkout."

"A commendable thought, I'm sure, but it doesn't mean that you don't have the right to get run-down."

"I s'pose not." Cyn could see Harmony's eyes starting to fill with tears. "And there's something else. I really, really want a baby before it's too late."

"Oh, sweetie."

Cyn sat holding her for a few moments, gently rocking her back and forth. "You know, I think maybe you should get this no-period thing checked out. I'm sure it's nothing, but it would be best to see a doctor."

Harmony promised she would.

"Look," Cyn went on, "why don't you come and have lunch at Mum and Dad's? The whole family's going to be there. Mum always cooks too much and they'd love to see you. It'll cheer you up."

Harmony said she'd love to, but she had to go out and choose a bathroom suite. She wiped her eyes with the heel of her hand. "The builder's going mad because I can't make up my mind. The thing is I'm hovering over the bidet—so to speak. I mean yer upper classes think they're totally naff, but I just read this article about how the French don't get yeast infections. What do you reckon?"

Cyn said it was entirely up to her, but she agreed she couldn't exactly see Hugh Grant sitting astride one.

She arrived at her mum and dad's just after one. As she walked toward the house, she decided not to say anything about Chelsea. Her dad and brother, being lawyers, would insist on taking legal action. Then, when she told them how she had taken matters into her own hands, the whole family would start beating their chests and climbing the walls with fear. She didn't want to give her parents anything else to worry about. They had enough to contend with, what with Grandma Faye staying with them while new central heating was being fitted at her flat. She rang the bell. Jonny answered.

"Hi, J."

"Watcha." They exchanged kisses. Even though they were now both in their thirties, Cyn still felt odd kissing her brother. She couldn't help it. In many ways she would have been more comfortable kicking Jonny's legs from under him, pinning him to the floor and refusing to let him up until he agreed, on pain of particularly excruciating and lengthy Chinese burn, to stop drawing anatomically correct genital features on her Barbie and Ken dolls.

She hung up her coat and asked him what was new. "You know, same ole. Oh, there is one thing . . ." His face broke into a grin. "Me and Flick have finally decided to get married."

"Oh, J, that is fantastic!" She threw her arms round him. Jonny and Felicity had been living together for three years. It was time. "So, when's the big day?"

"Second week in May. Flick's desperate for a spring wedding."

"Blimey, doesn't give you long."

"Tell me about it. Mum's already doing preliminary sketches for ice sculptures."

"But I thought it was traditional for the bride's family to do all the organizing."

"Yeah, but, you know, Flick's mum's broke."

When Flick's father died a couple of years ago, he left no life insurance and a pile of debt. At one time he had been a hugely successful wine merchant, but for two decades or more he had drunk more than he had sold. Flick's mum, Bunty, who was in her sixties, lived in the country. Although she hunted and continued to be invited to all the best parties, she had barely a bean to call her own. She wasn't nearly as well-to-do as Hugh's parents, but like them she fell into that category of elderly poshies down on their luck, quaintly referred to in polite circles as "distressed gentlefolk."

Jonny and Flick had offered to pay for the wedding, but Barbara wouldn't hear of it. No child of hers was going to pay for his own wedding. Jonny said, "Dad butted in at this point and said, 'You know, Barbara, I think maybe we should hear Jonny out on this,' but she bashed him over the head with her oven glove." The upshot was that Barbara and Mal were organizing and paying for the wedding.

"So far," he continued, "Mum is refusing to invite the Canadian cousins, after they didn't make the effort to fly over for Uncle Sid's funeral in 1984. Grandma Faye says let them come, but sit them next to the kitchen. Dad says don't invite them because it's two couples less and he'll save money. Flick thinks we should be a bit daring for once and go for a reception with a Hawaiian theme. Grandma says that's fine so long as we can still have the cocktail fish balls, the melon balls, the matzo balls and the chocolate fountain." By now Cyn was falling about.

"Wait," he said. "It gets better. Because Flick is Catholic, we have a major problem about where to hold the ceremony. You should have been here five minutes ago when Flick calmly announced that she would like to get married at the Blessed Virgin in Highgate. Grandma practically had a stroke. I think her precise words were: 'Why don't you just stick a knife in me and have done with it?' "

"And what about you? What do you want?"

"I just want to get married—don't really care where. Having said that, I have totally put my foot down about the Hawaiian theme. I've told Flick that I will agree to love, honor and cherish her, but nobody, not even her, is going to get me in a church, synagogue or wherever, wearing a garland of flowers and a sodding grass skirt."

"Oh, I don't know," Cyn giggled. "I think with your full hips, you could carry it off."

"You really think so?" Jonny said, starting to walk down the hall wiggling his bum.

"Hey, J . . ."

He turned to face her. She reached out and put her arms round him. "God," she said, feeling her eyes filling up, "suddenly my little brother's all grown up."

"Yeah, so grown up I'm thinning on top and going gray." He ran his hand across the top of his head. "I think it gives me a certain gravitas, though, don't you?"

She assured him it did. Jonny was only thirty and yet physically and emotionally he was careering into middle age. Unlike Harmony, who would probably still be slapping Clairol on her pubes at ninety, Jonny appeared to be embracing getting older. He seemed perfectly content, now that their father had retired, to be running the high street law firm Mal had set up thirty years ago. It didn't seem to bother him that the work involved nothing more thrilling or challenging than conveyancing, drawing up divorce petitions and helping rich, vindictive old ladies add codicils to their wills. He made no secret of the fact that he couldn't wait to settle down, buy a nice house in a nice suburban neighborhood where he and Flick would raise three nice kids and an Old English sheepdog named Prince.

Flick's take on life was much the same as Jonny's—conservative and intensely practical. That of course was her attraction—along with her being Catholic, a bit posh and in possession of a well-developed stiff upper lip. In other words, the antithesis of the intense, arty, constantly emoting Jewish girls he'd been out with in the past.

It wasn't that either of them was dull or lacked humor. Flick in particular was an immensely game, jolly soul, but neither of them was a risk-taker. Jonny was a firm believer in letting the rest of the world take wild gambles and chances. He would keep his bank account in the black and carry on paying into his pension plan, thank you very much.

The difference between Cyn and Jonny was, of course, that Cyn had come to see how emotionally and spiritually confining playing it safe could be. She had never actually challenged Jonny on the subject because she thought it would sound like she was judging him, but she'd sort of skirted around it. A couple of times she'd asked him about his ambitions and whether there were any dreams he wanted to fulfill.

"Haven't you ever gotten the urge to jack it all in and do something wild like going round the world on a Harley?"

"What? To get taken hostage and shot in Colombia? No, thanks. A villa in Tuscany's more my style. You know, I think Mum's illness made me realize early on that the only things that matter in life are to be healthy, in a loving relationship and financially secure. So far I've scored three out of three. And do you know what, Cyn, I'm the happiest bugger I know." Maybe he was. Or maybe he just convinced himself he was. It often occurred to her that deep down, he had doubts about the way he lived his life the same way she had doubts about hers.

Cyn followed Jonny down the hall, him telling her that it would be her turn to tie the knot next and her making the point that in order for it to be her turn, she would need to find a man prepared to marry her.

"What about Neil Applebaum from school? Apparently his Tourette's is really under control. Maybe you should give him a ring."

"Hah, hah."

"Just a thought," he laughed.

In the kitchen, Barbara was standing next to the stove, molding fish cakes with yellow-rubber-gloved hands. "Hi, darling," she said to Cyn. "Jonny told you his wonderful news?" She gently placed a couple of fish cakes in the frying pan and took a step back as the oil hissed and spattered. Then, holding out her rubber-gloved hands in front of her like a surgeon breaking off in midoperation to have his brow mopped, she presented a cheek for Cyn to kiss.

"It's fantastic." She kissed her mother, who smelled of Body Shop White Musk and minced fish. Cyn could feel Barbara examining her face. "You OK, darling? You look a bit peaky. Everything all right at work?"

"Yeah, I'm fine. Just a bit tired, that's all."

"I knew it. Those people you work for are pushing you too hard. I've a good mind to pick up the phone and . . ."

"Mum! Don't you dare. I'm thirty-two, not five. What would you do, demand they let me have an afternoon nap?"

Barbara shrugged as if to say, "Look, I worry, that's all." Cyn gave her another kiss that said, "Sorry, I know you do."

"Cyn, you're a clever girl," Grandma Faye called out from the table in the Alpine breakfast nook. "What rhymes with *tumor*?"

"Come again?" Cyn said, baffled. Jonny explained that one of Faye's best friends had died a few days ago, aged 104, and since the woman had no close family still alive, Faye had been requisitioned into writing a rhyming obituary for the deaths column in the local newspaper.

"I dunno, Grandma," Cyn replied, going over to kiss her. "What about *humor*?"

"Let me see if that scans." Faye lifted her glasses to her forehead, brought the writing pad close to her eyes and squinted. " 'You never heard a moan from Estelle Silverstone / She bore her tumor with great humor.' Great. That works for me."

"Brill," Cyn said, stifling a giggle. She and Jonny exchanged a look as they sat down at the orange pine table.

"So, Mum," Barbara called out, "what did Estelle die of?"

"Childbirth . . . She was a hundred and four. What do you think she died of?"

It was as much as Cyn and Jonny could do to keep straight faces. Barbara said, "Well, pardon me. I was only asking."

Cyn asked Grandma Faye how she was. Faye shrugged. "Oh, you know, *comme ci, comme ça*. My blood pressure's up, I've started getting shooting pains in my back, my stomach's a bit iffy—I get this terrible acid. And my circulation's not what it was. But you know me, I'm not one to complain."

Cyn looked at Barbara, who was looking heavenward and

clearly beseeching the Almighty to speed up central heating work at Faye's flat.

"You know," Grandma Faye whispered, moving in toward Cyn, "it would be nice if you found a young man by the time Jonny gets married. All your cousins are married or engaged. You're the last. Sometimes I think you're too fussy. Who was that nice boy down the road who used to go to your school? Had a bit of a twitch."

"Neil Applebaum," Jonny said, grinning. "I already suggested him, but Cyn's not interested." Cyn kicked Jonny's shin under the table, making him wince with pain.

"Shame," Faye sighed. "You're such a beautiful girl, Cyn. I don't know why somebody hasn't snapped you up. You know, if you found somebody, you'd be making your mother so happy."

Faye was right, it would make Barbara happy if she found a man. It was hard to believe that Barbara had been a bit of a feminist in her day and that when Cyn was a teenager, her frequently repeated mantra was "Little girls made of sugar and spice grow up to be cheesecakes."

In her midforties, most likely spurred on by having beaten cancer, Cyn thought, Barbara enrolled in a women's studies course at the local adult education college. Cyn still remembered overhearing her mother telling Grandma Faye that she and some of her fellow students had gone along to this women's group where everybody stood around in a circle using their makeup mirrors to "make friends with their vulvas" and Grandma Faye replying, "Wouldn't it be better to take it to a car mechanic?"

These days, with Cyn not married, the "A woman needs a man like a fish needs a bicycle" poster that had been stuck to the fridge door for years was long gone. Barbara had given in. After years of fighting her off, she freely admitted that she had—horror of horrors—"turned into my mother!" and gotten in touch with her yenta within.

"You know . . ." It was Barbara from across the kitchen. Cyn wrinkled her face. She was sure her mother was about to remind her of yet another article she'd read in the *Daily Mail* about women's fertility declining after the age of thirty-five. When it turned out to be more of her thoughts about the wedding reception, Cyn's face relaxed. "I'm not sure," Barbara went on, "about having all these balls on the dinner menu. Maybe it would be better to go for the melon balls, but drop the matzo balls and the fish balls."

"Funny, I didn't know fish balls dropped," Grandma Faye said, winking. She may have been eighty-four, diabetic and getting a bit frail, but her wit was as robust as ever.

Just then Flick came in. She'd been out on an errand for Grandma Faye and her cheeks were flushed with the cold. Flick was what Faye described as a "hardy English rose." She was blonde and pretty with perfect cream skin, sturdy thighs and a whopping great bum. (Jonny had a thing for women with big behinds.)

"Hi, Cyn," she said brightly, kissing her on both cheeks. "Wow, fab skirt." It was a dusky pink and black Marc Jacobs rip-off she'd bought at Topshop for thirty quid. "God, I'd give anything to have your figure. I'm just so huge and galumphing."

Flick was forever running herself down like this, which made Cyn feel awkward and guilty at the same time. She felt guilty for having been blessed with a good figure and awkward because there were only so many times she could trot out the same white lie about Flick not being remotely huge or galumphing. The unfortunate truth was that Flick did have something of the hockey-playing fairy elephant about her. Today Cyn decided to change tack. "Come on, Flick, I'd give my right arm and a certain amount of offal to have skin like yours."

"Clarins Beauty Flash Balm," she said, waving away the compliment. "Nothing to do with me."

"I keep telling her she's beautiful." Jonny shrugged, looking at Cyn. "But she just doesn't seem to get it."

Flick bent down and kissed him. "You are just biased, Pooh Bear."

At this point Grandma Faye broke in: "So, Felicity, did they have some indigestion tablets up at the shop?" Flick passed her a tube of Tums. It seemed that since Flick's suggestion that she and Jonny get married in a church hadn't quite caused Faye to have a stroke, the old lady was now playing the gastric reflux card.

"You can chew a couple of these after meals," Flick said kindly, "but don't overdo it. These chalky medicines aren't good for your kidneys."

"Thank you, my darling. You are an angel. I think maybe I'll take one now." Grandma Faye started to grapple with the foil on the Tums packet. Cyn couldn't help thinking how her stiff, gnarled finger joints clashed with her perfectly manicured scarlet nails. Suggestions of church weddings aside, Faye adored Flick. It was partly because she was sweet and thoughtful. It was also because she was a nurse. At last Grandma Faye had somebody permanently on hand to offer advice and counsel about her ever-increasing list of ailments. "Felicity, darling," Faye said, starting to chew the Tum, "maybe you could take my blood pressure again after lunch. I brought my sphygmomanometer. Oh, and my urine tester kit is in my handbag. I think my sugar might be up again. If I go to the bathroom after lunch, would you take a look?" Flick assured her it wouldn't be a problem. Cyn watched Jonny give Flick's hand a quick squeeze as if to say: "Look, I know she's a pain, but thanks for being so patient." Flick returned the squeeze with a kiss on his forehead.

"You know," Grandma Faye chuckled, digging Cyn in the ribs, "if these two ever hit hard times, they could make a fortune giving cooing lessons to turtledoves."

"You're just a bitter and twisted old woman," Barbara broke in, bringing a plate of Marks & Spencer crudités and sour cream dip to the table. "Help yourself, Flick. Don't be shy."

"Look," Faye said to Barbara, "I'm a widow who hasn't had sex in thirty-nine years and it's starting to get to me."

It wasn't just Faye who thought the world of Flick; the whole family did. Cyn loved her not just because she was jolly and easygoing, but because she was one of the few people she knew who—body image aside—completely lacked any edge or agenda.

In Cyn's opinion Flick's only fault—and it wasn't much of one—was that she had no sense of style. Clotheswise, she nearly always went for rugby shirts over cords. Occasionally, she would vary things with a chunky knit polo neck. She owned several, all in primary colors with a teddy bear or Bart Simpson motif on the front. She clearly felt the need to hide her plumpness behind baggy shirts and humor. Of course, Jonny, who lived in fleeces and tapered-leg Levi's when he wasn't at work, neither noticed nor remotely cared.

Their flat, which Flick had decorated herself, was a monument to magnolia. When Cyn tactfully suggested introducing some color, Flick had gone to Peter Jones and bought a couple of washed-out, Holiday Inn–style landscapes and some pale peach silk flowers. Hugh, who had gone to the house-warming party with Cyn, had pronounced it "more neutral than Switzerland."

The place wasn't entirely without a stylistic "twist," however. Flick had decided to "go a bit mad" by introducing a cockerel theme. There were china cockerels on kitchen display shelves, stenciled cockerels on kitchen cupboard doors. There was a cockerel wallpaper border in the living room and even a painted cockerel on the loo lid. Jonny said he was completely in awe of Flick's home-decorating skills. Cyn said she was, too.

By now Barbara had put the fish cakes in the oven to keep warm and was busy frying chips. Barbara made the best chips: crispy on the outside, exquisitely, mouthwateringly fluffy in the middle.

Gripping the table and letting out a loud "Oooph," Faye pulled herself off her chair. As she set off to fetch cutlery to lay the table, Cyn noticed how her movements stuttered. It was a few seconds before her legs got going. Twenty years ago she had been buxom and bustling like Barbara. These days her Lycra leggings looked positively baggy. Even so, she hadn't given up on her appearance. She was wearing green eye shadow and a purple sparkly sweater with eighties shoulder pads, and her hair was as big, blonde and stiff with Elnett extra hold as ever.

Barbara called over to Jonny and asked him to open the wine. "I left the corkscrew on the counter next to the sink." Jonny got up from the table. "Your dad'll be down in a minute," Barbara went on. "He's upstairs on eBay." After much soul-searching, Mal had finally decided to sell all his old Beatles and John Lennon records. Since he had them on his iPod, he couldn't see the point of hanging on to them. "He's really excited. The bidding's gone up to over £500."

Cyn couldn't help thinking it was a shame. She remembered each one of those LPs and their covers. Her mind went back to when she and Jonny were small and they would sit for hours with Mal in the shed, listening to music. Mal wore flared jeans back then and he still had hair. She remembered how proud he was of his perm. He'd wanted to dye it blonde, but Barbara put her foot down on the grounds that it would make him look like Harpo Marx. She remembered curling up on her dad's lap while Jonny sat at Mal's workbench painting his latest Airfix model. Every so often Mal would get up and put another John Lennon LP on the old stereo he kept in the shed. *Imagine* was his favorite. They all joined in at the Ooh-hoo, hoo-oo-oo bit.

"It's £550 now, actually," Mal corrected Barbara as he came in. He went over to the table where Jonny was pouring out the wine. Since he had been downstairs when the others arrived, it was only Cyn he kissed hello. "You look pale. You OK?"

"God, I've just had this from Mum. I'm fine, honestly."

"If you say so. So, has anybody else seen that Smart Car parked outside with an ad for hemorrhoid cream on the door?" His tone was all hammy innocence. It was perfectly obvious that her father knew it was her car.

Jonny instantly reverted to twelve-year-old pest and burst out laughing. "God, your company's making you advertise arse cream? But I thought they liked you. Talk about giving you the bum's rush."

"Jonny, that's enough," Barbara scolded. "Stop teasing your sister."

"They do like me," Cyn said. "There's been a huge mix-up, that's all, and I'm sorting it out."

"Of course, piles are the final taboo," Grandma Faye said. "They come to us all in the end. I think it's wonderful that Cyn is lifting the lid on them and bringing them out into the open for everybody to see."

"So," Mal said to Cyn, "moving swiftly on, I read in the

paper that your company just got the Sainsbury's account. You know, you really fell on your feet when you got that job. Talk about the hot place to be."

"I know." Cyn smiled, wondering how on earth she would explain it when it got out that she had been sacked by PCW for impersonating Chelsea Roggenfelder.

Mal picked up a carrot stick and dipped it in the sour cream. "You'll never guess what I just bid for on eBay and got."

"Omigod. Not more rubbish." It was Barbara. She was tipping chips out of the wire net onto paper towels. "Mal, we have a wedding to pay for." Jonny butted in at this point and reminded her that he and Flick had offered to pay for the wedding. Barbara told him he was a good boy, but the cost of the wedding was all taken care of. "Apart from the money," Barbara carried on at Mal, "you're turning the house into a junk shop. I've got that bit of filthy Concorde tail fin in the spare room gathering dust, along with the chunk of Berlin Wall and two Darth Vader costumes in the living room."

He made the point that it was all ephemera and would be worth a fortune one of these days. Barbara said she didn't care what it was or how much it would be worth, she wanted the whole lot moved to the garage.

"So, come on, Dad," Cyn said, "what have you bought?"

He tucked his T-shirt into his tracksuit bottoms. His sizable paunch meant the jeans were long gone. "An oxygen machine."

"An oxygen machine," Barbara repeated. "What? There's not enough air in Edgware?"

Mal explained that they were all the rage in L.A. "Madonna's got one. They super-oxygenate the brain so that you think more clearly. They cost three thousand new. This was a snip at seven-fifty."

"But my friend Sidney Jaffe," Faye piped up, "you know, with the emphysema—he gets an oxygen cylinder delivered every week for free. I'm sure he'd have let you have a go on it."

"This is different . . ."

"How can it be different? Oxygen is oxygen."

At this point Barbara brought a pile of plates to the table and Cyn and Flick went to fetch the fish cakes, chips and bowl of salad.

"OK, let's forget the oxygen," Barbara said, passing out plates. Now that the food was cooked, the tension was visibly retreating from her face. "Look, I don't want to rain on Jonny and Flick's parade, but I have an announcement to make. Your dad already knows." Her face broke into a smile.

"Oh, God," Jonny said in mock horror. "Me and Cyn are going to have a baby brother or sister."

"Jonny," Barbara said, handing him a plate, "I know I look good for my age, but I'm sixty-two."

"I've got it," Cyn laughed, "you're leaving Dad for Russell Crowe."

"Wrong again. The only man in my life, apart from your father, is Dr. Atkins, God rest his soul."

"And if you don't mind me saying," Faye said, "I think you should ditch him."

"Mum, I was a size eighteen last month. Now I'm a sixteen."

"Wonderful, so you can die from kidney failure and high cholesterol and be the thinnest woman in the cemetery."

"Faye, give it a rest," Mal said. "You know how Barbara struggles with her weight. She's doing really well."

"Well, pardon me for caring."

"Fish cake, anyone?" Flick broke in brightly, sensing the tension and looking distinctly ill at ease. "They look really yummy. I'll pass them around, shall I?" Flick had been brought up in one of those stiff middle-class families where friction and disapproval were rarely acknowledged and where conversation—particularly over the dinner table—was limited to anything pertaining to hitting balls with various kinds of sticks.

"Come on, it's OK," Jonny said, grinning and gently placing a hand on Flick's arm. "You should know by now, this is just my family letting off steam. It's nothing terminal." But his reassurance didn't stop Flick from leaping up and starting a tour of the table with the plate of fish cakes.

"Just a half of one for me, Flick darling," Faye said. "Any more disagrees with me." An eye roll from Barbara. Flick put the plate down on the table and started to cut a fish cake in two. "You know," the old lady went on, "it's meant to be healthy for people to let off steam. Cyn told me her therapist calls it 'venting.' My family never vented. That's why they all died early of colon disease."

"OK," Mal came back. "So, smoking, pollution and eating food packed with toxic chemicals had nothing to do with it. They all died of not arguing."

"Mal, don't start," Barbara muttered.

"Who's starting?"

"You are. You always have to start." Barbara cleared her throat and took a deep breath. She was calming herself down, but probably only for Flick's sake. "Anyway," Barbara brightened. "Back to our news." She paused. Then: "Dad and I are taking in a lodger. Well, not so much a lodger as a refugee." She explained he was from Tagine, a small French-speaking island republic off the coast of West Africa. A couple of years ago there had been a violent military coup. The place was now governed by an oppressive military dictatorship and anybody who dared challenge the regime risked being tortured and shot. "Our refugee is a chap called Laurent Cinnamon.

He's a left-wing activist who was part of the guerrilla group that organized a countercoup a few months ago."

Jonny said he remembered reading about it in the papers. "It failed and the rebels were executed, weren't they?"

"Most of them were, but Laurent managed to escape. He arrived in London just over a month ago. He needs some-where to stay while his asylum request is being processed. We're expecting him in a week or so."

"Omigod, an illegal immigrant!" Faye slapped her hand to her chest. "If the neighbors find out they'll lynch you."

"He's not an illegal," Mal pointed out, letting Flick put two fish cakes on his plate. "He's doing everything by the book."

"That's right," Barbara said. "And just try and imagine for a moment how he must be feeling. He left his family without having a chance to say good-bye and he's got no idea when he'll see them again."

Jonny asked Barbara what he did for a living. "In Tagine he was a teacher. He wants to retrain here and start a new life." She helped herself to salad. "You know, I'm really look-ing forward to him coming. It's years since I helped anybody or did anything for a good cause. Your dad's agreed to help him prepare his legal case."

"But how do you know his story's true?" Jonny pro-tested. "For all you know he could be lying through his teeth and be part of some slave-trading, drug-smuggling cartel. Dad, I'm not sure you and Mum should be getting into something like this."

"I have to admit, it does seem a teensy bit risky," Flick added, licking fish cake batter off her fingers.

Mal explained he had a contact in the Home Office and had managed to see the paperwork relating to Laurent. "I'm satisfied he's genuine."

"Well, I think taking in a refugee is a great idea," Cyn

said. "Mum needs a project and it's been ages since Dad did any legal work. Plus the country is crying out for teachers. I'm really proud of you both."

"Listen," Faye said, pulling a fish bone out from between her teeth, "did I ever tell you the story of how my grandfather smuggled himself out of Poland in a milk cart?"

"Yes," they cried in unison.

# Chapter 8

Barbara spent most of Sunday trying to find a suitable wedding caterer. It went like this: she would phone a company, jot down a couple of sample menus and then ring Cyn to get her reaction. It was odd, Cyn thought, that Barbara didn't phone Flick and Jonny first, but she supposed Barbara didn't feel as close to Flick as she did to her own daughter, and Jonny, being a bloke, wasn't likely to have views one way or another on whether sole goujons had had their day.

After Cyn had given her opinion, Barbara would phone Flick. Depending on Flick's reaction, the company ended up on Barbara's no list, the maybe list or the definite maybe list.

At one point a dispute arose over salmon and dill Wellington. Barbara thought it was a sensible, safe bet and virtually presented it as a fait accompli. "Nobody ever complains about salmon," Cyn agreed, but tentatively suggested it sounded a bit run-of-the-mill and maybe they should explore some other possibilities. Barbara then phoned Flick, who said pretty much the same. When Jonny agreed with Cyn and Flick, Barbara got all huffy and defensive and phoned Cyn again. By now Barbara was practically in tears because everybody was criticizing the salmon option without coming up with an alternative. She said she was trying desperately to do her best and felt unappreciated. Cyn was still trying to make her understand that their reservations about the salmon weren't meant as a criticism and how much everybody loved and appreciated her, when Jonny rang Cyn's mobile. Soon she had Barbara blubbing in one ear and Jonny in the other saying that Barbara seemed to be losing it, he and Flick were wilting under all the pressure and could Cyn try and persuade their mother to calm down. Somewhere in the middle of all this Mal rang Jonny and only half-jokingly offered him ten thousand quid if he and Flick would elope.

All Cyn had wanted to do that day was curl up on her new cream Ikea sofa and read the Sunday papers. Instead the papers lay folded and untouched on the coffee table and she spent the day with the phone clamped to her ear, trying to negotiate a peace settlement over salmon and dill Wellington. She supposed something positive had come out of all the pandemonium. At least it had taken her mind off the Chelsea Roggenfelder situation.

"But we have to move fast," Barbara said when Cyn tried to persuade her yet again that they might regret making too hasty a decision over the menu. "Fein Platters is offering a twenty percent discount if we use them. The thing is, I have to let them know by Tuesday. They do this wonderful cocktail buffet, but I'm not sure about vol-au-vents. Are they passé or are they having a revival like rum baba and prawn cocktail? What do you think?"

"Look, Mum, why don't we just . . ."

"You're right. We shouldn't risk being ironic. People might not get it. OK, scrub the vol-au-vents. Now, the curried chicken tartlets sounded a bit more like it. On the other hand they might be a bit too spicy. There's your uncle Lou's colostomy to consider. Maybe we'd be better off with mini chicken Kievs and veggie puffs." And so it went on: Barbara suggesting it would be fun to have a Tony Blair impersonator handing round canapés, Jonny saying it was naff and Flick asking if Cyn had any thoughts on gospel singers.

"Gospel singers? At a Jewish wedding? You know, I'm not sure it would go down too well."

"But we could get them to do some Jewish songs."

"Even then," Cyn said, trying to imagine the Willesden and District Black Gospel Singers letting rip with a rousing, hand-clapping version of "Sunrise, Sunset" from *Fiddler on the Roof*.

Flick said she took the point. "Look, Cyn," she went on, "that wasn't the real reason I phoned. There's something really important I'd like to ask you. I would have brought it up yesterday over lunch, but there was so much going on, what with your mother's refugee and Grandma Faye's gastric reflux."

"Ask away," Cyn said, praying that Flick wasn't planning on the wedding guests playing giant Jenga or indoor minigolf.

"Cyn, you know I think of you as the sister I never had . . ."

Cyn immediately felt her eyes filling up. "Oh, Flick. I'm really touched. I don't know what to say."

"Just say yes."

"To what?"

"I'd like you to be my maid of honor."

Cyn was lost for words, but not in a good way. All she could manage was a less than heartfelt "Wow." This was followed by a long pause during which she had a vision of a giant purple, hoop-skirted, puffed-sleeved meringue covered in bows and lace. Jeez, she'd have to ask Rhett Butler to be her date. "Wow . . . Your maid of honor? Wow!" She was aware that this was now her third wow.

"Please, please, please say yes," Flick pleaded. "I can't wait to go out and choose you a dress. It will be fab, just fab!"

No, it wouldn't be fab. It wouldn't be remotely fab. It would be dire. She couldn't do it. There was no way. Not in a million years. No. No. No.

"Of course I'll be your maid of honor! I can think of nothing I'd love more. I'm thrilled that you asked me."

"Jonny said you would be," Flick squealed. "Ooh, Cyn, this is fantastic. Really fantastic. Let's speak next week and make a date to go shopping. By the way, just a thought. Instead of the gospel singers, what about a band of medieval minstrels?"

Cyn went to bed and dreamed that Flick hired an electronic rodeo bull for the wedding reception. Joe from therapy was in the saddle. He looked unbelievably gorgeous in his dinner suit, especially with his tie and shirt undone. One large, firm hand gripped the reins, the other he waved high in the air. She watched his body and hips writhe and thrash as the saddle pitched wildly. The longer he stayed on, the louder the whoops and cheers from the guests. Finally the bull stopped. Joe dismounted to wild applause and strode over to Cyn. His face was one huge grin. As he took her in his arms and held her to him, she closed her eyes, breathed in his heady, musky, sweaty smell. A second later his lips had found hers.

The next morning, just before eight, the phone rang. Cyn was still asleep. She sort of came to, reached out from under the duvet and groped for the receiver. "Mum, please," she begged groggily. "It's the middle of the night. I'm all salmon Wellingtoned out from yesterday. Can we talk later?"

"It's not your mum, it's me." It was Hugh.

"Hi, Me. Wassup?"

"I'll tell you in a minute. For the moment, I'm more interested in finding out what you mean when you say you're all salmon Wellingtoned out."

"Wedding menu stuff. Jonny and Flick are getting married."

"That's great. Moozzle tov."

"Actually, that's mazel tov, but thank you anyway."

"You're welcome," Hugh said. "By the way, you do know it's nearly eight o'clock. Shouldn't you be getting ready for work?"

"Christ, it isn't, is it?" She sat up and squinted at the clock on her bedside table. It was. She swung her feet onto the carpet. "Bloody alarm didn't go off. Now I'm going to be late. Look, Huge, I've gotta go."

"But you don't know why I rang."

"Oh, right." She rubbed some sleep from the corner of her eye. "So, why did you?"

"Well, it's just that I've got an early start and a mad day and I know I won't get a chance to call you. I thought we could have dinner at my place if you haven't got anything else on. I thought you needed cheering up, what with this Chelsea thing. I tried asking Harms, but she's got a couple of late appointments at the salon." Cyn said she would love to come.

"So, do you reckon you'll see this impersonation scheme through?"

"I'm in too deep to get out of it now."

"You know something, gorgeous, I really have to admire your balls."

She giggled. "Fine, but can it wait until later?"

"Hah, hah." He said he would see her about eight and they could order in a curry.

Fifteen minutes after putting down the phone she was

showered and dressed. Somehow, in the time it took to toast a crumpet, she managed to roughly blow-dry her hair, put on her mascara and give Morris fresh food and water.

"You will never guess the dream I had last night," she said, closing Morris's cage.

"Hot, sweaty, jungle shag," he squawked, head tilted appealingly to one side.

"Not quite," she said, smiling. "But you're in the right ballpark."

When she got to the office, Luke was standing with his headphones on, having one of his moshing water cooler moments. She gave him a wave, but he was too far gone for it to register.

The moment she sat down at her desk, a chirpy but irritating junior copywriter named Ade came over. He was always telling crap jokes with pointless punch lines. They were made worse by him being in possession of a voice totally incapable of inflection. He announced that he had found "this wicked hemorrhoid joke" on the Internet. She listened politely, tittered at the appropriate point and then, when it looked like he was going to hang around for a general gossip, she gave him a broad smile, said she would love to chat, but she was up to her eyes in work. He didn't seem remotely put out and tootled off to find somebody else to annoy with his hemorrhoid joke.

She was being perfectly truthful when she said she had work to do. First, what with all the Chelsea stuff, she had gotten behind with her other work. Sainsbury's was waiting for her to submit a proposal for a TV commercial and she hadn't even begun to think about it. On top of that, she realized on the drive into work that she hadn't sent Gazza the final cost breakdown for the Droolin' Dream commercial. She assumed that Chelsea had been planning to take them to the meeting with Gazza and the marketing people and they were on her computer. She couldn't help feeling anxious. If the figures weren't there, things could get difficult. She could always get a copy from somebody in the finance department, but not without questions being asked. All in all, it would be much simpler if Chelsea had the figures.

She went over to Chelsea's computer, which still hadn't been switched off. She went into the Droolin' Dream file and found the cost breakdown straightaway. Easy. Yesss. She let out a long breath. Five minutes later she was sitting at her own computer, e-mailing the figures to Gazza. She signed herself: "Cyn—PA to Chelsea Roggenfelder."

She'd just finished when she saw Luke coming toward her, doing that lopey-jiggy walk of his. As she watched him, she couldn't help wondering what it was that twenty-something women found so attractive about men who wore their jeans so low that they exposed four inches of boxer short.

Having only vaguely acknowledged her, since he still had his headset on, Luke stood beside her desk, sifting through envelopes. At the same time he was making low *tch-tch-ktksssh* sounds and jerking his head like a rapping rooster. He put three letters on her desk and then immediately took one back.

"Ooops, sorry. That one's addressed to Chelsea." She waited for him to wander off, but he didn't. Instead he took off his headphones and hung them round his neck.

"You know, this really weird thing happened with Chelsea the other day." He had a south London accent and spotty skin that was pink and dry from Clearasil overuse.

"Really?" Cyn said. "What?"

"Well, I was in the ladies' toilet and—"

"Hang on. You were in the ladies' room?"

"Yeah."

"Any particular reason? Like you wanted to try out the hand lotion?"

"Der. I'm not a perv. The cleaner had gone for 'er break and forgotten to put in fresh soap and new toilet rolls. Somebody asked me to do it. Look, I made sure there was nobody in there before I went in."

"OK, go on."

"Right, well, anyway. I was in the end cubicle fitting a toilet roll, when Chelsea comes in—except I didn't know it was her until she got on her mobile and I heard her voice. Anyway, she's begging this bloke to help her with something . . ."

"Hang on, Luke. Why are you telling me all this? I mean, it just sounds like gossip." She'd always thought Luke was a bit idle and an MP3 short of an iPod, but she had never had him down as a gossip.

"No, it isn't. I'm telling you because she sounded really upset. She was crying and begging this bloke to help her and everything. It totally freaked me out. She sounded like my sister, Kelly, when my dad refuses to give her money. And that's pretty bad. I mean, Kelly can really turn on the waterworks, but this was much worse. I know nobody likes Chelsea much, but I've seen you two chatting and I thought that if she's in trouble, maybe you could help her." She was reassessing her view of Luke. Maybe he wasn't the brightest of lads, but he was a sensitive, caring soul.

"She kept repeating the same thing over and over: 'Please, just this last time. I'll never ask you again.' And 'Charlie' was mentioned a few times." He looked around to check nobody was eavesdropping. "You know what I reckon? I reckon she could have a drug habit." Luke explained that his elder brother was in rehab. "I saw what he went through and I wouldn't want the same to happen to Chelsea."

"Luke, you're a really sweet lad, do you know that?" He colored up.

Cyn supposed it was possible that Chelsea had a drug habit, but she was so into healthy eating and food supplements, it didn't seem likely. On the other hand, hadn't she read somewhere that the reason everybody in L.A. snorted cocaine was because it helped them absorb vitamins faster?

The begging conversation Luke described reminded Cyn of the fraught exchange she'd heard Chelsea having on the phone the other day. She'd been talking to a chap called Charlie then, too. She'd said he was her brother.

"Were any other names mentioned?" Cyn said.

"Yeah. She kept going on about a bloke called Skippy, saying how she really appreciated him helping out with Skippy, but she desperately needed something else. I reckon he's her dealer. And she also kept talking about a bust."

It was as much as Cyn could do to keep a straight face. Skippy was definitely not Chelsea's drug dealer. Skippy referred to the Skippy peanut butter account she had just finished working on. She had come up with a spectacular, potentially award-winning new TV ad. Cyn's mind began churning. Wasn't there an American ad agency called BUST? Standing for Benning Uberdorfer Samuelson and somebody? It was beginning to make sense.

"OK, Luke, don't worry. Just leave it with me. Chelsea's in hospital now, so I'm sure she's not taking anything she shouldn't. Thank you for coming to me and I will talk to her."

"You promise? Because my brother got really violent and everything. Crack nearly ruined his life."

"Don't worry, Luke. I really will deal with it."

He seemed relieved. "Thanks, Cyn."

The moment he disappeared Cyn turned back to her computer and went onto Google. She typed in *Charlie, Bust,*

*Advertising, Los Angeles*. She scrolled down the page—past all the sites devoted to the legalizing of cocaine—until she came to something that caught her attention: www.bust-ads.com/charlie-taylor. The Taylor bit didn't quite make sense, though, because she was expecting to find Chelsea's brother, who would be called Roggenfelder. But she clicked on the link anyway.

From what she could tell, Charlie Taylor was the "T" bit of the BUST partnership. She looked at his CV. He was the son of Max Taylor senior. From 1962 to 1973 Max senior had been Sargent Roggenfelder's partner. Cyn sat back. So, Charlie wasn't her brother, he was the son of her father's business partner. They were friends. He could even be an ex-boyfriend. Whatever his relationship with Chelsea, one thing was certain: Charlie Taylor was a shit-hot ad man. If Chelsea hadn't been begging him for money—which had never made sense, bearing in mind her wealth—what had she wanted from him?

Was it possible that despite her brilliance, Chelsea didn't have a creative bone in her body? Was it possible that she was getting this Charlie to help her? That would explain why she was always so quiet at those preliminary brainstorming meetings. She said nothing because she had nothing to say. But why go into advertising if she knew she was crap at it? It didn't take Freud to work it out. She would put money on Chelsea being an only child. She must have done it to please her father.

Cyn spent the rest of the morning trying to navigate her way through her feelings. She still felt hurt and monumentally furious with Chelsea, but now—assuming her theory was correct—she also felt sorry for her. Hugh and Harmony would say she was being pathetic, but she couldn't help it. She thought about phoning Chelsea and attempting some kind of heart-to-heart. Bit by bit, Cyn's courage returned. Chelsea was the last person on earth to hold up her hands and beg forgiveness. Emotionally damaged she might be, but there was still no doubt in Cyn's mind that Chelsea Roggenfelder needed to be taught a lesson. Carrying on with the impersonation plan was the only way to get through to her.

It was lunchtime before she got round to checking her e-mail. There was one from Gazza.

> *cyn please could you pass this message on to chel . . .*
> *howzit going in rain forest? thanks for sending figures*
> *which will stick in executive microwave to see how they*
> *defrost with powers that be upstairs but sure there'll be*
> *no problemo. big night out tonight with lads from accounts.*
> *promises to be wild with a capital mad. let's make date*
> *as soon as you're back.*
> *xx gazza*

Cyn groaned out loud at the mention of the date. Then she wondered what a load of accountants got up to on a wild night out. What did they do—find somebody to gang audit?

The intimidatingly grand house that Hugh was looking after for his parents' friends was just a few paces from Harrods. It was a formal, echoing museum of a place, full of dark oil paintings and hefty, lumpen antiques. This was a house where pompous dinner guests had competitive conversations about Wagner and Schiller and an infinitive had never dared be split. Whenever she stepped inside, Cyn got the urge to play naked Twister with the Red Hot Chili Peppers on the stereo at full blast.

"You OK?" Cyn said to Hugh as he took her coat. She was aware that his face matched the gray of his suit.

"I've lost my job."

"You're kidding."

"Nope. They want me out at the end of the week."

"But why would they want to get rid of you? I thought you had more customers than you could handle."

"I do. Despite that, the Surrogate Boyfriend scheme isn't making the profit the company had hoped for. So they're winding it up and I've been given the boot. The rotten part about it is that my boss took me out for this expensive lunch. I thought he was going to offer me a pay raise. Then he tells me my job doesn't exist anymore."

"Oh, Huge."

"It gets worse. Two minutes after sacking me he picks up his glass of wine and says, 'You know, Hugh, this is great. We should do it more often.' "

She put her arms around him. "I am so sorry. Look, if there's anything I can do. I mean, if you run short of money . . ."

"Thanks, gorgeous, I appreciate it, but don't worry, I'll be fine. Something will come up." He led her across the chessboard entrance hall, toward the drawing room.

"I'll phone Harvey Nicks—see if they need any personal shoppers." He pulled off his tie, opened the top button of his shirt and draped himself languorously over a maroon chaise longue. He looked like Noël Coward in a decline.

Cyn sat opposite him on an upright mahogany chair with a tall carved back that dug into her spine. "Blimey, where did they find this, Anne Boleyn's death cell?"

He didn't react. "No news about the screenplay, I take it?" she said and immediately wished she hadn't. If he'd heard anything he would have said. Now all she'd succeeded in doing was making him more miserable. She thought it best not to mention that with one thing and another she hadn't gotten round to reading it yet.

"*Rien, ma chérie,*" he said crossing his spider legs. "Harms offered me a job at the salon, at reception, which was awfully sweet of her."

"She offered me a job, too, if this Chelsea thing goes tits up. We could work there together. It'd be fun."

He managed a smile. "So, how are things with you?"

"Oh, you know . . . there's a new bloke who's joined my therapy group and I think I fancy him."

"Not good. Steer clear of mad people, that's my motto."

"That's what Harm said."

"Goodness, me and McFarmsworth agreeing. That has to be a first."

"But I'm in therapy and I'm not mad," she said, repeating what she'd said to Harmony.

"Just because you're not doesn't mean to say he isn't."

"Anyway, nothing's going to happen." She explained about Veronica's rule.

"Well, let's all sing hallelujah and give thanks for Veronica," he said. "Now, then, why don't we order some food? These friends of my parents keep telling me to help myself to anything I fancy from the wine cellar, so I've chosen two bottles of a rather exceptional Château Lafitte. Of course, drinking vintage Lafitte with curry is a bit like mixing Armani with Gap, but I don't care. I just want to get trolleyed." He went off to the kitchen and came back with the takeaway menu, the wine and two glasses.

She watched him pour the wine. "I'm pretty sure I've worked out why Chelsea stole my Droolin' Dream idea."

"Go on."

She explained about Luke overhearing Chelsea's conversation with Charlie Taylor and how she was pretty certain it was Charlie who was coming up with Chelsea's ideas. "It's all about impressing her father."

"And now you feel sorry for her and you've lost your nerve."

"OK, I admit I had a bit of a wobble when I found out, but no, I haven't lost my nerve."

"Good girl. What she did to you was nothing short of evil. You have every right to get your own back. The woman has it coming."

She sipped her wine. "You're right."

They were studying the takeaway menu and discussing various job options for Hugh when the idea hit her. "Omigod. I've got it."

"What?"

"I think I may have a job for you. My mum is trying to organize Jonny and Flick's wedding and everybody thinks it's too much for her and that she's losing the plot. Why don't I try and persuade her to take you on as her wedding planner? It wouldn't pay much, but it would tide you over."

Hugh didn't seem particularly thrilled by the prospect. The only thing that was going to cheer him up was a call from Warner Bros. to say his screenplay was the best thing they had seen in decades and could he fly out to L.A. immediately, first class, at their expense, for preliminary discussions about casting. She got up and went to sit next to him on the chaise longue. "Come on, Huge." She took his hand. "You organize spectacular parties. Harmony's fortieth for a start. She still hasn't gotten over the way you turned her living room into an Arabian tent. And she wasn't the only one. People did double takes when they came in and saw what you'd done. You found rugs, cushions, hookahs. It was like a film set. You organized musicians, dancers, the most wonderful caterers. Don't you remember those waitresses in veils and Aladdin pants handing round dishes of pistachio Turkish Delight? It was a magical evening. Everybody said so. You're really gifted, Huge, and this is an emergency."

"In what way?"

"OK, I wanted to spare you this, but I can see now that I have no choice . . . Flick's considering gospel singers or possibly a band of medieval minstrels."

Hugh sat bolt upright and slapped his hand to his chest in a gesture of high-camp self-mockery. "For the love of God! Tell me it isn't so."

"Would I joke about something like this? And she also wants me to be maid of honor in a purple lace meringue."

"Purple? Ouch." He was himself again now. "That is bad."

"Well, she hasn't actually said purple, but I know that's how it will end up. Huge, if nothing else, you have to rescue me." She could tell he still wasn't sure. "Please. If you do it, I promise you'll get to wear one of those cute little headset things."

"Really?" he said, camping it up again. "You'd really do that for me?"

"Huge, you're my best mate. I'd do anything for you."

He let out a long breath. "OK, this does seem like an emergency. I agree. It has to be stopped."

"I'll speak to Mum. Why don't I do it now?"

"Oh . . . kay," his voice had gone all flouncy again. "But whatever the deal, I'm holding out over the headset, right?"

"Right." She got up and went over to the phone, which was sitting on a small but ugly Jacobean table with thick twisted legs. "Put it on speakerphone," Hugh said.

Cyn dialed the number and let the phone ring a dozen or so times. She was just about to put the receiver down when Barbara picked up.

"Hi, Mum, it's me. Why did you take so long to answer?"

"I was waiting for a call from Fein Platters."

"I don't understand. Wouldn't that mean you'd pick up straightaway?"

"Absolutely not," Barbara insisted. "I'm playing hard to get."

Cyn wasn't quite sure where the logic was in this, since it was Barbara trying to hire Fein Platters rather than the other way round, but she decided to let it go. "Look, Mum, I've been having some thoughts about the wedding. It's going to involve you in so much hard work, so I was wondering how you'd feel about taking on a wedding planner."

"A wedding planner?" She seemed intrigued. "Goodness, it never occurred to me. They're all the go, aren't they? Sylvia Gold from the synagogue Ladies' Guild had one when their daughter got married. She didn't stop showing off about it. I remember the planner would always ring during our fund-raising meetings. I'm sure Sylvia organized it. She would get all lah-di-dah and say, 'Sorry, ladies, do excuse me. It's Bianca, my wedding planner.' But they cost a fortune. Your dad would really kick up."

"Not necessarily. Hugh's just lost his job and I told you what a wonderful fortieth birthday party he did for Harmony. I thought he'd be perfect to organize the wedding. It would take all the pressure off you. And he'd charge loads less than a real wedding planner."

"Hang on a minute," Hugh whispered. "A chap's got to eat." Cyn shushed him.

"Ooh, a *gay* wedding planner," Barbara was saying. "Gay men have got so much style and flair . . . such panache. I'm sure Hugh has got loads more flair than Sylvia's Bianca."

Hugh was rolling his eyes. "Got a wedding to organize?" he trilled. "Feeling overwhelmed? Don't know where to turn? Why not let Super Faggot come to your rescue? That's Super Faggot—first for fabulous functions." Cyn waved her hand in an attempt to shut him up.

"And isn't Hugh the *Honorable* Hugh Thorpe Duff?"

"He most certainly is," Cyn said. She turned to Hugh and gave him the thumbs-up. She knew precisely where this was going.

"I thought so," Barbara came back. "Not that I'm a snob or anything. I mean, you know me. I don't have a snobbish bone in my body."

"Of course you don't," Cyn said, realizing that even an old-fashioned, dyed-in-the-wool leftie like her mum could be seduced by class—particularly if it meant getting one over on Sylvia Gold. Or, in this case, two, since Hugh was both gay and exceedingly posh.

"I don't want to go too upmarket, though, particularly with the food. I don't want people to feel intimidated. We must still have Grandma's chocolate fountain and I thought deep-fried ice cream with black cherries might be fun."

At the mention of deep-fried ice cream, Hugh put his head in his hands.

"And do you think Hugh would come with me to My Daughter's Wedding and help me choose my outfit?"

"She has to be joking," Hugh muttered. "There's actually a shop called My Daughter's Wedding? I can't do it. I can't. You'll have to tell her. It's all too much."

"Mum, I know Hugh would absolutely love to help you choose an outfit." She looked at Hugh, whose mouth was making a series of contorted expressions as if he were having a stroke in installments. "Actually, he's right here and he's desperate to talk to you. Why don't you have a word?"

"You will pay for this, Fishbein," Hugh hissed, making slitty eyes. "You will pay for this, big time."

He snatched the phone. "Mrs. Fishbein! It's so wonderful to speak to you. How *are* you?" He covered up the phone, turned to Cyn and pulled another face. "I hate you. I hate you."

Cyn giggled and listened to her mother asking Hugh if he was sure he wouldn't mind helping her choose a wedding outfit.

"Mind? Of course I wouldn't mind. I would love nothing more." Another murderous look at Cyn.

"I was thinking of something in salmon," Barbara went on. Again he covered up the phone. "Now she wants to color coordinate with the main course!" He threw a cushion at Cyn.

"Salmon. Hmm. I can see that would be very you."

"Or aubergine, or pale lemon. Or avocado, maybe."

"Yes, any of those could work."

"You know, Hugh," Barbara said, "I think it would be wonderful to have you as our wedding planner. Of course, I'll have to talk it over with Jonny and Flick and Cyn's father, but I'm sure they'll all agree it's a brilliant idea."

"I do hope so," Hugh said. "And I promise you that I will do my absolute best to make Jonny and Flick's wedding absolutely perfect."

"I'm sure you will," Barbara said.

After Hugh put down the phone, he collapsed onto the chaise longue and lay there in a swoon, hand draped melodramatically over his brow. "Just tell me one thing," he said to Cyn. "Does your mother ever select colors that aren't based on food?"

# Chapter 9

The following evening, Cyn had to take the bus to therapy. Jonny's car was having its brakes relined and he had a meeting with a client after work, somewhere out in the sticks. Since he and Flick only had the one car between them, he asked if he could borrow Cyn's. "This bloke's a really important client. I wouldn't ask otherwise."

"And you think the Butt-Mobile is going to create the right impression on this really important client?" she asked. Jonny said he'd park it on the next street.

Cyn only just made it to her session on time. First she had to wait twenty minutes for a bus and then it started to rain. The entire journey was stop-start in the wet rush-hour traffic. She was the last to arrive—apart from Joe, who had sent a message to Veronica saying he had been stuck in a meeting and would be there as soon as he could.

As she walked in she saw that Jenny-with-the-plait was minus the plait. Her hair had been cut into a short bob and dyed blonde. Whereas the bob rather suited her, the color most definitely didn't. It was a cheap, tarty platinum blonde that collided spectacularly with her pale skin, mumsy skirt and long fawn cardigan. She looked like a Sunday school teacher on the game. Everybody was busy admiring the new hairdo, though—even Clementine. It was the first time Clementine had ever exercised tact in the group. Cyn decided that was a definite breakthrough.

"So you went for the chop," Cyn said to Jenny. "It looks great."

Jenny thanked her and said she couldn't begin to describe the trauma of losing the plait. She was wringing her hands as if she were reliving a mountainside air crash in which the survivors had been forced to eat each other. "I'll never forget what it felt like as the hairdresser cut into it. I cried for two days. I suppose it's a natural grieving process, though. The only thing that has gotten me through it is making a cushion and stuffing it with the hair. I felt it was important to keep it—you know, like you would keep a relative's ashes."

It went on like this for twenty minutes: Jenny sharing her pain and anguish, Veronica doing lots of empathetic nodding and people offering Jenny the box of tissues. In the end, Clementine, who had been shuffling from buttock to buttock for a while, seemed unable to contain her exasperation any longer. "For God's sake, Jenny, stop this bloody wittering. You can always grow your hair again." Jenny went all pathetic and said she felt Clementine was telling her she was being boring, to which Clementine replied, "You are being boring." Then Jenny said that even if Clementine was cross with her for going on, she still wanted to thank her for having the courage to be so honest about her hair and giving her the incentive to get it cut. Clementine grunted and muttered that Jenny was welcome. It was quite obvious that Jenny's helpless-little-me act was infuriating her.

Joe arrived just as Jenny's post-traumatic tress ended. Cyn had begun to think he wasn't coming after all and couldn't get over how disappointed she'd felt. When the door finally opened and he walked in, she felt a rush of excitement. He apologized for being late and sat down next to Cyn, where there happened to be a spare seat. Clementine, who was sitting opposite them, looked daggers at Cyn, but Cyn barely noticed. Joe smelled deliciously of the cold and she was filling her lungs with him. He started to take off his jacket.

"I love your shirt," Clementine simpered to Joe. "That blue really suits your coloring."

"Thank you," he said, looking more than a little self-conscious.

"So, Cyn," Ken said, clearly jumping in to stop Clementine from flirting with Joe again. "How are things with you?"

Cyn didn't hear him at first because she was struggling with her own jealous feelings about Clementine flirting with Joe. The comment about the shirt had made her flinch. She realized that she was jealous. Ken asked again how she was. Finally she came to and said she was trying to stop her mother from having a breakdown over her brother's wedding.

Sandra Yo-yo, who had said virtually nothing so far, suddenly perked up. "I really don't feel comfortable discussing mothers and weddings. A friend of mine from school got married last week and my mother has gone into an even deeper decline." Ken asked her in what way. His head was tilted to one side. There was a caring-sharing frown on his face. At that moment, he looked every inch the priest.

"There are three loos in my mother's house," Sandra explained, "but yesterday when I went round I noticed not one of them had any blue water."

Nobody seemed to know quite how to react to this. Cyn broke the silence by saying that she could identify with Sandra. "My mother and grandmother are desperate for me to find a man."

"Same with my mother," Ken said morosely. Then he realized what he had said. "Goodness, no. I mean she wants me to find a woman. I'm not . . . you know, that way." From the way he behaved every week toward Clementine, nobody thought for one minute that he was.

After the session, everybody began gathering up their bags and coats. Cyn noticed that as Clementine passed Joe on her way to the door, she paused for a couple of moments and gave him the briefest of winks. Joe returned it with a rather self-conscious half-smile. At the same time, Clementine seemed to brush her hand down the side of his jacket. Cyn thought this was a strange way of coming on to him. Did the woman have some kind of fabric fetish? A second later, Clementine had disappeared out of the door. Cyn knew the flirting was just Clementine being Clementine, but for the second time that evening she felt her insides perform an uncomfortable flip.

She stayed behind to use the loo.

It wasn't until she got outside that she saw the rain. It was falling in lumps. She stood on Veronica's porch and pulled up her coat collar. It was a good ten-minute walk to the bus stop. She cursed herself for not having brought an umbrella. Head down against the wind and rain, she set off down the garden path. She turned into the street. The pavement was so drenched it looked like somebody had poured varnish over it. After half a dozen paces, a car went past. A second later she heard the tires braking in the wet. She looked up and saw the car was being driven by Joe. As he reversed and pulled up alongside her, he leaned across the passenger seat and opened the door. "Come on, hop in," he said. "You're going to catch your death." He saw her hesitate. "Look, I know it's against the rules," he said, "but it's a filthy night and you're already soaked." Just then an icy blast of wind and rain took her breath away. She didn't need telling twice. The next moment she had slipped in beside him. "I really appreciate this. Thanks."

"No problem."

She could feel the water trickling down her face. She began wiping it away with her hand. "Here, use this," Joe said, producing a clean, folded handkerchief from his jacket pocket. She took it and thanked him. "Right, where to?" he said. "Crouch End, isn't it?" She couldn't believe he had remembered where she lived. She said the bus stop would be fine, but he insisted on taking her home.

"This is really embarrassing," she said as he pulled away. "What do we talk about?"

"Well, I guess it has to be something safe and totally unconnected with therapy. Why don't you start?"

"OK, this weather's really foul."

"Isn't it, now?" he said in that delicious Kerrygold accent of his.

"The weather forecasters always get it wrong."

"Don't they? In fact they hardly ever seem to get it right."

"Too true." They fell into an awkward silence. Finally she said that since they appeared to have gone as far as they could with the weather, it was his turn to think of a topic.

"OK," he said, "what's your worst vegetable?"

"Cauliflower. Hate it."

"Me, too," he said. "What's your favorite color?"

"Don't have one."

"Me neither. What's your favorite pop song?"

" 'Bohemian Rhapsody.' No question."

"No! That's my favorite, too! I don't believe it. Right, let's try something else. M&M's or Smarties?"

"Definitely Smarties."

"Me, too. OK . . . nights in or nights out?"

"Nights out in the summer and nights in in the winter."

"You know what? This is getting spooky."

She was laughing now. He was flirting with her, but she didn't mind. In fact she was thoroughly enjoying it. "OK," he said, "what's the longest word you've ever gotten in Scrabble?"

"I have absolutely no idea."

"Mine's *caterwaulings*," he said. "I was twelve. It was when I was at boarding school. This irritating know-all in my class challenged me to a game. He thought he could slaughter me. Anyway he put down *cater* and I added *wauling* across a triple-word score, using up all my letters in one go. I think I scored about a hundred points. God, that felt fantastic. Funny, isn't it, how you never forget things like that."

"What about the *s*?" she said

"The *s*?"

"The *s* in *caterwaulings*."

"Oh, right. He'd put that down earlier at the end of another word."

Cyn said it reminded her of the time when she was eight and she was the only person in her class who knew the meaning of the word *negligible*.

More silence. It was then that Cyn noticed the BMW logo on the car steering wheel. On the whole Cyn didn't pay much attention to the make of car people drove, or what it said about their income, but she couldn't help thinking that the film-editing business must pay better than she imagined.

Her eyes moved from the logo to Joe's hands. As he made a left turn, she thought how solid and capable they looked. In fact the whole of him looked solid and capable. He drove steadily with an easy confidence. Joe was one of those calm, levelheaded men, she decided, who always made you feel safe.

They were approaching Muswell Hill Broadway. "There's no such word as *caterwaulings*," she said.

"There most certainly is."

"There isn't. I mean, you don't say, 'I couldn't sleep because of all the *caterwaulings.*' It's *caterwauling*—no *s*." It felt comfortable squabbling with him. It was as if she'd known him forever.

"You're wrong. There is such a word. Look it up if you don't believe me." He pulled up at traffic lights. "I don't know about you, but I could murder a beer. There's a pub over there. Do you fancy a drink?"

"Joe, I would love to, but we can't . . ."

"Oh, get away with you." He'd lapsed into the Irish again. "The shrink police won't catch us there. And I won't tell if you don't." He was grinning, egging her on. "I would have thought that after the way you've stitched up this Chelsea woman, breaking Veronica's rules would be child's play."

She laughed. "OK, go on," she said. "Why not?"

"Great stuff." She was flattered that he seemed so delighted.

Cyn insisted on buying the drinks to say thank you for the lift. They found a quiet table at the far end of the bar. "So, what uniform would the shrink police wear?" she said, laughing. They decided on pince-nez and revolving bow ties.

They chatted away and she found herself telling him about her interview at PCW and how she'd managed to get the job on the strength of coming up with the "salmon that doesn't turn pink in the tin" line.

He asked about the Chelsea situation. She brought him up to speed and said she kept having moments of guilt. "You shouldn't feel guilty. She hurt you, and in a sense you are at war. When you are at war—even one you didn't start—you're forced to do nasty things. That's the nature of it. You either fight, or do the Buddhist thing and walk away. I think they call it 'yielding.' "

"I guess there are moments," she said, "when I wish I could be all Buddhist about it. Maybe I should put my trust in Karma and leave her to get on with it."

"Do you really think you could do that?"

"Probably not," she smiled.

"Few of us can. You want Chelsea to get her come-uppance in the here and now, so that you can enjoy it—not in the afterlife."

"You're right. Sod blinkin' Karma, I say." She raised her glass and they toasted the flouting of Karma.

She moved the conversation on to his job and asked him how he got into film editing. He told her that after his English degree, he'd done a course at the London College of Printing. She asked him what films he had worked on.

"Oh, nothing major. A few things that never made it to the big screen." He began swirling the last inch of beer around in his glass. "Now I do the occasional film, but it's mainly TV work. A lot of science documentaries."

" 'Fraid I don't watch too many of those. But I did see that one recently about the woman with the fourteen-stone tumor. That was brilliant. It took the surgeons hours and hours to remove it. She needed fifty pints of blood apparently. You didn't edit that, I suppose?"

"Definitely not," he said, his face contorting with horror.

She asked him what he was working on at the moment. He said he happened to be working on a film at the moment— a low-budget British science fiction movie. She expected him to say a bit more about it, but he didn't. Instead he went back to his beer swirling. Why was he so uneasy talking about his work? Was she seeing him in action? Seeing him keep his distance? On the other hand, maybe he was unhappy in his job or just being modest. Whatever, it would be wrong to push him.

"So, what brought you to therapy?" he said. As soon as

she was talking about herself, he brightened up. She told him about Barbara's cancer and the pressure she'd felt to be good and not rock the boat. He listened and really seemed to understand. She'd talked about this part of her life many times, but there was something about the way he listened, the questions he asked, that made it feel especially good sharing it with him.

Since he clammed up about his work, she hadn't expected him to open up about his family, but he did. He started to describe the playroom full of toys that were lavished on him instead of love. "Later on, when I was at boarding school, my mother used to send me designer leather jackets and shoes. I used to write long letters back telling her how much I missed her and asking when she was coming to visit me. I'd get a postcard from some exotic location telling me how busy she was."

"See, you do feel something," she said gently, realizing his eyes were filling up. She reached out and placed her hand on top of his.

"Sorry, I don't usually get like this. Now I've embarrassed you."

"Hey, no, you haven't. Not remotely."

When they got outside, the rain had stopped and Cyn said she could quite easily catch the bus from there. He wouldn't hear of it and insisted on taking her the rest of the way.

On the way home, he seemed much more cheerful and they started telling each other daft jokes. "I've got a good one," he said. "What's the difference between ordinary therapy and group therapy?"

Cyn shook her head.

"They supply bunk beds instead of couches."

"That is dreadful," she said, but it made her laugh. Soon

the conversation got round to comedy in general. She told
him that Woody Allen was her all-time top stand-up.

"Mine, too." She shot him a doubtful look. "No, this
time I'm not kidding." He explained that he had spent a year
working in New York after he graduated from the London
College of Printing and started buying old records of Woody
Allen doing stand-up. "Have you heard the moose routine?"

"Heard it?" She laughed. "I practically know it by heart."
She told him that her father was a huge Woody Allen fan. "If
he wasn't listening to John Lennon or the cricket, it was
Woody. He used to joke that since he didn't know the man, it
was overly familiar to shorten his name and refer to him as
Woody. He always insisted on calling him Wooden."

Joe laughed. "So he loved the moose routine?"

"It was his favorite."

"The moose mingled!" they shouted out simultaneously,
then cracked up. Joe was wiping his eyes.

"The Berkovitzes," he continued, "who were wearing a
moose suit, win and the moose . . ." He could barely contain
himself, ". . . the moose comes second." They were both
roaring now.

By the time they reached Cyn's flat they were had moved
on to British comedy. They agreed that *The Office* was cringe-
makingly hysterical, that *Fawlty Towers* was the funniest British
sitcom ever and that a special Nobel Prize category should be
invented for Eddie Izzard. They couldn't agree on the funniest film ever. Cyn said it was *Some Like It Hot,* Joe insisted it
was *Life of Brian*.

"You know," he said as they pulled up outside her flat,
"I've really enjoyed this evening."

"Me, too. I can't remember the last time I laughed so
much."

"Me neither." His soft brown eyes were locked on hers.

She wondered if he wanted to kiss her as much as she wanted to kiss him.

"So," Cyn said, "I guess I'll see you in therapy next week."

"I guess."

He looked like he was psyching himself up to say something. Maybe he was about to suggest they went out again. What would she say? Would she just sod Veronica's rule and say yes?

He interrupted her thoughts. "Right, well, bye, then," he said.

She felt a wave of disappointment. "OK, see ya." She opened the car door and slid out. He leaned across and wound down the passenger window. "By the way," he grinned, "don't forget to look up *caterwaulings* in the dictionary."

"You bet I won't," she said.

He gave a final wave and drove off.

As soon as she got in, she went hunting for her Scrabble dictionary. Naturally, *caterwaulings* was listed. She felt irritated at being proven wrong, but at the same time, curiously turned on.

# Chapter 10

No sooner had Cyn arrived at the office than her phone started ringing. It was Chelsea to say that despite Cyn's reassurances that everybody at Droolin' Dream knew she was in hospital, she couldn't bear being out of contact. Since Gary Rossiter was away she had just phoned his boss at Droolin' Dream to promise him she would be back on the case the moment she was better. Cyn nearly choked on her chococcino muffin. She felt the color drain from her face. The game was up. "I see," Cyn said, her voice barely more than a whisper. "So now you know, I suppose the two of us have some talking to do."

"Now I know what?" Chelsea said briskly. "What talking do we have to do?"

"Sorry, I thought you said you'd spoken to Gary Rossiter's boss."

"No, I said I'd called him. He wasn't there and this ditz brain woman on the switchboard had no idea where he was."

"He wasn't? She didn't? God, that's fantastic."

"What? How is it fantastic?"

"Sorry, no, sorry, I didn't mean that. It isn't at all fantastic. It's appalling. Bloody useless switchboard operators—complete pains in the arse."

"Cyn, you seem a bit wired. Are you OK?"

"Time of the month," Cyn blurted. "Brain meltdown. Be fine when I've had some chocolate."

"You know I have this wonderful herbalist." (She pronounced it 'erbalist in the faux French way Americans prefer and which drives British people insane.) "I'm sure she could help you. I could give her a call if you want. It's no problem, I have her on speed dial. And since you mention it, I couldn't help noticing once or twice that you seem to suffer from premenstrual bloating. Maybe she could give you something for that, too."

Waddabitch. Apart from the occasional postcurry distension, Cyn's stomach was always flat and firm—even though she did say so herself. Teeth, buttocks and hair clenched, Cyn told Chelsea that she was touched by her concern, but she would rather soldier on.

"Well, if you're sure."

Cyn said she was. "Look, don't worry, I know where Gary Rossiter's boss is." Know *where* he was? Bloody hell, she didn't even know *who* he was.

"Great, I was hoping you might. That's why I'm calling."

Cyn needed to think fast. She had to get Chelsea off the scent. She couldn't let her make contact with anybody at Droolin' Dream. OK, so where was Gazza's boss. Where? Think?

"He's er . . . he's in the States."

"Oh? How come?"

"Droolin' Dream is trying to take over Krispy Kreme. It's all incredibly hush-hush. Nobody is meant to know. Apparently he and the Krispy Kreme people are holed up at some hotel out in the wilds. The negotiations are so delicate that he's in-structed people not to contact him."

"That's totally absurd. First you tell me Gary Rossiter is walking in the Himalayas and now his boss has disappeared, too, and can't be reached. What about his PA?"

"I think she's on leave until he gets back."

"This is total BS. How can these people go out of contact like this and still call themselves businessmen? You know what? I'm going to speak to their chairman."

Please. God. No. Cyn swallowed hard.

"Look, Chelsea, you're getting yourself all worked up over nothing. Everybody at Droolin' Dream knows you're out of action and, like I told you on the phone the other day, Gary doesn't want to put any pressure on you."

"Really?" She was starting to calm down. "He said that?"

"Absolutely. They are all concerned about you and just want you to get better."

"Well, I have to admit that's very sweet." As Chelsea re-laxed, Cyn's heart rate started to come down. Then Chelsea sent it straight back up again. "You know, maybe I should e-mail them all, just to say how much I appreciate their con-cern."

"No! Don't do that! You mustn't. I mean, you can't. Your laptop's still here in the office."

"Cyn, are you sure you're OK? I can phone the herbalist in a second." Cyn managed to compose herself again, said she was fine and that she would e-mail Droolin' Dream on Chelsea's behalf.

"OK, if you don't mind."

"No problem," Cyn said, raking her hair with her fingers. "So anyway, how are you?"

"Well, I'm still in pretty bad shape. My back's painful and I'm still having to lie flat. I'm not even allowed up to pee. Right now, the doctors have no plans to let me go home."

"Well, you just rest," Cyn said. "And I'm always here if you need me."

"Thanks, Cyn. I really appreciate all you're doing. I'll just hold on and wait for Gary to get back."

"Probably best," Cyn said. She put down the phone and sat rubbing her temples. The situation was not looking good. Despite her saying she would wait for Gary to get back, Chelsea wasn't going to give up trying to make contact with Droolin' Dream. Sooner or later—and most likely sooner—she was going to find out what was going on. Of course, Cyn wanted Chelsea to find out, but not before she had the commercial—her commercial, the one she had thought up—in the can and ready to be broadcast. She had to move fast.

She e-mailed Gary Rossiter from Chelsea's laptop to say she was back from the Brazilian rain forest and was busy working on a script for the Droolin' Dream commercial, as well as looking for a director.

*By the way,* she wrote, *am v busy at the moment, could you please carry on e-mailing my assistant, Cyn, who will check my mail regularly and pass on messages.* Then something else occurred to her. Gazza probably had Chelsea's mobile number. *Also my mobile number has changed.* She gave him her own number, signed off and pressed *send*. There was a desperate, heart-stopping few moments when she realized she had signed off as Cyn rather than Chelsea, but somehow she remembered how to retrieve recently sent e-mail, change the signature and send it again.

Of course Gazza would e-mail straight back, pressuring her to go out with him. She would just have to think up another excuse. This time it would have to be one that would put him off for good.

She spent the rest of the morning phoning commercial directors. PCW had a pool of four or five they used regularly. Most of them were booked up until the summer. Two said they might be available this month to do the Droolin' Dream commercial. Both agreed to meet her for a drink to chat about it. After lunch she finally got down to writing her proposal for Sainsbury's. The rest of the afternoon was taken up with brainstorming meetings in the large trailer. Her mind was so taken up with Droolin' Dream that she found it hard to focus on radial tires, Ketchips or what women "really" wanted from nail polish remover beyond the blindingly obvious.

More than once she found herself thinking about Joe. In fact she'd hardly stopped thinking about him since they'd said good-bye the night before. What had happened last night? Had they made a connection? She thought they had, but maybe for him it had been nothing more than a pleasant but fairly insignificant couple of hours. She knew that she should see it that way, too. It had been fun to break the rules, but they were both in therapy. Veronica was right. If they got together it would change the dynamic of the group. They would both have to leave. Last night was as far as it could go.

When she got back to her desk, the phone was ringing. "Cyn, it's Joe."

She gave a start. "Joe?" she said frowning with confusion. "Therapy Joe? But how did you get this number?"

"Look, I'm sorry. I know how this must look, but I promise I'm not stalking you." He sounded tense, as if he'd spent hours psyching himself up to making the call. "It's just that this morning when I got into my car I found your Barclaycard on the floor. It must have fallen out of your pocket. When we were in the pub you happened to let slip where you worked, so I thought I should ring you before you panicked and canceled the card."

"That's really kind of you, but I hadn't even missed it." She thought back to the previous evening. On her way to therapy she'd stopped at a cash machine to get fifty quid. The machine had been a few yards from the bus stop. The bus had come along just as she was collecting her money. She'd shoved the cash and her card into her coat pocket. On the bus she'd transferred the money to her wallet. Somehow she'd managed to forget about the card and left it in her pocket. "I thought it wouldn't be a good idea returning it to you at therapy next week, because then everybody would know we'd met up." She took the point.

"How's about I put it in the post?" he said.

"No. Best not. It might get lost or stolen." He suggested sending it by courier, but they both agreed that wasn't the safest option either.

She thought about what to do. "Look, could we meet somewhere and then you could give it to me?"

"Sure. When?"

"Tonight's no good because I'm having dinner at my parents'. What about tomorrow after work?"

"OK." He paused. Then he cleared his throat. "Listen, you're probably going to think I'm way out of line, here, but I really enjoyed your company last night."

"I really enjoyed yours, too."

"And I know this is breaking every rule in the group therapy book and Veronica would probably say it's going to harm our emotional development no end, but would you like to do something tomorrow night? Perhaps we could see a film?"

"Joe, that's really nice of you . . ." OK, Cyn, be strong. This man may be devastatingly cute, not to mention intelligent, kind and funny, but he was also emotionally damaged. She would develop real feelings for him, only to have him panic and walk away. She would be left fractured and in pieces. And yet, and yet . . . She'd had so much fun last night and he had really opened up to her about his childhood. Apart from him not wanting to talk about his work—which might be put down to nothing more than modesty—she'd gotten no sense of him keeping her at arm's length. He'd come across as such a normal, regular sort of a guy.

Joe took her hesitation as a no. "Look, I understand if you don't want to. It was wrong of me to ask. I think I should hang up now. I'll drop the card at PCW reception and that way we won't have to meet. Let's just pretend this conversation never happened."

"No, Joe. Wait," she heard herself say. "I'd love to go to a film."

"You would? That's great. But what about Veronica?"

"Oh, bugger Veronica."

"Hmm, I'm not sure she's the type who takes kindly to being buggered."

This made her laugh.

"I noticed that Screen on the Green is showing *Some Like It Hot* tomorrow—for one night only."

Cyn hadn't seen it for ages. "Sounds great." As she had meetings with her two prospective directors starting late the following afternoon and didn't think she would be able to get away before seven, they agreed to meet at the cinema.


It wasn't just Cyn who was having dinner with her parents that night. Hugh and Harmony were coming, too. Barbara had arranged the dinner so that they could discuss the wedding. Naturally, Jonny and Flick would be there, which meant Cyn could get her car back. Barbara had also insisted on inviting Harmony on the grounds that "the poor girl is living in a hotel and can't possibly be eating properly."

The plan was that Cyn would take the tube to her mum's

and meet Hugh and Harmony there. Then, just as she was leaving work, she discovered a message from Harmony on her voice mail. "Cyn, I'm at 'Ewge's. You'd better get over here. He's having a major attack of the miseries and has taken to his bed. I've done all I can, but he's absolutely refusing to get up."

Of course, his depression had come on because he'd lost his job and heard nothing from Warner Bros. about his screenplay. Cyn found herself feeling a mixture of sympathy and irritation. She was desperately sorry that Hugh had been sacked and that he was struggling to get recognition for his writing, but at the same time she wanted to tell him the only way to succeed was to keep going and develop a skin thick enough to cope with being ignored and rejected. If he couldn't do that, then he might as well give up. She supposed it was easy for her to talk. She loved her job and earned a decent salary—although for how much longer she didn't know.

As well as being upset for Hugh, she was also concerned for Barbara. Not only had her mother gone to all the trouble of cooking dinner and now he was about to let her down at the last minute, but more important, he might decide the wedding planner job was too much for him as well.

"So, how bad is it?" Cyn said later to Harmony, who was looking stunning in a pale pink pleated miniskirt and a black and pink Chanel cardigan.

"Pretty bad." She drew heavily on her cigarette. "He's reading *Angela's Ashes*."

"Well, at least it's an improvement on *Final Exit*, which is what he read after his last novel was rejected. Has he started putting vicious reviews on Amazon yet?" Harmony said not as far as she knew. Cyn threw her coat over a chair and the two of them headed upstairs.

The bed was a dark oak antique four-poster. Hugh, pale and unshaven and wearing black silk pajamas, was propped up on a mountain of expensive-looking pillows doing his best to look feeble. An open copy of *Angela's Ashes* was lying facedown across his knees. Cyn stood there taking in the maroon silk bed canopy, the matching curtains and wallpaper, the portraits of stern-looking sixteenth-century aristocrats with no eyebrows. "Blimey, it's Henry the Eighth's bedchamber," she said. Hugh let out a tiny moan, but otherwise didn't respond. Cyn and Harmony looked at each other and rolled their eyes. Cyn went over and sat on the bed. "Come on, Huge," she said, taking his hand, "please don't get down. Warner Bros. will get back to you eventually, but meanwhile you have to carry on writing." He refused to make eye contact with her. Instead he stared off into the distance.

"You know, I met this really great guy last night," he said. "Turned out we had loads in common. He shares my love of theater, music, cinema."

"That's fantastic."

"Yeah, he and his wife even have a son called Hugh."

"Ah."

He turned to look at her, all puppy dog eyes. "Where did it all go wrong?" he said weakly. "Why am I such a failure?"

"Listen to me," Cyn retorted. "You are not a failure, OK? You're just struggling and that's hard. And as far as a relationship's concerned, there's somebody out there for you, I just know it. As for the writing, getting established takes time. You have to be patient and hang in there."

Harmony stubbed out her cigarette, climbed up onto the bed and lay next to Hugh, head on his shoulder. "Cyn's right, and meanwhile here you are living free in this great big gaff, helping yourself from the wine cellar. I mean, have you thought for one moment how the rest of the world lives? For example, did you know that seventy-five percent of the mentally ill live below the poverty line?"

"Christ," Hugh said, "that means twenty-five percent are doing OK. See, even drooling, matted-haired loons are more successful than me." He closed *Angela's Ashes* and put it on the bedside table. "Do either of you ever think about your funeral?"

"Sometimes I think about me gran's funeral," Harmony said. "Me dad turned up pissed, broke a flower off one of the wreaths and put it in his buttonhole."

Hugh said his grandfather had died in the garden digging up a cabbage for dinner.

"Ah, how did your grandma cope?" Harmony asked.

"She got the cook to open a tin of peas."

"No, I didn't mean . . ." Harmony stopped herself—partly because she had suddenly gotten the joke and partly because, like Cyn, she'd noticed that the vague twitching at the corners of Hugh's mouth was turning into a smile.

"Come on, Huge," Cyn said, nudging him with her elbow, "you're not doing yourself any good lying here moping."

"Do you really think I'll make it one day?"

"Without a doubt. You just have to keep the faith."

"It's like me and the salon," Harmony added. "There were times at the beginning when I was in serious debt. I had creditors hassling me day and night. For two years I barely slept with the worry. All I could think about was giving up, but somehow I found the strength to carry on."

"Yeah," Hugh said, "and then Justin came along with his magic wallet."

"OK, so my luck changed. Yours will, too. Me mam

always says that the devil doesn't crap in the same place forever."

He seemed to perk up a bit more. They were making headway. Harmony got up and went over to his wardrobe and pulled out a pair of jeans and a white Paul Smith shirt with tiny roses up the front panel. "Bet this looks great on you," she said about the shirt.

"Yes, well, I have been meaning to debut it."

"Come on, then," Cyn said, urging him on. "How's about I run you a shower? It'll make you feel better."

His face suddenly slumped again. "Thanks, gorgeous, but I just don't think I'm up to it."

Cyn asked him whether it was just the shower he wasn't up to—or was he also not up to going to her mum's for dinner and being her wedding planner.

"All three," he said, sounding more feeble than ever.

"OK, fine, but you have to phone Mum and explain."

"Can't you do it?"

"No," she said indignantly, "you're the one letting her down. Of course, she will burst into tears and develop sudden shooting pains in her chest because she's already told two hundred of her closest friends that the Honorable Hugh Thorpe Duff, fiftieth in line to the throne, is organizing her son's wedding."

"But I'm not fiftieth in line to the throne. I'm not anything in line to the throne."

"That's not the point. The point is, she's told everybody you're doing the wedding and now she'll have to suffer the humiliation of un-telling everybody. If the blubbing and chest pains don't make you feel sufficiently guilty and have you caving in, she will bring out the big guns and bore you into submission. You might even get her lecture on the 1926 General Strike, in which she'll make a cogent and eloquent case for renationalizing the railways and argue that if her grandfather didn't get depressed with no money coming in and nine children to support, then what right have you. "

"OK, I'll get up."

"Sound choice," Cyn said with a smile.

# *Chapter* 11

In the end, they all went to Edgware in Harmony's car. Cyn phoned Barbara along the way and made up a story about the traffic being bad, to explain why they would be a bit late. "Thanks for not squealing on me to your mum," Hugh said.

"Come on, Huge, as if."

Hugh, who was sitting in the front next to Harmony, began drawing a cuff out from under his jacket sleeve. "You two are right," he said. "Once I have a new writing project on the go, I'll be fine. Sorry for being such a pain in the arse." They assured him that was OK.

For a few minutes nobody spoke. Cyn sat trying to pluck up the courage to tell them about her date with Joe. Finally she decided it would be wrong to hold out on them.

"Look, I know you're both going to think I'm mad," she said, "but Joe—the guy from therapy—asked me to go out with him and I said yes."

"You're mad," Hugh and Harmony said in unison. Then Harmony went on about how she'd promised faithfully this wasn't going to happen.

"I know, I know." She told them about him picking her up in the rain, going to the pub and her credit card falling out of her pocket. "We had a real laugh last night. He seems so normal."

Hugh made the point that being in therapy, Cyn should know enough about mental health "to understand that your average nutter doesn't sit in the corner rocking obsessively and ranting about the laser beams in their heads. They suppress their lunacy. I suppose we all do it to some degree."

"Right," Cyn leaped in. "Maybe it is just a question of degree. Perhaps he does have a few problems, but when we were in the pub he really opened up about his childhood. I'm convinced he's not as badly damaged as you think."

"Cyn," Harmony said, looking at her in her rearview mirror, "has anybody ever told you denial ain't just a river in Egypt?" She rolled down her window and flicked cigarette ash onto the road.

Barbara answered the door. Her hair had been freshly set and she was in a jazzy red blouse and navy trousers. She was also in a tizz. Her potatoes had turned to water in the pan and she was on the phone to the plumber who had rung to make an appointment to come and fix some guttering. She did a quick round of hello kisses and told them to make themselves comfortable in the living room. "Mal's in there. He'll make you all a drink." Cyn asked if there was anything she could do.

"Actually, there is. You could come into the kitchen and fetch the peanuts and olives."

A minute later, Cyn was standing in the living room holding two of her mother's cut-glass (in Hugh's honor) nibbles dishes. Mal was sitting on the sofa, wired up to the oxygen machine he'd bought on eBay. He had a plastic tube coming out of each nostril. These joined up and formed one tube at about chin level—exactly like a stethoscope. The single tube connected with a device the size of a shopping cart on wheels, which sat on the floor beside him, making a gentle, rhythmic pumping sound. Harmony was sitting next to him, her face etched with concern. "So, 'ow are you doing, Mr. Fishbein?" As she put her arm round him, Mal looked both flattered and bemused.

"Oh, you know, the odd ache and pain, but I can't grumble."

"Good for you, Mr. Fishbein, that's the spirit. Never say die, eh? Cyn never said a word . . . you know"—Harmony nodded toward the oxygen machine—"about any of this."

Cyn tried to interrupt and put Harmony straight, but Mal got in first. "Great, isn't it? Cost me seven hundred and fifty quid on eBay."

"Oh, my God. You mean not only did you have to pay for it, but you were forced to buy it secondhand? What sort of a heartless, cruel world do we live in? The National Health Service used to be the jewel in this country's crown, now look at it, a complete shambles."

Cyn tried to break in again, but this time Hugh, who seemed to know what the machine was, pulled on her arm and gave a mischievous wink.

"I wouldn't expect to get something like this on the NHS," Mal said. "I mean, after all, it is a bit of a luxury."

"A luxury? I can't believe the bravery of the man."

Mal was looking confused, or at least pretending to. Cyn was certain he knew precisely what was going on. He wasn't setting Harmony straight because he was enjoying having a young, beautiful woman put her arm around him. He asked her if she fancied a go. Harmony looked taken aback. Hugh was stifling giggles and giving Cyn a look that said "Please, please don't spoil the fun."

"That's very kind of you, Mr. Fishbein, but I think your need is greater than mine."

"Madonna's got one, you know," Mal said.

"Geddaway. But she's such a health fanatic. I would never have taken her for a smoker. Is it terminal? How long have they given her?"

"About fifty years," Cyn broke in, putting the nuts and olives down on the coffee table. "Dad's not ill, the oxygen is meant to increase brain power. Half of Hollywood owns one."

"What?" Mal said, starting to laugh. "You thought I was dying?" He slapped his thigh—rather theatrically, Cyn thought—and roared. Harmony stood up, red faced. "Why didn't you tell me?" she hissed at Cyn. "You just let me carry on and embarrass myself."

"She tried," Hugh said, "but I wouldn't let her. I was just having a bit of fun, that's all. Sorry. Forgive me? Please?" He gave Harmony a squeeze. She tried to fight him off, but it was pretty halfhearted. "Well, at least you've cheered up," she said, starting to see the funny side. "I suppose we should be thankful for small mercies, but I'll get you for this, Thorpe Duff. Just you see if I don't." She smacked his arm, but not so that it hurt.

Still chuckling, Mal took the tubes out of his nose and got up from the sofa.

"Thanks for coming to the rescue over the wedding," he said to Hugh. "I love Barbara, but I've spent the last few days in the shed keeping out of her way. She's been getting herself so worked up over caterers and whatnot she was beginning to sound like Nigella on helium."

Hugh smiled and promised Mal that there would be no

more panics and Jonny and Flick would have *the* most perfect wedding. At this, Mal got hold of Hugh's arm and took him to one side. "Just one thing," he lowered his voice. "If you could take it easy, you know, on the money side of things."

"Point taken, Mr. Fishbein."

"And here's another point," Barbara said, bustling into the room with a bowl of Kettle Chips. "Misers don't make great husbands."

"You're absolutely right, my sweet," Mal said to her. At the same time he was winking at Cyn. "But misers make brilliant ancestors . . . So . . ." He started rubbing his hands. "What's everybody having to drink?"

Mal was handing round drinks when Grandma Faye, who had never met Hugh or Harmony, appeared. She was particularly taken with Harmony, whom she described as the spit of the young Elizabeth Taylor. Mal said he hoped she meant the film star rather than the tortoise.

She practically curtsied when Cyn introduced her to Hugh. He seemed to think she was tremendous fun and was happy to sit on the sofa with her while she listed all the side effects she was getting from her new blood pressure pills. "You know," she said in a voice that everybody could hear, "it's such a shame you bat for the other side. I mean, a good-looking boy like you—it's such a waste."

Before Cyn had a chance to tell Barbara that Hugh had a brilliant sense of humor and wouldn't be remotely offended, she had shot across the room. "Mum, try these olives," she said, practically thrusting the bowl in her mother's face.

Faye helped herself, turned back to Hugh and carried on: "Are you absolutely sure you're that way inclined? I mean, there must be drugs they can give you—hormones or something." By now Barbara was in a full-scale panic. Faye refused to let her get a word in, so all Barbara could do was stand there and watch, popping olives like Valium. But it got worse. "I had twin cousins who were gay," Faye continued. "Both became rabbis. My father always called them the fruit Jews."

Hugh cracked up. "This woman is priceless. Mrs. Fishbein, you are so lucky to have a mother as gloriously witty and entertaining as Faye." Faye was positively glowing.

"Yes, well, she certainly keeps us all amused," Barbara said chirpily, wiping her palms down the sides of her trousers and glaring at Faye.

Because Jonny had to pick Flick up from the hospital and then they got caught up in roadworks, they didn't arrive until everybody was about to sit down to dinner. Having drooled over Harmony's outfit, figure, makeup and hair, Flick must have spent a full five minutes apologizing for her appearance. "I didn't have time to get changed and I look like such an old frump-bag in my nurse's uniform." Harmony shot Cyn a look of mild desperation. She'd only met Flick a couple of times, but she'd immediately picked up on how insecure she was about her figure and her constant need for reassurance.

"Stuff and nonsense," Hugh said, brightly. "I bet you have all the male patients begging you to give them bed baths." Flick gave a self-conscious giggle. "You have a wonderfully voluptuous hourglass figure." He stood behind her and placed his hands either side of her waist. "Look how perfectly you go in here. Your bust and hips are in perfect proportion." Flick had now turned crimson and was fiddling with her hair. "You are going to look fabulous on your wedding day," he insisted. "Simply fabulous."

"Gosh, don't know about that," Flick said with a horsey snort.

As they all sat down, Cyn shot Hugh a look that said "you are a genius."

Tonight they were eating in the dining room. Barbara

had clearly made the decision that her alpine breakfast nook did not befit an honorable. She had also gotten out the best cutlery and the Portmeirion Botanic Garden dinner service.

"Please start, everybody," she said. Then she turned to Hugh, whom she had insisted sit next to her. "I hope you like melon. I wasn't sure whether to get honeydew or cantaloupe. In the end I decided on honeydew. Much better flavor. And the ginger sprinkled on top just gives it a lift, I always think."

"I agree. This looks absolutely delicious, Mrs. Fishbein."

"Please. Call me Barbara."

"You know, Barbara, I was just admiring your curtains. Wonderful color."

"How clever of you to notice. They're new. I thought avocado with a salmon thread worked really well."

"Doesn't it?" Cyn watched him looking around, taking in Barbara's filigree photo-trees and Canaletto prints. Four or five hung round the room in heavy gilt frames with gold viewing lights above them. Whatever he was thinking—and she could guess—he wasn't letting it show for a second. Quite the reverse, in fact. "You know, Barbara, you have a truly original eye."

"Goodness? You really think so?"

"*Sans doute. Sans doute.*"

"Flatterer," she giggled, practically batting her eyelashes. Hugh had worked his magic. From here on in, any suggestion he made about the wedding would be met with her unquestioning, wholehearted and overwhelming approval. She was his—wedding cake marzipan in his hands. "I get my eye for interior design from my father," she said, patting her hair. "He was in soft furnishings."

"What are you talking about?" Faye butted in. "Your father sold brushed nylon sheets and pillowcases off a stall in Ridley Road market."

Barbara grimaced at her mother. "There were cushions, too," she protested. "And curtains."

Faye gave a shrug and said she didn't remember any cushions and curtains.

"Anyway, Hugh," Barbara went on, "I really want to thank you for agreeing to be our wedding planner. It was all getting a bit too much for me on my own."

"You can say that again," Mal muttered, stabbing a melon chunk.

"What was that, Mal?" Barbara said, narrowing her eyes.

"Nothing. I just said it looks like rain."

Flick, who remained as sensitive as ever to the atmosphere chez Fishbein, suddenly produced a sheet of paper out of her bag. "Look, everybody," she cried, "I've done some sketches for Cyn's bridesmaid dress. I had a mooch round the shops, but everything seemed so restrained and boring. So, I thought, why not design my own?" She passed the paper over to Cyn, who was sitting next to Hugh and Harmony. The sketches were all pretty much the same—variations on the hooped lace meringue Cyn had been dreading. "I thought apple green would be just perfect."

Cyn dug her fingers into Hugh's thigh.

"Come on, gorgeous," Hugh whispered, "at least it's one up on purple."

"How do you work that out?"

He ignored her. "Yes, these might work," Hugh said to Flick.

"Thank you," Cyn hissed. "Thank you very much."

"Although," he went on, "I've been having a few thoughts about the wedding and I was thinking maybe we should keep it very simple."

"I like simple. Simple's good," Mal said, eagerly. "In fact the simpler the better."

Barbara dug him in the ribs and told him not to fill up on bread because there was chicken casserole coming.

"I know it's a cliché," Hugh said, "but less really is more."

"Oh, you are so right, Hugh," Barbara simpered. She turned to Flick. "I really think we should take our lead from Hugh. Simple elegance should be our catchphrase."

Flick looked a tad deflated.

"As it's a spring wedding," Hugh continued, warming to his theme, "I thought we should go for soft yellows and creams with touches of fresh spring green and maybe a hint of blue to remind us of the clear blue summer skies to come."

Barbara was practically swooning. Even Flick seemed to have come under his spell. "Gosh, that does sound awfully romantic," she said, reminding Cyn of Jenny in her therapy group. Flick turned to Jonny, who was sitting at the far end of the table. "What do you think, darling? You haven't said much."

Jonny didn't answer. His head was down and he appeared to be deep in concentration.

"Darling?" Flick repeated.

"Wonderful. Great," Jonny mumbled without looking up.

"What's wonderful?" Flick said.

"Whatever you just said."

"I didn't say anything. Hugh did."

"Jonny," Barbara said, "do you mind telling us what you are doing down there?"

"OK, I'm sorry," Jonny said, placing a copy of the *Law Society Gazette* on the table. "It's just that this whole wedding thing is starting to get me down. There's just no letup." Mal said he would drink to that.

Flick looked as if she was about to burst into tears when the doorbell rang.

"Who's that?" Mal frowned. Grandma Faye said they could all sit guessing, or he could get up and open the door. He went out into the hall. Barbara got up and hovered by the dining room door. "Ooh, I think he's here," she cried.

"Who?" Cyn said.

"Our refugee. We weren't expecting him for another couple of days. Thank goodness I did that big food shop yesterday." She was bursting with excitement and turned to Faye: "Mum, please don't say anything to embarrass him. Remember, he's a stranger in a strange land."

At that point Mal walked in dwarfed by a six-foot-six, blonde-haired, blue-eyed Aryan god, whose denim jacket barely concealed an Arnie six-pack and hod carrier's arms.

"Everybody," Mal said, "I'd like to introduce Laurent Cinnamon."

Everybody was taken aback by the sight of Laurent Cinnamon, but Barbara more than most. Her expression practically screamed disappointment. Cyn had no trouble reading her mother's thoughts: this wasn't how it was meant to be. Laurent was meant to be black, not Dulux Brilliant White. She'd desperately wanted to show off her brave black revolutionary (preferably complete with tribal markings and African caftan) to all her lefty, *Guardian*-reading friends and make them feel jealous and inadequate because they weren't doing their bit for mankind, like her. Now this chap had turned up looking like a Von Trapp son on steroids.

*"Bonsoir,"* Laurent said, with a wave and a broad Chiclet smile. By now everybody was on their feet, hands outstretched.

"Laurent, welcome to our home," Barbara managed to gush. She immediately began fussing about whether he was hungry and whether he had a problem with honeydew melon.

"*Le melon*—eet is wonderfool. *J'adore le melon.*"

"Please say if it isn't. I can offer you papaya, pineapple, mango, guava, coconut . . . And are you warm enough? Our wretched climate must take a lot of getting used to. I could find you a woolly. Or maybe you'd like me to turn the heating up?"

"*Non,* I am fine, really. Except maybe I could use *la toilette*?"

"Of course, of course," Barbara said. "I'll show you to the downstairs cloakroom." As Barbara led Laurent to the door, Harmony fell back onto her chair. "Wow, will you look at that?" she whispered, her glazed eyes locked on Laurent's disappearing, peach-perfect butt. "Is that perfection or what?"

"It is," Hugh replied, "and what's more, it is all mine."

"For Chrissake, 'Ewge, don't be ridiculous. He isn't gay."

"Er, hello, stone-washed denim jacket over stone-washed jeans. I think so."

"Rubbish. He's just got provincial taste, that's all. Didn't you see the way he looked at me as he came in? He is so straight."

"What? With a name like Laurent Cinnamon? Please."

"He's from bloody French West Africa, what do you expect him to be called? I'm telling you, he's straight." Harmony turned to Cyn. "Cyn, tell 'Ewge that Laurent is definitely straight."

Cyn said she wasn't sure. "But don't you fancy him?" Harmony said. "I mean you're always saying how blonde, gentile-looking men give you the hots."

"Not like they used to," she said wistfully, thinking about Joe's dark hair and eyes. "Plus I don't go for muscle-bound hunks. Laurent is way too Tarzan for me."

"Well, he can call me Jane and invite me to his tree house anytime," Harmony said. She turned to Hugh. "A fiver says he's straight."

"Right, you're on."

At this point Barbara came back carrying a chair for Laurent. "Put Laurent next to me," Grandma Faye said. "Come on, budge up, everybody. Let's make some room."

When Laurent returned, Grandma Faye smiled and patted the empty chair. Cyn could tell she was smitten and wishing she was a decade or six younger. "It's funny, Laurent," she said, taking his hand, "coming from Africa, I think we were all expecting you to be a bit more cinnamon colored."

Like Hugh, Laurent seemed to take an immediate liking to Grandma Faye and appeared not to be remotely offended by the cinnamon remark. Over Barbara's chicken casserole and some fried plantain, which she managed to whiz up in ten minutes, he explained that his ancestors had been French Catholic missionaries who had gone to Tagine in the eighteenth century. "Zey fell in love wis ze place and stayed on. Many missionary families did. Zese days zere are quite a few white people. But we all get on. Zere is no, 'ow you say?, racial tension."

"Is it very beautiful?" Harmony said, leaning in toward him, chin in hand.

Laurent began swirling wine around in the bottom of his glass. "Tagine ees very poor, but it ees paradise on earth. Ze sun is always shining, ze beaches are made of soft, white sand. At dusk, eet feels like warm silk under ze feet. Ze sea is liquid turquoise and jade . . ." His voice trailed off. "Zen ze trouble began." He said that Tagine—which was about the size of Wales—had been ruled for fifty years by an ineffectual but benevolent dictator called Henri Elysian. "When Elysian died, ze military simply seized control. Zey kill hundreds of people—anybody who opposed zem and got in zeir way—doctors, nurses, teachers. Suddenly Tagine ees in the grip of zees madmen who are robbing ze people. Zey 'ave increased taxes, ze hospitals 'ave no medicines, schools have been burned down. People are going hungry and ze very young and ze very old are dying."

Nobody interrupted him. Everybody sat in silence, trying to absorb the horror Laurent described. Harmony seemed to be particularly affected. Cyn could see her eyes filling up. "As long as I bloody live," she whispered to Cyn, "I will never understand the evil in this world. What kinds of monsters kill babies?" Cyn, who was struggling to keep her own emotions in check, put an arm around Harmony.

Laurent was explaining how he helped set up an underground movement to fight the military regime. "We want to bring democracy to Tagine. As I'm sure you read in your newspaper, we eventually stage a countercoup, but eet fail. Nearly all of us die." He was starting to choke on his words. "By some miracle, I was spared and now I am 'ere wiz you."

"And most welcome you are, too," Barbara said, placing her hand on top of his.

"I will help you present your case to the Home Office," Mal said. "It's clear that you have enemies in Tagine who would persecute you if you went back. I really can't see it's going to be a problem getting you asylum here."

"Sank you. Sank you so much. What can I say?"

"You don't have to say anything," Barbara said. "It is an honor to have you. Now, then, who's for pudding?"

Barbara started collecting plates. Laurent immediately got to his feet to help her.

"Laurent, you really don't have to," Barbara said. "You sit down. Mal and I can manage." But he insisted.

"So, Laurent," Harmony said, shooting a quick look at Hugh. "Do you have a girlfriend back in Tagine?"

"*Non*. No girlfriend." Hugh grinned a valedictory grin.

"For the last few years zere 'as been no room in my life for women. But I live in 'ope." Hugh's face fell.

Laurent picked up some plates and followed Barbara into the kitchen.

Harmony turned to Hugh, hand outstretched. "Right," she grinned, "I think that's a fiver you owe me."

# Chapter 12

When Cyn arrived at Screen on the Green, Joe was at the sweets counter, buying popcorn. He was wearing a trendy short black raincoat with the collar turned up, which she thought made him look particularly sexy. She snuck up behind him. "Hiya."

He spun round. His startled expression morphed into a broad smile. "I didn't know if you preferred your popcorn salted, sweet or with toffee," he said, "so I got all three." He picked two cartons up off the counter. Underneath his raincoat, a packet of toffee popcorn was sticking out of his jacket pocket. She couldn't help laughing.

"Now you see why I'm really in therapy," he said, laughing along with her. "I suffer from this obsessive need to please."

"Well, consider me well and truly pleased. Pleased and delighted. Thank you."

"So which one would you like? Or we can share them all."

She said sharing would be good. He asked her to take the carton sticking out of his jacket pocket. "It's too big and I think it's going to fall out any second." As she rescued the carton, a piece of paper came with it and landed on the floor. He bent down and picked it up. She watched him as he unfolded it and stood reading it.

"Oh, God," he said with a slow shake of his head. "This is all I need."

"What?"

He handed her the piece of paper. On it was a handwritten note. It said *Give me a call sometime, Clementine.* Underneath she had listed her home number, her mobile number, her work number, her e-mail and her fax. "I think she wants to go out with me."

Cyn burst out laughing. "You think?"

He carried on staring at the paper. "She must have slipped the note into my pocket during last week's therapy session. Maybe I'm a bit dozy, but I never noticed."

Cyn had a realization. Her mind shot back to the end of the therapy session when she'd noticed Clementine stop to wink at Joe. Afterward she'd run her hand down the side of his jacket. Clementine had been doing more than coming on to him, she'd been slipping the paper into his pocket. Cyn thought about telling him what she'd seen, but she didn't want to give the impression she was bothered about Clementine flirting with him or that she had been spying.

"So what are you going to do?" she said.

"Well, I'm not planning to phone her, that's for sure. The poor girl really does have problems. You can't help feeling sorry for her. I'd like to let her down gently, though. Maybe I should just take her to one side after the next session and tell her it's not on. I'd hate to humiliate her in front of everybody. On the other hand, I know what Veronica would say—that it would do her more good to face up to this in front of the group."

Cyn said it was up to him. Although for personal as well as therapeutic reasons, she couldn't help thinking that

Clementine shouldn't be allowed to get away with hitting on Joe, she loved the idea of him not wanting to hurt her. It made him seem even more sexy. "This is all too weird," he said. "Here I am breaking Veronica's rules to see you, while at the same time trying to work out the correct way to put off another woman in the group."

If Cyn had been a bloke she would have no doubt said something like "Wow, mate, two women interested in you, don't knock it." But since she wasn't a bloke and since she was also anxious for him to tell Clementine he wasn't interested, she didn't.

An usherette showed them to their seats. They were early. The trailers hadn't even started. As they took off their coats, Cyn noticed how perfectly Joe's fitted lavender-and-white check shirt showed off the outline of his upper body.

He had clearly noticed what she was wearing and told her how great she looked. She thanked him, but decided to say nothing about how she'd been up at six thirty that morning, clothes strewn over her bed, in an attempt to find an outfit suitable for the meetings she had with the two putative Droolin' Dream directors and then for their date. After umpteen try-ons she decided everything was either too smart or too dressy. In the end she plumped for a coffee-colored, low-waisted A-line skirt. The heavy cotton had a wonderful satin sheen. It was dressy, but the color made it smart at the same time. She loved the way it hugged her hips and flared out into knee-length box pleats. She teamed it with a dark brown scooped-neck Lycra top with three-quarter sleeves. Pointy brown suede boots with spiky heels topped the whole thing off.

After spending an hour on her makeup and straightening her hair with her new ceramic straightening irons, she thought she looked pretty hot—both professionally and sexually. Her illusion was shattered when she got to work and Brian Lockwood, who was filling in for Graham Chandler, declared, "Ooh, look, everybody, Cyn's come as a poo." Several women came up to her to tell her that she looked gorgeous and not to take any notice because even though it was barely ten o'clock, Graham had already been at the Famous Grouse, but it did nothing for her self-image. That lunchtime she took a cab to Oxford Street and found a top, almost identical to the one she was wearing, in cream.

"Here's your Barclaycard," Joe said, taking it out of his wallet and handing it to her. He asked her about her day and she started telling him about her meetings with the directors. "One of them seemed particularly enthusiastic, so I've pretty much decided to go with him." She wasn't sure how it happened, but soon she was telling him about Laurent Cinnamon. When she told him how Grandma Faye informed Laurent that they had been expecting somebody a bit more cinnamon colored, he laughed so much that he almost choked on his popcorn.

"Joe," Cyn said when he had recovered, "there's something I need to ask you. I hope you won't mind."

He seemed intrigued. "Go on," he said.

"What's your name?"

"My name?"

"Yes. I only know your first name."

"Oh, right. Of course you do. I'm Joseph Dillon. Joseph Connor Dillon to be precise."

"Pleased to meet you, Joseph Connor Dillon." She held out her hand, which he took. "I'm Cynthia Ruth Fishbein."

"Pleased to meet you, too."

Joseph Dillon. Joseph Dillon. She was sure she knew that name from somewhere. "Your name seems familiar," she said. "I'm trying to work out where I could have heard it."

"Beats me," he said with a laugh. He sounded genuinely perplexed, but she was sure she detected a sense of unease in his face.

"I love the name Cynthia," he said, changing the subject. "It was my grandmother's name. We were very close. I adored her."

"I hated my name when I was a kid," she said, "but I made my peace with it a while back." She told him the Yoko story, which amused him no end.

"Oh, I've got something for you, too," she said, starting to root around in her bag. She was looking for the handkerchief he'd lent her the other day when he rescued her from the rain. She'd washed and ironed it. "I know it's here somewhere." As she located it, her hand brushed against her mobile. It was vibrating. She quickly handed him the handkerchief and took the phone out of her bag. "Oops, forgot to turn it off." She was about to hit *end* when Joe said she shouldn't ignore the call on his account.

"You sure? It seems incredibly rude."

"Don't be daft. Quick, take it, before they ring off. By the way, thanks for returning the handkerchief. You really didn't need to."

She pressed *connect*.

"Chel, it's me, Gazza. Got your e-mail. So, how was the rain forest? Wet with a capital pissed-it-down, I bet."

"God! Gazza." She put her hand over the phone. "It's my contact at Droolin' Dream," she whispered to Joe.

"Sorry," Gazza said, "have I caught you at a bad time?"

"Actually, this isn't such a great time. I'm in the cinema and the film's about to start. Can I call you back tomorrow?"

"Sure," he said, "but it was just a quickie. I wanted to check if we were still on for that curry."

What? Bloody hell. She hadn't had a chance to think up

another excuse to get rid of him and now he had caught her completely off guard. She was racking her brain for something to say when she noticed the cinema charity bucket being passed along the row in front. People were being asked to give money to the Gay and Lesbian Alliance. In an instant she had her excuse.

"Gazza," she said softly, "I haven't been completely honest with you. There's something I haven't told you."

"What?"

"Well, you see, the thing is . . ."

"Sorry, I can't hear you. I'm in the car. You're cracking up."

She got up from her seat. "That any better?"

"Chel, I can barely hear you."

Cyn was completely unaware that by now the cinema had filled up. She was too busy angling her phone so that Gazza could hear. "How's that?"

"A bit better, but you'll have to speak up."

"OK. The thing is," she said, raising her voice. "I don't go out with men."

"You don't? Why? . . . You need to shout."

"I'm a lesbian," she bellowed.

"How do you mean, a thespian? . . . Oh, I get it, amateur dramatics, that sort of thing?"

"No, I'm not a thespian, I'm a les-bi-an. I don't go out with men because I'm a lesbian."

The whole place erupted with laughter. A few women were whistling and applauding. One of them shouted, "What are you doing Saturday night?"

Her entire body prickling with embarrassment, Cyn fell back onto her seat. To say she wanted to be swallowed up by the ground and pile driven to the earth's core was an understatement. Her instinct was to run, but since she and Joe—who was looking highly amused—were in the middle of the row, it would have meant pushing past all these tittering people, which would have been even more embarrassing.

"Look, Gazza," Cyn said, sliding down on her seat in an attempt to disappear. "I'll phone you tomorrow and we'll have a proper chat, I promise. Now really isn't a good time." Without giving him a chance to protest she hit *end*.

"Gazza at Droolin' Dream was trying to get me to go out with him," Cyn whispered to Joe. "I can't stand him and it was the only excuse I could think of. I'm not a lesbian. I'm really not."

"I think I'd already worked that out." It was his laugh, the soft, sexy way he said it, that made her heart take a tiny leap. "But if you don't mind my saying, wouldn't it have been simpler to have told him you had a boyfriend?"

"Believe me, a bloke like Gazza wouldn't have been put off by me having a boyfriend. He'd have just seen it as a challenge."

Cyn assumed that by *boyfriend* Joe was referring to a mythical boyfriend rather than himself, but as she looked at him looking at her with those brown eyes of his, she rather wished he had been talking about himself.

Some Like It Hot was as hysterical as she remembered and more. Her favorite scene, the one with Marilyn Monroe and Tony Curtis on the yacht, made her think of the time she tried to seduce Hugh when they were at university.

It was a mild night and as they strolled along Upper Street trying to decide where to eat, they made each other laugh rattling off lines from the film. Eventually they got on to *Monty Python*. He knew the Cheese Shop and Parrot sketches by heart, as well as a couple she barely remembered featuring Jean-Paul Sartre and a couple of old bags called Mrs. Premise and Mrs. Conclusion. "Oh yes, I remember," Cyn said, going into a perfect Python old-bag squawk. " 'You don't want to come home from Sorrento to a dead cat.' " As they fell about, yet again, Cyn got the same feeling she'd experienced the other night when they were together—that she had known him for years.

Eventually they went to a Lebanese place Joe knew and said was pretty good. Over meze and beers they started talking about the film again.

"That script just sparkled, don't you think? Some of those comic lines were pure genius. I'd have given anything to have written it." Cyn was about to pop a piece of pita bread into her mouth, but she stopped. She was looking at him. He seemed thoughtful, far away. She got the impression he wasn't just saying that he would have given anything to have written it. He really meant it.

"Does that mean you don't like being a film editor?" she inquired.

"No. I love what I do. I wouldn't want to change." She thought he was protesting too much. She wasn't sure if she entirely bought the denial. He picked up his glass of beer. "So, tell me some more about this Laurent Cinnamon."

She carried on looking at him for a few moments. "You don't like talking about your work much, do you?" she said gently.

"It's not that." There was the familiar uneasiness. He couldn't look her in the eye. "It's just that the actual process of film editing isn't that fascinating to people outside the business and I worry that I'm being boring, that's all."

"Well, I don't think I could find you or it remotely boring." He seemed flattered by this. "So, come on," she continued, "have you had thoughts about writing?"

"Maybe," he said, looking at her now.

"Screenplays?"

"Possibly."

"It's never too late, you know." She told him about Hugh and the struggle he was having. "The rejections get him down, but he keeps going. I should get the two of you together."

"That would be great," Joe said. "And you're right—I should give it a go."

"Remember, it was you who told me how important it is to take risks."

He dipped a piece of pita bread in the baba ghanouj. "I know. I guess I find it easier to counsel other people than take my own advice."

"Don't we all," Cyn said. "But if you don't make it . . . well, at least you tried. And you've still got your job, so nothing has been lost. My gran's always telling me how life's too short not to try and make your dreams come true."

"Your gran's right," he said softly, holding her gaze in his. "You do have to try and make your dreams come true." He carried on looking at her. It felt like one of those moments where, if they hadn't been sitting at opposite sides of a table, he might have kissed her.

"Cyn, I was wondering," he said, breaking the silence. "Are you into walking?"

"Well, if you mean around Selfridges, I love it. It's as good as going to the gym. I've calculated that five laps of the lingerie department burns off over three hundred calories."

"You're really funny, you know that?"

She grinned. "I do my best."

"No, seriously. I was thinking that if the weather's good on Saturday, I might drive up to the Peak District and do a bit of a hike—nothing too strenuous. I'd really love it if you came with me." It suddenly occurred to her that despite all evidence to the contrary, Joe was going to turn out to be one of those wholesome woolly-hatted rambler types who carried beef paste sandwiches in his knapsack and collected recordings of British birdsong.

"It's funny," she said, "you don't strike me as the hiking kind."

"Oh, God, now you're thinking I'm some earnest, knobbly-kneed twonk."

She gave a nervous laugh. "God, no. The thought never occurred to me." She paused and gave him a slightly coy look. "I bet there's no way you've got knobbly knees."

He thanked her for the vote of confidence. "I'm not into walking in a big way. It's just that we used to do weekend hikes at boarding school and I sort of got into it. These days I find it more interesting than the gym."

"I can see that," Cyn said. She was trying to look enthusiastic about his proposal, but inside she was feeling less than eager. The Selfridges remark hadn't been completely flippant. Although she liked the countryside, she preferred to appreciate it in her own way: lunch in a pretty oak-beamed pub, complete with log fire and stretched-out Labradors, followed by a gentle afternoon stroll through a picture-book village. This would be punctuated by prolonged walks around an artsy-crafty, knick-knacky shop full of homemade fudge, plasticized William Morris–design shopping bags and earthenware egg cups declaring they were a "Souvenir of Frisby-on-the-Wolde" or wherever. Cyn wasn't what you might call a rambling person. She couldn't help feeling that if God had wanted people to ramble, he wouldn't have invented the four-wheel drive.

"Oh, I love hiking," she gushed. "I adore it."

"Really? So, you've got boots and all the gear?"

"Absolutely. Compass, waterproof jacket, map holder thingy, the lot."

After dinner they swapped phone numbers, which Veronica-wise felt especially wicked. Then he walked her to her car. His was parked a few streets away. A bit of her didn't want him to come with her because it meant he would see the Anusol ad again and she would have to put up with another load of bad jokes. She decided to tell him how she'd ended up with the Anusol car. Because he already knew about Chelsea stealing her Droolin' Dream idea, he didn't think it was remotely funny. "God, that woman deserves all she gets. I wish I could be there when she gets her comeuppance." Finally they reached the car. She could see the corners of his mouth starting to quiver. "Still, you could have a brilliant bumper sticker."

"What?"

"Something like—'If you're not a hemorrhoid, get off my arse.' "

"Et tu, Joe?" she said feigning deep hurt. "Et tu?"

"Sorry," he smiled. "I just couldn't resist it."

She reached inside her bag for her keys.

"Once again, I had a great time," he said.

"Me, too," she whispered, looking up at him. He moved closer. She hadn't noticed until now that his nose was covered in tiny freckles. He cupped her face, making her stomach do a flip. His warm breath was on her face. She closed her eyes, felt her head starting to swim. It began with little kisses on her lips. Then he wrapped her in his arms so that her breasts were tight against him. Finally her mouth yielded and he was deep inside her, his tongue hard, probing and urgent against hers. If he hadn't been holding her she would have fallen.

"Wow," she said as they finally pulled away.

"Wow," he repeated softly, trailing his finger along her nose and down to her chin.

Four times they tried to say good-bye and four times it ended with another glorious kiss. It was only when a gang of teenage boys went by making *wwrrooar* noises that they started to feel self-conscious and decided to really call it a night.

"So, I'll pick you up on Saturday," he said. "Say half past seven?"

"Half past seven? In the morning?" In her book, on a Saturday or Sunday anything before ten o'clock counted as the middle of the night.

"That was my initial thought," he grinned, "unless, of course, you fancy making it evening and trekking in the dark."

"No, no, seven-thirty's fine. Perfect, in fact. I always say there's nothing like getting off to an early start."

"Fantastic. See you then, then." He gave her a final quick kiss on the cheek.

"By the way," she called after him. "I looked *caterwaulings* up in the dictionary and you were right, it does exist. Sorry I didn't believe you."

"That's OK," he said. He carried on walking. Just before he turned the corner, he turned round to wave.

# Chapter 13

The following evening Cyn met Harmony for a drink. Harmony had phoned during the day to say she was going to a dinner party round the corner from Cyn's flat and why didn't they get together beforehand.

The White Horse, Cyn's local, was heaving. In a couple of hours, England was due to play Brazil in some World Cup warm-up game and people were already piling in to watch on the pub's three wide-screen TVs. There was barely any breathing space, let alone a table.

Cyn's discomfort was made worse by her footwear. Underneath her suit trousers, she was wearing hiking boots. For the second lunchtime running, she'd dashed up to Oxford Street to go shopping. This time it was to buy walking gear. Contrary to what she had told Joe, she didn't own so much as a PowerBar.

Hugh said he would come with her since he was going to be up in town anyway. He seemed to have bounced back from his disappointment over Laurent being straight, and in anticipation of a long-overdue tax rebate, he had decided to go window-shopping for cuff links. "You know, gorgeous, I wish you weren't getting involved with this Joe," he said as they walked arm in arm down Oxford Street. "I'm really worried for you." Of course she did have reservations about Joe, but she assured him she was a big girl and could take care of herself. He shrugged and let it go.

Hugh wandered around Millets looking down his nose like Joan Collins in Wal-Mart. "Urrgh," he shuddered at one point, tentatively prodding a fleece and instantly withdrawing as if it might bite, "this stuff is so synthetic you could wash it and it wouldn't even get wet." Meanwhile, a helpful but rather dorky lad painstakingly kitted Cyn out with everything she would need: socks, rucksack, waterproof jacket, fleece, bobble hat, gloves, flashlight, map cover on a string, hiking pole and things called gaiters. These turned out to be waterproof covers to protect her trouser bottoms.

She came out of the changing room and presented herself to Hugh. "Dah, dah! What do you think?" He took one look at the hiking pole, red-and-white fleece and matching bobble hat and declared: "My God, alert the jury, we've found Waldo."

Cyn admitted she felt a bit ridiculous in the red fleece and hat. "But they're low on stock and it's all they've got left. Anyway, I'm going for a hike in the Dales, not a sashay down the runway." Nevertheless Hugh insisted on going through all the shelves and eventually found a black fleece and matching ski hat without a pom-pom.

The lad in Millets insisted it was vital she break in the walking boots. Taking his advice to heart, she'd worn them all afternoon at the office. It was now after seven, which meant she'd had them on for nearly six hours. They were hard and unyielding and as she and Harmony stood by the pub door, contemplating fighting their way to the bar, Cyn started to fantasize about the rather naff foot spa her aunty

Lilly had given her for her birthday a few years back, which she'd ended up taking to a charity shop.

Because the pub was so packed, Cyn suggested they find somewhere else, but Harmony said she didn't have much time and that on a night like this, everywhere would be crowded. "Let's get a couple of drinks and take them outside. It's not cold."

It took them a full five minutes to force themselves through the crowd of jostling, blaring young blokes and reach the bar. Most were still in their work suits with their shirts and ties undone. A few were wearing jeans and England shirts. One or two dorks were wrapped in red-and-white flags.

Cyn insisted the drinks were on her. She was just paying when Harmony spotted a couple of people getting up from a table. "Quick, see if you can grab it," Cyn shouted over the din. "I'll bring the drinks over."

The table was near the door where the decibel level wasn't quite so fierce. Cyn put the drinks down and started taking off her coat.

"Look, hon," Harmony said, rooting round in her bag for her fags, "don't take this the wrong way, but I can't help noticing you're wearing hiking boots with work trousers. Don't you think pointy kitten heels would work better?"

"Ha, ha," Cyn said, sitting down. She explained about Joe and the hiking trip. "I'm trying to break them in and they're really rubbing my toes and the backs of my feet." Harmony suggested that might be because she was wearing them over sheer knee-highs rather than thick woolly socks.

"So, did you remember to buy flares?" Harmony asked. She flicked her Bic and lit up.

"Flares? Don't be daft. When did you last see a fashionable hiker?"

"No, you dope. I mean flares," Harmony said letting out a trail of smoke. "You know—to send up, if you get stranded."

"Harms, this is a walk in the English countryside, not the final scene in *Titanic*."

"Well, you can't be too careful." Cyn told her she sounded like Grandma Faye.

"So, you've really fallen for this Joe, then?"

Cyn swirled the ice in her glass of Coke. "I think I have. He kissed me last night."

Harmony gave a soft snort. "Oh, great," she said, her voice full of sarcasm.

"It was actually. In fact it was mind-blowing . . . God, I wish you and Hugh would stop worrying. Joe is so normal. He's the one pursuing me."

"But don't you see?" Harmony leaped in, flicking ash into an ashtray. "That's classic. He loves the thrill of the chase. But when he's hooked you, he loses interest. I bet you anything his problems have nothing to do with his inability to be emotionally intimate. This guy's into power. The chase is all about power. It's what feeds his self-esteem. Men like him don't do relationships. They aren't interested. There's no buzz."

"Blimey, when did you start subscribing to *Psychology Today*?"

"Very funny. It was a quiz in this month's *Cosmo*: 'Can You Spot a Bastard?' "

"Well, I'm sorry," Cyn said. "I just don't see it. Joe is kind, funny, intelligent. He's also not remotely into power. In fact he's very modest. He hardly ever talks about his work. I mean, how often do you come across that in a man? Usually they have these giant testosterone-fueled egos and don't stop going on about themselves."

Harmony shrugged. "Maybe he's hiding something."

"Like what?"

"I dunno. He could be some kind of con man."

"OK, the moment he tries to sell me a time-share apartment in Florida, I'll ditch him."

"All I'm saying is be careful and don't rush into anything."

"I won't and I am being careful. Promise."

Harmony took her hand. "It's just that I love you and I don't want to see you get hurt."

"I know. I love you, too." She took a mouthful of Coke. "Hugh came with me to buy my hiking gear today. He seems to have gotten over Laurent not being gay."

"Yeah, I phoned him this morning to check if he was OK about it. He seemed fine. Said he didn't have time to talk because he was busy with wedding stuff and needed to keep the line free. Apparently he was waiting for some harpist woman to call him back." While Cyn tried to imagine what "You're the One That I Want" would sound like being played on the harp, Harmony sat staring into her vodka tonic. "I'm thinking of asking him out."

"Who?"

"Laurent. Who else? I just think he is the most beautiful man I have ever seen. The moment he walked in, I got goose pimples all over."

Cyn made the point that the perimenopause didn't seem to be affecting Harmony's libido. "By the way, have you been to the doctor yet?"

"Yeah. He did a blood test to check my hormone levels. Said he'll phone me with the result . . . The thing is, with Laurent, it's more than just fancying him. I mean, this is a man who put his life at risk for something he believed in. When he started talking, I could see there was a real fire in his soul. D'you know what I mean?" Cyn said she did.

A load of blokes were chanting "Inger-l'nd, Inger-l'nd" and clapping. The match was due to start in a few minutes. Cyn suggested it might be time to leave. They were gathering up their coats when Cyn spotted him in the crowd. Even though his face was painted white, with a red St. George's Cross along its entire length and breadth, he was still clearly recognizable.

"Omigod. It's him."

"Who?"

"Gazza."

"Sorry, none the wiser."

"He's the bloke from Droolin' Dream. The one who thinks I'm Chelsea."

"Bloody hell."

Cyn explained about him fancying her. As she looked up she realized he had seen her. "Bugger, he's coming over. OK, you have to pretend to be my girlfriend."

"I am your girlfriend."

"No, my lesbian girlfriend." More rushed explanation.

"So, you be the butch one," Cyn said, "and I'll be the feminine one."

"Er, hello, correct me if I'm wrong, but you are the one wearing hiking boots. I, on the other hand, have just had a French manicure and I'm wearing Voyage. I think it's clear to the casual observer which one of us looks like the lesbianator."

Cyn took in Harmony's itsy-bitsy floaty dress, her hair in a pretty chignon, held in place with a diamanté comb. "I know, but you've got brothers who are car mechanics. You'll be better at talking butch."

"What do you want me to say?" Harmony was starting to panic.

"I dunno. You'll think of something."

They sat back down. A second later Gazza was standing

in front of them. "Chel! This is amazing! Of all the bars in all the world, you had to walk into mine." He was swaying slightly and his speech was a bit slurred. He'd clearly had a few.

"Gazza! I had no idea you lived round here."

"Actually, I don't. I'm just catching up with some mates who do."

She hoped her relief wasn't too obvious. "I tried to get you a few times today, but you weren't answering."

"Another team-building day," he said, turning toward Harmony. Under the grease paint, his face was becoming one giant leer. "So, this is the little woman, eh? Chel, you are one lucky lady and I mean lucky with a capital Wrrruuurrrh." He slurped some beer from the pint glass he was holding.

Cyn could tell Harmony was balking at being referred to as "the little woman." Nevertheless, she stood up and shook his hand. "Watcha," she said, in a voice that had dropped at least nineteen octaves. "I'm Harmony. How they hanging?"

Cyn was practically splitting her sides. "Harmony's a car mechanic," she said, praying he didn't recognize her true identity from all her TV appearances.

Harmony, bless her, didn't miss a beat. "That's right."

"Geddaway. A great-looking bird like you, I don't believe it. You're never a car mechanic." Gazza was swaying so much he almost spilled his beer.

"I am, really."

He wasn't having it. "Yeah, right." He stood there, trying to marshal his thoughts. "OK, I have an Audi that drifts to the left on a straight flat road, meaning I have to keep correcting the steering. What's the cause?"

Harmony didn't hesitate. "Most cars tend to drift to the left because of the natural camber of the road, but this sounds more serious. Worn out suspension bushes, I'd say."

"Blimey, that's exactly what the garage said. God, a

beautiful sexy woman who knows about cars. What more could a fella want? You know, I'm wondering if maybe I'm a lesbian." He came closer and looked round to check he couldn't be overheard. "Don't suppose, you know, you'd be interested in having a bit of a party—if you get my meaning? You know, the three of us—back at my pad in Winnersh?"

Cyn told him he'd had too much to drink. She and Harmony got up to leave.

"You see, I reckon you two would give up being lesbians once you'd experienced Gazza magic."

"Bye, Gazza," Cyn said. "I'll speak to you tomorrow, when you've sobered up."

"You'll regret it if you don't at least give it a try," he called out after them. "I could make my ex-girlfriend come all night long. And I mean come with a capital O. Think about it."


To give Gazza his due, he rang Cyn at work the next morning, to apologize. "Sorry, Chel, I was pissed with a capital Rat-arsed and totally out of order. Look, I hope this won't affect our professional relationship." When she assured him it wouldn't, he seemed truly relieved. She was starting to feel really guilty about deceiving Gazza. He was a twonk, but an affable one, she decided. She told him that she had found a director and that she would let him know as soon as they'd set a date to start filming. "By the way," he said, "I've worked out the main sell lines we need to get across in the script. I'll e-mail them to you now."

She decided to take the afternoon off and start work on the script at home. That way there would be nobody looking over her shoulder, asking awkward questions. Nobody would mind her leaving early. There were no meetings planned and since Brian-the-boozer Lockwood had taken over from Graham, everything had gotten rather lax.

Before she left, Luke came over and asked if she'd seen Chelsea yet and broached her drug habit. Cyn reassured him that she would speak to her soon. "At the moment, she's still in a great deal of pain. I'm not sure she can cope with a full-scale intervention right now. But don't worry. I will do what's required. You can rely on it." Luke seemed satisfied and ambled off. As she watched him go, Cyn smiled to herself. "Oh yes," she said out loud, "you can absolutely rely on it."

On the way home, she stopped off to pick up a Greek salad for lunch. Morris nattered away quietly in the background while she sat at the kitchen table stabbing bits of feta and reading Gazza's e-mail on her laptop. He had listed more than a dozen selling points—essentially a load of adjectives like *fresh, light, fluffy, satisfying, inexpensive* and so on—which he wanted to be worked into a twenty-second script. Oh, and then there was the key point, that Low Nuts were low in fat. Gazza also wanted that mentioned at least six times.

She sat there reminding herself of the scenario: the sixties women sitting round a kitchen table complaining about their weight and how hard it is to diet. Then in comes the Audrey Hepburn look-alike with the box of Low Nuts.

Once she'd finished eating, Cyn took her laptop into the living room. She decided she would be more comfortable sitting on the sofa. She plumped up some cushions and took her time arranging them against the sofa arm. When she finally sank onto the sofa, feet up, she carried on fiddling and altering the position of the cushions until she was perfectly comfortable. Only then did she reach out onto the coffee table and pick up her computer.

Laptop in place, she realized the act of stretching out had altered the position of the cushions. She reached behind her back and adjusted them yet again. "OK, right," she said, giving a cushion one last tug, "let's get going." She typed: *Droolin'*

*Dream commercial.* She pressed the *return* key twice, indented and typed: *Scene 1.* She paused and added a colon. Then she linked her fingers and bent them back so that her knuckles cracked. "So, what's my opening line? C'mon, think. Think." Nothing. More knuckle cracking was followed by more cushion tugging. She turned her attention to the laptop and began playing with font size and trying to decide between print styles—should she go for Courier or Times New Roman? After two or three minutes she decided the only way to get her brain in gear was to make a cup of coffee.

She got up, went back into the kitchen and filled up the kettle. "So, Mo," she said, going over to the birdcage and peering in through the bars. "It's been ages since we had a talk. How you diddling?"

"Need a leg over," he said in a perfect imitation of Keith Geary. "Need a leg over."

"Same ol', same ol', then. I, on the other hand, have big news. I've met a man and I think I'm falling in love. His name's Joe. And he is just gorgeous. And I mean gorgeous with a capital cute." God, Gazza was getting inside her head like one of those ridiculous Christmas pop songs. "I've never met anybody like Joe before. He's funny, kind and ever so cute. He kissed me last night and it was so unbearably blissful that I thought I was going to pass out. What do you think of that?" She found a piece of cucumber on the counter, which had come from her salad, and pushed it through the cage bars. "Gorgeous Joe," he squawked. "Love Gorgeous Joe." Then he pecked the cucumber greedily from her fingers.

Cyn took her mug of coffee back to the sofa, but try as she might, no words would come. It was odd, writing scripts usually came quite easily to her. This one was different, though. Her entire career depended on it. The upshot was, her mind had frozen.

She typed: *Scene: Sixties kitchen. Three women are sitting at a Formica kitchen table.* She followed this with another colon.

When the words still wouldn't come, more displacement activities followed. These included picking at the dry skin on her bottom lip, booking an eyebrow wax and test-driving her new *Sex and the City* bunny vibrator—five times.

Finally she decided to have a bath. There was no point getting dressed again, so she decided to change into her pajamas. Her new hiking boots were sitting on the floor at the end of the bed. She decided to put them on for a few hours—but over thick hiking socks this time—in one last attempt to break them in.

By seven o'clock, due to frequent displacement walks around the flat, the boots were feeling much more comfortable. Scriptwise, she'd only written two lines and was struggling. When the phone rang, she couldn't have been more grateful. She would have happily chatted away to a loan company or wrong number, just to get a few minutes' break. But it wasn't either of those. It was a distinctly careworn Hugh, phoning to give her a progress report on the wedding arrangements. He'd finally booked the tent, and after spending the entire day on the phone had finally found a rabbi and a priest prepared to perform a joint blessing after a civil ceremony. The bad news was, he'd made no progress with the food and entertainment. The "simple elegance" idea had lasted five minutes, it seemed. Barbara was still fixated on deep-fried ice cream and Flick was talking white stretch limos and suggesting that instead of confetti, each guest should be given a children's tube of bubbles and a wand. "I thought it was a rather sweet idea," Hugh said, "until she started making noises about having a steel band playing 'I'm Forever Blowing Bubbles.'"

Cyn had just gotten off the phone with Hugh when

Harmony rang in a state of wild excitement to say she'd phoned Laurent and asked him out. "I'm picking him up in an hour. God, my heart won't stop racing. I feel like a sixteen-year-old getting ready for her first date. I've already tried on a dozen outfits." Cyn told her to have a wonderful time and ring her afterward with all the details. A few minutes later Barbara rang, equally hyped, to say did she know Harmony had asked Laurent out? Barbara couldn't stop going on about what a lovely boy he was. Apparently, nothing was too much for him. He couldn't do enough around the house and he'd even gotten Grandma Faye working out. "You should just see the pair of them going at it on the living room carpet." Cyn said that really would be a sight to behold. "Oh, by the way," Barbara said before she hung up, "your dad's feeling a bit under the weather. He thinks he might be coming down with flu. If you ask me, those nasal tubes in that oxygen machine of his were full of germs." Barbara didn't seem remotely perturbed, so Cyn told her to wish Mal better and that she would phone tomorrow to see how he was.

It was well after midnight when she finished the script. In the end it wasn't at all bad, even if she did say so herself. She'd managed to capture the right lighthearted tone, at the same time as getting in a reasonable selection of Gazza's selling points. Of course it would probably need some last-minute rewrites when they came to filming, but for now she was happy.

She made herself some Marmite toast and hot chocolate, which she took back to the sofa. When she'd finished, she picked up the script, intending to give it a final read-through, but she could barely keep her eyes open. She had just begun to nod off, when the phone rang again. She gave a start and reached onto the floor for the phone.

"Cyn, it's me, Harms. You awake?"

"Not really," Cyn said blearily.

"Great, 'cos I just had to ring like I promised and tell you I had *the* most fantastic evening with Laurent." If it was possible, she sounded even higher than she'd sounded a few hours ago. "He wouldn't let me pay for anything. Of course he's got practically no money, so we ended up taking this long romantic walk by the river, eating hot dogs and putting the world to rights. Cyn, he is a truly good man. A real visionary. He's got all these amazing ideas about how to make the world a better place . . ."

"Harms, that's wonderful, but I've been working all evening and I really am . . ."

"I mean, you want to hear him on fuel emissions and global warming."

"I'm sure it's fascinating. The thing is . . ."

"And famine. He says it's not so much financial aid countries like Ethiopia need, as education in modern farming methods."

"So they say . . ."

"And he thinks religion is one of the major causes of all the hatred and misery in the world. You know, the idea of my team being better than your team. I'd never thought of it like that."

"It's a good point, but . . ."

"He is dead brainy. I reckon he could give Hugh a run for his money. God, Cyn, men with brains are just *so* sexy, don't you think?"

"Absolutely . . ."

"Oh, and to top it off, he's also the most brilliant kisser. Bloody hell, I think I might be in love. Anyway, look, don't be offended, I'd love to stay up yakking, but I really need to hit the sack."

"It's OK, Harms, I'm not remotely offended. Night, night."

Cyn put down the phone. She did her best to get herself up off the sofa, but her legs simply refused to engage with her brain. Instead she rearranged the cushions one last time and fell asleep. She was still wearing her hiking boots.

# Chapter 14

In her dream, the intermittent buzzing sound was coming from a chain saw being wielded by Mr. Levinson from downstairs. For some reason he had gone crazy and was in the street carrying out a ferocious attack on a twenty-foot mountain of Droolin' Dream Low Nuts. With every long, piercing buzz, Mr. Levinson wrought more carnage. Huge, gleaming gobbets of strawberry jam spurted onto the pavement, hedges and car windscreens. In the distance a police officer was crouched behind the open door of his patrol car, megaphone in hand. "Sir," he called out, "step aside from the doughnuts."

Slowly, Cyn started to come to. In the space of a couple of seconds she realized that the buzzing was coming from the intercom, Joe was downstairs, it had to be half past seven and she had overslept. "Oh, God, no. Bloody hell." She leapt off the sofa, making her head go all swimmy because she'd gotten up too quickly and ran to the intercom. "Hi, Joe, come on up," she said, pressing the door release. She looked in the hall mirror and tried to flatten her psycho morning hair, but it was having none of it.

"I am so, so sorry I'm not ready," she started to gabble as

she let him in. "I was working late last night on the script for the Droolin' Dream commercial and I overslept."

"That's OK," he said brightly. "We've got plenty of time." As he kissed her on the lips a goose pimple shiver went up her back. This was caused by sexual excitement, tinged with the fear that her early morning breath might have been less than sweet.

She thought he looked unbelievably sexy in his khaki parka, black scarf and well-worn hiking boots (and not remotely wholesome—at least not in the meat-paste-sandwiches-and-birdsong-records sense). By contrast she was standing there in her ancient brushed cotton floral pajamas with a question mark over her breath, feeling about as sexy as Granny Clampett. "Let me just jump in the shower. I'll be ten minutes."

"Don't panic. Honest, we'll be fine. By the way, the boots look great. I'd never have thought of teaming them with pajamas."

She looked down at her feet and felt herself turn crimson. "Ah, yes . . . the boots." She'd already told him she owned loads of hiking gear, so she could hardly say she was breaking them in. "I, er . . . I slept in them . . ." And why had she slept in them? In case of a sudden middle-of-the-night trekking emergency? "I slept in them to save time. That's it. Always takes me ages to get them on."

"But you're about to have a shower. Presumably you're going to take them off?"

"Ah, yes. Silly me. I didn't think of that."

He stood there looking at her, a bemused expression on his face. She suggested that while she got ready he go into the kitchen and make them some coffee. "You can say hello to Morris."

"Morris?"

"He's a mynah bird. I'm looking after him for a bloke at

work. Chats away like mad, but don't be embarrassed when he starts going on about his lack of a sex life."

She headed off to the bathroom. "Hi, Morris," she heard Joe say, "pleased to meet you, I'm Joe."

"I'm Joe. I'm Joe. Gorgeous Joe. Gorgeous Joe."

For the second time in less than five minutes, her face was burning with embarrassment. She had to stop having heart-to-hearts with Morris. They were just too dangerous. She charged back to the kitchen before Morris could do any more damage. She couldn't tell if Joe's bemused expression was new or left over from their conversation about her hiking boots. "Don't worry," Cyn said brightly, "he calls everybody gorgeous, don't you, Morris? The milkman, the postman—even old Mr. Levinson downstairs." She turned to Morris. "Say 'gorgeous Mr. Levinson.'" Silence. "Come on, Morris." Not a word. "Morris, show Joe how clever you are." She was virtually pleading with him now. "Don't be shy. Say 'gorgeous Mr. Levinson.'" But Morris was having none of it. For once he was keeping his beak firmly shut.

"Doesn't seem to be in the mood," Joe said. "Don't worry. I'll put the kettle on. You go and get ready." He said that as it was particularly cold out, she might want to put on some extra layers.

Cyn headed back to the bathroom, but not before putting a tea towel over Morris's cage. Had she turned round and looked back into the room she would have seen Joe pulling off the cover and starting to engage Morris in more conversation.

When she returned five minutes later dressed in hiking gear, the cover was back on the birdcage and Morris was quiet. She'd hemmed and hawed about whether to include the plastic map holder and waterproof gaiters in her ensemble. Because of her confusion earlier, she couldn't remember if Joe had been wearing them. Deciding he probably had, she fastened the map holder string round her neck and pulled the gaiters up over her trouser bottoms. All she remembered for certain was that he hadn't been carrying a hiking pole— although he could have left it in the car. Since her hiking pole was retractable, she decided to play it safe and stash it in her rucksack.

"Wow, you really are a serious hiker," he said, taking in the gaiters. He wasn't wearing any. Nor was he wearing a map holder. Thank God, she wasn't carrying the hiking pole. She already felt like the school swot who turned up every day with an immaculately pressed blazer and freshly polished protractor.

"Yes, I did a few walks last year," she lied. "The Dales, Hadrian's Wall, the Lake District, that sort of thing. I think it's essential to have the right gear and be prepared." To prove her point, she reached into her pocket and pulled out her compass and PowerBar.

"You're right. Even though it's almost spring the weather can still close in. You can't take any risks." He handed her a cup of coffee. "By the way, I love how you've done up this flat. You've got great taste."

She thanked him and said she simply worshipped at the temple of Ikea, like most people.

"Maybe, but not everybody knows how to pull a look together."

Just then she noticed Hugh's Siamese twin screenplay— which, to her shame, she still hadn't gotten round to reading— lying open on the kitchen table. "Hugh's your gay writer friend, isn't he?" Cyn nodded. "I hope he won't mind, but I couldn't resist flicking through it . . . You know, it's quite in-spired."

"Really?" God, had she gotten Joe all wrong? Did he go in for the same sort of turgid, pretentious stuff Hugh did?

"Does this guy know how funny he is? I've only read the outline and a few pages of the script, but this has all the makings of a hilarious black comedy."

OK, now she got it. She gave a soft laugh. "I think you've got the wrong end of the stick. Hugh's pretty earnest. He doesn't do hilarious—at least not intentionally."

"Well, I think this has real comic potential. A film about one Siamese twin facing the electric chair is so impossibly macabre and gruesome that you could only play it for laughs. With the right handling, the right director, it could really work."

"You really are passionate about writing," she said softly.

He gave a self-conscious look that suggested the comment had knocked him off balance. "I suppose I am."

"You really ought to give it a go. There are loads of writing classes you could join if you need help getting started."

"I know. Maybe I'll check a couple out." He said he would like to read the screenplay through carefully and if he still felt the same about it afterward, he knew a couple of film producers who might be keen to take a look at it. He asked her if she thought Hugh would mind him taking the script away to read.

"Mind? He'd be over the moon. Warner Bros. doesn't seem to be in any hurry to get back to him." She didn't say Hugh would be less than over the moon about *My Brother, My Blood, My Life* being made into a comedy, but they would cross that bridge when—or more to the point if—they came to it.

In the end they got under way just after eight thirty. "You know," she said, pulling her seat belt across her, "us seeing each other outside therapy feels really wicked. It's like we're a couple of naughty kids bunking off school for the day."

He said he felt the same. "Maybe we should buy booze and find something to set fire to . . . On the other hand we could just listen to some music." He suggested she choose something from his pile of CDs in the glove compartment. She went for a *Sixties Greatest Hits* compilation. For nearly an hour they sat singing along to all the old classics. Round about Newport Pagnell, "Unchained Melody" came on and they agreed it was a crying shame that great songs became instantly debased once they were used in films or commercials.

When they weren't singing, they talked about holidays, books, places they'd been, places they'd like to go. The only thing off-limits was any discussion of people in the group. They decided this would be disloyal.

Cyn couldn't get over how the time just melted. At one point he started reminiscing about Dublin and told her how as a student he dived naked into the River Liffey on a dare and got caught by the police. She made him laugh by telling how she hated roast lamb as a child and that she always used to secrete her portion into her Barbie and Ken trailer that she kept under the dining room table for that purpose.

"So," she said, at one point, wondering if she could finally draw him out about his job, "you still working on this science-fiction movie you were telling me about in the pub?" He said he was. She asked him how it was going.

"Oh, you know. Coming along." She suspected that was all she was going to get.

"Are you based at one of the big film studios?"

"Yeah, Pinewood."

"You know, Joe," she said gently, "I'd really like to hear about your work. I'm interested in finding out more about what you do. I promise I won't be bored."

"OK, last week we digitized our rushes ready for the Avid off-line."

"Oh, right," she said, blinking with noncomprehension.
"See, you're bored already," he said, smiling.

It was true she hadn't understood what he was saying, but
she wondered if he was trying to blind her with science in order to put her off asking more questions.

As they carried on listening to the music, she noticed he
had no Pinewood Studios parking permit stuck to his windscreen. Hugh had a friend who worked at Pinewood. He'd
given her a lift home once. She'd spotted the parking permit
and remarked on how glam it looked. It was odd Joe didn't
have one, she thought. On the other hand, maybe it had
come off. The road-tax permit on her old Peugeot used to fall
off all the time—particularly in winter when there was loads
of condensation on the windscreen.

The traffic was clear until just before the Nottingham turn-
off, when it came to a complete standstill. For an hour and a
half they barely moved. According to the traffic news on the
radio there had been "an incident" and "considerable delays
could be expected." They had no choice other than to sit
it out.

When the traffic eventually cleared it was lunchtime and
they were starving. They stopped at the next service station
and gorged themselves on a surprisingly edible all-day English
breakfast. Later on in the loo, she divested herself of the map
holder and gaiters.

They arrived in Ribbledale just after two. It was snow-
cold, but the sky was bright blue with the occasional splodge
of white meringue cloud. Since the weather was so bitter,
the place wasn't at all crowded. They headed out of the car
park. Joe had his rucksack slung over his shoulder, but there
was no evidence of a hiking pole. She decided to keep hers
hidden.

They made for the narrow river that lay a few yards ahead. Tiny ripples on its surface twinkled in the strong light. Gnarled, bent-over trees covered in a delicate haze of new green clung to the muddy bank, their branches skimming the water. In the distance, majestic emerald domes presided over the skyline.

"Isn't this just grand?" Joe said, turning his face to the sky and taking in a lungful of air. Cyn agreed it was. It was even grander when Joe took her hand as they negotiated the stepping-stones across the river.

Soon they came to a wooded area covered in a thick carpet of tiny white flowers.

"They're wood anemones," he said. "Did you know that the wood anemone propagates mainly by means of creeping underground stems?"

"Wow, I'm impressed," she said, secretly wondering if he really was going to turn out to be a hill-walking nature nerd after all. "How do you know all that?"

"Oh, I'm a bit of a nature buff on the quiet." Her face must have registered a certain unease, which he picked up on, but he said nothing to relieve it. Instead he let her carry on wondering about him, let the silence stand between them. It must have been a full ten seconds before his face finally broke into a grin. "Not really. We just passed a sign asking walkers not to trample the wood anemones. The rest, for some ridiculous reason, I just happen to remember from school biology."

She was still giggling when he reached out and tilted her face up toward him. The next thing she knew he was planting a kiss on her lips. "You know which bit of you I especially like?" he said. She shook her head. "It's your eyes. They're the most exquisite shape. Like two perfect almonds." He ran his finger over her eyebrows and lids. Soon he was kissing her again, but properly this time. She felt herself melt into his arms, the familiar ache, the quivering in her stomach. She could have happily let him ravish her right there, among the wood anemones.

As they set off again he took her hand in his. It was big and warm. She enjoyed its firmness, the way it swamped hers. At one point a twitchy-nosed squirrel went scuttling across their path.

"You know," she said, "sometimes in the winter when it gets really bitter, I worry about the animals getting cold."

"Yeah, I know what you mean. You wonder how the cows manage without Chap Stick."

She burst out laughing and as they carried on along the riverbank they came up with more absurd ways to protect the animals from the elements—tiny thermal vests with special spike covers for hedgehogs; wetsuits for ducks.

Somehow talking about animals got them onto reincarnation and Cyn said she'd often wondered if people came back as animals and vice versa. Joe said he definitely believed in reincarnation. She saw the teasing expression on his face, but decided to play along. She asked him how long he'd believed in it.

"Oh, ever since I was a young gerbil," he said. More laughter. Eventually Joe said, "How d'you fancy having a go at climbing that peak over there? I've done it before. It's small and the incline is pretty gentle. Shouldn't take more than a couple of hours. And there's this great pub on the other side where we can get a drink and some food."

A gentle incline? From where she stood the slope looked practically vertical and he'd promised this outing wasn't going to be strenuous. The other day on the StairMaster she'd set the level at a pathetic three. This was going to be ten times harder. She would be gasping for breath after about two minutes. She was going to die. She was so going to die. He must have seen her expression. "If you feel you're not up to it, we could always keep to the river."

"Not up to it? Who's not up to it?" she said, determined not to let him think she was a wimp. "I'll race you. Last one to the top buys the drinks."

In fact the slope was far more manageable than she'd imagined. But she still found it tough going. There was no question which of them would be buying the drinks. It helped, though, that every so often they stopped to admire the scenery and kiss. She loved the scenery, but she loved the kissing more.

They'd been going about an hour when her boots started giving her trouble. First they started rubbing the backs of her ankles, then the sides of her feet. She managed to carry on without saying anything. If it got no worse she would be just about OK. But it did get worse. She could feel the skin being scraped away. Every so often she grimaced in pain. "You all right?" Joe asked at one point.

"I'm fine," she panted. There was no way she was about to confess she was wearing new boots that she hadn't broken in. "I'm just a bit out of shape, that's all."

"What you need is some kind of an incentive to keep going."

"You're right," she said. "Promise me there's a Dolce and Gabbana outlet store at the top and I'll be there in no time."

It was another forty minutes or so before they reached the summit. She tried to ignore the pain and concentrate on the glorious view, but it wasn't easy. A couple more times Joe asked her if she was all right. Each time she managed to reassure him she was.

"I'm really glad you agreed to come today," Joe said as they started to make their way down the other side of the peak.

"Me, too." She gave him a smile, but by now the pain at the backs of her feet was excruciating. It was so bad, she stopped talking. They carried on making their way down in silence. Soon she was starting to hobble. "Sorry, Joe. I have to stop for a bit." She sat down on the freezing damp grass, undid her boot and tugged it off. Blood was oozing through the back of her sock. It was the same on the other foot. She pulled off one of her socks. This really hurt because the blood had congealed and stuck to the wool. The back of her bare foot had gone past the blister stage and was now red-raw.

Joe was crouching in front of her, looking closely at the foot and grimacing. "God, you poor thing. That must really hurt. Why on earth didn't you say? I knew something was up. It's these new boots of yours, isn't it?"

"What makes you think they're new?" she said defensively. "I just look after them, that's all."

"Is that right?" he said, barely disguising his amusement. "And is that why everything else you're wearing looks so new, too?"

She could see no point in keeping up the pretence. "OK, I give in. You've rumbled me."

"You haven't done much proper walking, have you?"

"Not as such," she said.

"But you should have said your boots were killing you," he said gently. "What an idiot you've been."

"Sorry," she said meekly.

His concerned expression turned into a grin. "I'm flattered you wanted to impress me, though."

"OK, let's get one thing straight," she shot back, full of indignation. "I was not trying to impress you."

"Really?"

Again she felt cornered. She couldn't lie to him. "OK, maybe I did want to impress you. But only a bit."

He began opening his Eastpak. "I think I've got some of that fancy artificial skin stuff in here, somewhere." Tenderly and with great care he patched her up. Even though she was in pain, feeling his hands on her bare feet was intoxicating. When he had finished, he started nibbling and licking her toes. Even though it was just playful messing around, she thought she would die from the pleasure. Here she was freezing cold and hurting and still managing to have fantasies about the two of them naked in bed and him going down on far more than just her toes.

The artificial skin protected her feet and took away most of the pain, but by the time they reached the pub, it had started to peel off. There was no way she could contemplate walking back to the car. Even if she hadn't been in pain from her feet, it wouldn't have been wise. It was five o'clock and it would soon be dark, but more to the point, the sky had turned from AOL blue to an ominous light bruise. Joe suggested they have a drink and a quick bite at the Cross Keys and then get a taxi back to the car park.

Since it was still early, the bar was almost empty. When they asked to see the bar menu, the landlord—a rather anxious, high-complexioned chap in his sixties, whom Flick would have described as an old fussbudget—was full of apologies and said they didn't start doing proper food until seven. "But I'd be more than happy to do you a Ploughman's or some sandwiches. Now, then, fillingswise, we've got cheese, chicken, ham and roast beef. I think there might even be some prawns left. I can go and check if you like. If you fancy something hot, I could do you toasted cheese and ham, but I think the sandwich maker might still be on the blink. Or bacon perhaps? Of course you'd have to wait a few minutes for that." Cyn said she would have a Ploughman's and a pint of bitter. Joe ordered a pint as well and a couple of rounds of roast beef sandwiches.

"Will that be with horseradish or without?"

"Er, with, please."

"White or wholemeal?"

"Wholemeal."

"Butter or spread?"

"Butter, please."

"Hah. You won't be saying that in a few years when your cholesterol count's six point six. Mind you, mine's not as bad as the wife's. Doctor said her arteries are more furred up than a yak's back in winter."

While Joe waited for the drinks, Cyn sat herself down at a table next to a huge inglenook fireplace decked out with horse brasses and leather bellows. A pile of logs burned and crackled in the hearth. Two ginger cats were curled up in front of it, fast asleep. She leaned down and started to stroke one of the cats. The creature gave a muffled squawk at being disturbed and then began to purr.

"The food here is every bit as good as you said it was," Cyn told Joe as she plastered her doorstep chunk of crusty bread in pale unsalted butter. She cut into the dense strong cheddar that came in a thick moldy rind. "Here, you have to try some of this cheese." She cut him a small piece and popped it into his mouth. It felt so natural to be sharing her food with him and he seemed more than happy for her to steal crisps and bits of salad off his plate.

When they'd finished eating, the landlord came over and asked them if they could do justice to a nice plate of "the wife's sherry trifle." They both agreed that they could more than do it justice.

"This is wonderful," Joe said, spooning up trifle.

"Yeah, and it's dead easy to make."

"No, I meant this. Us. You and me."

"I know. Feet aside, it's been a perfect day. Absolutely perfect."

Joe looked at his watch. "Look, I don't want to be a killjoy, but I really think we should get going. When I was getting the drinks, the landlord mentioned they were forecasting snow."

"And for once they got it right," Cyn said, staring out of the window. Outside it looked like a scene from one of those glass snow globes. The wind had come up and swirling flakes the size of fifty-pence pieces were piling up on the ground. "Christ," Joe said. "It's a real blizzard out there."

"I hope you've got somewhere to stay tonight," the landlord said, clearing away their plates. "I wouldn't like to chance a long drive. Not if I were you. Not in these conditions. Oh, no. Definitely not. Another hour or two and it'll be drifting to kingdom come."

Cyn and Joe exchanged anxious glances, wondering what to do. "These scientists say bloody planet's warming up," the landlord went on. "No blinkin' sign of it in these parts."

"Don't suppose you do accommodation here, do you?" Joe said.

"Aye, as a matter of fact we do. I think I've got a couple of rooms left. I'll have to check with the wife that they're made up. You see, she handles all the bookings. I keep to the pub side. I don't step on her toes. She doesn't step on mine, so to speak. She's upstairs with her mother just now. Ninety-two years young she is. We converted the top floor into a granny flat when she hurt her hip. So many people these days see the elderly as a burden, but not my missus. She's an angel. Nothing's too much for her. She shouldn't be long, though. So, what are you looking for? A twin, I presume?"

Joe looked distinctly uneasy at the mention of bedroom arrangements. He looked from the landlord to Cyn and back again, clearly not sure how to play this.

"Yes, we'd like a twin, please," Cyn said, giving Joe's thigh a squeeze, "with a double bed if possible."

# Chapter 15

The landlord took Cyn and Joe up to the pale blue Laura Ashley chintz bedroom and then spent a full ten minutes pointing out its most noteworthy features. There were the tea- and coffee-making facilities, the barrel of shortbread—"homemade by the wife"—the individual radiator thermostats and the newly installed shower in the en suite bathroom that apparently "worked a treat" until somebody in another room ran a tap or flushed the loo. To make doubly sure they wouldn't be caught unaware, he directed their attention to the piece of laminated card he had stuck to the mirror over the washbasin, informing guests to "beware of fluctuating water pressure and temperature."

The second he left, they fell back onto the soft double bed giggling. Joe had just started to kiss her when there was a gentle knock and the landlord poked his head round the door. In a fraction of a second, Cyn and Joe went from prone to bolt upright.

"Me again," said the landlord. "Just a word about the smoke detector. It can be a bit sensitive. So if you're going to smoke, please, could you do it out of the window?"

Joe said it wouldn't be a problem since neither of them smoked.

"Oh, right you are. By the way, I've put the electric blanket on for you. Most of our guests find the medium setting adequate. Of course, if you would prefer a hot water bottle, you only have to ask."

"That's really kind of you," Cyn said. "But I think we'll be OK."

"You see, the wind really does rattle through these old window frames. By rights I could do with some double glazing. Chappie came to give us an estimate. I'll get round to it one day, no doubt. Right, then. I can't think of anything else." He nodded, offered up a tiny, self-conscious wave and closed the door. Joe pushed Cyn back down onto the bed.

"Ooh, I almost forgot," came the familiar voice. "What paper will you be wanting in the morning?" In an effort to create a respectable distance between himself and Cyn, Joe rolled to one side of the bed. The only problem was, he had misjudged the force required for said roll and ended up on the carpet, flat on his back, arms and legs outstretched like a stranded beetle.

"Is the gentleman all right?"

"Fine," Joe said, staggering to his feet, rubbing his left shoulder. "Absolutely fine."

"You want to treat your back with more respect. You can't be too careful with backs, I always say. Now, then, where was I? Oh, yes, newspaper. What shall it be?"

"Oh, whatever," Cyn said. "We really don't mind."

"You look like *Observer* people to me," he said. "I'll get that, then, shall I?"

"Fab."

"And we serve a full English breakfast in the saloon bar from seven thirty."

"Wonderful."

"Right, then. Anything you need, just shout. Me and the wife are only downstairs."

"Thank you, but I'm sure we'll be fine," Joe said.

The door closed again. They were fit to explode with laughter, but stifled it in case the landlord heard. To ensure they weren't taken by surprise again, Joe marched over to the door, locked it and put the key on the pine chest of drawers next to a furry hedgehog wearing a cap, miniature wire spectacles and an apron. He was still rubbing his shoulder.

"Come and sit down on the bed," Cyn said. "Let me do that."

She made him take off his shirt. His broad, muscular torso was firm and still tanned from the summer. She knelt behind him, pressing her thumb into his shoulder muscle.

"Ooh, that's good," he said, rolling his head.

"Some heat might help," she said. "What about a soak in the bath?"

He turned round to face her. "You know, I think maybe I'd prefer a shower . . . I'm sure there's room enough for two."

"I was thinking precisely the same," Cyn smiled, feeling her heart rate speed up. He stood up, pulled her to her feet and began kissing her. This time their kissing was deep and urgent. She could feel the outline of his erection against her. She pushed her pelvis toward him. "Come on, let's get this off," he whispered.

He pulled her fleece up over her head. Then he took off her T-shirt. This was followed by two thermal vests. "Sorry about those," she said. "If I'd known how today was going to end, I would have put on my best silk undies."

"Don't be silly," he said softly, pulling her bra strap down off her shoulder. He started kissing her throat. She threw back her head, so that the tendons in her neck were stretched and taut like lift cables. She felt him unhook her bra. He stood for a moment or two, gazing at her breasts. He cupped one in his hand, lowered his mouth to her nipple. The gentle nibbling and biting made her gasp. Moisture was seeping from her. She was aching to feel him inside her. She'd taken off her boots downstairs in the bar, so it was easy to slip out of her trousers. As she stood there in her pants she undid his jeans belt. He looked down, watching her hands. She undid his zipper and ran the back of her hand lightly along the contour of his erection. His breath was coming slow and heavy. She tugged on his jeans and pants, releasing him. His penis sprang out, strong and thick. She sat back on the bed and covered the tip with her mouth. As her tongue caressed him, he dug his fingers into her shoulders and let out a long sigh.

"Let's get in the shower," he whispered. He took her hand and led her toward the bathroom. She found herself looking at his sturdy, muscular legs and remembering the comment he'd made about her thinking he was a knobbly-kneed rambling type. "I knew you had gorgeous knees," she giggled. He looked confused for a moment and she had to remind him of their conversation. Then he thanked her for the compliment.

"By the way, remember the problem with the water temperature," she said as he reached inside the cubicle and turned the control. While the water heated up, he pulled down her pants and kissed her bush. Then he asked her to sit down on the edge of the bath.

"Open your legs," he said.

She did as he asked. He knelt down in front of her and trailed his fingers over her opening. She thrust against his fingers, but he made no attempt to go inside, which drove her wild with frustration. "Please. Please touch me."

"Soon."

He pulled her up. The shower cubicle was full of steam. He stepped inside. "The temperature's fine," he said, holding out his hand for her. She took his hand. The hot needles stung her body—especially her raw feet. His arms were around her and he was kissing her again. Ignoring her feet, she floated into the pleasure. When they finally pulled away, he smiled at her and pushed her flat wet hair out of her eyes. Despite the temperature she was trembling. There was a tube of shower gel at their feet. He picked it up and squirted some onto his hands. As he rubbed it in a caress over her breasts, she let out a tiny whimper. She held out her hand and asked him to squirt some gel onto her palm. She rubbed soap over his chest and followed the line of dark hair that led to his bush. Her hand curled around his penis and slid along the shaft. She watched him bite his bottom lip with pleasure.

"Spread your legs again," he said.

Her head was spinning now. "You'll have to hold me," she said, "or I'm going to fall down."

Her head resting on his shoulder, she parted her feet. His soapy hand began to glide over the inside of her thigh. Slowly, lingering here and there, he brought it higher. And higher. Until. As he parted her and began gently exploring her, she gripped his neck, brought her mouth to his. As his fingers probed her, she thrust her tongue into his mouth, desperately trying to communicate how much she wanted him to make her come. With the lightest touch, his fingers slid over her vulva. She needed him to go harder, faster. She pressed her hand on top of his, urging him on. "There's plenty of time," he whispered. He began licking her neck and the inside of her ear. He toyed with her between her legs, the same way he had when he had been stroking her thigh. It was one step forward, three steps back. He left her teetering on the edge. "Please! Please!"

"Sshh. Just relax."

By now she was having real trouble keeping upright. He sensed this. "Would you be better lying down?"

Before she had a chance to reply the decision was taken out of her hands. In a second, the warm, soothing water had turned to ice. They both screamed. Cyn leaped out of the cubicle and grabbed a bath towel, while Joe moved his body away from the jet of water and reached for the temperature control. He stood frantically turning the dial. After three or four seconds he still couldn't make the hot water come back on, so he gave up.

"Can't say we weren't warned," he laughed as he stepped out of the cubicle and picked up a towel.

"The electric blanket's on in the bed," she said, shivering. "I'll race you."

He chased after her, caught her and the two of them fell onto the bed. As he kissed her he parted her legs. She whimpered as he began rubbing her juices over her vulva. She arched her back, bucked like a horse. "I want to feel you inside me," she cried out. He made her turn onto her stomach. Then he placed a couple of pillows under her middle, so that she was forced onto her knees. He was spreading her juices over her buttocks now. Slowly, his fingers moved down toward her vulva. He was opening her. Then she felt it, the first thrust. Then another and another. Deeper and deeper. Harder. Faster, but his fingers were back on her clitoris. The touch was strong and rhythmic now. He was giving her precisely what she wanted. He was drawing firm clockwise circles over her. Her breath was coming in tight rasps. Soon it was too much to bear and she felt the familiar juddering and quivering inside her. His grinding became slower, harder. She could feel his body tense, sense him gritting his teeth. There was one final thrust. Then, finally, he relaxed.

Afterward she lay in his arms while he pushed tendrils of damp hair out of her face.

"I think I just went to heaven," he said.

"Me, too," she said, kissing his chest and letting out a long, slow breath.

"So, how does it feel, getting more and more wicked by the day?"

She furrowed her brow. "How do you mean?"

"Well, first you hatch this devious plan to get your own back on this Chelsea woman and now you're making passionate love to somebody from your therapy group, which I'd say is more than just breaking the rules. Veronica would probably see it as psychotherapeutic heresy. Don't get me wrong, I totally approve. It's one of the things I adore about you."

She found herself blushing at the "adore" bit. "I'll tell you how becoming even more wicked feels," she said, rolling onto her back and staring up at the ceiling. "Bloody, bloody brilliant. Having barely broken a rule in my life, I'm getting really good at it. There's something so exciting about it. Of course I worry about the Chelsea situation backfiring, but this, you and me . . . it feels so right."

"For me, too." He tilted her face toward him and held her gaze in his. "I want you to know that I have never felt this way about any woman I have been out with. It's a complete first and it feels wonderful."

She snuggled into him again.

"You've taken a fair old risk getting involved with me," he said, "and I'm not talking about breaking Veronica's rules. I've never been in a long-term relationship. Most women would have run a mile."

"I'm not most women."

"Now, isn't that the truth?" he smiled, kissing her forehead.

"I guess we need to be honest with the group, though," she said. "We can't pretend nothing's going on."

"I know. We have to own up, but let's not talk about it now. It can wait."

They were starting to feel cold and decided to get in under the sheets. "Oh, this is bliss," Cyn said, feeling the warmth of the electric blanket underneath her. Then a thought occurred to her. "God, I hope I left Morris with enough food and water. I'm sure I did, but we'll really need to get going early in the morning."

"No problem."

"Talking of food and water, do you fancy a cuppa and a piece of shortbread?"

"Maybe in a minute," he said. He suddenly looked pre-occupied, she thought.

"You OK?"

"I'm fine. You know, today really was one of the most wonderful I can ever remember. I loved every second . . ."

"Me, too."

He gave her a quick squeeze. "I'm glad, but there's something we need to talk about."

"I know."

"You do?" He swallowed hard.

"Yes. You've got to decide how to handle the Clementine situation. So, are you going to confront her in the group about her giving you her phone number?"

"I haven't decided. No, it's not that. There's something else. The thing is . . ."

Just then her mobile started ringing. She picked the phone up off the bedside cabinet and looked at the caller display. It was her mother. "Sorry, Joe, it's my mum. If I switch the phone off now while it's ringing, she'll realize and get offended." She flipped the lid.

As Barbara started speaking, the color drained from Cyn's face. "Oh, my God, when did it happen? . . . OK, don't worry, I'm on my way. The thing is, it's going to take me a while. I'm in Derbyshire with a friend. We spent the day walking. Now there's heavy snow, but I'll be there. One way or another." Usually by now her mother would have been cross-examining her, wanting to know how she'd spent her day and what friend she was with, but she said nothing apart from "OK, darling. Take it easy. Drive carefully."

Cyn leaped out of bed.

"What is it?" Joe said, looking alarmed.

She was snatching clothes up off the floor. "It's my dad. He's in hospital. He collapsed at home a couple of hours ago. They've established it's not a heart attack or a stroke, but beyond that, the doctors have got no idea what's the matter with him. Apparently they're doing loads of tests." She looked down at her hands, which had started to shake.

The landlord, whose name they finally discovered was Don, couldn't have been more kind. He refused to accept a penny for the room and, even though it was Saturday night, he had a pub full of people and they were short staffed, he insisted on giving them a lift back to their car. Although it had stopped snowing, the country roads were like narrow, snaking ice rinks. Since Don drove an old army-issue Land Rover with snow chains, navigating the lanes wasn't too much of a problem. What worried Cyn and Joe was how they would cope in a car.

"Just keep in a low gear and take it steady," Don advised. "Remember, if you go into a skid, don't brake, turn into it."

Cyn and Joe thanked him for everything. "My pleasure," he said. Then he turned to Cyn and laid his hand on her shoulder. "I hope your dad is OK."

"So do I," she said.

They took Don's advice and crawled along the country roads. Cyn didn't say much because she was worrying about what was wrong with Mal and fearing the worst. Joe was quiet, too, because he was concentrating on the road.

It took them nearly two hours to reach the motorway. Surprisingly, this wasn't nearly as treacherous as they'd expected. There was plenty of snow piled up on the hard shoulder and median strip, but the road itself was relatively clear.

For once the sand trucks had gotten out in time and done their job.

"You know," Cyn said as Joe pulled out to overtake a van, "I couldn't bear it if anything happened to Dad. And God knows how Mum would cope. She'd be devastated. Absolutely devastated. She gives him a hard time, but she adores him."

"Come on," Joe said gently, "you're jumping the gun here. Your dad is relatively young and fit. You said he'd been feeling a bit under the weather. This could turn out to be nothing."

"But what if it turns out to be something?" She paused. "Joe, I'm really scared."

He reached out for her hand and gave it a reassuring squeeze. "I'm here," he said. He turned to look at her—just for a second. There was a warmth and sincerity in his expression that convinced her he really meant what he said.

They reached the King George in Edgware about eleven. Joe dropped her off at the entrance to the emergency room. They both agreed he shouldn't come in, as this wasn't the time to introduce him to her family. When he asked her how she would get home, she assured him that Jonny would give her a lift.

As they stood by the electronic doors, he wrapped her in an enormous hug. "Promise you'll call me as soon as you know anything," he said.

"Promise." She kissed his cheek.

"Good luck."

"Thanks." She turned to go and stopped in her tracks. "God, I forgot. There was something you were trying to tell me back at the pub, just before the phone rang. What was it?"

"Don't worry," he smiled. "It'll keep."

———

The ER was the usual dingy National Health Service deal: rows of plastic seats screwed to the floor, a television blaring away in the corner, besieged junior doctors looking as if they could sleep for a month.

Barbara, Faye, Jonny and Flick had colonized some seats next to the severely dented coffee machine.

Cyn wanted to run over to her mother, but couldn't. Despite several layers of Elastoplast on the backs of her feet, her boots were still rubbing. Instead she half jogged, half hobbled. Barbara was fiddling with a ball of tissue. She looked hunched and small. "Hi, Mum," she said, sitting down next to her mother and putting her arms around her.

"Oh, sweetie, you made it," Barbara said, returning Cyn's hug. She was so distressed she didn't seem to notice Cyn's hiking gear. "I was so worried about you in all that terrible snow."

"It wasn't too bad once we hit the motorway." Cyn turned to Jonny. "So, what's the news?" Old traditions died hard—particularly when people were under stress. Since Jonny was the male member of the family, she expected him to be in charge.

He shrugged. "Bugger all. They're still doing tests." He said he was cross that the paramedics hadn't brought Mal to the Royal, where Flick worked. "She knows all the staff there and we might have gotten more sense out of them." He was tight-lipped and fiddling with the change in his pockets.

"Come on, Bear, sit down," Flick said gently. "They're doing their best. These things take time." She turned to Cyn. "How about a cup of coffee? It's just about drinkable." Cyn said a coffee would be great.

"If you call chicken-soup-flavored coffee drinkable," Faye piped up.

"Hi, Gran. You OK?"

She said she was fine. "Cyn, tell me, what do you look like? This is a hospital. There are nice young doctors here. Couldn't you have made an effort? You look like you've been hiking. How are you ever going to find a boyfriend dressed like that?"

Cyn didn't say she had already found one. It wasn't the time or place. "I have been hiking" was all she said.

"Since when did you hike?" Faye persisted.

"Since I realized there's lots of lovely countryside that I've never seen."

"So who did you go with?"

"A friend."

Grandma Faye assumed she meant a girlfriend and gave a shrug as if to say "I give up."

Meanwhile, Jonny wanted to carry on discussing how the coffee could have tasted of chicken soup. "There's no chicken-soup button. It's just tea, coffee or hot chocolate."

"I'm only telling you what I tasted," Faye said.

Barbara was sipping tea. "He was fine until a few hours ago," she said. "All he had was a bit of a temperature. The next minute he was lying on the bedroom floor unconscious. I thought I'd lost him." She paused. Her face became a frown. "You know, Mum, you're right. The tea tastes of chicken soup, too."

"What did I tell you?" Grandma Faye said, turning to Jonny. "See? I'm not mad. Your mother agrees with me." With that she pootled over to a young couple sitting with a little girl whose arm was in a makeshift sling. "Excuse me," she said, sitting herself down next to the mother, "but can't help noticing you've got coffee from the hot drinks machine. Tell me, would you say it tastes of chicken soup?"

Barbara sat shaking her head. "My husband could be dying and what does my mother do? She seizes the opportunity to conduct a market research campaign."

"I'm sure she doesn't mean to be insensitive," Flick said. "It's just her way of coping with the stress." She handed Cyn a plastic cup of coffee and turned back to Barbara. "Mal's in good hands. I'm sure it's nothing too serious. It might be nothing more than the flu and his temperature just shot up."

Barbara nodded. "Maybe you're right. At least it's not his heart."

Just then a young male doctor appeared, draping his stethoscope round his neck.

"Mrs. Fishbein?"

Barbara shot to her feet. "That's me. I'm Mrs. Fishbein."

"I'm Dr. Goldman," he said, extending his hand and offering Barbara a warm smile. "Just to let you know that we won't have the results of your husband's blood tests until the morning, but I'm pretty certain this is nothing to worry about. I've just finished examining him and from what I can tell, this is nothing more than a rather nasty case of mumps."

"Mumps?" Barbara fell back onto her chair, her face exuding relief tinged with disbelief. "Are you sure?"

"I'm as certain as I can be at this stage."

Barbara turned to the rest of the family. "Did you hear that? Mal's got mumps. Thank God. Mumps? Who'd have thought? That's wonderful news, Doctor. Absolutely wonderful. Thank you."

"It's on the increase again since the rumpus over the MMR vaccine and so many parents stopped vaccinating babies. When children get it the symptoms are usually quite mild. In adults they can be far more severe. Mr. Fishbein's neck and groin area are very swollen."

"So why did he collapse?"

"His temperature suddenly went very high."

"See, what did I tell you?" Flick smiled.

Faye, who had reappeared the moment the doctor arrived, looked particularly concerned. "Dr. Goldman, you said my son-in-law's groin was very swollen. Tell me, will it affect his fertility?"

"Mum, for God's sake," Barbara hissed. "Mal's in his sixties. What does it matter?"

"I'll tell you why it matters. What if you died? Mal might want to get married again, start another family. He needs to know that everything's in working order."

"It's so reassuring to know my mother spends her time thinking about my death."

Faye shrugged. "I'm just trying to be realistic, that's all. Accidents happen. Five years from now you might go out and get run over."

"OK, but Mal would be nearly seventy. Do you mind telling me what woman in her right mind would want her baby and her husband in nappies at the same time?"

Unlike the rest of the family, who were used to this kind of exchange between Faye and Barbara, Dr. Goldman was looking distinctly uncomfortable. "Mr. Fishbein's fertility could be affected. If it's important, we could make an out-patient appointment in a few weeks to check his sperm count."

"I assure you, that won't be necessary, Dr. Goldman," Barbara said, still looking daggers at Grandma Faye.

"Fine. For now, though, we'll keep him in overnight for observation. I'm pretty sure we can let him go home tomorrow. I'll make sure he has plenty of painkillers. Then all he will need is lots of rest, fluids and Tylenol to keep his temperature down. By the way, have you and your family all had mumps?"

"I have," Barbara said, "and my children had it when they were little. Mum, what about you?"

Grandma Faye waved a dismissive hand in front of her. "Of course. When I was growing up in the East End we got everything—whooping cough, scarlet fever, diphtheria, typhoid. Only the strong survived."

"Mum, I know for a fact you did not get typhoid or diphtheria." Barbara turned back to Dr. Goldman. "Thank you for everything. I can't tell you how relieved we all are." He shook her hand again and reassured her Mal would be fine. She asked if they could see him.

"Absolutely. He's still in a cubicle. The porter will be along in a minute to take him up to the ward."

As everybody set off toward Mal's cubicle, Barbara noticed Cyn was limping. "What on earth happened to you?"

"It's nothing. Just a few blisters."

"You sure? I mean, if it's more serious, you could ask one of the nurses to take a look."

Cyn reassured her she was OK. As they carried on toward the cubicle, Grandma Faye held back. Cyn watched her go over to Dr. Goldman. He was pushing coins into the coffee machine. She tugged at his sleeve. "Dr. Goldman?"

"Yes?"

"Tell me, do you have a girlfriend?" Cyn's ears pricked up. She spun round and went limping over. She had to rescue the poor man. "Actually, I do," he said, coloring up.

"I see," Grandma Faye said, clearly disappointed. "So, is it serious?"

"We're engaged."

"Oh, congratulations." She nodded in Cyn's direction. "This is my granddaughter, Cynthia. Don't be put off. She usually dresses much nicer than this. Try to imagine her without the sweater and muddy boots. Anyway, she would love to meet a nice Jewish doctor. I don't suppose you have any colleagues you could introduce her to?"

"Gran," Cyn cried. "Please. That's enough." She grabbed her grandmother's arm and mouthed an apology at Dr. Goldman. He seemed amused more than embarrassed.

"I was only trying to help," Grandma Faye said to Cyn as Cyn dragged her toward Mal's cubicle.

———

Everybody piled into the tiny curtained-off cubicle. Mal was lying back on a pile of pillows, drip in arm, looking distinctly puffy about the face. But more than anything he looked exhausted. He raised his hand a few inches in greeting. "It seems it's going to be a while yet before you get to spend all the life insurance money." He grinned at Barbara.

"Behave," she scolded gently. She bent down and kissed him on the forehead. "I've been climbing the walls with worry. We all have."

"Really?"

"Of course."

"That's nice." A contented smile formed on Mal's face.

Everybody could see he was struggling to keep his eyes open, so they each gave him a quick kiss, wished him better and said good night.

The next day, Mal came home with, in his own words, "testicles the size of melons." "Every time he needs the loo, it's a major production," Barbara said on the phone to Cyn. "His bits and pieces are so swollen and heavy he can hardly walk. The poor man needs a sling."

"Wow, thanks for sharing that," Cyn said.

# Chapter 16

When Cyn phoned Joe on Sunday morning to let him know her dad was going to be OK, he couldn't have been more delighted or relieved. "I hated seeing you so worried," he said.

She thanked him for getting her to the hospital.

"No problem. I was just glad to help. So, how are the feet?"

She told him they were getting better, but she was still having to wear several layers of Elastoplast to stop her shoes rubbing.

"Ouch. Sounds really uncomfortable . . . By the way, I wanted to say again that the other evening—the bit before the phone rang—was one of the most wonderful I can ever remember."

"Same here. I'm so sorry it ended the way it did."

"Will you stop being such an idiot?" he laughed. "There is absolutely nothing to apologize for." She loved the way he called her an idiot. He said it with so much affection.

"Sorry," she said.

"And will you stop saying sorry?"

"OK, sor—" Now she was laughing.

"Look, changing the subject," she went on, "we need to work out how we're going to handle the next therapy session. Like I said the other night, I think we have to come clean and tell the group that we've been seeing each other."

"I know. And I've also got to sort out the Clementine situation. It's all getting very complicated, and what makes it worse is that it's all going to have to wait because I'm going to miss the next couple of sessions."

"How come?"

"The second week I've got an important meeting in Glasgow I can't get out of and I'm going to miss this Tuesday's session because I've decided to go to Dublin to see my mum."

"Wow, that's a bit sudden."

"I know, but I've realized I need to talk to her about what happened to me when I was a kid. She's not getting any younger and if I leave it any longer it might be too late. I just phoned her to ask if it was OK to come and she said yes."

"So she was pleased you wanted to see her?"

"It was hard to tell over the phone. To be honest, she seemed a bit wary. I only ever see her at Christmas and I think she got the sense that something was up."

Cyn told him she thought he was doing absolutely the right thing by going.

"I hope so," he said. He paused. Then: "So, are you absolutely sure that when we tell everybody we've been seeing each other that Veronica will insist we leave the group? I've only been there two minutes. It seems a shame. They're a funny old lot, but I was getting to like them."

He sounded really sad, she thought. "Joe, please don't worry about leaving. Veronica will understand. It can't be the first time something like this has happened, and I'm sure she'll help us find new groups."

"But that takes time," he said. "It was a couple of months

before Veronica got an opening and I was able to join your group." He seemed really put out at the thought of having to wait. Therapy had clearly become very important to him.

"Don't worry," she said. "In the meantime, you've always got me. I'm a great listener."

"I know you are," he said warmly. "You're right, there's no hurry."

But she got the feeling there was.

The first thing Cyn did when she got into the office on Monday morning was phone Interflora and send flowers to Don and his wife at the Cross Keys to say thank you for all their help. No sooner had she put the phone down than Barbara rang to say that if she was planning to come and see Mal that day, she shouldn't leave it too late. Apart from still being in pain and too weak to get up other than to stagger to the loo, he was finding it almost impossible to stay awake in the evenings beyond about six o'clock. Cyn said not to worry. She would take a couple of hours off work and get there about four.

When she arrived, the front door was open. She was greeted by a studenty-looking girl trying to maneuver herself and a black cello case through the slightly-too-narrow doorway. "You sure you can manage?" Barbara said in her faux bright, for-God's-sake-mind-the-new-paintwork voice that only Cyn recognized. As the girl turned round to reply in the affirmative, she caused the case to swing violently to one side and take a chunk out of the door frame. "Oops," Barbara said with wild understatement. "Not to worry."

The next moment it had swung the other way and knocked over four empty milk bottles that began rolling down the garden path. The girl apologized and, offering Cyn a taut smile, scurried down the garden path—inasmuch as it was possible to scurry carrying a cello.

"We'll let you know," Barbara called out after her. Cyn

retrieved the milk bottles and put them back down on the front step. "Thanks, darling," Barbara said as she let her in. "The cellist was Hugh's idea. I have to hand it to her, she played beautifully, but her choice of music wasn't that great. Between you and me I can't quite picture opening the dancing at the wedding to Klaus Huber's *Transpositio ad infinitum* for virtuoso solo cello." Barbara closed the door. "We've got another act to see, though. They're due in half an hour. Why don't you stay and listen? Hugh and Flick are here. I'm sure they'd appreciate your opinion."

Cyn said she would love to stay. "So, how's Dad?"

Barbara said his temperature was down, but he was still on painkillers. "Why don't you pop up and see him?"

Mal was lying in bed, propped up on a pile of pillows and surrounded by newspapers and magazines. A bowl of nectarines and a barely touched cup of tea—probably cold—sat on the bedside table. He was fast asleep with his iPod headphones on. Cyn tiptoed toward him and gently took them off. He half opened his eyes and smiled at her. "Hi, sweetie." His voice was croaky with sleep.

"Hi. How you doing?" She leaned over and kissed him.

He eased himself into a more upright position. "Not bad, but I'm still feeling so weak. I try getting up, but five minutes later I just want to be horizontal again. It's so frustrating."

"Don't worry. You just have to go with it. You'll soon get your strength back."

Just then the doorbell went. They heard Grandma Faye answer it. "That'll be Jonny," Mal said. "He promised to take the afternoon off to help with the auditions. He's late. Flick won't be pleased."

There was a thumping on the stairs and Jonny came in.

He took one look at Mal's swollen face and neck and announced, "Hey, it's Puff Daddy."

"Very funny," Mal said. "By the way, I thought you were supposed to be here an hour ago."

"Meeting with a client ran over. Don't worry, I phoned Flick."

Just then Grandma Faye appeared, breathless from the stairs. She was wearing a purple leotard, black Lycra pedal pushers and a purple headband. She looked like a senior citizen from *Fame*. "Wow, Gran, get you," Cyn said.

Faye beamed at the compliment. "Laurent's been getting me doing some gentle exercises to help my joints. I'm really getting into it. I even went out and bought a sports deodorant." She turned to Mal. "So, how you doing?"

"How would you be if you were me? The district nurse comes every morning. In sixty-four years, my testicles have never received so much attention from a woman. The tragedy is I'm in too much pain to enjoy it."

Everybody laughed. "I was just about to put the kettle on," Faye said. "I wondered if you fancied another cuppa." He thanked her and said he was fine. "I didn't manage to finish the last one." She went over to the bedside table and picked up his cup and saucer. Reminding him to just shout if he wanted anything, she went back downstairs.

"Actually, there is something I'd like," Mal said. He was looking at Jonny. "I was wondering if you could do me a favor."

"Sure."

"I don't think I'm going to be up to preparing Laurent's case for the Home Office. Would you do it? You know the score; we have to convince them that if he returns to his country under its present regime, he would be likely to face summary imprisonment or execution for his political beliefs.

It shouldn't be difficult because his case was well documented by Amnesty International at the time of the coup there."

Cyn watched Jonny hesitate. It wasn't that her brother didn't care about Laurent, he did. Jonny had been as distressed as everybody else the other night when Laurent talked about life under the military dictatorship in Tagine. It was just that he knew precious little about immigration law. Suburban conveyancing and divorce cases were his specialties. Taking on Laurent's case meant going beyond what was familiar and predictable. Cyn knew this would make him feel anxious and insecure.

"OK, I'll do it," Jonny said, breezily. "No problem."

Cyn could see the look of surprise and pleasure on her father's face. Mal had never said as much, but he had often hinted to Cyn that he felt guilty about encouraging Jonny to join his law firm straight from university. "If he'd traveled a bit, seen some of the world, done some charity work . . . even smoked a bit of pot . . ." Then his voice would trail off, but Cyn knew what he was trying to say: if Jonny had done some of these things, maybe he might have developed a more adventurous spirit. Cyn could never bring herself to risk upsetting her dad and telling him what she knew: that Jonny's need for security had begun when he was little, with Barbara's illness. Maybe traveling and finding something more imaginative to do after university than joining his father's legal practice would have helped, but probably only in the short term. Cyn suspected that her brother's need to play it safe and not take risks were so deep-seated that whatever he had done, he would always have turned out the same.

"Good boy," Mal said, smiling up at Jonny. "I started making some notes. I've got them all on disc."

When Mal began to look tired again, they left him to sleep.

"You sure you don't mind taking on Laurent's case?" Cyn

asked Jonny as they walked downstairs. "After all, it's not really your thing."

He gave a shrug. "I know, but getting to grips with immigration law will give me something to think about other than this blinkin' wedding. Plus it's for a good cause and it's not as if it's going to be more than a onetime thing. I just hope I don't bugger it up."

Jonny carried on into the living room while Cyn popped to the loo. She was just coming out when the music started. She found herself stopping to listen. After a few seconds she began giggling. Somebody, or rather a group of somebodies, was playing "Like a Virgin." What was more, they appeared to be playing it on Peruvian pan pipes.

She walked into the living room and stood by the door so as not to interrupt the performance. Gathered at one end of the living room, in front of the smoked-glass wall unit-cum-cocktail cabinet, were six Peruvian pipers in traditional black hats and brightly colored ponchos. Sitting at the dining table, drinking tea, eating miniature Danishes and jigging about to the music were Barbara, Flick, Grandma Faye—still in her gym gear—and Jonny. Hugh was there, too, but he wasn't eating or jigging. He was shooting Cyn a pained look that said: "This has absolutely nothing to do with me, OK?"

Nobody seemed to notice the look. Instead they were all merrily singing along: "Like a vir-ir-ir-ir-gin, touched for the very first time." Hugh put his head in his hands.

Faye, meanwhile, tiptoed over to Cyn and pulled her into the living room. "Come on, darling, join in. Aren't they wonderful? They're called The Lima Dreamers." She lifted her hands over her head and began stabbing the air with her forefingers. "Like a vir-ir-ir-ir-gin . . ."

Cyn surveyed the scene. With the exception of Hugh, who was now sipping his tea looking like the queen at a pub karaoke night, everybody was having a ball. High on all the clapping and singing along, The Lima Dreamers were seriously into the Madonna vibe. Flick was clapping wildly, although her claps bore little relation to the rhythm of the music. Barbara was tapping her foot and knocking back the Danish. Grandma Faye was boogying in her purple leotard. Even Jonny was getting into the groove.

This was not the real world, Cyn decided. Ponchoed Peruvians did not descend on ordinary suburban houses and start playing "Like a Virgin" on pan pipes, egged on by gyrating grannies in leotards. There was no doubt in her mind that they were trapped in a Magritte painting and were about to be joined by a puffing steam train and a group of little bowler-hatted men parachuting down on their umbrellas.

The Lima Dreamers were a hit with everybody. Even, as it turned out, with Hugh, but not for artistic reasons. He'd had his eye on one of them, a cute chap in a pink and orange poncho called Gustavo, but when he'd gone to ask for his phone number it turned out Gustavo's English was virtually nonexistent and Hugh gave up. "I know the language of love is meant to be universal, but it gets pretty boring after a while."

Cyn approved of the Lima Dreamers, too, and could see how in an ironic way they would liven things up during dinner. After they had gone, Hugh tried to argue the case for something a bit more upmarket and restrained, but Grandma Faye made the point that this was a wedding, not a wake.

"OK," Hugh said, summing up. "We're agreed, then, that

The Lima Dreamers will play during dinner. Later on, they will hand over to the dance band."

Everybody nodded. "Fine," Hugh said in a tone that exuded resigned acceptance more than excitement. He looked worn-out, Cyn thought. It was pretty obvious that Barbara and Flick had reverted to type and were far less committed to "simple elegance" than they had been at the first meeting to discuss the wedding. They were clearly having second thoughts about Hugh's muted, classy approach to the nuptials. He seemed to be happy to back down—fed up, no doubt, with fighting a losing battle, not to mention overseeing the tussles that were surely going on between her mother and Flick, her mother and Grandma Faye, and her mother and Mal. Looking at him now, he seemed pathetically grateful just to have everybody in agreement. Pen in hand, his eyes surveyed his to-do list. He added a couple of ticks. "Right, the ceremony and the tent are sorted, as are the flowers. Everybody's agreed we're going with bubbles instead of confetti. The invitations should be here in a day or so. This brings us to outfits . . ."

Flick took the floor and said she had abandoned the idea of having dresses made because nobody could do them in time.

"Well, I'm planning to get my outfit at My Daughter's Wedding in Mill Hill," Barbara said. "They have wonderful wedding and bridesmaids' dresses. Why don't we all go together?"

"Mill Hill?" Hugh said in a voice that suggested he had been thinking more Notting Hill.

"Yes." She explained to Hugh that it was run by a woman named Bernice Greenspan whom she knew from the synagogue Ladies' Guild. "I got my dress for Jonny's bar mitzvah there."

"In 1989," Cyn added, not altogether helpfully.

"And I'm sure we bought you several bridesmaids' dresses there," Barbara added.

"We did," Cyn said, remembering all four polyester pastel creations.

"Anyway, I know for a fact that Bernice still carries a wonderful collection of dresses and wedding outfits." She suggested that they all—and by that she meant herself, Flick, Cyn, Grandma Faye and Hugh—meet up at My Daughter's Wedding on Saturday morning.

"Ooh, this is going to be so exciting," Flick squealed, clapping her hands. She turned to Jonny. "You hear that, Pooh Bear? I'm going to get my wedding dress. And I'm sure there'll be something utterly perfect for Cyn."

"Excellent," Jonny said with a thin smile. He didn't look so much tired and frazzled as bored.

Cyn reached under the table and squeezed Hugh's thigh as if to say "Please, please don't let me down on this one." Hugh turned to her and gave a quick wink. "OK," he went on, addressing the whole group now, "that just leaves the catering to sort out." He turned to Barbara. "We've had menus and sampled food from at least a dozen caterers. It really is make-your-mind-up time."

The problem was that Flick still wanted something "a bit out of the ordinary and ethnic-y" and Barbara was standing her ground, insisting that ethnic didn't work at big mixed-age-group parties. "We need to go for something undemanding that everybody will eat. I still think we should go for salmon. Or possibly halibut."

Everybody was putting in their two penn'orth when Laurent appeared. He was wearing battered old trainers and shorts. Judging by his red face and damp hair, he had just been for a run. He eased his way into the room, raising a hand in apology, picked up a book from the coffee table and started to make his way out. He was just going out of the door when he turned back.

"Excuse me," he said tentatively, "but I couldn't help overhearing. I know eet ees none of my business, but I do not understand why you cannot have ze ethneec and ze un-demanding." Nobody remotely minded him interrupting, but they all agreed combining the two would be ridiculously complicated.

"Not necessarily," Laurent said.

"Really?" Barbara said, indicating the spare chair next to her and inviting him to sit down.

"Absolutely. I could do eet. My mother—she was a won-derful cook and she taught me all she knew. Back in Tagine I often 'elp 'er to cook for beeg parties. Why don't I prepare some traditional African food along wiz some more tradi-tional dishes and we can 'ave a buffet, *non?*"

Silence fell. The words *bush* and *meat* suddenly hung in the air. It was only Cyn who noticed the expression on Laurent's face and realized he had decided to play up to their fears.

"I can do wonderful theengs wiz leopard and, *comment ça veut dire,* monkey brains."

Faces winced. Buttocks were clenched. Grandma Faye looked like she was about to keel over. The only people not participating in the wincing and clenching were Cyn, be-cause she knew Laurent was only teasing, and Hugh—who was always up for a bizarre new taste sensation. His latest passions were Heston Blumenthal's sardine ice cream and leather-flavored chocolates.

"Laurent," Barbara said, clearing her throat and going in search of her most diplomatic tone of voice. "I'm sure you can do wonderful things with that kind of meat. The thing is it's not actually kosher."

"Or legal," Jonny muttered.

"What about locusts? Zey are kosher, *non*?"

"Er, *non*."

"Maybe you like caterpillars. Or white ants?"

"Good grief, no," Flick cried out. "Definitely not."

"So no grasshoppers, zen?"

"I don't think so," Barbara said, shooting Hugh a for-God's-sake-help-me-out-here expression. Hugh was about to say something, but Laurent got in first. "Eet ees OK," he said, his face breaking into a broad smile. "I just make joke wiz you."

"Oh, thank the Lord," Barbara said, slapping her hand to her chest.

"But I meant it when I said I am magnifique cook. 'Ow about I prepare some beef wiz pineapple and coconut wiz a vegetable rice? Zen we could 'ave chicken in peanut sauce, fried plantains, sweet potatoes. And maybe I do some poached salmon and salads for ze less adventurous guests."

Cyn looked at Laurent's chiseled face, the thick, muscular neck and biceps, the six-pack bulging under his T-shirt. These days so many men were great cooks, but she could no more imagine Laurent in the kitchen than she could imagine Rambo doing needlepoint.

"Please let me do zees," Laurent went on. "It would be my way of sanking you."

Barbara told him he had done so much already. "You help around the house. You're working out with my mother."

"But I would like to do zees, too."

Barbara was trying desperately not to show it, but Cyn could tell she still wasn't convinced that Laurent was up to it. Sensing this, he suggested cooking them a special dinner the following week, to prove he really could cook.

"Why not?" Hugh said. He looked round the group and everybody seemed to be in agreement.

Grandma Faye turned to Laurent. "If you end up doing

the catering, can we still have the chocolate fountain and fish balls?"

Laurent's brow furrowed. "Fish balls. I see. Tell me, Faye, do your people eat any other part of ze fish?"

Only Cyn was able to stay for dinner. Flick and Jonny couldn't because they were eating out with friends—although Jonny made time to sit down with Laurent and explain that Mal had asked him to take over Laurent's asylum case. Hugh said he was meeting people, too, but confessed to Cyn that he wasn't really. "The truth is, I'm starting to wilt under the pressure of this wedding. If I don't spend the next three hours soaking in a Jo Malone lime-basil and mandarin bath, I think I shall probably die." Cyn suspected there was another reason he wanted to get going—although he was far too polite to say anything. Hugh was the only one of her family and friends who hadn't had mumps and she was pretty sure he didn't want to hang around chez Fishbein more than was strictly necessary.

He had said good-bye to Barbara and was putting on his coat in the hall, when Cyn came running out of the living room. "God, I nearly forgot," she said excitedly. "Joe's taken your screenplay away to read. He loved the outline and the first few pages. He's talking about showing it to one of his movie contacts."

"You're kidding."

"Would I kid about something like that?"

"Bloody hell."

"Fantastic, isn't it?"

"So have you heard from him? Has he said what he thinks? Does he like it? I mean, what did he say?"

"Huge, calm down. He only took it on Saturday."

"God, I don't know what to say. Maybe I should phone

him—you know, to explain some of the more complicated metaphors and talk him through my philosophical thrust. On the other hand maybe I shouldn't hassle him. He might think I'm insulting his intelligence. What do you think?" He was gabbling and running his hand over his head. Cyn had seen Hugh miserable and depressed a thousand times, but the twitchy neurotic artiste was a whole new look.

"What I think is that now that he seems to like your screenplay . . ." She lowered her voice in case Barbara was within earshot and might hear what she was about to say, "you have suddenly changed your mind about the madman I am going out with and had the most fantastic sex ever with on Saturday night."

"OK, you win. Maybe I did misjudge him. So, should I phone him or what?"

"Look," Cyn said evenly, "I'm sure Joe wouldn't mind you ringing, but he's not the type to mess you around. As soon as he's read it, he'll be in touch."

"OK, and you're sure he's got my phone number."

"Absolutely."

"And my mobile."

"Yes."

"What about my e-mail?"

"I gave him that, too. Look, Hugh, try not to get carried away. Joe is reading the screenplay, that's all. He can't commission it. He might possibly pass it on to somebody who might possibly know somebody who might, that's all."

"I know, but at least it's something." He was staring off into space. "God, Cyn, have you ever felt like your life is about to change—that it's your time?" Grandma Faye, who happened to be walking past, stopped and said, "Yes, it happens to every woman when she hits fifty."

Hugh laughed, waved good-bye to Faye and turned back

to Cyn. "It's going to work out, gorgeous," he said, gripping her hand. "I just know it."

Cyn was starting to panic and wish desperately that she hadn't said anything.

Faye and Laurent weren't staying for dinner either. Faye was playing bridge and Laurent had another date with Harmony.

"I like your brozzer," Laurent said to Cyn as they sat alone in the kitchen waiting for Harmony to arrive. " 'E 'as a generous spirit, like your parents."

She felt flattered on Jonny's behalf. "And what about Harmony? Do you like her?"

"Of course. 'Armony ees a very special person."

"She is. Harms and Hugh are my best friends."

He nodded. "She told me 'ow much she loves you."

"I love her, too," Cyn smiled.

"She ees complicated, though, *non*?"

"How do you mean?"

"She pretend to be tough, but I can see she ees vulnerable. She make ze jokes all ze time to try and 'ide eet, but I can see srough her." The man was truly multiskilled—sort of Rambo meets Jamie Oliver meets Frasier.

"She had a hard childhood," Cyn said. "There was no choice, she had to be tough."

"I know."

"She told you?"

He nodded. "We talk all ze time. Zere ees a chemistry between us. I have a feeling of coming 'ome when I am wiz her. Do you know zat feeling, Ceen?"

Cyn began stabbing a teaspoon into the bowl of sugar. "Oh, yes. I know it. I know it very well." She was thinking about Joe.

"Zen you understand, *non?*"

She carried on stabbing the sugar. "Laurent, please don't hurt her. Her last relationship just ended and she's very fragile at the moment."

"I know. Zees Justin. He was a fool, an *idiot, non?* I could never 'urt 'Armony. Never. You 'ave my word."

She believed him. Of course in the end it might not work out between them. But Cyn had high hopes. There was no doubt that Laurent possessed a heart as big as he was and that unlike Justin, he didn't seem to have a fear of commitment. In fact it was the very opposite. He desperately wanted to look after Harmony. She had managed to work her way out of poverty with only herself to rely on. Now she deserved a soft place to fall: a place that all the money in the world couldn't buy.

Harmony arrived looking like Sandy from *Grease* in a flared acid-yellow skirt with black polka dots. On top she wore a black button-through blouse with a turned-up collar and three-quarter-length sleeves. It suddenly occurred to Cyn that her best friends seemed to be forever at her parents' house. For a few seconds she felt about nine again.

Harmony could barely contain her excitement. "I just got the results of my blood test," she whispered. "I'm fine. Not remotely menopausal."

Cyn threw her arms round her friend. "Oh, hon," she said, squeezing her, "that's wonderful news."

"You were right. The doctor says my periods have been messing around because I'm stressed. He reckons working too many hours, doing up the house and the whole Justin thing just got too much. He says I just need to slow down and have more fun."

"But you've never slowed down in your life."

"I agree I might have to work on that, but in the meantime I'm going to start on the fun part. I'm taking Laurent back to my hotel where I have a bottle of Cristal on ice. This will be our third date. Time to move to the next level, I think." She gave Cyn a wink and turned to Laurent, who was coming down the stairs. "Come on, *chéri, allons-y*."

Laurent's face lit up when he saw her. He wrapped her in his arms, kissed her and told her how *magnifique* she looked. He was wearing old, indifferently fitting jeans and an ancient leather bomber jacket, which had never been trendy, even when it was new. But Harmony didn't seem to notice. As he scooped her up, she was all girlie giggles and fake swoon. When he finally let her go, she turned to Cyn. "Isn't this man just gorgeous?"

Cyn agreed he was.

"Oh, by the way, don't forget," Harmony went on. "Thursday night—party at the salon." Cyn had completely forgotten. Harmony had mentioned the party weeks ago and it had gone straight out of her head. She had poached some hot-shot stylist from John Frieda and was having a drinks do to welcome him. "I've got a stack of celebs coming. It'll be a laugh."

"OK if I bring Joe?"

"Of course. I think it's about time I checked him out." She turned to Laurent. "Cyn's going out with some guy she met in her therapy group. Me and 'Ewge are worried he might be bonkers." Laurent clearly had little understanding of what she meant by *therapy group* or *bonkers*. Harmony said she would explain later.

"Oh, God, you're not going to start giving Joe the third degree, are you?" Cyn said, "just because he's in therapy . . ."

"It's not just because he's in therapy. The man is thirty-six and has never had a proper relationship—remember?"

Laurent shrugged. "Eet can 'appen. Maybe he has not met ze right woman yet."

"Thank you," Cyn said to Laurent. "At last, somebody who understands." She turned back to Harmony. "Look, I know you mean well, but Joe and I are getting serious. You know how Gran's always going on about there being a lid for every pot. Well, I think I've found my lid. I really want you to be pleased for me."

Harmony looked sheepish. "Oh, Cyn, I'm sorry. Of course I'm pleased you've found your lid." But there was no mistaking the concern on her face.

Barbara boiled Mal a couple of eggs for his supper and took them up to him with some buttered toast and a cup of tea. While she was gone, Cyn made a couple of gin and tonics.

"Here, get this down you," Cyn said to Barbara as she came back into the kitchen. "You look like you could do with it." Her mother's face was taut and drawn. Cyn suspected it had little to do with organizing the wedding and everything with the shock of finding Mal collapsed on the floor last week.

"You read my mind." Barbara smiled. "Cheers." She swallowed hard. Cyn insisted she sit down. "I'll get the supper. Pasta OK? I found a jar of tomato sauce in the cupboard."

"Perfect." Barbara sat down, pulled out another chair and rested her feet on it. "This thing with your dad has been quite a shock." She took another slug of her gin and tonic.

"I know. We were all shaken up by it."

"I started thinking about him dying."

Cyn lit the gas under the pasta water and came and sat down at the table. "Mum, don't worry. Dad's got decades left." She took her mother's hand.

Barbara shrugged. "I hope so. I really love him, you know—more now than ever. Something seems to happen as you get older. The children are grown up, you're freer than you've ever been and life starts to be fun again. The love seems to get deeper, more intense. It's wonderful, but I've been wondering if it comes about partly because you know you might not have that much time left. "

"I can see how it might," Cyn said gently.

"Sometimes I look back and wonder where all the years went. It seems like yesterday that you and Jonny were babies. You used to wear this cute little rabbit sleep suit with ears. You looked so gorgeous. Do you remember the first time we took you on a plane and you asked if we were going to Heaven?"

"Yes, and you said we weren't exactly going to Heaven, but Ibiza was pretty close."

Barbara sat swirling the ice around in her glass. "My cancer really affected you, didn't it?"

Blimey. Where had that come from? Cyn was knocked completely off balance. She couldn't think what to say. "When I was ill," Barbara went on, "and Daddy had to look after you, you were so good. Too good. He reminded me the other day how he never had to shout at you."

"You talked about this with Dad?"

"Of course. Why wouldn't I? Tell me, is it the reason you're in therapy?"

Cyn looked down at her drink and up again. "Mum, now isn't the time for this. You've got enough to worry about."

"It is, isn't it? Please tell me."

Cyn took a sip of her gin and tonic. "I think it probably is. A lot of the time I find it hard to stand up for myself. I feel I have to be good all the time and I think maybe it's a legacy from having to be so good when you were ill." Barbara was looking forlorn. There were tears in her eyes.

"Oh, God, now I've upset you," Cyn said. "It's the one thing I promised I would never do. It wasn't your fault you got ill. I'm not blaming you. It's just that it affected all of us."

"It certainly affected Jonny. He told me."

"God, you really have been busy. He didn't tell me you'd talked."

"I'm sure he will. He said my illness made him feel insecure and frightened and that's why he's so scared to take risks now."

"He told me the same."

"Sweetie, I am so sorry." She pulled some tissue out of her trouser pocket and wiped her eyes.

"Sorry? What for? Mum, for crying out loud, you didn't choose to get breast cancer."

"I know, but you weren't much more than babies. I suppose a bit of me still feels responsible for what happened."

"You mustn't. It was out of your control."

"In my head I know that, but my heart is another matter."

"Oh, Mum." Cyn squeezed Barbara's hand.

"We should have talked about this years ago. It was my fault we didn't. When it was over you both seemed pretty OK and I didn't want to risk making you unhappy by raking it all up again."

"And all this time I've been desperate not to upset you."

Barbara smiled. "We've both been so stupid . . . So, is it good, this group?"

"I'm not sure. Some of the people are a bit weird." She paused—trying to decide whether or not to tell her mother about Joe. She decided that since they had started being honest with each other, she would. "I met a man there. His name's Joe. He was the friend I was in Derbyshire with."

"You met a man at your group? Is that wise? I mean, some of these people in therapy are terribly unstable."

What was it with everybody? Why did the whole world assume people in therapy were unhinged?

"He's not remotely unstable in the same way that I'm not unstable. Quite the opposite, in fact. He's lovely. He had a lousy upbringing, that's all." She decided not to say anything about his lack of a long-term relationship. Then she really would start to worry. Instead she said, "He's Irish."

"Catholic?"

"Yes."

"Oh, fantastic." Barbara smiled, her voice heavy with sarcasm. "Tell you what, you break the news to your grandmother, I'll alert the paramedics." Although Faye now adored Flick, her initial reaction to being told her granddaughter-in-law-to-be was Catholic had owed less to modern liberal thinking and more to late-nineteenth-century Yiddish theater.

"But you don't mind, right?"

"Sweetie, how can you even ask? If this Joe makes you as happy as Flick makes Jonny, I couldn't be happier and I know your dad will feel the same." She looked hesitant, as if she was psyching herself up to ask her next question. "Are you in love with him?"

"It's very early days, but yes. I think I am."

They were still hugging and crying when Cyn heard the sound of water boiling over. She leaped up and turned down the gas.

"So," Barbara said, "are you better now at standing up for yourself?"

Cyn tipped fusilli into the water. Once again she considered telling Barbara about the Chelsea affair, but she decided the time still wasn't right. What with the wedding and Mal's mumps, her mother had enough on her plate. She didn't need to know her daughter was doing something so reckless it was putting her in serious danger of losing her job. "I'm getting there," was all Cyn said.

"Good girl. You know, I'm really proud of you."

"Thanks."

"So are we OK?"

Cyn came back to the table and took her mother's hand again. "Mum, we were never not OK. You can be a bit bossy and interfering sometimes, but I love you so much."

"And I love you, too."

Cyn returned to the counter and began spooning pasta sauce into a microwave dish.

"So, exactly when do I interfere?" Barbara said with the teensiest hint of defensiveness. "I mean, it's not like I'm on the phone every five minutes telling you how to live your life. Just because I care about you and want to see you happy, is that interfering? Is it so wrong that a mother should want to see her daughter happily married with children? No, go on, tell me. I'd really like to know . . ."

# Chapter 17

The next day Cyn e-mailed Gazza to let him know that the auditions for the Droolin' Dream commercial had been arranged for the following Monday and that Dan, the director, was aiming to start filming the following week. Gazza came straight back to say he was happy for Cyn and Dan to be in charge of the auditions, but he would be there for the filming.

*By the way, got a freebie boxed set of k.d. Lang CDs and wondered if you would like them. Thought they might be up your street.* She couldn't help laughing. She hated lying to Gazza. In his own clumsy way, he meant well. She e-mailed back to say she would love the CDs.

She also got a voice mail message from Chelsea to say her back was improving gradually with physiotherapy and she would be leaving hospital in ten days or so. "I won't be ready to come back to work for another couple of weeks, but I will be stopping by the office to check how everything's going. Also, I want to go to Slough to see the Droolin' Dream people. I hope Gary Rossiter will be back from his vacation by then."

Cyn's heart lurched. The moment Chelsea got back, she

would find out what had been going on behind her back and there would be an explosive, probably public confrontation. The new Cyn felt she could cope with this, but she needed to be certain it would be Chelsea who was going to end up exposed and humiliated. What scared her was that the opposite might happen and that when Graham Chandler got back from New York, it would be she who was out on her ear.

The fact remained that Cyn possessed no hard, incontrovertible evidence that Chelsea had stolen her idea. Luke's evidence was useless since he believed the potentially incriminating conversation Chelsea had had in the loo was with a drug dealer called Skippy. Only Cyn knew that it was with Charlie Taylor, the ad man in L.A. who was supplying all her ideas.

Somehow in the next ten days, Cyn had to prove that Chelsea was a fraud and that when Charlie refused to come up with any more ideas for her, the fear of being found out had driven her to steal Cyn's Droolin' Dream proposal. Her task seemed so impossibly ridiculous that it was almost funny. "Right, not much pressure there, then," she laughed out loud.

She was still preoccupied with all this as she sat in the coffee shop across the road, drinking cappuccino and waiting for Joe to arrive. He was flying to Dublin from City Airport. Since his flight wasn't until three and the PCW office was pretty much on his way, he and Cyn arranged to meet up for a quick bite. He texted her to say he would be another fifteen minutes or so.

"Sorry I'm late," he said breathlessly. "Couldn't find anywhere to park."

He sat down opposite her and reached into his jacket

pocket. He pulled out a plastic bag, which clearly had a book inside. "I found this yesterday in a secondhand bookshop. I thought it would be perfect for you." He put the bag on the table in front of her. She looked puzzled. "Go on, open it," he said, smiling.

She opened the bag and took out a battered paperback. The moment she saw the title she burst out laughing and read it aloud. "*Take a Hike—The Couch Potato's Guide to Country Walks.* That's brilliant. I love it." She realized in that moment how little she minded being teased by him. In fact she adored it. It brought with it an intimacy that she had rarely felt with a man.

She reached across the table and kissed him. The kiss turned into something slightly more than a peck. It wasn't until they pulled apart that they realized the waitress was standing next to them waiting to take their order. With a certain amount of embarrassed throat clearing, they asked for a couple of ham-and-cheese paninis and two more cappuccinos.

While they waited for their food to arrive she started telling him how worried she was about not being able to prove it was Chelsea who stole her idea rather than the other way round.

"I'm wondering if I should phone this Charlie Taylor," she said. "See what he has to say."

"You could try, but I'm not sure he would say anything. You told me that his father worked with Chelsea's father. There's a family connection. At the end of the day he's bound to stay loyal to Chelsea, no matter what he really thinks of her."

"Yeah, you're probably right. I need to give this some thought. Maybe there's another way of approaching him."

Their cappuccinos arrived. As he sat scooping up the froth, a faraway look came over him.

"So," she said, suspecting what was the matter, "all geared up for seeing your mum?"

"I guess so," he said quietly, still looking down at his coffee.

"You sound like you might be getting cold feet."

He abandoned his froth scooping and looked at her. "A bit, maybe."

"That's understandable. Seeing her is going to be hard, but I reckon it'll be worth it." She decided to tell him about her heart-to-heart with Barbara the night before. "Turns out she always suspected her illness had taken an emotional toll on Jonny and me, and she's been carrying the guilt around for all these years. My only regret is that I didn't say something sooner. It would have helped both of us."

"Come on," he said gently, "you did what you thought was right. You can't start blaming yourself."

"I know, but it's hard not to." She paused. "In the group you said you weren't angry with your mother. In fact, if I remember rightly, you said you didn't feel very much at all toward her. So, has that changed?"

"Maybe. I'm not sure. You know, I realize I need to be in therapy and it is definitely helping, but I'm still not very good at all this *feelings* stuff." His face broke into a smile. "I guess it's a bloke thing."

She shrugged. "Not all men find it hard. What about Ken?"

"He's been a priest—you'd expect it."

She thought for a moment. "What about Woody Allen? And then there's Ross from *Friends*."

"OK, first, Ross isn't real, he's made-up. Second, they're both American. Americans don't do anything other than talk about their feelings. I mean, Oprah's practically had every citizen's inalienable right to emote written into the Constitution."

She gave a gentle laugh and said she got the point.

"Having said all that," he went on, "maybe I have started feeling a bit angry. I was only eight when Mum sent me away—not much more than a baby. I think about being this little mite all alone in that vast school with nobody to talk to but Bostik."

"Bostik?"

He looked a bit uncomfortable. "Bostik Bear. His eyes kept falling out and Mum used to glue them back on with Bostik. And the name sort of stuck, as it were." He smiled at the joke.

"You know what I think?" Cyn said.

"What?"

"I think you're frightened that if you start opening up to your mum, you might explode with all this rage that until now you've kept locked inside you, and she won't be able to handle it."

He nodded slowly. "It does feel like I'd be opening a massive can of worms."

"And that's not easy. After all, she's what, seventy?"

"Seventy-two," he said. "And on top of that my stepfather died a couple of years ago and she's all alone. I just don't want to give her any more upset."

Cyn reached out across the table and took his hand. "You won't be upsetting her. If she's anything like my mum, she knows how she hurt you. None of it will come as a surprise. She probably needs to talk just as much as you. It'll be a relief."

"You are very wise, Ms. Fishbein, do you know that?"

After lunch she walked him to his car. It was only as they stood with their arms around each other saying good-bye that she realized she hadn't mentioned Harmony's party on Thursday. She explained. "Please say you can come. I really want you to meet Hugh and Harms."

"Of course. I wouldn't miss it. Plus it'll give me a chance to talk to Hugh about his screenplay. I've finished it and it really is as brilliant as I first thought. A mate of mine from Paramount is in town. I gave it to him to look at."

"Omigod! Huge'll be over the moon."

"I know, but I don't want to get his hopes up. Nine times out of ten, these things come to nothing."

"Don't worry, he understands that," Cyn said.

"OK, so see you Thursday, then. And enjoy therapy tonight—if *enjoy* is the right word."

"Joe, you know I could always tell the group about us seeing each other. It's just that I can't help feeling it needs to be done sooner rather than later."

He wouldn't hear of it. "Our relationship is half my responsibility and we have to tell them together. I don't want you taking this whole thing on your shoulders. Now, promise me you won't say anything."

"God, I love it when you take control," she said, making out she was joking, but secretly she was starting to feel quite horny.

He laughed and made her promise she wouldn't say anything. "OK, see you Thursday," he said, lowering his head and kissing her. She felt his hand slide under her top.

"C'mon, you've got to go," she giggled.

"I don't have to." His hand was moving toward her breast. "You could play hooky from work and we could go back to my place for the afternoon."

"I can think of nothing I'd rather do, but your mother's expecting you."

"S'pose." He kissed her thoroughly and then, reluctantly, he pulled away. Somewhere in the background country and Western music was blaring from a car radio. "Do you know what you get if you play country and Western music backward?" he said.

She thought he was being serious. "No idea. What do you get?"

"Your wife back, your truck back, your dog back."

She burst out laughing and gave him one last peck on the cheek. "Stop making nervous jokes and just go," she said.

Once again Cyn was the first to arrive at therapy. As she sat down, she saw a note written by Veronica lying on the table in the middle of the circle. Apparently it wasn't just Joe who couldn't make it. The note explained that Clementine had phoned that morning to say she thought she was coming down with flu. Cyn couldn't help feeling a moment's disappointment that Clementine wasn't going to be there. Sharp-tongued as she could be, Cyn couldn't help admiring her wit and her ability to say exactly what she thought. When she wasn't there Cyn missed her.

As the rest of the group arrived, the usual hiyas and how-are-yous were exchanged. Jenny kicked off with an emotional and rambling update on her state of mind about her haircut. Apparently she had gotten over the initial shock and was working her way through anger toward acceptance.

No sooner had Jenny finished than Sandra Yo-yo burst into tears. Apparently she'd been shopping for jeans in Selfridges, where she'd had an unfortunate run-in with their new BodyMetrics computer. "You type in your vital statistics and it creates this 3-D image of your body and comes up with the make of jeans that will fit you best."

There was silence and some uncomfortable shuffling. Sandra had been gaining weight lately and, judging by the tears, it was clear that her BodyMetrics experience hadn't been a positive one. "I crashed the damned computer and this mechanical voice booms across the entire floor: 'Error. Error. Sandra Feldman is unfittable. Sandra Feldman is unfittable.' I nearly died with the humiliation." Tears tumbled down her cheeks. Jenny handed her the box of tissues.

To make her feel better, everybody started sharing stories of their most humiliating moments. Jenny said she once went to a job interview wearing a sweater she had just taken out of the dryer and it wasn't until she came out of the interview that she discovered she had a pair of knickers stuck to her back.

Then Sandra stunned everybody by saying that when she was nineteen—in a unique moment of rebellion against her mother—she'd had sex in a cornfield. Afterward she developed an infection and her gynecologist found a kernel of corn inside her.

"Sounds like a severe case of corn on the knob," Ken the ex-priest blurted. He immediately turned scarlet and said, "Good Lord, I can't believe I just said that."

But he couldn't help laughing. Veronica said it seemed to her that Ken's earthy side, which he always tried so hard to hide and that was absolutely vital if he was to have a sexual relationship with a woman, was, at some level, alive and kicking. "Would you like to say a bit more about that?"

It turned out that Ken wanted to say a great deal more about it—including the fact that one of the reasons he joined the priesthood was because his self-esteem was nonexistent and it was a way of avoiding female rejection. "Leaving was definitely a sign that I was changing and that I was becoming more confident. I've taken the first step. I just don't seem to be able to take the next one."

For the next hour, he became the group's sole focus as everybody tried to encourage him to get in touch with his inner letch.

———

Joe phoned on Thursday morning and suggested that before Harmony's party they have a quick drink at his place. She asked him how the trip to Dublin had gone.

"Fine. Far better than I imagined. I couldn't believe it. I'll tell you about it when I see you."

She said she would get there around six. She'd been longing to see Joe's flat. It felt strange being so intimate with somebody and not seeing where he lived. Since he owned a BMW, she wondered if his flat would be posh, too. On the other hand it could be pretty ordinary. Maybe she'd gotten it wrong and Joe wasn't as well-off as she'd assumed. Perhaps he was one of those men who spent all his money on his car. There were a couple of blokes at work who spent hundreds a month repaying loans on Porsches and lived like students.

She decided to wear her Carrie Bradshaw dress—so called because whenever she wore it everybody said it was soooo Ms. Bradshaw and all she needed was a Manhattan in her hand. It was an emerald-green empire line, with a wide floaty skirt and a black band and bow under the bust. She always paired it with a tiny emerald satin bag and matching stiletto sling backs and never told a soul it was another of her cheapo Top Shop rip-offs.

Joe's Camden flat was decidedly upmarket. It was on the tenth floor of a brand-new block overlooking the canal. He'd mentioned when they first met that he hadn't been there long and it was still looking a bit bare.

As she walked in he kissed her and told her how beautiful she looked.

"You don't look bad yourself," she said, taking in his expensive navy suit and lilac check open-necked shirt. He led her through the glass brick hall into the open-plan living room. Like hers, it had wooden floors and white walls. Unlike hers, it was at least thirty feet square. At one end there was a fabulous beech and granite kitchen. The other end was a wide horseshoe of floor-to-ceiling glass. She found herself catching her breath and virtually running to the window. "Joe, this view is absolutely stunning."

"It's why I bought the flat. On a clear day, you can see all the way to Crystal Palace." He came up behind her, gently removed her pashmina and laid it down on the sofa. She felt his lips touch her neck. She closed her eyes and let her head list to one side, her neck stretching like a cat's. When she finally turned to face him, he began stroking her hair. Finally he kissed her on the mouth.

As they pulled away he asked her what she would like to drink. "I've got wine, or there's a bottle of champagne in the fridge."

"Ooh, champagne would be lovely."

She began looking around. There was the brown leather sofa that she recognized from the Habitat catalogue, a trendy steel standard lamp and a couple of canvasses draped in cloths propped up against the wall. That was it, apart from three tall stacks of taped-up cardboard packing cases and an Apple Mac sitting on a computer table in one corner. The only light came from the windows and the spotlights in the ceiling.

"Sorry the place is in such a state. Would you believe I've actually been here three months? The problem is I've been so busy with work that I haven't had time to organize anything. The sofa only came last week. Before that I had to go to bed if I wanted to get comfortable."

"But it's going to be wonderful when you've finished. You're so lucky."

He handed her a glass of champagne. "I could always come and help you," she said. "I love furniture shopping. It would be fun."

"God, I'd love you to come shopping with me. I need all the help and advice I can get. And I could see from the way you've done up your flat that you know your stuff." She blushed at the compliment.

He led her over to the sofa and they sat down. He put the bottle of Moët down on the floor beside them. As she began sipping her champagne she noticed a photograph in a silver frame on top of a packing case. She got up and looked at it. A young, smiling woman in a flowery Laura Ashley smock dress was standing in a garden holding a baby. She was gazing down at the bundle in her arms, clearly smitten. She was also the image of Joe. "This is your mother with you, isn't it?"

Joe nodded.

"She's very beautiful," Cyn said.

"Isn't she? Even though her face has aged, she doesn't look that much different now."

"It's funny. After everything you've said about her, I'd imagined some haughty ice queen, but she doesn't look like that at all. Look at her. She clearly adores you."

"I know." She could see in his face that his emotions were starting to overwhelm him. "She gave me the photograph last night. She wanted to prove to me that she really did love me and that she never stopped."

"So," Cyn said, coming back to the sofa, "did she explain why she abandoned you?" He took a couple of swallows of champagne. She got the feeling that he didn't want to go back over it; that it was all too painful and that any second he would start telling her another daft joke like the country and Western one. She made no attempt to push him. She just sat there next to him, waiting until he was ready.

He drained his glass and picked up the bottle off the floor. Then he topped off her glass and refilled his own. Bit by bit, in fits and starts, the story emerged. Sometimes his eyes filled up. At other times he seemed so detached, so male, that Cyn felt he was telling her about something that had happened to somebody else.

It turned out that it wasn't long after Joe's mother, Sheila, got married that she realized she'd made a mistake. Joe's father was happy jogging along as an accountant, but she wanted excitement. He bored her. Then Joe came along and she felt trapped and alone with a child. When Joe was seven, she had an affair and divorced Joe's father.

Des, Joe's stepfather, was handsome, wealthy and provided Sheila the excitement she was looking for. He bred racehorses and had a string of famous clients. He was also a very powerful, controlling charmer who had swept Sheila off her feet. Once under his spell, she did everything he asked, including sending Joe away to school.

"So he was jealous of you," Cyn said. "He saw you as a rival for your mother's affections."

"Pretty much." She could tell by his face that he'd reached a part of the story that he found particularly upsetting. "Anyway, apparently she missed me so much she used to cry herself to sleep. She said she begged Des to let me come home, but he always refused. So she left me." Instead of the tears she would have expected, he offered her a half-laugh.

"So how does she feel about it all now?"

"Pretty bad," he said.

"I can imagine. The guilt must have been eating her up for years. But I don't understand. When you were older she could have said she was sorry and tried to build a relationship with you."

"It never occurred to her that I would forgive her. And my stepfather was still alive. He still had her under his control. When I stopped coming to see her—apart from at Christmas— she decided that was her rightful punishment."

"Jeez, what a mess. So, did you manage to tell her how you felt?"

"Yes, but I was so nervous about upsetting her. Plus I kept getting confused about what it was I actually felt. I just hope I made sense." He paused. "I also think I started to feel sorry for her. I wasn't expecting that."

"That's because you began to realize that it wasn't just you who missed out. She did, too. The point is, you've got time to create happiness in your life, but she's over seventy. She doesn't have much time left."

"I know. That's why I really want to start getting to know her. I've invited her to come and stay with me for a few days next month."

"That's great. You just have to keep talking. The more the two of you understand about each other, the easier it will get."

"I hope so."

"And it will take time," she reassured him. "You can't rush it."

His eyes locked on hers. "You know, you really are brilliant at all this therapy stuff. You'd make a great shrink."

"No, I wouldn't." She took his champagne glass from him and put it and hers down on the floor. Then she moved her body so that it was touching his and began stroking the inside of his thigh. "You see, I'm just not sure I would have the willpower to leave my sexy, good-looking male clients alone on the couch. I'd want to climb on there with them and start undressing them."

"I wouldn't mind that," he said, watching her start to unbutton his shirt. "Of course I'd have to be your only client." His shirt open, she began kissing his chest. Soon she was trailing her fingers lower and lower along the line of dark hair. His stomach quivered. She didn't have to feel him to know he wanted her, she could see the evidence quite clearly. She made a move to undo his belt, but before she could get there he had pulled down the straps of the green dress and was planting kisses on the tops of her breasts. She felt her nipples harden. Soon, his lips were on her neck, her shoulders, her mouth. His breath was coming in rasps. She felt her heart rate quicken. The champagne and his kisses were making her head spin. She found herself taking his hand and placing it under her skirt. "Wow, stockings," he murmured, fingering the lace tops. She let out a low sigh as he eased his hand between her legs and began caressing the skin above the stockings. His tongue surged inside her mouth. He tasted of champagne. He made her open her legs further and trailed his finger over the crotch of her panties.

Unlike his, her breathing had become slow and deep. With each breath, she took in the smell of him. She could feel herself floating. It was almost as if she was outside all this and it was happening to somebody else. He pushed her down onto the sofa and lifted her skirt above her waist. First he kissed her stomach, then he began tugging at her panties. He opened her legs and maneuvered his body between them. When he parted her with his fingers, she felt the warm air on her vulva. His first touch was so gentle, but as his finger slid over her, she couldn't stop herself from crying out. "Please, please." Another gentle caress was followed by another and another. The floaty feeling became even more intense. She was oblivious to everything except what she was feeling between her legs. Cyn the person had disappeared. Instead she was pure sensation, and her body and brain had become a place where ecstasy and excitement permanently collided.

Without warning, his fingers were inside her, thrusting hard and deep. She let out another cry. He carried on like this for maybe half a minute. Finally he changed tack and started going down on her with his mouth and tongue. The flicking became harder. She arched her back. A bit of her didn't want to come. She wanted to stay here, in this place hovering just on the edge, but there was no stopping it.

She lay there panting, waiting for her pulse to return to normal. "Oh, God," was about the limit of her conversation for the next few minutes.

He pulled himself on top of her. "Can I assume from your response," he said teasingly, "that what just happened was to your liking?"

"Oh, my God."

"I'll take that as a yes, then."

When she had finally recovered she made him sit up. She reached for his trouser belt and undid his fly. His erection was huge, rock hard and straining against his boxers. She pulled at the elastic waistband and released him. "OK," she said, gently blowing a warm breath onto the tip of his penis. "Your turn."

By the time she had gone to the bathroom to touch up her hair and makeup they were running seriously late for Harmony's do.

"Oh, I almost forgot," she said, coming back into the living room and opening her bag. "I printed this out for you from the Internet. It's a list of creative writing courses in north London. A couple of them look really good." As she handed him the piece of folded paper a look of what she could only describe as profound discomfort crossed his face.

"You OK?" she said.

"Yes. Fine." Only she could see he wasn't. Judging by the way his Adam's apple was moving up and down his neck, he couldn't stop swallowing. He opened the paper. "This is really kind of you," he said, scanning the list. "I don't know what to say."

"You don't have to say anything. It only took five minutes. I hope they're useful."

"I'm sure they will be."

"Joe, are you sure you're all right?" He was quite pale all of a sudden.

"I'm fine. I think I'm just hungry."

"Me, too. I haven't eaten since lunch. Look, Harmony's thing won't go on more than a couple of hours. We'll perk ourselves up with canapés and then go out to eat afterward."

"Actually, I've already booked somewhere. I hope you don't mind."

"Great."

As Cyn went to pick up her wrap off the back of the sofa, she noticed Joe's jacket—the one he usually wore to therapy—lying next to it. The paper with Clementine's contact numbers was poking out. She could just read the top one. For a split second her stomach lurched with suspicion. Why on earth would he hang on to it? She immediately felt guilty. He wasn't hanging on to it. He had simply forgotten to throw it away. It was easily done. Nevertheless she couldn't quite let it go.

"So, have you had any more thoughts about how to handle the Clementine situation?" she said.

He rolled his eyes as if to say "I'm trying not to think about it," which she couldn't help finding reassuring. "No. I keep putting it off. I really have to give it some thought."

He opened the front door and stood back to let her go in front of him. "By the way, over dinner there's something I really need to talk to you about."

She turned to face him. "God, the other night at the hotel—you were trying to tell me something then. Now I feel awful. What with Dad and everything, I completely for-got. I am so sorry."

"There's nothing to be sorry for."

"So, what is it you want to tell me? Is it something to do with your job?"

"Not really," he said. "Look, let's get going and talk later."

# *Chapter* 18

The salon was one giant air-kiss of A-list celebrities. Cyn turned to Joe and said the only person she didn't recognize was herself. As they made their way past the row of basins to the bar, they overheard Jerry Hall and Trudie Styler gossiping about kids and schools. Kylie Minogue was having a mock fight with Sting, who seemed to have had a few and was pretending to try to feel her bum. George Michael and Boy George were in a huddle bitching about Graham Norton's jungle-pattern shirt, which they decided had to have come from the *Lion King* gift shop.

Among the sartorial hits, there were the inevitable duds: Vivienne Westwood looked like she'd just been out riding with the prince regent, and Christina Aguilera gave every impression of having gotten her PVC hot pants off a stall at Shepherd's Bush market. Laurent, in his tapered stone-washed jeans and Vive Tagine Libre! T-shirt, didn't stand out for a second.

Harmony appeared out of the crowd, dragging a rather bemused and overwhelmed Laurent by the hand. Without doubt her dress belonged on the list of sartorial hits. She looked like Greta Garbo in her backless ivory satin halter neck. "God, you look amazing," Cyn said.

"D'you like it? Laurent helped me choose it." She was conspicuously unsteady on her feet. The salon had been closed all afternoon to get ready for the party; Cyn decided she must have been on the champagne since lunchtime. "Between you and me, I think the reason he likes the dress so much is because you can't wear a bra with it and he enjoys watching my nipples jigging about."

"What am I to do wiz her?" Laurent laughed with an open-palmed shrug. "She ees wicked, a vulgarian, *non*? Tell me, are all ze women in Liverpool so earthy?"

"Pretty much," Cyn said. "Particularly when they've had a few." She was just about to introduce Joe, but Harmony saved her the trouble.

"So, you must be Joe," she gushed, kissing him on both cheeks. "Well, I have to say, you are severely cute. Are there any more like you at home?" She turned back to Cyn. "I tell you, this man is a serious hottie."

Joe seemed to realize she was pissed and thanked her for the compliment.

"I just want you to know, though," Harmony said, holding him in her steely, slit-eyed gaze, "that little Cyn here is my best friend. Anybody who hurts little Cyn hurts me. And I don't take kindly to being hurt. Do we understand each other?"

"She's had a skinful," Cyn muttered to Joe. "Just ignore her."

The next second, Harmony was all smiles and asked them to excuse her because she and Laurent needed to mingle. "Ooh, look, there's Princess Michael of Kent."

"But why ees a woman called Michael?" Laurent said as they disappeared back into the crowd. "I do not understand."

———

A waitress appeared carrying a tray of champagne. Joe picked up two glasses and handed one to Cyn. "What was all that about?" He seemed amused more than anything. "I got the impression that if I put a foot wrong I could end up in a concrete pillar."

"It's my fault. I told her you were in therapy, that's all, and she's just a bit protective."

"In other words, she thinks I'm a complete nut job. Great."

Cyn smiled. "Don't worry. As soon as she gets to know you, she'll realize you're perfectly sane."

"OK, until then I'll keep away from cement mixers."

"Might be a good idea," she giggled, squeezing his arm, "just for your own protection."

Just then Cyn spied Hugh. "OK," she whispered to Joe as they made their way over to him, "whatever you do, don't tell Huge his screenplay was funny. He sees himself as a thinker and seeker after truth. Even suggesting that *My Brother, My Blood, My Life* is comedy would be tantamount to telling him he's intellectual plankton. He'll have a total hissy fit. Let's leave it to the bloke at Paramount to break the news."

"OK, fine."

Cyn and Hugh exchanged kisses. "Huge," she said, "I'd like you to meet Joe. Joe's been reading your screenplay."

Hugh took Joe's hand in both of his. "This is so kind of you. I really don't know what to say."

"Don't say anything yet. I've passed it on to an old mate of mine who's now this big hitter at Paramount and he's promised to read it. His name's Ted Wiener. He's very young and always on the lookout for anything a bit avant-garde. I gave him your number and e-mail."

"Bloody hell. I'm overwhelmed."

"Not half as much as I think Ted will be when he's read it. I think you are very talented."

"So, Joe, tell me honestly, in your opinion was it my attempt at post–existential nihilism that sold it to you?"

"Funny you should say that. I think maybe it was."

"And what about that scene in the condemned cell with the twins' mother? I really tried to create a collision of spiritual ennui and torment. "

"And I think you did it brilliantly,"

"Well, I have to say it's wonderful to find somebody who really understands what I'm trying to communicate." He turned to Cyn. "I have to say, you made a brilliant choice when you decided to start seeing this man. And thank you for showing him the screenplay."

"I didn't really. He just picked it up—which means I still haven't had a chance to read it. I feel really guilty."

"Don't. The important thing is that *My Brother, My Blood, My Life* is being read by people with true insight. What more could I want? Not that I don't value your opinion, of course . . ."

"It's all right, Huge," she said, offering him a reassuring smile. "I'm not offended."

The three of them stood chatting. After a few minutes Cyn spotted a chap she didn't recognize. He was tiny and South American looking. He was wearing a sleeveless sheepskin jerkin with the zip open, revealing a tan that was impossibly ocher, even for somebody from South America. "Anybody know who that is?" she said.

"Ah, you clearly missed Harmony's welcome-on-board speech. That is Atahualpa, the stylist she poached from John Frieda and our guest of honor. He's from Peru and, looking at him, he has a butt like a perfectly ripe cantaloupe." Hugh bit his bottom lip. "Sorry, chaps, you're going to have to excuse me." He turned to thank Joe again for all his efforts and the two men shook hands. As he walked away, Cyn stood smiling and shaking her head. First it was one of the Lima Dreamers, now this Atahualpa. What was it with Huge and blokes from Peru?

No sooner had Hugh disappeared than a short, bald, medicine ball of a man, a fat cigar in his hand, hovered into view, arms outstretched in greeting. "Son of a gun! I do not believe this." An obviously American man in his sixties threw his arms around Joe. "Jo-seph! Bubbie! How are you?"

"Barney! What are you doing here? You don't have a hair on your head."

"I'm with my wife. Brandy comes here to have her hair done whenever we're in London. She's over there, talking to Jerry Hall. So, how long has it been? Let me look at you." Now he was pinching Joe's cheek as if he were a little boy. "You've filled out. Success must agree with you. You still keeping fit?"

"I try, but you know what with work, it isn't always easy."

"Tell me about it," Barney laughed, slapping his paunch. He turned to Cyn and drew heavily on his cigar. "And precisely when," he said to Joe, "were you planning to introduce me to this vision of feminine loveliness standing next to you?"

Cyn couldn't help blushing.

"I'm sorry." Joe turned to Cyn. "This is Cynthia Fishbein. Cyn, I'd like you to meet Barney Weintraub. Barney is . . ." Joe cleared his throat anxiously, ". . . a work colleague."

"Hey, what's with the colleague? That's the extent of my intro? You're not going to say anything about me being this hot-shot film producer, who only last month was placed at number three in *Vanity Fair*'s list of top-ten movers and shakers?"

By now Cyn had picked up on Joe's awkwardness and hesitancy. She was in no doubt that he wasn't quite as pleased to see this Barney chap as he made out. She could see why. Barney Weintraub made Liberace look like an ego-free zone.

She extended her hand and said how pleased she was to meet him. Barney took her hand in both of his and kissed it.

"Young lady, the pleasure is all mine." Cyn couldn't help being amused. Barney Weintraub was a caricature of a lecherous Hollywood huckster circa 1939. She had no idea men like him still existed.

"Well, it's been wonderful seeing you again, Barney," Joe said, "but if you'll excuse us, Cyn and I were just leaving. We have a dinner reservation." Cyn had a clear view of Joe's watch. They weren't due at the restaurant for another hour.

"You know, Cyn," Barney carried on, completely ignoring Joe. "I gave this man his first big break. I was so impressed by his work in Britain that I hired him to come over to L.A. and write *Help, I'm Turning into My Dad*. And the rest, as they say, is history. It's been a smash in the States. So, remind me, when's it coming out in London?"

"I'm not sure. Christmas, I think." Joe's voice wasn't much more than a whisper.

"Christmas—he thinks." Barney looked at Cyn. "Can you believe the man? He makes out he doesn't even know when his own film is coming out. You know the trouble with you Brits? You're all too modest."

Joe gave a halfhearted smile. "Anyway, Cyn and I really should get going."

"It'll be a hit over here as well. I guarantee." He puffed on the cigar. "So I hear you're working on a Brit flick."

Joe nodded. He put his hand on the small of Cyn's back as if to say "Let's get going." But she didn't want to leave just yet. She had taken rather a liking to Barney and wanted to stay and chat. "Joe, why didn't you tell me you've worked on a Hollywood movie? I'm really impressed." She looked at Barney. "He's such a dark horse. He never talks about the films he's edited."

"Edited?" Barney looked mystified. Joe looked as if he

wanted somebody to shoot him. "Where did you get the idea that Joe edited it? He wrote the screenplay."

"I'm sorry," she said, frowning. "I don't understand." She looked at Joe, expecting him to step in and clear up the confusion. He didn't. Instead he stood there looking as if he couldn't make up his mind whether to kill Barney or make a bolt for it.

"And how's your new project going? I hear it's taking a long time to research. Something to do with shrinks—am I right?"

"Yes. That's right." Again Joe's voice was barely audible.

At this point Brandy appeared: thirty, tops, blonde, Pammie bust, not a single working muscle in her face. She was also six feet tall: the Empire State to his Guggenheim. "Barney, ho-nee, I've just been speaking to this totally awesome man. He comes from that funny little island in Africa where there's been all the violence. It sounds totally un-believable. I suggested to him we hold a black-tie fund-raiser—get lots of actors of color to support it. Whoopi could be guest of honor, we'd get Denzel and Eddie and Morgan and I'm sure *People* magazine would make it a cover . . ."

"Folks," Barney interrupted, his face beaming with I-am-the-luckiest-son-of-a-bitch-on-the-planet pride, "may I introduce Brandy." She just about managed to maneuver her face into an indifferent smile and offer Joe and then Cyn a limp but perfectly manicured hand.

"Bar-nee. Please." She tugged at his sleeve.

"I'm sorry," he said with a shrug. "I gotta go. What the little lady wants, the little lady gets. Great to catch up, Joe. And Cyn, it was truly a delight and a pleasure." Once again he took Cyn's hand and kissed it.

The Weintraubs turned to go. "Hey, Barney, do you mind?" Brandy hissed. "I've told you my head isn't in a good place right now. If you have to come on to women, does it have to be right under my nose? It's so totally humiliating."

"Oh, Daddy's sorry, baby. So who is this guy you want me to meet?"

Joe turned to Cyn and made a comment about Brandy and Barney deserving each other, which would have been what Cyn was thinking if she hadn't been preoccupied with something infinitely more important.

"So, you're a screenwriter?" she said. At this stage she was more confused than anything else.

"Yes."

"Just a screenwriter?"

"Yes."

"Not a screenwriter who occasionally moonlights as an editor?"

He was looking at the floor and rocking back and forth on his feet. "No."

"I don't get it. Why did you lie?"

"It's complicated."

"I'm listening."

"OK, but let's go and get something to eat. We can talk over dinner."

"No. I want you to tell me now. I need to know what's been going on."

"All right," he said, "but it's so noisy up here. We need to find somewhere quiet to talk."

She led him downstairs to the basement. It was the same minimalist deal as upstairs. Limestone floor, a line of sparkling white basins against one wall, mirrors and adjustable black leather chairs along the other. She leaned against one of the basins. "Joe, what on earth is all this about?"

He rubbed the back of his neck. "Shit. I really didn't mean for you to find out like this. First I want you to know how sorry I am. I've been trying to tell you the truth for ages. I was finally going to break it to you tonight. I am a screenwriter. After I wrote *Help, I'm Turning into My Dad,* I was approached by Rowan Atkinson's company to write another comedy, this time about group therapy."

She stood there letting the information sink in. "So you write comedies? That explains the whole Woody Allen and Billy Wilder thing." It also explained the BMW and the fabulous flat.

He nodded.

"Anyway, I knew nothing about therapy, so it was suggested that I get some firsthand experience . . ."

Cyn's heart lurched. "Hang on! Are you saying you infiltrated my group? That you're there under false pretences?"

"No. Yes. Not exactly. I was at first. Then it all changed."

"Omigod. So what are we to you? Sophisticated lab rats? You watch how we behave, hear about our struggles and experiences, and then you turn it into comedy?" She was starting to feel dizzy with shock and anger. She walked across the room and sat down in front of one of the mirrors. Her face looked white. Joe followed her and stood behind her so that they were both looking at each other in the mirror.

"Please hear me out. I was never ever going to use specific details. I just wanted to get some sense of what group therapy was like—the atmosphere, the way people speak, the body language, the way people behave toward each other. Veronica wouldn't let me join until I'd had a few one-on-one sessions with her and the irony was that after I'd seen her, I realized that I needed help—that I needed to be in the group."

"Oh, please. You expect me to believe that?"

"It's true. Everything I've told you about my family is the God's honest truth."

"Well, you know what, Joe, I don't bloody believe you."

Another thought struck her. "Christ, what was I in all this? The neurotic Jewish love interest?"

"Don't be ridiculous," he snapped.

"It doesn't sound ridiculous to me. From where I'm sitting it looks like you used me. Have you the remotest idea how that feels?"

"I can guess." He pulled up another chair and swiveled hers around so that she was facing him. "Cyn, I'm sorry. I couldn't be more sorry. If it makes a difference, yours wasn't the first group I tried to join. I tried three others and from the outset I was honest and up-front with each of them about the film. The therapists leading those groups didn't want to know. When the last group told me to sling my hook, I panicked. There's millions riding on the *Analyze Them* project. I've got the director and producer phoning me, nagging me day and night, wanting to know how soon they can see a rough draft of the screenplay. I knew the only way I was going to be able to join a group was to lie. I shouldn't have done what I did—it was appalling—but I want you to understand the reason."

"But even if I did understand, which I'm not sure I do, it's still no excuse."

"Tell me—after the way you impersonated this Chelsea woman—doesn't some of what I've told you ring bells for you?"

"Joe," she said, her tone positively polar, "don't even begin to compare the two. I didn't set out to deceive anybody. I arrived at Droolin' Dream fully intending to tell my contact there who I was. Things just got complicated and I was forced to lie. I'm not happy about it. I'm not happy about it one bit, but I had no choice."

"There's always a choice," he said. "We both chose to be dishonest."

"But you used people. You used me. You used the group."

"And you're using Chelsea."

"She hurt me. I'm just getting my own back. You used the group, and what for? As comic material. As entertainment. That's despicable. Utterly despicable."

He looked down at his hands. "I'll tell the group the truth. I promise."

"I should bloody well hope so." Something else occurred to her. "God, on top of everything else, you even let me find creative writing classes for you." Her eyes were filling with tears. "Christ! You just stood there while I humiliated myself tonight. How could you do that?" It was then that she noticed the cart and the bowl full of red hair dye sitting on it. Without thinking she picked up the bowl and dumped it over his head. He didn't move. Instead he just sat there in his plastic helmet, letting the gloopy mess trickle down his face.

"OK, I deserved that," he said. He pulled off the bowl. There was a towel lying on the cart. He picked it up and began wiping his head and face. She could see the dye had already stained his skin and was leaving red streaks on his face. Served him right.

"Well, one good thing has come out of all this," he said, managing a smile, "you've finally managed to get in touch with your assertive side."

"This isn't funny," she said.

"I'm not laughing. And I'm not proud of what I've done. I fucked up."

"Yes, you did. Big-time."

"I have been trying to tell you. I tried while we were out walking. I tried later on at the hotel and like I said, I was planning to tell you tonight over dinner. You have my word."

"I'm not sure what that's worth anymore." Her voice was quiet and trembling. "I'm going home now."

"I'll take you."

"No, I'd rather be on my own." She picked up her bag, walked over to the emergency exit—which was off—and pushed the bar. As she climbed the basement steps to the street, Joe grabbed her arm. "I really am sorry, you know. Please, just come and have dinner and let me explain everything."

"I think I've heard enough. Joe, I'm really not sure where this leaves us. Right now I feel like I don't ever want to see you again."

"I can understand that."

She pulled her arm from his grasp. "Taxi!"

# Chapter 19

She sat in the taxi staring out of the window, but seeing nothing. Despite his miserable upbringing—if that was even true—Joe had seemed so upright, so decent, so honest. The flaws in his character were all about emotional commitment. She would have been devastated—God knows—but she could have better understood it if he had taken her to one side tonight and dumped her. But this. A single tear trickled down her cheek.

Of course, she'd half sensed something wasn't right. It wasn't as if she hadn't wondered why he avoided talking about his job. Why hadn't she pushed him on it, insisted on an explanation? How could she have been so naive? On top of the shock and hurt, she felt like such a fool.

When she got home she took off her Carrie Bradshaw dress, left it on the floor with the rest of her clothes and fell into bed. She lay there replaying the tape of their relationship. There had been so much intimacy between them—not just sex, but emotional intimacy. She'd told him about her family, her childhood. She'd made herself vulnerable and she thought he had, too. She'd trusted him. She'd fallen in love with him.

Now he was telling her that their relationship had been nothing more than a farce and a sham. She had no idea how much of what he'd told her about his life was true. Maybe none of it was.

Chinks of daylight were beginning to appear through the curtains by the time she fell asleep. When her alarm woke her at seven, her head was pounding. She thought about taking the day off and working from home, but doubted whether she'd get anything done. Instead she took a couple of Tylenol, fed Morris and took a long hot shower.

She was just pulling into the PCW car park when her mobile rang. The caller display told her it was Harmony. "What happened to you two last night?" she said, sounding more than a tad put out. "The pair of you buggered off without even saying good-bye."

"I'm sorry, Harms. I was so upset I wasn't thinking."

"What were you upset about?"

Cyn told her.

"Bloody hell. I can't believe it. How could he lie to you like that? Still, at least you know he isn't mad. Not that it helps."

She told Harmony about the hair dye.

"That showed him," Harmony said. "Good for you."

"Do you know, it felt fantastic."

"God, to think I was about to eat humble pie and tell you how great I thought Joe was. So I take it you've finished with him?"

"I didn't come out and say it, exactly. I just ran off. But I don't see how I can forgive him. The way he used me—not to mention the group—is inexcusable."

Harmony didn't say anything for a moment. "Look, I don't want it to sound like I'm backpedaling here and I'd be the first one to say his behavior was appalling, but something's just occurred to me. Don't you think it's great the way Joe's been helping 'Ewge? I mean, he's a screenwriter and he's going out of his way to help a potential rival. You have to admit that's a pretty generous thing to do."

"Or he's just feeling monumentally guilty," Cyn said skeptically.

"Maybe. I dunno. Look, how's about me and 'Ewge come round tonight to help you drown your sorrows?"

"I'd really like that," Cyn said.

They said good-bye and Cyn flipped her phone shut. So was Joe simply bad? (For bad, read damaged, emotionally scarred—whatever you wanted to call it.) Or was he a good man who had done a bad thing? If he was really sorry and if he was prepared to confess to the group and deal with their hurt and anger, didn't he deserve a second chance?

Joe was right, maybe she didn't have the right to get all snotty and climb on her moral high horse, when here she was stealing somebody's identity and lying to poor old Gazza. Trust was vital in a relationship, but so was forgiveness.

She was still mulling all this over when Hugh and Harmony arrived around eight, bearing four bottles of Merlot and a mountain of Chinese. "You know," Harmony said, spreading pieces of duck over her pancake, "years ago before my mum was born, my granddad cheated on my nan. I remember asking her once if it had been hard to forgive him."

"What did she say?"

"She was a tough old bird, my nan—from that generation of women that just got on with life, no matter what it threw at them. Anyway, she said she recognized my granddad wasn't perfect, that no human being was, and she took a leap of faith. Turned out to be the right choice. As far as we know he never put a foot wrong again."

"But she never knew if she would be able to trust him again."

"That's what I said. Her view was that no matter how close you are to a person and no matter how long you live with them, you can never really know them and you can never really trust them. Taking him back was a risk, but Gran always said, 'If you don't risk, you don't live.' " Harmony started to smile. "And judging by your recent performance, it's not like you're scared of taking the occasional risk."

It was ironic. Cyn remembered Joe saying exactly the same thing to her soon after he joined the group. She looked at Harmony. "I don't get it. You seem to be telling me I should forgive Joe. Why the change of heart? You hinted at it on the phone this morning. Until today you've done nothing but warn me against him."

Harmony shrugged. " 'Ewge and me have been doing some talking. We both feel that Joe really did put himself out over the screenplay. Maybe he's not all bad. Perhaps he does deserve a second chance."

Cyn turned to Hugh, who nodded his agreement. "Having said that," Hugh went on, "it's not me who he lied to."

"I don't know what to do," she said. "I need some time to think this through." She pincered a piece of sweet-and-sour pork with her chopsticks. "Why don't we let it drop for a bit? So," she said to Hugh, "how did it go with you and Atahualpa?"

"Great. We're meeting up for a drink next week. I couldn't believe it. Turns out that he's doing a part-time film studies degree. We spent ages chatting about movies. He really knows his stuff."

"You know what, Huge, your luck is definitely starting to change. I can feel it."

He smiled at her. "I think you might be right." A pause.

Then, "Look, if you want me to, I can always tell this Ted Wiener bloke to get stuffed. I don't want you to feel as if I'm being disloyal by carrying on with this. I'll find a home for that screenplay on my own."

"Hugh," Cyn said, "I may be feeling a bit fragile at the moment, but not that fragile. Anybody trying to sell a screenplay to Hollywood needs all the help they can get. So, have you heard from Ted yet?"

"Yeah. He rang me today to say he was sitting down to read the screenplay and would get back to me. Whatever you say about Joe, he isn't without influence. I mean, when he told you his name was Joseph Dillon—didn't that ring any bells?"

She thought back to their first date at the cinema when he told her his name. "Very vaguely. I suppose I should have Googled him, but I just didn't think."

"If you had, you would have discovered, as I did, that Joseph Dillon is the hottest new comedy screenwriter around."

"Well, whoop-de-do. Shame he's such an unprincipled git." She could feel herself getting angry and decided to change the subject again. She turned to Harmony. "So, has Laurent moved in with you at the hotel?"

"Pretty much."

"God, it's really serious between you two."

Harmony flipped open the lid on a packet of Marlboro Lights and pulled out a cigarette. "I told 'Ewge on the way over. Last night Laurent told me he loved me."

Cyn loved Harmony and of course she was overjoyed and delighted for her, but she couldn't help feeling more than a pang of jealousy—not that she was about to let it show. "Omigod, that's wonderful," she cried. "And do you feel the same?"

"There isn't a doubt in my mind."

"But you've only known each other three minutes."

"I know, but I'm certain. He's certain. I've never felt like this about anybody before. I've asked him to move in with me when the house is finished. He said yes."

"Well, I hope for your sake," Hugh said, adjusting the crease in his trousers, "that he isn't just out for your money."

" 'Ewge, we've been through this," Harmony said, lighting up. "You saw what he wore at the party last night. He's so proud he wouldn't even let me take him out and buy him a new shirt. We don't go to restaurants because he can't pay. All he wants to do is get his asylum application approved and find a teaching job."

"But you'll always be earning shed loads more than him," Cyn said. "How's he going to cope with that?"

"I don't know. I'm not denying it might be a problem, but we are just going to have to find a way through. And if we don't . . ."

"You will," Cyn said. "If you love each other, you'll work it out." The moment she said the words, it occurred to Cyn that maybe they should apply to her and Joe as well. "I'm really happy for you. Honest." She reached out, took Harmony's hand and squeezed it.

"I am, too," Hugh said. "I'm sorry if I sounded negative. I just don't want you getting hurt, that's all."

"Look, it's a risk, but like Gran said: if you don't risk, you don't live. And you know me—tough as old boots."

But they all knew that she wasn't really.

After Hugh and Harmony had gone, she went into the kitchen, found a music station on the radio and began scraping plates and stacking the dishwasher. The loud music stopped her hearing the phone. She was on her way to bed when she noticed the message light flashing.

"Cyn, hi, it's Joe. Pick up if you're there . . . OK, you're not. Look, we really need to talk and sort this thing out. What I did was wrong and I'm not proud of it. I'll try you again tomorrow." She thought he sounded so sad, so genuinely regretful. A large part of her ached for him and wanted to forgive him, but not enough to pick up the phone.

The next morning, just after ten, Cyn pulled up outside My Daughter's Wedding. As she clicked the car lock, she saw Barbara, Grandma Faye, Flick and Hugh walking toward her. This was the beginning of some kind of omnibus episode of *Queer Eye for the Straight Bride, Bridesmaid, Mother of the Bride and Grandmother of the Bride*.

"Isn't this exciting," Flick trilled breathlessly to Cyn. "I just can't wait."

Decorwise, My Daughter's Wedding was a suburban take on Louis XIV's Versailles salon. The signature color was cerise. The walls, the carpet, the silk curtains, the velvet seats on the little gilt chairs, were all cerise. The only relief came from three white fiberglass Doric columns, two full-length mirrors in heavy gold frames and several cherubim and seraphim ascending to a badly stenciled, puffy cloud heaven.

Barbara walked in and said it looked just like her cousin Estelle's living room. "Apart from all the dresses, that is." The rack of wedding dresses ran the entire length of the shop. There seemed to be hundreds of them, their fat skirts billowing under clear plastic. They were arranged in a rainbow that went from pure white to latte. The bridesmaids' dresses, equally fat and billowy, occupied two slightly shorter racks. Beyond them were the mother-of-the-bride outfits. Inside the glass counter at the far end of the shop was a display of veils, sparkly paste tiaras and blue satin garters.

Bernice Greenspan, who had run My Daughter's Wedding for the best part of forty years, hugged Barbara and Cyn hello. The last time Cyn had been here was about ten years ago when she and Barbara and her cousin Rochelle had come to buy dresses for Rochelle's wedding. Being here yet again was giving Cyn a particularly poignant—especially given the state of her love life—sense of déjà vu: "Bridesmaid revisited," she said to herself grimly. She tried not to let it get to her, but it wasn't easy.

"Barbara," Bernice gushed, standing back to look at her, "I swear you've lost weight!"

"You think so? I have been trying. But look at you. You look sensational."

"Believe me, I don't feel it. Let me introduce you to my thighs, Oreo and Hershey."

It was true Bernice could have done with losing a few pounds. An uncharitable person might have decided she could have shed three of them simply by taking off her earrings and bracelets. Bernice's "less cannot possibly ever under any circumstances be more" interior design philosophy definitely extended to her appearance. As usual she was wearing too much: too much yellow, too much lip liner, too much Diorella, too much fake tan.

Grandma Faye took one look at Bernice's taut, plastic face and whispered to Cyn, "Well, I'll give her one thing, she looks remarkably lifelike."

Barbara introduced Grandma Faye and then Flick, who was looking as excited as a five-year-old on her first visit to the pick 'n' mix counter at the candy store.

"So, this is the bride! Now, then, I don't want you to worry about a thing. I am going to find you something absolutely stunning."

Hugh, who hadn't said much so far—although his face had spoken volumes from the moment he set foot inside the shop—ostentatiously cleared his throat. Bernice's remark had apparently put his nose severely out of joint.

"Oh, and this is Hugh," Barbara said. Pause for dramatic effect. "Hugh is our wedding planner and stylist."

"Ree-ally?" Bernice was clearly impressed. Barbara's satisfaction was causing her to glow so much, Cyn felt like asking for a protective lead sheet. Bernice shook Hugh's hand and said she was certain they would be able to work together.

"I'm sure we will," Hugh said.

"So, what thoughts have you had about a wedding dress?"

Flick opened her mouth to speak, but Hugh raised his hand. "Perhaps it might be better if I explain," he said. Flick looked disappointed for a second. Then she managed a smile. "Yes, of course. You've got far more ideas than me. I'm bound to get it all wrong." Cyn was starting to feel really sorry for Flick. Hugh meant well and his sense of style was impeccable, but this was about Flick's wedding, not his. On the other hand, without him, Flick did risk turning up to her wedding looking like a human Pavlova.

Hugh launched into his discourse on classic simplicity. Bernice looked Flick up and down and said she couldn't agree more. Hugh seemed surprised, as if he'd been expecting a battle with Bernice. She led Hugh over to the wedding dress rack.

Flick was practically jumping up and down with glee. "Oooh, I wonder what they're going to choose," she squealed. Over at the rack, Bernice and Hugh were busy pulling out dresses. Cyn could just about make out what they were saying.

"I thought something waisted that just skims the tummy and hips," Hugh said.

"I agree, and an extralong sleeve to add length to the arms. Maybe with a slight flare."

"My thoughts exactly." They were an unlikely pairing, but they seemed to have hit it off in an instant.

Ten minutes went by. Then: "OK, everybody," Bernice said, "we have found *the* most perfect dress." The dress draped over one arm, she made her way over to where the women were sitting on little gilt chairs. "Flick, prepare to be amazed." She started to pull up the plastic. "Now, it may need a bit of pinning and tucking, but don't worry about that . . . . So, what do you think? Isn't this just perfect?"

"Oh," Flick gasped, putting her hands to her cheeks. "Omigod, it's gorgeous. I would never have chosen something so elegant on my own." In front of them was a simple ivory silk gown—its only embellishment tiny diamonds and drop pearls edging the sleeves, wide V-neck and hem. "And just look at the back." Bernice turned the dress round. The wide V was repeated, and from it came a short, diamond-and-pearl-encrusted train. "Isn't it fabulous? And I've got the perfect veil and tiara."

When Flick came out of the fitting room in the dress, everybody's eyes filled up. Faye spoke for everyone when she declared that Flick looked like a princess.

Of course, then the inevitable happened and it was decided unanimously that it would be a mistake for Flick to buy the first dress she tried on. The upshot was, she tried on half a dozen more, only to come back to the first.

"So, you all really like it?" Flick said, back in the original dress. "Really, really?"

Everybody assured her they adored it, that Jonny would adore it, her mother would adore it and that all the guests would adore it.

To celebrate, Bernice made them all tea, which she served in pink and gold bone china cups. "Right," she said, offering round the box of M&S Belgian chocolate biscuits. "Time to turn our attention to the maid of honor."

"Again," Hugh said, pincering a finger of dark chocolate from the box, "I think we're looking at sophisticated, understated chic."

While Hugh and Bernice adjourned to one of the racks

of bridesmaids' dresses, Flick began looking along another one on the other side of the shop. "Oooh, look at this," she cried. "Now, this is stunning."

Cradling the dress, she came tearing over to Cyn, Barbara and Grandma Faye. She held it up in front of them. Cyn's stomach performed a series of horrified flips.

"I think what with my dress being so simple," Flick went on, "we can afford to go to town a bit with the maid of honor's dress."

Cyn prayed the dismay she felt wasn't showing on her face. She stood there taking in the satin bows around the hem, the frills, the net underskirts, the pale peachness of it all.

"Oh, Cyn, isn't it just to die for?"

"No doubt about it," Cyn said, aware that even Barbara and Faye, who were by no means gifted in matters sartorial, were exchanging pained glances.

By now Hugh had made a mercy dash to Cyn's side. "Hmm," he said to Flick. "I can see where you're coming from, but I have to say that I'm not altogether convinced."

Cyn watched Flick's face fall. "Oh, right. Well, if you say so."

"You see, with Cyn's complexion I think we should be looking at something a bit more—"

Cyn couldn't listen to any more. "Flick," she broke in, "take no notice of Hugh. I adore it. It's absolutely perfect. If it fits, we'll take it."

"We will?" Flick said.

"We will?" Hugh said.

"We will?" Barbara and Grandma Faye said in unison.

"Absolutely," Cyn said.

"An excellent choice, if I may say so," Bernice said, obviously not one to sabotage a sale.

Cyn put on the dress and stood looking at herself in the

fitting room mirror. She was in no doubt that the design had been a collaborative effort of Cinderella's ugly stepsisters and Elton John.

When she came out of the fitting room, Flick clapped her hands and pronounced it perfect. "Utterly perfect."

And as far as Cyn was concerned, that was the only thing that mattered.

# Chapter 20

It took another two hours to choose outfits for Barbara and Grandma Faye. In the end, Hugh and Bernice persuaded Barbara to go for a sleeveless full-length silk dress and matching coat. Everybody agreed that the soft champagne color looked wonderful with her dark skin and auburn hair. Grandma Faye chose a lavender suit with a Peter Pan collar and buttons made of tiny clusters of slightly darker lavender crystals. "You're absolutely sure this color doesn't make me look like the Queen Mother?" she said.

They were still trying to convince her it didn't when Cyn's mobile started ringing. She could see from the caller display that it was Joe. She flipped the lid and began moving away so that she was well out of earshot.

"Hi, it's me." He sounded nervous and tentative, she thought. "I don't know if you got it, but I left a message on your machine."

"Yes, I got it."

"So do you think we could get together and talk?"

"OK, but not now. I'm with my mum and my gran. We're buying outfits for my brother's wedding."

"Oh, right. The thing is, tonight I'm off on this Glasgow trip I told you about the other day." She felt relieved. His going away would leave her with more thinking time. "This Scottish director I know wants to spend a few days brainstorming some ideas for a new project," he went on. "I can't get out of it because he's taken time out specially. I'm back on Wednesday, though. I thought if you're not doing anything, maybe we could get together in the evening."

"Why not?" she said, not exactly brimming with enthusiasm.

"Look, before I go, I want to tell you again that I didn't join the group to *steal* anybody's life. Like I said, I only lied because I panicked when no other groups would have me. Along with telling the group about us, I fully intend to come clean about the film and the way I've deceived everybody. I'll take the reprimands I deserve and then I'll leave. At least that'll make our relationship easier—if we still have a relationship. But you know, the funny thing is that since I've been in the group I've realized I actually do need therapy. The whole thing has become much more than just a research project. It became about me."

"Joe, I really will think about everything you've said. I promise. But I can't talk here. I have to get back to Mum and everybody."

"OK. But please don't let one act of gross stupidity get in the way of us."

"I'll see you on Wednesday," was all she said. She was still angry, but she also knew she still loved him.

Cyn closed her phone and went over to the counter, where Faye was insisting on paying for Flick's wedding dress. "I want it to be my present," she said.

"But you've already bought us all that dinner service we wanted. This is too much."

"Don't be silly. It's my pleasure."

Flick threw her arms around Grandma Faye and said she didn't know what to say.

"You don't have to say anything, sweetie. Just have a wonderful wedding."

Cyn felt Barbara's hand on her shoulder. "Sweetie, you OK?" Her mother's face was frowning with concern. "You seem a bit tense. Who was on the phone?"

Cyn guessed the hurt must be showing on her face. Being in the bridal shop, seeing all the joy and excitement on Flick's face, had made her realize just how high her hopes for her relationship with Joe had been. She had allowed herself to think they might have a future together. But that was before she'd found out he'd deceived her. Now, since she wasn't sure if she could forgive him, she had no idea what the future held.

"I'm fine," she said to Barbara. "It was just somebody calling me from work with some ridiculous query that could easily have waited until Monday."

"It's the same with my nephew," Bernice piped up. "He's in advertising as well. His mother says his phone goes twenty-four-seven. He's so stressed he's got an irritable bowel. I said to him the other day, 'Bradley, if you carry on like this, your bowel won't be just irritable, it'll be bloody furious.' But you can't tell him. He thinks he knows it all."

"He's young. What can you do?" Barbara shrugged. Then she turned back to Cyn. "You sure it was just work?"

"Positive." She turned her smile on to full beam, but she could tell her mother wasn't entirely buying it.

Hugh shot off home because he was anxious to see if there was an e-mail from Ted Wiener. Flick said she would come back to Barbara's to pick up Jonny, who was there keeping

Mal company. Cyn said she'd pop in, too, as she hadn't seen her dad for a few days.

She arrived behind everybody else because she'd stopped off to get gas.

Barbara answered the door and said Jonny and Mal were in the living room watching the soccer game. "I'll be in with tea in a minute. You go and see your dad."

"Where are Flick and Grandma?" She said Faye had gone for a lie down and Flick was on the phone to her mum, telling her about her dress.

Cyn went into the living room. Mal was sitting on the sofa in his dressing gown. He still looked tired. It was the first time she'd noticed how thin he looked. He must have lost at least a stone.

"Hi, Dad," she said, kissing his cheek. "How are you doing?" She sat down next to him.

"Not too bad. I just wish I could get my appetite back. I'm desperate to put some fat back on."

"Dad, stop worrying," Jonny said from his armchair, where he was staring into the TV screen. "It's just a matter of time . . . Ooh, penalty! Come on, that has to be a penalty!"

"That's what the doctor keeps telling me," Mal said.

"And he's right," Cyn said. "I know it's frustrating, but you just have to go with it."

Just then Harmony poked her head round the door. She waved at Cyn.

"I just popped over to pick Laurent up. We're off. Your mum said it all went well at the bridal shop."

"Really great. You should see Flick's dress. It's gorgeous. I shouldn't say too much in front of the bridegroom, but it's got—" Suddenly Jonny and Mal were shushing them.

"Listen to this," Mal said. Cyn turned toward the TV. The soccer game had finished and the news was on. Harmony came properly into the room and stood behind the sofa.

". . . just received confirmation of a second uprising in the West African republic of Tagine. After three days of civil unrest, the military dictatorship of Colonel Moses Papaya has been deposed. The tiny paradise island, which witnessed the deaths of hundreds of its people eleven months ago . . ."

"My God, this is brilliant news," Harmony cried. "Now he's free to go back and see his family whenever he wants. I can't believe it."

She ran back to the door and yelled to Laurent to come down. As she waited for him to appear, her face started to fall. "God, I hope that doesn't mean he's going to run off and leave me."

"Don't be daft. Laurent loves you," Cyn assured her. "Of course he isn't going to run off." Cyn was doing her best to smile. So were Jonny and Mal, but it wasn't easy for any of them. They weren't thinking about Laurent choosing to leave Harmony. What had occurred to them was that after this news, he might be forced to.

A couple of moments later, Laurent came in. "I was listening on ze radio, upstairs."

Harmony ignored his shocked expression and threw her arms round him. "I am so happy for you. This means you can go home to visit. Your mother will be over the moon." She stepped back to look at him. Her face became a frown. "I don't understand. Why the long face?"

"Eet ees wonderful for my country," Laurent said. "Eet ees ze best possible news. Eet ees everysing we fought for, but . . ."

"But what?" Harmony said.

"Don't you see? Eet means I cannot stay 'ere. My country ees at peace. I 'ave no reason to be 'ere. My asylum claim ees bound to be refused. Zey will send me back."

"Don't be silly. Of course they won't. I mean, you still have enemies over there. The people you fought still want to kill you."

"I imagine that by now zey are either dead or een prison."

Harmony turned to Jonny. "Is that true? Will the government deport him?"

"I think you have to be prepared for that."

She asked Mal if he agreed. He looked grim-faced and said he was afraid he did.

The color had drained from her cheeks. "But Laurent was going to move in with me. It's all sorted. He was going to get a teaching job. We had a future planned. OK, what if we got married? Then the Home Office would have to let him stay."

"They'd assume it was a marriage of convenience," Jonny said. "Laurent would be deported instantly and you could face prosecution. Look, try not to panic. Nothing is going to happen overnight. I am going to carry on with Laurent's claim, but I'd be lying if I said I thought it was going to be successful."

"So what are you saying? Does he have some chance of being granted asylum or are you just going through the motions?"

"Let's just wait and see," Jonny said.

"But we can't just sit here and do nothing. Surely there's something more we can do. I mean, aren't there politicians we can lobby?"

Laurent put his arm round her. " 'Armony," he said gently, "we 'ave no choice. Jonny will do his best."

"I know he will. I don't doubt that for a minute, but—"

Laurent shushed her. "Come on. Let's drive to ze Heath and go for a walk."

Eventually Mal said he was feeling tired and went upstairs for a lie down. Flick and Barbara were in the kitchen getting started on the seating plan for the wedding. Cyn and Jonny were on their own in the living room.

"You look as unhappy about all this as Harmony and Laurent," she said to him.

"I am. Apart from anything else, I hate losing."

She couldn't help smiling. When they were children, Jonny always played to win. Once, when he was about eight or nine, he was playing Monopoly with her and lost. Afterward he had an almighty tantrum. This involved bending the board and jumping up and down on it until it was completely destroyed. Mal caught him, went uncharacteristically berserk and made him pay for a new board out of his pocket money.

"Mum told me the two of you talked about her cancer and the way it affected you. She and I had a similar talk."

"That's good. I'm glad. You know, I don't think I've ever felt as close to her as I do now."

"Me, too."

"I realize now how Mum's illness made me frightened of taking risks. All my life I've assumed that being brave can only end in disaster. I think I'm starting to change, though. Getting involved with Laurent's case has helped."

"In what way?"

"I suddenly found something I felt passionate about. I think it's time for me to move on professionally. I've decided to take on more asylum cases. Just one or two to start with, just to see how I get on. Then we'll see. I know some people come to this country and try to cheat the system, but I believe everybody has the right to the best possible life, free of persecution, and if that means wealthy countries taking them in, so be it. If this country hadn't taken in our great-grandfather, we probably wouldn't be here now . . . God, help me down from my soapbox."

"No. It's important you've found something that inspires

you and gives you satisfaction. In thirty years' time you won't look back and say 'if only.' "

"That's what I'm hoping."

"What does Flick say?"

"I thought she'd be scared about me trying something new, but she's all for it. I think she's really proud of me."

Cyn took his hand. "So am I, and I know Mum and Dad will be, too."

On her way home Cyn phoned Hugh to tell him the news about Laurent. "Christ, first bloody Justin lets her down and now this. How did she take it?"

"Not good."

"You know, I think my dad's got a couple of contacts at the Home Office. I'll give him a ring and see if he can put in a good word."

"I know she'd appreciate that. So, anything from Ted Wiener?"

"No, but I'm hanging on in there."

"Good for you. By the law of averages something's got to start going right for one of us."

He gave a small laugh. "So, have you made a decision about Joe?"

"Not yet," she said, "but he explained a bit more about why he did what he did, and I'm starting to understand."

"Sounds like you're moving in the right direction," Hugh said.

When she got in, she hung up her coat and went to check her messages. There was only one. It was from Keith Geary saying he would be back from Korea late Sunday night. Although he wasn't involved, his call was a sudden and unpleasant reminder of work and the Chelsea affair.

Keith thanked her for looking after Morris and asked if she could bring him into the office on Monday.

"I'm going to miss you, Mo," she said a little later as she sat at the kitchen table, toying with a tuna salad and feeding Morris bits of tomato through the bars of his cage. Morris's head made little jerky movements as he demolished the tomato.

"Miss you. Miss you. Miss gorgeous Joe." She knew perfectly well that Morris had no idea what he was saying and that his last comment was simply a random statement made up of sounds that meant nothing to him. Nevertheless, it made the hairs on the back of her neck stand up.

"You know what, Mo, I really would miss him like crazy if we split up." The bird was sitting on his perch, his head listing appealingly to one side. She poked her fingers through the bars and gently stroked his beak.

She didn't sleep well that night, but her wakefulness had little to do with Joe. There was something more immediate and urgent playing on her mind. Sometime during the next week Chelsea was coming into the office. When she did, Cyn would confront her about stealing her proposal. The problem was that she still had no irrefutable proof that the idea hadn't been Chelsea's idea all along.

She lay in bed, gazing up at the ceiling. "Hi, God, it's me, Cynthia Fishbein. Look, I appreciate how busy you are, what with all the violence and famine in the world, and I know we haven't been in touch since Brad married Jennifer, but I was wondering if you could see your way clear to helping me prove that Chelsea really did steal my proposal."

She tossed and turned for twenty minutes. When sleep refused to come, she turned on the bedside light. She reached

down onto the floor and picked up one of the Sunday newspaper magazines that had lain there for a week, unread. As she
opened it, two or three bits of junk advertising fell out onto
the duvet. She began picking them up. One of the leaflets
was a Gadget Shop promotion, advertising digital recorders
that could be used to tape phone conversations. As she sat
looking at it, an idea started to form in her mind. Suppose she
phoned Charlie Taylor in L.A. Was there even the faintest
chance that she could get him to admit he was responsible for
coming up with Chelsea's advertising campaigns? She knew it
was a long shot. Charlie had close links to the Roggenfelder
family and whatever his true feelings toward Chelsea were, he
was bound to remain loyal. He would also want to protect
his own reputation. If the advertising world found out how
he had been helping Chelsea deceive PCW it wouldn't do his
career much good. It might even destroy it.

Of course, an admission from Charlie wouldn't actually
prove Chelsea stole the Droolin' Dream proposal. On the
other hand it would prove she was a cheat and a liar.

She carried on staring at the picture of the tape recorder.
The longest of all possible shots it might be, but phoning
Charlie had to be worth a try. She tore out the newspaper ad
and slipped it under her bedside light.

The Droolin' Dream auditions were due to start at ten on
Monday morning. Dan, the chap she had chosen to direct the
commercial, had offered to hold them at his office in Soho.
This suited Cyn since holding them at PCW would have
meant people asking awkward questions. The downside was
she had to drive all the way to PCW to drop Morris off and
then head back into town.

In the end she got to PCW just after nine. Keith's face lit
up the moment he saw Morris.

"Morris. Me old mucker," he said, taking the cage from

Cyn. "So, how you diddling, then? Have you missed me?" Keith put his face up to the cage and began making little kissing noises.

"Miss gorgeous Joe," Morris squawked.

"Who's he when he's away from home?" Keith said, grinning. "Look, Morris, if you've been having doubts about your sexuality, you know you can always talk to me about it."

"Don't worry," Cyn said, "it's my problem, not his."

Keith looked up at Cyn. "What? You're having doubts about your sexuality?"

She set Keith straight. Then she said her good-byes to Morris and turned to go.

"Oh, by the way," Keith called out after her, "I got you this to say thank you for having Morris." He put the cage down on his desk and picked up a large glass jar. "It's called kimchee," he said, handing it to her. "It's a bit of a delicacy in Korea."

"Sounds exotic. What's it made of?"

"Basically it's cabbage that's been pickled in a jar, buried in the earth and left to rot. It smells a bit odd, but believe it or not, it's delicious."

"Putrefying smelly cabbage? Wow, thanks, Keith. You shouldn't have. You really shouldn't."

She stashed the kimchee in the tiny luggage compartment at the back of the Smart Car. Eventually, of course, it would end up in the bin, but since it was a present she didn't have the heart to dispose of it immediately. It seemed more respectful somehow to store it somewhere that could be regarded as halfway between her flat and the bin. The car was perfect. Her thinking was that it would stay there for a month or two. During that time she would forget about it. When she came across it again she would decide that by now it had to be off (not that kimchee probably went off, since it was off to start with) and feel guilt free about chucking it.

She arrived in Soho just before ten and only had to drive round for fifteen minutes to find a meter, which wasn't bad going.

Dan's office consisted of three rooms above a French patisserie on Greek Street. In Cyn's experience most commercial directors were flash types who drove Porsches with personalized license plates. Dan wasn't like that. It was one of the reasons she'd chosen him. He was in his midforties, bookish, with wispy hair and weird wire-framed German glasses. Although he was a talented director of commercials, his real passion was directing TV documentaries. Because the TV work tended to come in fits and starts and he and his wife had four kids to support, the ads helped pay the bills.

Cyn and Dan were due to see more than forty actors. The upshot was that they'd decided to hold the auditions over three days. Cyn had told everybody at PCW who mattered that she wouldn't be back in the office until Thursday. Since people were always disappearing to visit clients in various parts of the country, nobody seemed particularly bothered.

Cyn had never seen so many Audrey Hepburn wannabes. Two or three actresses actually turned up wearing little black dresses, pearls and long black gloves. One—a pinched-faced woman with thinning shoulder-length gray hair, who couldn't have looked less Audrey-like if she'd tried—even produced a cigarette holder "in order to find my motivation." When Cyn explained that her "motivation" was being provided by a box of low-fat doughnuts, she got all sniffy and "I've-actually-appeared-with-Branagh-at-the-Royal-Shakespeare-you-know" about it and left. Cyn had been tempted to ask: "What as? Third crone?"

By the end of Monday they had seen so many oddballs and no-hopers that they were beginning to think they wouldn't find anybody. Then on Tuesday at half past five, just as they were on the point of adjourning to the Red Cow across the road to drown their sorrows in double vodkas, they found the three fat women all at once. They were sisters from Bexley Heath who had absolutely no acting experience. The only reason they knew about the audition was that one of them cleaned the office of the theatrical agent Cyn had taken on to find actors. But they were outspoken, funny and totally fearless. In other words, perfect.

Finding the women cheered her up no end. The only thing bringing her down was the Joe situation. Even after what he'd told her about panicking, the other therapy groups refusing to let him join and having the director and producer breathing down his neck, she still couldn't work out what to do. Her heart wanted to forgive him, but her head was telling her to beware. On the drive over to Veronica's she thought about discussing her dilemma with the group. In one sense talking about it would be easy because Joe wasn't going to be there. On the other hand she didn't want to be put in the position where she was forced to identify him. That would mean admitting their affair. Of course she was all in favor of confessing, but she believed it wasn't her responsibility alone and that it should be done when they were both there. Nor was she about to tell the group that he had deceived them as well as her. He needed to do that. In the end she decided that raising the issue was going to be too complicated and that she should just let it go.

The session began and immediately lapsed into one of those silences Cyn hated. She sat examining her nails, feeling her usual urge to say something, anything to fill the void. She looked at Clementine, who was sitting on the other side of the circle. "So, are you feeling better after your flu?"

"I'm fine. It never really developed."

"That's good," Cyn said.

Empty seconds ticked by. Jenny sneezed. Ken handed her the box of tissues. Still nobody spoke. Cyn cleared her throat. "I, er . . . I've got this problem." She was aware of everybody's eyes—particularly Veronica's—suddenly focusing on her. "I've been seeing this bloke. I really care about him. The problem is he's deceived me."

"In what way?" Veronica asked gently.

Oh, great. It had happened exactly the way she'd predicted. Veronica had put her on the spot and she would end up identifying Joe. She wished she hadn't started this. "In what way?" Veronica prompted.

"He told me he did one thing for a living and it turned out he did something else."

Clementine burst out laughing. "Oh, come on. Get over yourself. He said it to impress you. If I had a quid for every guy who told me he was a roadie for Coldplay, I'd be a very rich woman."

"Well, I can really feel Cyn's suffering," Jenny piped up. "I think what this man has done is very hurtful."

"You know something, Jenny," Clementine shot back, "I reckon you were the kind of kid who stayed awake at night worrying about the way the ranger treated Yogi and Boo Boo."

Jenny sat there, utterly mortified, but saying nothing. Cyn was about to say something cutting to Clementine, but she didn't get a chance. The door opened and Joe came in. He took a seat between Ken and Clementine. Cyn found herself blinking with shock. First, she hadn't been expecting him. Second, he'd had his hair cut. Short. Really short. He'd practically been scalped. On the whole, that Justin-Timberlake-goes-to-Auschwitz look didn't appeal to her, but Joe had a great-shaped head and on him it looked sexy. At the same time as finding him sexy, she also felt guilty. He'd obviously had to cut his hair to get rid of the red hair dye she'd poured over his head.

He and Cyn exchanged uneasy glances. "Didn't you tell the group you were going to be away this week?" Cyn said.

"Yes, but my meeting in Glasgow finished early and I managed to catch an earlier flight."

Judging by the way everybody was looking at him, the rest of the group was more interested in his unexpected haircut than in his unexpected arrival.

"Blimey," Ken said matily, "if you were in the Marines they'd send you home to grow your hair." Joe reddened and said he was experimenting with a new look.

"Well, I think it looks fantastic," Clementine simpered. "I adore that strong, tough-guy look on a man. I bet you have muscles to match."

Veronica shot Clementine an arctic look that wiped the flirty smirk off her face. Then she turned to Cyn. "So you were saying that this man let you down by lying about his job."

Cyn felt like making a bolt for the door. She didn't want to discuss this with Joe in the room. It would embarrass her and hurt him. Instead of saying anything she looked at Veronica and gave a reluctant half-nod in answer to her question.

"Maybe you would like to say a bit more about how he hurt you?" Veronica said.

Cyn's eyes darted round the room. She was looking in every direction except Joe's.

She didn't say anything because she had no idea what to say to get herself out of this mess.

"Is it *very* painful?" Jenny asked, her concern bordering on the melodramatic.

"A bit," Cyn said meekly, by way of understatement.

"Remember, we're all here for you," Jenny added. Cyn looked at her and smiled her thanks. The seconds passed. Cyn kept shifting in her chair, trying to come up with a convincing story.

"Come on," Sandra Yo-yo said. "You know what they say. Better out than in."

More silence.

"You know," Joe said, finally, "this bloke might be really sorry for what he did and be desperate to make it up to you."

Ken asked him what made him think that and Joe said it was just a feeling.

Cyn finally turned to look at Joe. "OK, suppose he is sorry. What difference does that make? It doesn't mean I can trust him."

"So, you don't think he deserves a second chance?" Joe went on. "Surely you've done things in your life that you're not particularly proud of."

"Of course I have, but . . ."

"And isn't love about forgiveness as well as trust?"

"Ah, Joe's right there," Ken said. "As it says in the book of Matthew: For if you forgive men when they sin against you, your heavenly Father will also forgive you. But if you do not forgive men their sins, your Father will not forgive your sins."

"Hang on," Cyn said to Joe, "what makes you think I love this man?"

"I don't know. Maybe . . . a little bird told him." He said the little-bird bit as if it were in quotation marks. Hang on . . . Morris? Morris told Joe she loved him? It must have been when he came to pick her up that day they went walking. God, she'd Super Glue Morris's beak if she ever got hold of him. By now she was turning crimson with embarrassment. Veronica looked confused and said she didn't understand where the bird fitted into all this. Joe said it was just a thought, and Veronica knitted her eyebrows as if to say it was a rather strange one.

"And I suspect this guy loves you, too," Joe said. "Of course I don't know him, but has it occurred to you that maybe he sits at home at night thinking about little else other than getting married and making babies with you?" Bloody hell, Joe was telling her he loved her. Suddenly every inch of her skin was tingling. Until now she hadn't realized how much she had wanted to hear him say it.

"And men do spend time thinking about these things, just like women," Ken broke in, looking in Clementine's direction, with what Cyn took to be a longing expression.

Cyn was staring at Joe, still processing the "he loves you, too" bit. "He does?" she said in the faintest whisper.

"I'm positive he does," Joe replied. "Isn't it possible that this chap is a good bloke who just made a mistake? Maybe he was under pressure of some kind and couldn't help it."

"Joe's right," Sandra Yo-yo said. "I think you owe him a second chance."

"I think maybe I do," Cyn said. She watched Joe's face light up.

"Wow, that's fantastic," he said. Then, clearly realizing it might look as if he was referring to himself, he quickly added, "I mean, that's fantastic for your bloke—whoever he is."

Nobody seemed to know what to say next and another of those familiar therapy silences fell. As Cyn carried on looking at Joe, she couldn't help noticing his expression gradually change. He seemed to be growing uneasy. He started to bite his bottom lip. He raised his eyebrows at her, as if to say "Well, here goes." He was going to do it. He was going to tell the group about their affair and how he'd lied about his identity. She gave him an encouraging nod. She desperately wanted to tell him that when he got to the subject of their affair, she would be there taking her share of the responsibility. Then, as he opened his mouth to speak, Veronica raised a hand to stop him.

"I'm glad you made it to the group this week, Joe, because I have something very important to say that concerns you."

Jeeeeezusss. Cyn knew precisely what was coming. Veronica was going to expose their affair before Joe could. Joe threw back his head and stared up at the ceiling as if he was waiting for it to fall on him. Cyn wanted to take his hand, tell him she was with him and that it would be OK.

"Yesterday," Veronica continued, "I received a note. It was an anonymous note, which I'm pretty sure was sent by a member of this group. I would like to say that I find the idea of anybody sending anonymous letters quite despicable, and I sincerely hope that the person who sent it will have the courage to own up. Having said that, I felt that there was probably some truth in the letter's contents."

Bloody hell. Who turned them in? Who? They'd been so careful. How could anybody have found out?

"It would seem that two members of this group have been seen out together and it would seem that they are conducting an inappropriate relationship. One is Joe. The other is . . ."

Cyn's head was in her hands.

"The other is Clementine."

For a second Cyn thought she'd heard wrong, but she knew she hadn't. She was starting to shake and feel sick, as if she was about to keel over. She sat with her eyes closed, pressing her eyelids. It all made sense. She understood why he hadn't thrown away Clementine's list of phone numbers. What was more, he hadn't been in Dublin last week, seeing his mother, and Clementine hadn't been ill. The two of them had been together. She would stake her life on it.

"Oh, for God's sake," Clementine snapped, "this is ridiculous and utterly laughable." But Cyn could see from the smirk on her face that she was looking decidedly pleased with herself.

Cyn found herself standing up. "Would you all excuse me?" she said. "I don't feel very well all of a sudden. I . . . er . . . I think I might be coming down with something." Without looking back, she gathered up her coat and bag and headed for the door.

Had she turned round she would have seen Joe sitting gobsmacked and paralyzed with shock.


She supposed she should be more angry with Joe than she'd been the other night at the salon when she found out about the screenplay, but she wasn't. She was completely numb. Discovering that Joe had done something else to hurt her was a bit like somebody hitting her over and over again, and finally she shut off and stopped feeling anything.

If she was angry with anyone, it was herself. How could she not have realized what was going on? Of course he was seeing Clementine. She found herself thinking again about the list of phone numbers. She couldn't believe she had convinced herself that he had simply forgotten to throw it away. This was a man who admitted to being scared of emotional commitment. The moment things started to get heavy, he'd moved on, just as he always did. Clementine was his new conquest. Not only that, but she would be able to provide him with more fodder for his screenplay. Part of her wanted to feel sorry for Clementine, but she couldn't. At the same time as being used, Clementine had taken Joe from her. It was then that the pain kicked in. Even though she knew Joe wasn't worth shedding any tears over, she couldn't forgive Clementine for stealing him.

She'd been driving for about five minutes when her

mobile rang. She reached inside her bag. The caller display said it was Joe. She flipped the lid.

"Cyn, you have to believe me. I did not have an affair with Clementine." He sounded breathless and utterly distraught.

"Joe, save it. I'm fed up with the lies." Then, having decided he wasn't worth shedding any tears over, she found herself letting rip. Somehow, out of the numbness and shock, rage had surfaced. "Joe, you are pond life, that's what you are. Actually, thinking about it, that's an insult to pond life. What you are is the scum that lives on the top of ponds. Now just crawl back into your sewer and don't try to contact me again." She slammed the phone shut, aware that she had mixed her metaphors and that pond life lived in ponds, not sewers—hence the name *pond life*—but she didn't care. She'd made her point.

She found herself wondering who the anonymous letter writer was. It could only be Jenny, Ken or Sandra. Despicable as the act was, she realized she didn't have any bad feelings toward whoever had written the letter. The truth had come out and as far as Cyn was concerned that was the only thing that mattered.

She decided that whoever had done it must have seen Clementine slip Joe her phone number and then perhaps seen the two of them together. It was possible. She'd once bumped into Sandra Yo-yo in Accessorize.

It wasn't until she went to bed that the tears came. They cascaded down her cheeks. She heard herself sobbing like a child. How could he tell her he wanted to marry her and make babies with her, when all the time he was seeing Clementine? It was so cruel, so wicked. What kind of a sick, warped individual was Joseph Dillon?

At some stage she dropped off. When her alarm woke her the next morning, her pillow was a sodden mess of foundation, mascara and tears.

# Chapter 21

The frantic activity of the next few days came as a blessing. She had virtually no time to think about Joe.

First thing on Wednesday she was back in Dan's office auditioning actresses. They were still looking for their Audrey. All morning, women came and went, one disappointment following another. Then, after lunch, a dark-haired, gamine-faced girl walked in. Cyn noticed her eyes straightaway. They were the color of chestnuts. She was wearing a twin set and high sling backs. When she spoke she revealed a patrician voice that could have cut crystal. Cyn and Dan knew she was the one.

From then on, when Cyn wasn't in meetings with set designers or the people in charge of costume and makeup, she was in a huddle with Dan, going over the storyboard and making last-minute script changes.

She also found time to go to the Gadget Shop and buy the cassette recorder she needed before she could make that long-shot call to L.A.

Joe rang several times a day, but she wouldn't take his calls. Each time he left a message, begging to talk to her. "Cyn, this isn't what you think. I have not been seeing Clementine. You have to believe me. I can explain. I love you so much. Please phone me." He sounded like he was starring in some tacky made-for-TV romance. He even came round to her flat. Mr. Levinson from downstairs told her that on two occasions he'd come home to find a man outside the building, ringing her bell. Both times she'd been with Harmony.

Whenever she felt the sadness and anger were over-whelming her, she would phone Harmony or Hugh or go and see one of them. Since they'd both decided they liked Joe and that he was essentially a decent bloke—albeit one who had made a serious mistake by lying to Cyn about why he had joined the therapy group—they'd been flabbergasted when she told them about his affair with Clementine. They both agreed he just didn't seem the type. Cyn accused them of being naive and said there was no *type*. "OK, then," Hugh said, "why did he decide to help me?" The first time Hugh had asked her that question, she had put Joe's kindness down to his feelings of guilt about hurting her. Now she seriously doubted whether Joe possessed the capacity to feel guilt. She told Hugh she couldn't answer his question.

Hugh suggested she come and stay with him until she was feeling a bit stronger. She thanked him, but said she would rather be on her own. She knew he would only try to jolly her up and make her go to parties. Harmony offered to come and stay with Cyn. "I'll make you bacon butties," she said. "All that fat'll keep your strength up." Cyn didn't take her up on her offer either. She knew Harmony was worried sick about Laurent's possible deportation and that she wanted to spend all her time with him. "We are totally refusing to give up hope," Harmony said when Cyn asked her how things were going. "We just have to pray something will work out. Hugh's dad has spoken to his mate at the Home Office, so we're waiting to see if that has any effect."

It wasn't just Harmony and Hugh who were able to lift

her spirits. Barbara kept phoning with various updates on Mal and the wedding, which also helped take her mind off Joe. Barbara was so excited about everything that for once she didn't notice that Cyn seemed down. Cyn was grateful. Barbara had enough to worry about with the wedding. Finding out that Cyn had broken up with a boyfriend would only add to her stress.

Barbara's most important news was that Mal had started eating and was putting on weight. Not only that, he had just bought an air-conditioned pith helmet on eBay, which meant he was definitely on the mend. Weddingwise, she was in a panic because the disposable cameras for the tables that had been promised a week ago hadn't turned up. On the other hand the trial-run dinner Laurent had promised to cook had been an absolute triumph—even if his fish balls had been a bit big. Apparently, Grandma Faye had remarked that they'd been more like whale balls. On top of her panic about the cameras, she was also having problems with her thigh, bottom and midriff shaper, which Sandra had recommended she wear under her dress. "I'm wearing it around the house, but it's so tight. I feel like an Egyptian mummy—sort of Tutankhamen-does-Lycra."

The other thing keeping her distress at bay was her obsession with trying to get the commercial shot and in the can before Chelsea and Graham Chandler got back. Cyn was determined to see Chelsea knocked off her perch and it seemed to her that the only way to do that was to turn her own Droolin' Dream proposal into a first-rate commercial. By doing that she would be proving to Graham—post the Pickersgill Double Glazing fiasco—that she wasn't the hopeless flake he probably now thought she was and that she deserved to be promoted.

———

They started shooting the Droolin' Dream commercial on Friday. Cyn had told Dan she would be late because she had a meeting with her nail polish remover client, which she couldn't cancel at short notice as the chap was flying down from Glasgow.

After the meeting she came out of the large trailer and practically collided with Graham.

"Graham! It's you," she said, instantly realizing the crassness of her statement.

"Really?" he said brightly. "And there was me thinking I was Ivana Trump." Despite his jokey manner, he looked tired and crumpled. He had obviously come to the office straight from the airport.

"So, did everything get sorted in New York?"

"Just about, but it was a close thing. At one point it looked like the U.S. operation wasn't going to survive. But things are looking much better. Speaking of things looking better, how's Chelsea? I heard what happened."

"She's fine. She said she would be popping into the office sometime this week."

"Good." He put his hands in his pockets and began turning over loose change. Cyn could see he was starting to feel awkward. "You know, at some stage we need to sit down and talk about how things are working out for you here. Your idea for the Droolin' Dream advertisement was less than inspiring and then I heard how you lost us the Pickersgill Double Glazing account. I've just read Cyril Pickersgill's letter, dropping the account. It's absolutely venomous. I don't even want to know how or why you got Keith's bloody mynah bird to start imitating the old duffer. Having said the man is a nightmare, I'd love to have seen his face."

"I didn't do it on purpose, you know. I can explain—"

Graham held up his hand to stop her. "You know, Cyn,

we had such high hopes for you, but I'm worried that the job's becoming too stressful for you."

No! That simply wasn't true! The job only got stressful when Chelsea Roggenfelder made it stressful by stealing her ideas. Cyn simply couldn't listen to any more of this. She had to tell him what Chelsea had done. "Look, Graham, I need to talk to you about my Droolin' Dream proposal . . ."

"I agree, but not now." His tone was one that wasn't about to countenance protest. "I'm jet-lagged, I've got a backlog of work a mile high. I'm afraid it will have to wait until the end of the week."

"But it's really important," she persisted. "There are some things you really need to know."

"I'm sure there are, but I'm sorry, they are simply going to have to keep."

"OK, fine," she said thinly. She realized that as an apparently underperforming junior copywriter, she wasn't exactly at the top of Graham's priorities.

She went to her desk, picked up her Filofax and flicked through until she found the address of the sound stage where the Droolin' Dream commercial was being filmed. She headed for reception, giving Luke a hello wave as she went. He came running over.

"Cyn, have you managed to speak to Chelsea yet about this drug thing?"

"No, but she's popping back briefly this week. I'm sure we'll get a chance to talk." An understatement if ever there was one.


Cyn was just pulling out of the PCW car park when her mobile rang.

"Gorgeous, it's Hugh. Guess what?"

"What?"

"No, go on. You have to guess."

"Omigod! You've heard from Ted Wiener."

"He's only gone and bought my screenplay. He's crazy about it."

"No!"

"Yes!"

"You're kidding."

"I'm not."

"No!"

"Yes!"

"No!"

"OK, can we please stop this?" Hugh said, finally. "Ted Wiener really loves it. Of course it's going to need some rewrites, but in the meantime he's optioned it, which basically means he's paying me shed-loads."

"How many shed-loads?"

"Fifty thousand shed-loads."

"Bloody hell. Dollars or pounds?"

"Pounds."

"No!"

"Gorgeous, you're doing it again."

"Sorry. Oh, Huge, this is fantastic. I don't know what to say. Well done. You really deserve this."

She wondered if Ted Wiener agreed with Joe that *My Brother, My Blood, My Life* was a comedy. She wasn't sure how to broach it. Hugh was so obsessed with being seen as a "serious" writer that he was bound to take any suggestion that his screenplay was a comedy as a personal slight. In the end, he raised the issue himself.

"Of course it took someone as inspired as Ted to see the piece for what it is. He described it as, and I quote: 'a dark, deeply disturbing, black comedy.' I always knew a clown lurked somewhere inside me. Somehow I managed to harness it without realizing. Artistically speaking I think I have finally discovered where I need to be." He didn't say anything for a moment. "Look, I know how wretched you're feeling just now. I'm sorry to keep banging on about myself . . ."

"Hey, you've just had some great news. You have every right to bang on."

"OK, but I just want to say that I'm thinking about you and if you need me, I'm always here."

"I know, Huge. I really appreciate that."

The sound stage——on a small studio lot in Battersea——was like a scaled-down aircraft hangar. It was heaving with set builders, camera people and lighting men. Then there were the runners and production assistants: frantic girls with head-sets and belly button rings running around waving clipboards.

Dressing rooms ran off to the sides, while at one end there was a massive trestle table loaded with rolls, croissants and miniboxes of cereal. Cyn made a beeline for the table and helped herself to a bacon, sausage and egg roll. As she bit into it she spotted Dan giving instructions to one of the cameramen and went over to say hi.

"Everything OK?" she said as the cameraman left. Egg yolk was running down the side of her mouth. She wiped it with the back of her hand.

"Fine," Dan said. "We should be ready for a first run-through in a few minutes. By the way, have you any idea who that strange-looking bloke is over there?"

Dan jerked his head. It was Gazza. He was wearing a backward baseball cap and a black T-shirt with Film Crew written across it. He was sitting in a director's chair, reading the *Sun*.

"That's Gary Rossiter," she said. "He's the client. Prefers it if you call him Gazza."

Dan rolled his eyes. It was then that it hit her. It was all this talk of names. Bloody hell, how could she have let this happen? What with all the upset and confusion in her life, it simply hadn't occurred to her. Dan called her by her real name and Gazza thought her name was Chelsea. She had two choices: either she could keep the two men apart—not really doable without the day turning into one of those ridiculous farces where people keep getting shoved into cupboards. Or she could make up some story. "By the way," she said, "Gazza's got this thing about odd nicknames. He calls me Chel. Don't know why. Best if you just go along with it." Whoever invented that saying, Cyn thought, about weaving tangled webs when we practice to deceive, didn't know the half of it.

"He calls you Chel?"

"Yes."

"For no reason?"

"That's right. He's a bit eccentric, but he's lovely when you get to know him. Why don't you come over and meet him?"

Dan gave her a look as if to say "God, why do I always end up with the bloody weirdos?" and followed her to where Gazza was sitting.

"Great to meet you," Gazza said, shaking Dan's hand. He turned to Cyn. "Thought I'd get into the spirit of the occasion. What do you think of the outfit? I wore it when I videoed my school's production of *Hello, Dolly!* Haven't put it on since. Thought I'd get it out for an airing."

Dan rolled his eyes while Cyn assured him it was most appropriate.

"Of course," Gazza went on, "I know a thing or two about filmmaking . . . So, how about at the end, doing the doughnuts CGI? That means computer-generated image."

"Yes," Dan said thinly, "I know what it means, but why?"

"I just thought it would be great if the doughnuts could fly."

"Fly?" Dan repeated flatly.

"Yeah, and morph. One of them could morph into like . . . an Orc or something."

Cyn noticed a vein throbbing on the side of Dan's forehead. "Great idea," Dan said. "Perhaps we could also have the women morphing into hobbits?"

"I think what Dan is trying to say," Cyn stepped in, "is that having doughnuts morphing into Orcs might possibly take the commercial a bit off message."

"You're right," Gazza said. "Arty ads are OK for your Channel 4 audience, but it would go over the heads of most of the punters." He turned back to Dan. "But if you need any advice, don't hesitate to ask."

"I'll bear that in mind," Dan replied.

"Ooh, I nearly forgot," Gazza said to Cyn. With that he unzipped his shoulder bag and pulled out the boxed set of k.d. Lang CDs. "Thought these might appeal to you—you know, what with you being that way inclined. Not that I see you as a misfit or anything. And even if you were—not that you are—you're still entitled to be treated with respect. How does that old song go? All God's critters got a place in the choir—some sing low and some sing higher."

Cyn decided to rescue him before he dug himself in any deeper. "Thanks for the CDs. I really appreciate it."

"You're welcome, Chel. Anyway, I think I'll go and get a cup of coffee." He got up and headed toward the trestle table.

Dan turned to Cyn. "You told me you had a boyfriend."

"I did until recently, but we split up."

"So why would Gazza think you're gay?"

"It's complicated. It happened a couple of weeks ago. We got our wires a bit crossed over something. I think we should let sleeping dogs lie and not get him any more confused."

"Probably for the best," Dan said, amused.

He went off to have another word with the cameraman, leaving her alone. She was aware that her neck felt knotted and tight. The pressure was getting to be too much. First there was Joe, then all the Chelsea stuff and now there was the guilt she was feeling about Gazza. No matter how much she tried to justify it, she had deceived him. Not long from now she was going to have a great deal of explaining and apologizing to do.

"So," the Audrey character cooed, beaming into the camera, "with only sixty calories in each light, fluffy, scrumptious ball of deliciousness . . . do not doughnut, why not Low Nut?" She bit into a doughnut and made a face that was somewhere between discovering Dolce & Gabbana was being sold at garage sale prices and an orgasm.

"And cut," Dan called out. "Excellent." While the makeup girl went over to the actors and blotted their faces with powder, Dan got into a huddle with the cameraman. After a couple of minutes he announced they were going for a second take.

"OK, quiet, please, everybody . . ." A lad appeared with an electronic clapboard and numbers started flashing. Dan nodded at the actors. "In your own time . . ."

Cyn was sitting in a director's chair next to Gazza. She could hardly believe it was finally happening. The three fat women were sitting in the sixties blue Formica kitchen exactly as she'd imagined, speaking the lines that she'd written. She'd conceived, designed and helped bring the commercial to life. It was the first time she'd seen a project through on her own and she had never felt more proud.

Gazza winked at her as if to let her know that he was "pleased with a capital Over the Moon."

She continued watching, mouthing the actors' words,

concentrating on every expression and movement they made. She was so carried away that she barely heard the shouting and commotion coming from behind her.

"Will somebody please tell me what the hell is going on?" a voice yelled. Cyn's heart rate accelerated like a Harley on a speedway track. She knew that voice. It was Chelsea's. Dan called "cut" and along with everybody else, turned toward the door. This wasn't how it was meant to happen, Cyn thought. She hadn't bargained for this. In her fantasy, she was the one who challenged Chelsea. She was the one to go on the attack. That way she claimed the advantage. Then she noticed Chelsea wasn't alone. Graham was with her. She hadn't expected that either. Still, maybe it was no bad thing. Now at least she wouldn't have to tell her story twice.

"Who's she?" Gazza said to Cyn.

"A woman I work with. The chap with her is Graham Chandler, one of our CEOs."

Cyn was in the grip of a full-scale panic. She took a deep breath and waited. Chelsea got closer. The shouting and ranting got louder. The woman was doing her best to stride out, but she seemed to be hampered by a severely stiff back. She was leaning back, legs apart, hand in the small of her back. She looked like a heavily pregnant woman without the bump. The crew was standing around exchanging bemused looks. Nobody was saying a word. Cyn looked at Gazza, painfully aware that she was going to have to start explaining herself to him, sooner rather than later.

"Cyn," Chelsea snarled, waving her walking stick in the air like some batty old trout in an Ealing comedy. "I think you have some explaining to do, don't you?"

"How did you know I was here?" Cyn said.

Chelsea gave a smirk. "You're not as clever as you think. I was looking for you in the office when I saw your Filofax lying open on your desk."

Cyn flinched at her stupidity. "You know, Chelsea, I think it's you who has the explaining to do, not me."

"Me?" Chelsea came back with a snarl. Then she laughed. "Oh, that's cute. That's real cute. You steal my idea and now you're demanding an explanation from me? What sort of kooky, *Alice in Wonderland* world do you inhabit?"

"Cyn," Graham broke in icily, "I think Chelsea deserves an explanation."

At this point Gazza got up. "Chel," he said to Cyn, "why is your CEO calling that woman Chelsea when you're Chelsea?"

"She's not Chelsea," Chelsea said. "I'm Chelsea. Her name is Cyn. She stole my identity."

Gazza ran his hand across his forehead. "Sorry, I'm confused. So, Chel, when you told me your name was Chel, it wasn't really Chel?"

Cyn was feeling so guilty she could barely look him in the eye. "That's right," she said. "I lied to you."

He turned to Chelsea. "So, you're the real Chel."

"Let's get one thing straight, bozo. My name is Chelsea. It is not, never has been and never will be, Chel."

Gazza stood ruminating. "You know, now that I come to think of it, your voice does sound familiar."

"Of course it's friggin' familiar," Chelsea hissed. "Before I hurt my back and went into the hospital, we used to speak almost every day on the phone. In case it's escaped your notice, I have an American accent. Cyn does not."

Gazza turned to Cyn. "So your boss didn't insist you lose your accent because of the Cool Britannia thing?" Cyn shook her head. Chelsea let out another burst of laughter. "That's what she told you?"

"So could somebody please explain what is going on here?" Gazza said.

Dan said he wouldn't mind finding out either.

"This woman," Chelsea declared like some hard-nosed courtroom prosecutor, "stole my proposal and then tried to pass it off as her own. While her boss was away she took advantage of a weak, vulnerable colleague who was lying helpless in a hospital bed."

"Cyn, what do you have to say for yourself?" Graham said, sounding like he was moments from kicking her out on her ear.

Cyn pulled herself up to her full five-foot-four-and-a-half and went over to Chelsea. She was about to call her a conniving, cold-blooded, cruel, ruthless, talentless bitch and say she didn't know how she had the audacity to stand here lying, but she didn't. This was no time to lose her temper. Graham would think she was bonkers and she would lose all her credibility.

"You stole my idea," Cyn said calmly, "and you know it."

"Don't be ridiculous. Why would I steal your idea? I'm the most talented creative at PCW. Everybody knows that. You, on the other hand, have been lurching from one blunder to the next. Actually I feel sorry for you. It's obvious you've had some kind of a breakdown. Nobody in their right mind would steal the proposal after Graham had read it and already knew it was mine. You know what, sweetie, I really think you need to get yourself some help."

Cyn didn't say anything. Instead she bent down and picked up her handbag. From it she took a small cassette player. "The quality may not be very good, but I think it will explain everything. Yesterday I made a phone call to a man named Charlie Taylor. For those of you who haven't heard of him, Charlie is president of the biggest advertising agency in L.A. A long time ago Chelsea's father and his father were partners."

For the first time, Chelsea was starting to look edgy. "Oh, come on, please. Do we really have to listen to this garbage?"

Cyn pressed the *play* button: "Hello, may I speak to Mr.

Taylor, please?" Cyn paused the tape and explained that the voice was hers. She asked everybody to excuse her bad American accent. Then she pressed *play* again.

"May I ask what it's concerning?"

"Just say it's Chelsea Roggenfelder." (Cyn had decided that pretense was the only way to get past Charlie's assistant.)

"Oh, Ms. Roggenfelder, hi. Just putting you through . . . Mr. Taylor, I have Ms. Roggenfelder on the line."

"Chelsea, what do you want now? How many more times do we have to go through this? I've told you, it's over. I can't keep doing this. I have a business to run. If you can't come up with your own ideas for ad campaigns, then get the hell out of the business. It's not right for you. Instead of trying to impress your father, find yourself a shrink. You have issues with your dad that you're just not dealing with. I came up with the Skippy campaign and that's it. No more. Finito. The end."

Cyn switched off the machine, reliving the utter astonishment she had felt on the phone last night as Charlie spilled everything without her having to say a single word.

Cyn turned to Chelsea. "When Charlie refused to come up with a proposal for the Droolin' Dream campaign, you decided to steal mine. For the record, I found out about Charlie Taylor from Luke, who overheard you on the phone to him."

"Luke? Luke?" she spluttered. "What does he know? He's nothing. He's just the goddam gofer, for Chrissake. Why would anyone believe him? This is an outrage. I am going to sue your ass. Then I'll sue Luke's ass. This is slander. It's a violation of my human rights. It's, it's . . ."

"It's the truth," Cyn said quietly. She glanced across at Graham, who looked completely stunned.

"The hell it is," Chelsea roared. "You framed me. That guy on the tape is just some actor you found." She turned to Graham. Her face was red. She was starting to look pathetic and desperate. "Graham, you have to believe me." There was a nervous laugh. Her eyes were pleading. Cyn could tell that deep down she knew it was all over. "Can't you see that this is just a cheap, squalid attempt to discredit me? You have to do something. Cyn is the one who needs help, not me."

Graham let out a slow breath. "Come on, Chelsea," he said gently. "I'm going to take you home." He reached out to put an arm round her.

"Get away from me," she hissed, slicing the air in front of her with her hand. "I don't want any of you near me." A moment later she had spun round and was marching toward the main door. Cyn and Graham looked at each other as if to say "So, do we go after her?" Meanwhile, embarrassed glances were exchanged between the other spectators as they shifted uncomfortably on their feet.

Cyn found herself chasing after Chelsea. As well as recognizing that the woman was bonkers and needed help, there was something else she needed to say to her.

She found Chelsea outside, leaning against the wall of the building. She was staring up at the gunmetal sky, her breathing heavy with rage, her arms folded in childlike defiance. Cyn stood beside her, but Chelsea didn't acknowledge her presence. She simply carried on gazing skyward.

"I know I'm not blameless in all this," Cyn said, suddenly aware of the cold and wishing she had a coat. "I did steal your identity. I was angry, but that was no excuse. I shouldn't have done it."

Chelsea didn't say anything. Nor did she make any attempt to look at Cyn. They stood there in silence for maybe a minute. At one point Chelsea ripped a leaf from a low, overhanging tree branch and began shredding it.

"You have no idea what it was like when I was growing up," Chelsea said eventually. Her voice was soft now but there was no mistaking the bitterness. She turned to look at Cyn.

"To say my father had huge expectations of me is probably the understatement of the century. By the time I was seventeen I knew I didn't want to go into advertising, but he wouldn't listen. I even did my own thing for a few years, but he was devastated and we grew apart. Finally, to make him happy, I caved in and took the job at PCW. I knew straightaway I'd done the wrong thing. My dad thought up some of the most successful advertising campaigns in America. He was a genius and he expected me to live up to that. I knew I never could, but I also knew that just being me would never be enough for him. He always wanted more. The only way I was going to gain his respect was to surpass him."

Cyn's eyes were starting to fill up. "I'm sorry," she said, placing her hand gently on Chelsea's arm. "I'm so sorry."

Chelsea ignored Cyn's demonstration of sympathy, but she seemed happy to let her hand stay there, stroking her arm. "What are you sorry for?" Chelsea said. "I stole your proposal. That is unforgivable." She released the handful of leaf shreds. The chilly breeze carried them off briefly before allowing them to float down onto the pavement.

"And stealing your identity wasn't exactly an act of Christian charity. Having said that, I was pretty angry—not least of all about you making sure I got the Smart Car with the Anusol ad. Why did you do it? What had I ever done to you?"

"Nothing. You had done absolutely nothing to me." By now Chelsea's eyes were glassy with tears and she was swallowing hard. "It's just that you are so talented and I was eaten up with jealousy. I hated seeing you succeed and I wanted to hurt you. It started with the car and then I stole your proposal. I have no defense other than to say I wanted success so much, it became an addiction. I couldn't allow myself to fail. I just couldn't." Finally the tears started to tumble down her cheeks. "God, I'm such a mess."

"You are now, but things can change. Charlie's right. It's important to get some help so that you can discover the real you. When you've done that, you need to introduce her to your dad."

"Cyn, why the hell are you being so nice to me, after everything I've done to you?"

"First of all, I feel guilty because I'm not completely without blame in all this. Second, I know from my own up-bringing how a troubled childhood can affect a person. It doesn't excuse what you did and I'm still angry, but it does explain it."

"So, what do I do if my father refuses to accept the real me?"

"Come on. It's not like you're a thief or a murderer. All you are is somebody who isn't very good at the advertising business. If he can't accept that, then he really isn't worth the trouble. But my guess is he had no idea how much pressure he was putting on you, that he'll be mortified to find out how it affected you and all he'll want to do is make it up to you."

Chelsea sniffed and wiped a tear with the heel of her palm. "I don't know."

"You have to give it a try."

Chelsea shrugged. "Maybe I do."

It was then that Cyn noticed Graham standing just a few feet away.

"I take it you heard all that?" Chelsea said to him.

He gave her a half-smile and nodded. "Most of it. Come on, let's go," he said. As he turned to Cyn his expression changed. Suddenly there was steel in his eyes. "I spoke to Gary Rossiter briefly and made my apologies," he said briskly. "Luckily for you, he seems to be a remarkably generous chap. Nevertheless, you and I need to talk. Two o'clock—my of-fice. I'm not remotely happy about the way you handled this situation." She felt sick. There was no doubt in her mind that she would be clearing out her desk a few hours from now.

After Graham and Chelsea had gone, people drifted off to get coffee. Dan and Gazza held back.

"For what it's worth," Dan said to Cyn, "I'd have probably done the same thing in your position. The woman needed to be taught a lesson."

"I know," Cyn said, "but I could probably have come up with a more grown-up way of dealing with it. Look, it was wrong of me to keep you out of the loop. I should have told you what was going on."

He shrugged. "I don't think it's me you have to apologize to." He nodded in Gazza's direction. The man was looking utterly forlorn. As Dan went over to join the rest of the crew, Cyn went up to Gazza.

"I am truly sorry. I didn't set out to deceive you. It's just that the first time I met you at the Droolin' Dream office, you were convinced I was Chelsea. You wouldn't let me get a word in and the whole thing just spiraled out of control."

He didn't say anything. His hands were in his pockets and he was looking down at the floor.

"Gazza, please say something. Shout, scream, but don't go silent on me."

After a second of two he finally looked up. "I know people think I'm a bit of a prat."

"No, they don't . . ."

"Yes, they do, but it may surprise you to know that I'm not a total plank. I would have understood and I'd have helped you if you'd let me. All you'd have needed to do was explain."

"But I didn't know you would help me. I didn't know

you. I was so angry with Chelsea, I wasn't thinking straight. I just wanted what was mine and I didn't think further than that."

He nodded. "No, you didn't."

She couldn't remember the last time she'd felt so ashamed. "I've got a meeting with Graham this afternoon," she said. "He's probably going to sack me, which means somebody else will be in charge of the Droolin' Dream account. At least you won't have me around anymore."

"Chel, I said I wasn't a plank and that means I have enough brains to know a good thing when I see it. This ad is going to be fantastic with a capital Terrific and I want you around until we've finished. If Graham sacks you I shall have something to say about it, believe me."

"I'm not sure it'll do much good." She paused. "So what's happening? Are you forgiving me?"

He managed a smile. "In time I think I'll manage to get over it. I just can't believe I let you convince me you'd changed your accent because it didn't fit in with PCW's Cool Britannia image."

"Bearing in mind I came up with it in about three seconds, I thought it was pretty inspired."

She was so glad Gazza hadn't shouted at her—even though she'd had it coming. She found herself thinking about how she'd laid into Joe on the phone and called him pond life. Not that he hadn't deserved it. She couldn't help missing him, though, and she knew it would take a long time before she could put their relationship behind her. No matter how much somebody hurts you, she thought, it's impossible to love them one day and simply stop the next.

"By the way," she said to Gazza, "there's something else I lied about."

"I know, you're not a lesbian."

"Bloody hell. How on earth did you guess?"

"I didn't. It was supposed to be a joke. You mean it's true?"

Her face was contorted with guilt. Then she nodded. "You kept asking me out and . . ."

He let out a long sigh. "I know. You don't have to say any more. I was coming on too strong. It's a fault. You're not the first woman to have said it. When I like somebody I just get a bit carried away, that's all."

"But I shouldn't have said I was a lesbian."

"So that other woman, the woman you were with that night in the pub, she isn't gay either."

Cyn shook her head. "So, do you want your k.d. Lang CDs back?"

"Nah, you can keep them."

"You sure? I really do like k.d. Lang."

"Then have them. I'd like you to." They decided to go and get some coffee. "You know," Gazza said, "the Audrey Hepburn bird is really fit. Do you reckon she might be up for a film and a chicken vindaloo later?"

# Chapter 22

Graham said that what Chelsea had done to Cyn was appalling and despicable. "There can be no question of her keeping her job at PCW. Having said that, I realize she's a complete basket case and deserves a modicum of sympathy. I suggested she go back to the States, get some therapy and later on I can help her find another job in advertising, but in a noncreative role. She wasn't interested, though. I think she wants to discover where her real talents lie and make a new life for herself."

"That makes sense," Cyn said.

"Yes, but what doesn't make sense is the way you handled this situation. Chelsea couldn't help herself, but you could." Oh, boy, was the axe ever about to fall. "When this thing blew up, you should have come to me and told me what was going on. Instead you went over my head and took things into your own hands. Your arrogance is mind-blowing. Plus you deceived Gary Rossiter. A less decent and forgiving bloke would have told PCW where to go and then leaked the story to *Campaign*. Overnight our name would have been mud."

"But I thought if I came to you, you wouldn't believe

me. As far as you knew, Chelsea was the most talented person here. You had enormous respect for her. Meanwhile I was messing up left, right and center. Only this morning you said you weren't sure if things were really working out for me at PCW. Then when Chelsea confronted me just now at the studio, you turned to me and you said she deserved an explanation. Your mind was already made up. If I hadn't made that tape recording, you'd still believe her version of events."

Graham put his elbows on the desk and made a steeple with his fingers. "OK, I admit I might have taken some convincing, but that doesn't alter things. What you did threatened the whole company."

"I realize that now. I'm sorry."

"And I'm sorry I didn't see through Chelsea."

"How could you? If it hadn't been for Luke overhearing her on the phone to Charlie Taylor, the real story would never have come out."

Graham sat back in his chair. "I'll speak to him later and thank him for what he did. Maybe we should think about giving him a bit more responsibility. I always thought with Luke that if brains were taxed he'd get a rebate. Maybe I was wrong. Do you think he could cope?"

"I think he deserves a try." Cyn resolved to give Luke a talking-to about leaving his iPod at home and sharpening up his act.

"By the way, Gary Rossiter speaks very highly of you. He thinks you're amazingly talented."

Cyn smiled. "He just fancies me."

"No, it's more than that. And he's right. Your Droolin' Dream is a fantastic concept. It perfectly captures the zeitgeist. How long before you finish filming?"

"Three or four days. So does that mean you're not going to sack me?"

"No, I'm not going to sack you. I was furious, but I was never going to sack you."

"Thank you. Thank you so much." She was shaking with relief. "That's really fantastic. I don't suppose . . ." She was going to ask him if he could have a word with the Anusol people about modifying the ad on the side of her car, but Graham had already been more than generous for one day. There was no point pushing it. Instead she stood up and went to the door. It was a walk of less than ten feet. Somehow she managed to fit in at least half a dozen more thank-yous.

Since Graham prided himself on his honest and open management style, the moment he'd gotten back to the office after taking Chelsea home, he had called a staff meeting to tell everybody what Chelsea had done. The upshot was that no sooner did Cyn come out of Graham's office than dozens of people came up to hug her, pat her on the back and tell her how much they admired her. Few took the she-was-emotionally-damaged-and-couldn't-help-herself position. Keith Geary, who had loathed Chelsea more than most, had even been out and bought champagne to celebrate. Cyn found it hard to join in the revelry. Not only did she feel sorry for Chelsea, she felt monumentally guilty about stealing her identity.

"So, when I heard Chelsea on the phone in the ladies' room that time," Luke said at one point, "she wasn't talking to her drug dealer? He was really the bloke who was inventing all her ad campaigns?"

Cyn nodded. "You know, Luke, if it hadn't been for you, I would never have been able to work out what she was up to. You're a bit of a hero in all this. Thank you." She gave him a squeeze. Luke was glowing, partly with embarrassment at being hugged and partly because it was probably the first time in his life anybody had ever paid him any real attention, let alone described him as a hero.

Because Gazza and the people at Droolin' Dream wanted the commercial finished as soon as possible, they carried on filming over the weekend. This suited Cyn partly because she was anxious to get the ad finished as well, but also because she thought Joe might try calling round at her flat again. At least she didn't have to deal with him being downstairs ringing the doorbell and refusing to go away. Having to talk to him; having to listen to him begging her to take him back while she still missed him, while she still loved him, would just be too painful. What was even more painful was having to constantly fight the bit of her that wanted to pick up the phone and tell him about the Charlie Taylor tape and describe in every glorious, magnificent detail how she'd finally gotten her revenge on Chelsea.

By Tuesday, a rough cut of the Droolin' Dream ad was ready. Cyn organized a screening in the large trailer. Dan was there, along with Graham and all the other creatives. When it was over, there was a spontaneous round of applause.

"Well done," Graham said. "This is fantastic. Absolutely fantastic. I know it's going to be a huge success." He turned to the rest of the group. "I hope you will all join me in wishing Cyn every success as a senior copywriter." The applause started up again. Cyn felt herself turn pink with delight. "I'm not sure I entirely deserve this," she said to Graham. "But thank you. I promise I won't let you down."

"I know you won't," Graham said warmly. "By the way, I thought you'd like to know that your promotion comes with a company car. What would you say to a VW Beetle?"

"What would it be advertising?" She was imagining goose-stepping bratwursts or an image of Adolf Hitler pigging out on sauerkraut and going, "Some people think I was a sour Kraut, but this is the real thing!"

344                    Sue Margolis

"No advertising, this time. I absolutely promise."
"In which case, I'd say thank you. Thank you very much."

She decided tonight's would be her last therapy session. The only reason she was going was to finally confess to her relationship with Joe. It wasn't that she felt she needed or even deserved the group's forgiveness. It was more like wanting to draw a line under everything that had happened, so that she could get on with the next part of her life. Then she would say good-bye. She knew she would have to leave. For a start, the group wouldn't let her stay after she'd had an affair with a group member, but there was another reason for leaving. What had happened between her and Joe had, in a sense, been a blessing in disguise. During the huge row at the salon, she'd allowed herself to get truly angry. She hadn't hidden her feelings. Nor had she decided they weren't worth expressing or that she would be a bad person if she came out with what was on her mind. She'd just let rip. Getting angry didn't scare her anymore. She didn't need therapy anymore.

She had no idea if Joe and Clementine would be there. Given the choice she'd rather they weren't. Seeing them— Joe especially—would cause her emotions to crash-land again. But it was vital that the group heard her version of events. Afterward she would say good-bye and wish them all well.

Cyn made sure she was a few minutes late. That way she didn't have to chitchat with people—particularly Joe and Clementine—before the session began. When she arrived everybody was sitting in silence. Joe was unshaven and looked like he hadn't slept for days. Even Clementine seemed uneasy. Cyn took a seat well away from both of them and refused to make eye contact. As she took off her coat she was aware of a more general discomfort. It seemed to hang in the air like stale cigar smoke. She had no idea what had been said after she'd left last week, but it was obvious nobody wanted to go there. Cyn decided to take the initiative, but Joe got in first.

"I said it last week and I want to say it again. Clementine and I have not been having an affair."

"That's right," Clementine said. "OK, it wasn't for want of trying on my part. I admit I gave Joe my phone number, but nothing happened."

Cyn found herself giving a contemptuous snort. Still she refused to look at Joe.

"We would both like to know who wrote the note," Joe continued.

Veronica's eyes went slowly from one person to the next. Cyn could almost see the green Kryptonite rays penetrating each person's brain.

"Joe, for God's sake put an end to this nonsense," Cyn burst out. "Why are you lying? You were having an affair with me and you were seeing Clementine at the same time. That's the truth, isn't it?"

There was one of those cinema audience gasps that happens when a character gets his brains blown out or finds a severed horse's head in his bed. "No, that isn't the truth," Joe said with forced evenness.

By now Ken was looking utterly crestfallen. "Here's me finally plucking up the courage to go speed dating at the Immaculate Conception of Our Lady, while Joe waltzes in and seduces two women practically overnight. I'd give anything to have a bit of what he's got."

"Look, for the last time," Joe shot back, "I did not seduce two women . . ."

"OK, so you seduced one," Jenny snapped. Her anger seemed to have come from nowhere. Everybody turned to look at her. "At least you don't spend your entire life being ignored, the way I do. It's not fair. I hate it and I just wish I knew why it happened."

As Clementine opened her mouth to speak, Jenny flew to her feet. "Say something clever," she hissed, "and I swear I'll . . . I'll . . ." Clementine recoiled in genuine terror.

"Well, Jenny, I don't think anybody is ignoring you now," Veronica broke in. "While it is undoubtedly a good thing that, like Cyn, you have managed to get in touch with your inner devil, may I remind you that physical violence is not acceptable in the group."

Jenny sat down and took a couple of deep breaths. "It was me who wrote the letter to Veronica," she said. "It was cowardly and I'm not proud of it, but I'm just fed up with being bullied by Clementine. That comment she made last week about me lying awake worrying about the way the ranger treated Yogi Bear and Boo Boo was typical. I can't stand it anymore." She burst into tears and turned to Joe. "I'm sorry I involved you," she sniffed. "You're a good, kind man and I've got nothing against you."

"Hang on," Cyn said, finally looking at Joe. "You really weren't seeing Clementine?"

"Absolutely, categorically and emphatically not."

"But you hung on to her list of numbers. I saw it sticking out of your jacket pocket the night we went to Harmony's party."

"Clementine works for *Vogue* and a friend of mine has a daughter who's about to leave university and is desperate to get into fashion journalism. I was going to check if it was OK with Clementine if I passed on the numbers. I just thought Clementine would be a useful contact."

Cyn could barely take in what she was hearing. She'd spent a week trying to stop having feelings for Joe. Suddenly she could start loving him all over again. She sat there, stunned.

Her mind suddenly went back to the night she won the Smart Car and she first observed that good news could be as much of a shock as bad.

Joe turned back to Jenny. "You know, for somebody who doesn't have anything against me," Joe said, "you have a funny way of showing it. Why on earth didn't you just confront Clementine?"

Jenny shrugged. "I tried lots of times, but I'm not as quick-witted as her." She was looking at Clementine now. "You're so confident and haughty and you have an answer for everything. Not a week goes by when you don't make me feel inadequate or stupid. I know I can be a bit saccharine and earnest, but I'd rather be like that than the kind of person who goes round constantly hurting people the way you do."

"But I thought you knew I was just making fun," Clementine protested. "It's the way I am. I don't mean anything by it. It's all bravado. Deep down I'm not at all confident. I'm a screwup who can only feel good about herself when she's picking up men. Of course I didn't exactly have the best role model. I mean, you try having a mother who was the bloody Hooker Laureate and see where it gets you."

"The Hooker Laureate?" Cyn repeated incredulously, trying not to laugh. "Are you saying she serviced the royals?"

"She had 'By Royal Appointment' tattooed across her left buttock. She saw to them all. And it wasn't just the men, believe me. She had more than one duchess on her books."

There was a group squirm. Cyn assumed she wasn't the only one imagining Clementine's leather-clad mother going down on some coroneted and ermined old dowager.

"But you've never mentioned any of this," Jenny said.

"I was too ashamed."

Veronica suggested it was time for Clementine to start examining her past, maybe in some one-on-one sessions. Clementine agreed, but only if Jenny was made to leave therapy. She said her anonymous letter was wicked and cruel and tantamount to physical violence and that she had no place in the group.

"Look," Joe interrupted, "since we're talking about kicking people out, there are a few things I need to say."

He hesitated for a few seconds and then began to tell his story. All of it. He left nothing out. When he got to the bit about his affair with Cyn, she said a few words of her own. She told the group how guilty she'd felt and how they were always intending to own up and leave.

"As far as deceiving the group about what I do for a living," Joe said, "all I can say is that I'm desperately sorry. I showed a flagrant lack of respect."

"You did," Veronica said. "I think there is probably a great deal of hurt in the room right now."

"Ah, deception," Ken said, gazing into the distance. "The wicked worketh a deceitful work: but to him that soweth righteousness shall be a sure reward. Proverbs eleven, verse eighteen."

"God, so you're like this hot-shit screenwriter?" Clementine said to Joe, completely ignoring Ken. "Have you any idea who might play me? Charlize Theron would be good. She was fabulous in *Monster*."

Cyn was waiting for somebody to say that this wasn't really the issue, but nobody did. Even Veronica was self-consciously twisting an end of hair round her finger as if the words *Dame, Judi* and *Dench* had all just come to mind at the same moment.

"You know," Ken said, "Richard Chamberlain was wonderful as the priest in *The Thorn Birds*. Do you think he would be too old to play me?"

"Oprah could play me," Sandra said. "I know she doesn't do much acting anymore, plus she is black of course, but if we could persuade her to do it, I think she'd really be able to identify with my struggle over my weight."

Joe was quick to make the point that he had come to therapy to do research and that none of the film would be based on people in the group. Cyn could see from the looks on their faces that they were all the tiniest bit disappointed.

"I don't understand," she said. "Aren't any of you angry?"

"I feel hurt and I do feel Joe betrayed us," Sandra said, "but I think he's been terribly brave to face us all like this and I would hate him to leave the group. Although if he stays I think it should be as one of us, not as an observer. "

"I agree," Ken said. "After all, who amongst us is without sin? All have sinned, and come short of the glory of God. Romans three, verse twenty-three."

Clementine felt the same. "Joe was under stress, he panicked and made a mistake. He's said he was sorry. I think we should all move on." She said that if Joe stayed on she promised not to hit on him anymore.

Joe was clearly overwhelmed and said he didn't deserve their generosity. He agreed to think about staying on.

Sandra then suggested to Clementine that it was a bit hypocritical of her to forgive Joe while insisting Jenny was thrown out of the group. "I mean, Jenny confessed, too. It can't have been easy. I think she's been just as brave as Joe."

Clementine was reluctant, but eventually, with a bit of persuading from Ken, she conceded the point. "Guess we're both a couple of basket cases," she said to Jenny, her expression distinctly conciliatory. "I'm sorry I bullied you."

"And I'm sorry I dealt with it the way I did."

Ken was looking at the two women and smiling a beatific smile. Cyn felt herself cringe again. Unless she said something, any moment now the man was going to do a *Golden Girls* and call for a group hug.

"I just want to say I'm leaving," Cyn said. "This will be my last session." She explained that although she wasn't entirely proud of it, getting her own back on Chelsea had changed her. "That and pouring hair dye over Joe's head," she said, offering him a grin. He met her grin with one of his own and gave the top of his head a self-conscious rub.

"I think it is probably the right time for you to leave," Veronica said to Cyn with something verging on affection. "You have come to the end of a very long journey. I think you are finally where you need to be."

Cyn's eyes found Joe's. "Definitely," she said.

When the session was over, everybody, including Veronica, hugged and kissed Cyn good-bye. They all said how much they would miss her and wished her well. Jenny said she would never forget the way she stood up for her. "I'll always be grateful for that."

Soon everybody had driven off and it was just Cyn and Joe left alone on the pavement. For a few seconds they just looked at each other. Then Joe cupped her face in his hands and kissed her.

"I love you," he said.

"I love you, too."

A second or two passed. "You know," he went on, "something really changed in me when I met you."

"How do you mean?"

"From the beginning, you and I felt so right. The whole fear-of-commitment thing just seemed to fade away." He shook his head as if he still couldn't quite believe it. "The thought of you and me not being together actually fills me with dread. I don't pretend to understand exactly what happened. Veronica would probably say that being with you somehow helped me resolve my trust issues. But a bit of me thinks it's simply taken until now to meet the right woman. Whatever—all I know is that I want to be with you."

"And I want to be with you, too," she said, her face melting into a smile.

He didn't say anything for a moment. "I'm sorry I hurt you."

"You didn't mean to. It was rotten of me to assume you were seeing Clementine. I should have given you a chance to explain. And for the record, I don't really think you're pond life."

He smiled. "Actually, you said I was less than pond life. If my memory serves me correctly, you said I was the scum that lived on the top of ponds and I should crawl back to my—"

"OK, you don't have to rub it in. I know what I said. But I was angry."

"You had every right to be," he said. "It didn't look good. So, are we finally sorted?"

She nodded. "We are so sorted."

"Cue credits and slushy music?"

"I think so, don't you?"

He drew her gently toward him and kissed her again.

# *Postscript*

Cyn and Joe had been premature deciding to let the cred-its roll. There were several more important scenes to go. For a start, there was the one a month later where they decided to move in together. It made sense since Joe was practically living at Cyn's flat anyway.

After he officially moved in, Cyn decided to take a couple of weeks off work. She went to the gym in the mornings while Joe worked on his screenplay. In the afternoons they went for long walks on the Heath, followed by tea and cake at Louis's Patisserie, or shopped for furniture, rugs and blinds for his flat. They would live there eventually, but had decided to hold off moving in until they'd made it comfortable.

After the way he'd lied to Veronica and the group, Joe had thought about abandoning the *Analyze Them* project, but Cyn convinced him there was no need as long as he kept his promise not to re-create the characters from the group in the film or steal their stories. His only problem was that he'd been with the group such a short time, he hadn't done sufficient research to write the screenplay. Then one day, a few weeks before he moved in with Cyn, he happened to be calling Barney Weintraub and Brandy picked up.

They chatted for a few minutes and he ended up telling her about his predicament. It was the best thing he could have done. Apparently her therapist knew a therapist who had a friend in L.A. who ran Attention Seekers Anonymous. It turned out that a branch had just opened in London. When Joe phoned to say he was writing a screenplay about group therapy and could he come along to the group as an observer, they practically begged him to come. The group met twice a week, and after a month Joe had more material than he knew what to do with.

As far as his own therapy went, he had decided to leave Veronica's group and make a fresh start with a new, male therapist who he hoped would help him sort out some of the issues still hanging over from his childhood.

If they didn't go walking or shopping, they stayed in and made love until it got dark. Joe took to referring to those afternoons as "living in Cyn," which made her laugh. Afterward they would open a bottle of wine and cook pasta. When they had finished eating they would snuggle up on the sofa and watch *Friends* and *Seinfeld* reruns. At some point Cyn would let out a soft, contented sigh. She'd come to realize that "feeling at home" wasn't about four walls, it was about people—or in her case one particular person. With Joe, she knew she had come home.

A few days before Jonny and Flick's wedding they decided they wanted to do something utterly daft and frivolous. Joe suggested a day trip to Euro Disney. Cyn had never been and thought it was a brilliant idea.

She hadn't realized that the most important scene of all would be played out there. After they'd done the scary rides like Thunder Mountain and the Matterhorn, from which she had emerged each time with her stomach feeling like it was about to eject her entire Eurostar champagne breakfast, Cyn suggested they go on something a bit more gentle. "I know, what about It's a Small World?"

"Cyn, how old are you? Thirty-two or two?"

She made a pouty kiddie face. "Please? Come on, we've spent the whole morning on the scary rides, and it looks so pretty."

After much protest, Joe finally gave in, but she had to practically drag him onto the ride. They climbed into a carriage. About to get in behind them was a Scandinavian-looking couple with two blue-eyed children with white-blonde hair, aged about three and five. Suddenly the three-year-old boy peed on himself. Clearly humiliated by what he'd done, the poor little mite burst into tears. His parents did their best to soothe him and calm him down, but he wasn't having any of it and started crying even louder.

"You know," Joe said, turning to Cyn, "that could be us in a few years."

"What, peeing on ourselves as we attempt to board the It's a Small World ride?

"No," he laughed. "I meant that could be us, trying to cope with small children."

"Hang on—when you say us . . ."

"I mean you and me. As in a couple."

As their eyes locked, she felt her heart rate crank up several notches. "Joseph Dillon, are you asking me to marry you?"

"Absolutely." He moved in closer and began trailing his finger down her cheek. "So, what do you say?"

She didn't have to think. "Yes, please," she said.

Just then the ride started. They missed most of it because they were snogging, so afterward Cyn insisted they go round a second time.

Cyn didn't want to steal Jonny and Flick's wedding thunder, so she said nothing to her family about Joe's proposal. She knew the moment Barbara found out there would be no holding her back. Before you could say *marquise diamond,* she would have placed an advertisement in the "Social and Personal" column of the *Jewish Chronicle* announcing her daughter was engaged to a famous, drop-dead gorgeous Hollywood screenwriter.

By now, though, they'd met Joe two or three times and everybody had said how much they liked him. Barbara was particularly smitten and not just because of who he was. "Watching the two of you together," she told Cyn, "you just seem to be a perfect fit for each other. You know, I remember just before your dad and I got married, Grandma said the same thing about us. And look how we've lasted."

Joe seemed to be completely at home with the Fishbein clan. He was happy to talk soccer with Jonny—they were both Arsenal fans—or listen to Mal while he spouted forth about the e-sniping software he'd just found that could put in a bid on eBay within a hundredth of a second of the end of an auction. He didn't mind one bit when Flick demanded to hear about all the celebs he'd met or when Grandma Faye got him in a corner and started recounting long, complicated stories about the war and how her brother-in-law had been sentenced to eighteen months in Pentonville for selling black-market onions.

The final scene was Jonny and Flick's wedding. Of course the ceremony, which took place in a tent in Barbara and Mal's garden, wasn't the actual wedding. Since Flick was Catholic and Jonny was Jewish, they did what they'd always planned and had a civil ceremony a couple of days before, followed by lunch for the immediate family at a swanky French restaurant on the river. Then, on Sunday, a rabbi and priest blessed the marriage, and Flick and Jonny—surrounded by what Barbara, for catering purposes, insisted on referring to as fifty couples—exchanged the vows they had written. As far as everybody was concerned, that was the real wedding.

It went like a dream. Well, almost. The spring sun shone, not just in a namby-pamby-occasionally-poking-out-from-behind-the-clouds kind of a way. It really shone and there was actual warmth in it. Mal, who everybody said looked ten years younger since he'd lost weight, gave Flick away. She looked exquisite in her pearl and diamond wedding dress and—as it should be—Jonny couldn't take his eyes off her. The blessing took place under a white canopy garlanded with narcissi and blue hyacinths. Flick carried a bouquet of lilies of the valley.

Barbara and Mal stood next to the bride and groom, along with Grandma Faye and Flick's rather gung-ho mother, Bunty. She had spent the morning knocking back the sherry, holding forth on the delights of hunting and three-day eventing and giving every impression that she hated getting dressed up and would have been infinitely more comfortable in a pair of old jodhpurs and a hacking jacket coated in Labrador hair. Cyn stood a few feet behind the others in her *Gone With the Wind* peach creation, looking like a giant version of one of those tacky toilet-paper-roll covers. But her appearance was the least of her worries. After all the effort she'd put in to ensure she would be the perfect bridesmaid, what had happened seemed so unfair.

The day before the wedding she'd had her eyebrows shaped and her underarms and legs waxed. She'd also had a deluxe manicure (Joe asked if it was deluxe because it came with fries). When she got back she put on a face pack and sat down and wrote a thoughtful and loving message in the wedding card she'd gotten for Jonny and Flick. She'd already given them their present: a Lazeee Nights Ultra Camper camp bed. Cyn had wanted to get them something more imaginative and stylish, but Flick had specifically requested the camp bed, on the grounds that their flat only had one bedroom and they were desperate for somewhere other than the sofa to put visitors.

Thinking she was being superorganized, Cyn draped everything, including her dress, over the passenger seat of the Smart Car, which she was still driving because her company VW Beetle hadn't arrived yet. She wasn't worried about the dress getting creased because there wasn't a natural fiber in it.

She spent the night alone as Joe's mother was over from Dublin and staying at his flat. He and Sheila had a long way to go, but they were gradually getting to know each other again. Joe had wanted Cyn to meet her, but they both agreed it was probably too early. "You've still got lots of talking to do," Cyn said. "My being there will just complicate things. I'll come the next time you get together."

On Sunday Cyn woke up with that breathless birthday morning feeling she'd always had as a child. Cyn loved weddings. She loved the buildup: the last-minute panics that always seemed to involve a drink spillage and a famously capable aunt taking control and sprinkling liberal amounts of salt over the upholstery. She loved the way the top floor of the bride's parents' house became Bride Central—a girlie locker room full of antsy, hyped-up women charging around in their underwear trying to glue on false eyelashes and calm their nerves with Baileys. She loved seeing the bride walk down the aisle, filled with hope, optimism and anticipation. Most of all, though, she loved the smell: the heady collision of perfume, flowers and herring hors d'oeuvres.

The ceremony wasn't until four. Barbara had said to come over about one o'clock because that's when the hairdresser and makeup artist were arriving. Cyn stayed in bed all morning, exchanging sexy text messages with Joe, drinking coffee and reading the Sunday papers.

She got up at midday, had a shower and pulled on a pair of jeans. As she left the flat, quietly pom-pomming "The Wedding March," she couldn't help congratulating herself on how organized she'd been. She stepped into the street, filled her lungs with warm spring air and clicked the car lock. Even before she'd finished opening the door, she recoiled, hand clamped over her nose and mouth. The stench hit her like a slap or a sudden blast of heat. Some hooligan must have broken into her car overnight and filled it with decaying, putrid, rancid rubbish. But when she steeled herself to poke her head into the car, it was exactly as she'd left it. The dress, her carrier bag of bits and pieces, were detritus-free. It occurred to her—rather stupidly—that the smell was coming from outside the car. She looked round for a rubbish truck. Nothing.

She threw open the driver's-side door and then went round and did the same on the passenger side. Desperate to find out what was causing the stink, she flung open the glove compartment and felt inside, desperately hoping her hand wasn't about to come into contact with a maggot-ridden rat. There was nothing apart from an ancient, half-finished packet of Doritos and a couple of dusty tampons in their wrappers.

It was only when she opened rear door that she saw it. "Oh . . . my . . . God!" It was as much as she could do not to retch. The lid on Keith Geary's jar of kimchee—the "rotting cabbage" delicacy he'd brought her from Korea—had blown. The tiny luggage space was covered in leaked, fetid ooze—which was now even more rotten than it had been to start with. When she looked closer she could see that the trail disappeared under the passenger seat. She rushed to the front of the car and picked up the dress. The hem was touching the floor. The outer layer of skirt—the bit everybody would see—looked perfect. It was only when she lifted it and looked at the petticoats that she saw the hems were damp with kim-chee liquid.

There was no time to sponge the dress—not that mere soap would have had any impact on the smell. Nothing short of incineration could have gotten rid of it. She drove to her mother's with the windows open and the air-conditioning on full.

Her parents' bedroom contained not only the hairdresser and the makeup artist but Barbara, Flick, Grandma Faye and Flick's mother, Bunty, all in various states of unease and un-dress. "Wow, it's *My Big Fat Jewish-Catholic Wedding,*" Cyn said brightly.

Barbara's hair had just come out of rollers and was being back combed. "Hello, darling," she said from under her spiky, Phyllis Diller fuzz. "Hang your dress on the front of the ward-robe." As Cyn hooked the hanger over the door, she missed seeing her mother's nostrils start to twitch. "Good Lord. What on earth is that smell? It's vile."

"God, yeah, it's disgusting," Flick said, adjusting her bosom inside her bustier. "Cyn, did you bring something in on your shoes?"

"No, it's not dog mess," Faye said. "It's definitely vege-table. Reminds me of the East End during the General Strike when the bins didn't get emptied for weeks."

"Have to say I can't smell a thing myself," Bunty piped up. She carried on drinking her tea and munching on a shortbread finger. Cyn put her olfactory immunity down to her having spent too many years mucking out horses.

Flick went over to the wardrobe and sniffed. "Uuurgh. Cyn, it's your dress. What on earth happened?"

Cyn sat down on the bed and explained about the kimchee and how the petticoats had soaked up some of the putrid liquid.

"But you're going to stink the place out," Barbara said. "It'll put everybody off their food. Why on earth didn't you keep the dress in your flat?"

"Because I was trying to be superorganized and I wasn't expecting a jar of kimchee to burst and leak all over my car."

Flick immediately went into ultracalm nurse mode. "I know, why don't we spray the dress with perfume?"

The upshot was that Cyn walked down the aisle behind Flick and Mal looking like an antebellum meringue and reeking of kimchee heavily laced with her mother's Youth Dew. Cyn caught several people grimacing and waving their hands in front of their faces. Joe mouthed to her that she looked fantastic, which was sweet, bearing in mind what she looked like, but even he pulled a face as she got closer. Then, just as the ceremony was about to kick off, her cousin Ben, aged four, yelled out, "Phwoarrr, who's farted?"

Everybody pretended not to have heard the remark and soon all the guests were dabbing their eyes with handkerchiefs. Cyn couldn't work out if the universal waterworks had been brought on by watching Flick and Jonny gazing into one another's eyes as they recited alternate verses of "Take My Breath Away"—their magnificently tacky choice of wedding vows—or the kimchee fumes.

After the ceremony Joe was collared by Grandma Faye, who introduced him to Uncle Lou with the colostomy bag, who in turn started to bang on in a voice that the whole of Edgware could hear about the difference in symptoms between diverticulitis and colitis. Cyn was about to go and rescue him when she saw Hugh—mercifully still mumps-free—striding out toward her. His hand was pressed against his headset earpiece and he seemed deep in concentration. "Sorry, gorgeous, can't stop," he said briskly. "Laurent needs some help deciding if the cherries should be poured over the deep-fried ice cream or served separately." Having just said he couldn't stop, he then did just that. "Good God, so it's you. Look, don't take this the wrong way, but there is something distinctly niffy about you."

"You've always known how to charm a girl." Cyn smiled. She told the kimchee story again, but he was in such a flap over the deep-fried ice cream, he was only half listening. "So," she said, "how are the rewrites going?"

"Hard work, but I'm coping. But what's been fantastic is that Atahualpa and I have decided to move in together. We're starting off in his flat, but it's tiny, so we've already started looking for something bigger."

"Oh, Huge. That's fantastic news."

"But what about you and Joe? I couldn't be more glad that you two finally got together. He's a great bloke. I knew you had him wrong." She wanted to tell him they were getting married, but she felt it wouldn't be right as her parents didn't know.

They both looked up to see Joe standing next to them. "I knew she had me wrong, too," he said to Hugh. "But I had a bugger of a job convincing her."

Hugh smiled and nodded. "Look, I just wanted to say how much I appreciate you giving my screenplay to Ted Wiener. It's not much, but I'd like to take the two of you out for dinner next week to say thank you."

Cyn and Joe said that would be great. Suddenly Hugh was pressing his earpiece again. "I'll phone you. Look, I have to dash. The Lima Dreamers have arrived and I need to show them where to set up."

He jogged off. "I was about to come and rescue you from my mother and grandmother," Cyn said to Joe.

"I didn't remotely need rescuing. They're great fun." A waitress came up to them carrying a tray of champagne. Joe took two glasses and handed one to Cyn. "Your grandmother's just been pitching me a film idea. Did you know her father escaped from Poland in a milk cart?"

"Oh, God, she's not telling that story again. I hope you reminded her they already made *Fiddler on the Roof*."

"I didn't have to. Your mother made the point rather forcibly. I have to say, they're a bit of a double act, those two."

Cyn gave a short laugh. "So, did they tell you about the kimchee?"

He said they did.

"I thought the dress was bad enough. Now I stink as well."

"Of course you don't stink. There's a faint trace of something, a slight aroma maybe, but the worst has gone."

"Promise?"

"You have my word." He gave her a kiss and a squeeze to make his point, almost making her spill her champagne. "And for the record, I love the dress. I'm a big Vivien Leigh fan."

"You are such a charmer, do you know that?"

"I'm telling the truth," he protested.

"Yeah, right."

Everybody agreed that Laurent's food was glorious. His fish balls, in particular, were a triumph. Even Uncle Lou with the colostomy bag tucked into a huge plate of chicken and peanut sauce. Everybody oohed and aahed over the chocolate fountain and deep-fried ice cream—which in the end was served covered with cherries. While the guests ate, the Lima Dreamers played easy-listening pop classics with an Incan twist.

Jonny made a speech thanking Flick for loving him and thanking Mal and Barbara for having him. Flick stood up and declared that this was the happiest day of her life, and then she presented Barbara, Bunty and Grandma Faye with huge bunches of flowers. Jonny's best man, another solicitor, made a supposedly hilarious speech that consisted of several ponderous references to Jonny fulfilling his contractual obligations later that night. Mal said how much today reminded him of his wedding to Barbara.

"I can't believe we've been married for nearly forty years."

"I can," Barbara heckled, which got a huge laugh.

He said the secret of a happy marriage was to make sure you didn't go to bed angry. "You have to stay up until the problem is resolved. Last year Barbara and I didn't get to sleep until March."

As the laughter died down he began reminiscing about Jonny and Cyn when they were babies. "It seems like yesterday we were celebrating Jonny's circumcision. It was then that we realized he had his mother's balls." Finally he turned to Flick, took her hand in his and said how proud and delighted he and Barbara were to welcome her into the family. "I know it's a cliché, but we really have gained another wonderful daughter."

Barbara had the last word. She said the celebrations couldn't have happened without Laurent and Hugh and all their hard work. She proposed a toast to them, and Cyn started the applause.

After the speeches, Joe disappeared to the loo. Harmony, whom Barbara had put at a table full of Cyn and Jonny's university friends, came over and helped herself to Joe's seat. As ever, she looked spectacular. She was wearing a full-length halter-neck dress in scarlet silk. "Everybody's talking about you and the jar of kimchee," she said. "I laughed so much I thought I was going to wet myself." She leaned forward and sniffed. "God, you're still pretty strong."

"Really? Joe said it was just a slight aroma."

"Depends on your definition of slight, I suppose." She looked across at Flick, who was chatting to a group of elderly relatives. "She looks so happy."

"So do you," Cyn said, deciding Harmony looked more than just beautiful. She looked positively radiant. For once she didn't have a cigarette in her hand. "I know—you've had some news from the Home Office, haven't you?"

"We have." She started fiddling with the napkin Joe had left on the table. "But it's not what you think." She paused. "Laurent has to go back. The Home Office has said there is no reason to give him asylum since the troubles in Tagine are over."

Cyn had no idea what to say or how to comfort her. "I am so sorry. I was sure Hugh's contact would be able to pull a few strings."

"He did his best, but he couldn't help. He said he was very sorry."

"I don't understand," Cyn said. "Why aren't you more upset?"

"I've decided to go back with him."

"How do you mean? What, for a holiday?"

"No, for good."

"Don't be silly," Cyn laughed.

"I'm not. I'm serious."

"Yeah, right. Come on, you'd hate it. How would you survive without Donna Karan and Joseph round the corner? And what about the business?"

"I'm leaving Atahualpa to run it and when the renovation work is finished on the Holland Park house I'm going to rent it out."

Cyn felt her laughter disappear. "Bloody hell, you're actually serious, aren't you?"

Harmony nodded. "Deadly. You know how unsettled I've been lately." She abandoned her napkin fiddling and looked directly at Cyn. "I just felt my life lacked purpose. Well, now I think I've found it. Brandy Weintraub, you know, who's married to Barney, the film producer—well, she's setting up a charity to help the schools and hospitals in Tagine get back on their feet. Laurent's so excited. He can't wait to get back and help rebuild his country, and I want be there with him."

"So what will you do?"

She shrugged. "Mop hospital floors, work in school kitchens. I don't care."

"But you don't go anywhere without straightening irons and a tube of Beauty Flash Balm."

"There's a first time for everything."

Cyn squeezed her hand. "You're my best friend. I love you, and I don't want you to go."

"You're my best friend and I love you, too. But we'll phone and e-mail and I'm definitely coming back here to have the baby."

"Baby?" Cyn cried. "You're pregnant?"

Harmony nodded.

"Omigod." Cyn threw her arms round her.

"Six weeks. Isn't it wonderful?"

Cyn felt her eyes filling up. "It's better than wonderful, it's bloody brilliant, that's what it is. I wondered why you weren't smoking. God, Laurent must be over the moon."

"Just a bit. Since I told him, he's barely stopped singing 'La Vie en Rose.'"

"Oh, this is fab, just fab." Cyn carried on hugging Harmony. "So, you'll come back for lots of holidays, then?"

"Lots. I promise. Plus I don't intend to completely neglect the business."

"And Joe and I and Hugh can come and see you?"

"Of course you can. Once we're settled, all of you can come for weeks, entire summers and Christmases if you want."

Cyn hesitated for a moment. She was desperate to tell Harmony she and Joe were getting married, but she felt it would be disloyal to her parents. In the end she decided she would burst if she didn't say something.

"Maybe Joe and I could even have our wedding there. On the beach perhaps."

Harmony pulled away, looked at her and blinked. "You're getting married?"

Cyn gave a series of excited nods.

"Oh, Cyn. I am so happy for you. For both of you. From what I've seen, Joe's a great bloke. And I know he'll make you happy. God, I can't believe we're both getting our lives sorted out. Come 'ere." More tight hugging and back patting.

"Listen, I'm going to tell Hugh in a minute, but not a word to Mum and Dad until after today. They'll only get up and make an announcement, and I don't want to upset Jonny and Flick."

"Don't worry," Harmony said. "I won't say a dickey bird." She paused. "Cyn, don't take this the wrong way, but I'm going to let go of you now. It's just that I'm worried your fumes might be getting to the baby."


By now Jonny had grabbed Grandma Faye and was leading her onto the dance floor. "Do you know 'Chattanooga Choo-Choo'?" she called out to the bandleader—the Lima Dreamers had left after dinner and been replaced by a more traditional dance band. "You've got it," he said. The band struck up. Arthritis or no arthritis, after two cherry brandies, Grandma Faye was cutting a rug like a youngster. Jonny could barely keep up with her, but that was mainly because he had two left feet. After a couple of minutes, Barbara and Mal joined them.

"I hope we look as good as that in thirty years," Joe said.

"Yeah, but suppose I'm all saggy and fat. Will you still fancy me?"

"Cyn, if I can sit here thinking how much I want to marry you when you smell like a city dump, I can cope with anything."

"But you said I didn't smell," she protested. "You said it was just a faint aroma."

"Aroma, stench . . . who cares?" he grinned. She tried to land a playful thump on his arm, but he caught her wrist. "Come on, let's dance. They're about to play our song."

"But we don't have a song," she said, "apart from 'It's a Small World.' "

He started laughing. "Believe me, it's not that. I've asked the band to play something really special."

"Oh, I get it. Very funny. You've persuaded the singer to come on and do 'Lady in Red,' only you've gotten him to change the words to: 'I'll never forget the way you *smell* tonight.' "

He had to practically drag her onto the dance floor. As the music started, he took her in his arms. She rested her head on his shoulder. The band was playing " 'Til There Was You."

# About the Author

Sue Margolis was a radio reporter for fifteen years before turning to novel writing. She lives in England and has also written *Breakfast at Stephanie's, Apocalipstick, Spin Cycle,* and *Neurotica.*

Don't miss
SUE MARGOLIS'S
other novels

NEUROTICA

SPIN CYCLE

APOCALIPSTICK

BREAKFAST AT STEPHANIE'S

Please turn the page for previews of:

NEUROTICA

and

APOCALIPSTICK

# NeuRoTiCa

If *he* always has
the headache,
why should you
suffer?

SUE
MARGOLIS

# NEUROTICA
## On-Sale Now . . .

Dan Bloomfield stood in front of the full-length bathroom mirror, dropped his boxers to his ankles, moved his penis to one side to get a better look and stared hard at the sagging, wrinkled flesh which housed his testicles. Whenever Dan examined his testicles—and as a hypochondriac he did this several times a week—he thought of two things: the likelihood of his imminent demise; and the cupboard under the stairs in his mother's house in Finchley.

It was a consequence of the lamentable amount of storage space in her unmodernized fifties kitchenette that Mrs. Bloomfield had always kept hanging in the hall cupboard, alongside the overcoats, macs and umbrellas, one of those long string shopping bags made pendulous by the weight of her overflow Brussels sprouts. From the age of thirteen, Dan referred to this as his mother's scrotal sac.

These days Dan reckoned his own scrotal sac was a dead ringer for his mother's. His bollocks couldn't get any lower. Dan supposed lower was OK at forty; death on the other hand was not.

By bending his knees ever so slightly, shuffling a little

closer to the mirror and pulling up on his scrotum he could get a better view of its underside. It looked perfectly normal. In fact the whole apparatus looked perfectly normal. There was nothing he could see, no sinister lumps, bumps or skin puckering which suggested impending uni-bollockdom, or that his wife should start bulk-buying herrings for his funeral. Then, suddenly, as he squeezed his right testicle gently between his thumb and forefinger, it was there again, the excruciating stabbing pain he had felt as he crossed his legs that morning in the editors' daily conference.

Anna Shapiro, Dan's wife, needed to pee right away. She knew because she had just been woken up by one of those dreams in which she had been sitting on the loo about to let go when suddenly something in her brain kicked in to remind her that this would not be a good idea, since she was, in reality, sprawled across the brand-new pocket-sprung divan on which they hadn't even made the first payment. Looking like one of those mad women on the first day of the Debenhams sale, she bolted towards the bathroom. Here she discovered Dan rolling naked on the floor, clutching his testicles in one hand and his penis in the other with a look of agony on his face which she immediately took for sublime pleasure.

As someone who'd been reading "So you think your husband is a sexual deviant"–type advice columns in women's magazines since she was twelve, Anna knew a calm, caring opening would be best.

"Dan, what the fuck are you up to?" she shrieked. "I mean it, if you've turned into some kind of weirdo, I'm putting my hat and coat on now. I'll tell the whole family and you'll never see the children again and I'll take you for every penny. I can't keep up with you. One minute you're off sex and the next minute I find you wanking yourself stupid at three o'clock in the morning on the bathroom floor. How could you do it on the bathroom floor? What if Amy or Josh had decided to come in here for a wee and caught you?"

"Will you just stop ranting for one second, you stupid fat bitch. Look."

Dan directed Anna's eyes towards his penis, which she had failed to notice was completely flaccid.

"I am not wanking. I think I've got bollock cancer. Anna, I'm really scared."

Relieved? You bet I was bloody relieved. God, I mean for a moment there last night, when I found him, I actually thought Dan had turned into one of those nutters the police find dead on the kitchen floor with a plastic bag over their head and a ginger tom halfway up their arse. Of course, it was no use reminding him that testicular cancer doesn't hurt. . . . What are you going to have?"

As usual, the Harpo was full of crushed-linen, telly-media types talking Channel 4 proposals, sipping mineral water and swooning over the baked polenta and fashionable bits of offal. Anna was deeply suspicious of trendy food. Take polenta, for example: an Italian au pair who had worked for Dan and Anna a few years ago had said she couldn't understand why it had become so fashionable in England. It was, she said, the Italian equivalent of semolina and that the only time an Italian ate it was when he was in school, hospital or a mental institution.

Neither was Anna, who had cellulite and a crinkly post-childbirth tummy flap which spilled over her bikini briefs when she sat down, overly keen on going for lunch with Gucci-ed and Armani-ed spindle-legged journos like Alison

O'Farrell, who always ordered a green salad with no dressing and then self-righteously declared she was too full for pudding.

But as a freelance journalist, Anna knew the importance of sharing these frugal lunches with women's-page editors. These days, she was flogging Alison at least two lengthy pieces a month for the *Daily Mercury*'s "Lifestyles" page, which was boosting her earnings considerably. In fact her last dead-baby story, in which a recovering postnatally depressed mum (who also just happened to be a leggy 38 DD) described in full tabloid gruesomeness how she drowned her three-month-old in the bath, had almost paid for the sundeck Anna was having built on the back of her kitchen.

Dan, of course, as the cerebral financial editor of *The Vanguard,* Dan, who was probably more suited to academia than Fleet Street, called her stuff prurient, ghoulish voyeurism and carried on like some lefty sociology student from the seventies about those sorts of stories being the modern opiate of the masses. Anna couldn't be bothered to argue. She knew perfectly well he was right, but, like a lot of lefties who had not so much lapsed as collapsed into the risotto-breathed embrace of New Labour, she had decided that the equal distribution of wealth starting with herself had its merits. She suspected he was just pissed off that her tabloid opiates earned her double what he brought home in a month.

But what about Dan's cancer?" Alison asked, shoving a huge mouthful of undressed radicchio into her mouth and pretending to enjoy it.

"Alison, I've been married to Dan for twelve years. He's been like this for yonks. Every week it's something different. First it was weakness in his legs and he diagnoses multiple sclerosis, then he feels dizzy and it's a brain tumor. Last week he decided he had some disease which, it turns out, you only get from fondling sheep. Alison, I can't tell you the extent to which no Jewish man fondles sheep. He's a hypochondriac. He needs therapy. I've been telling him to get help for ages, but he won't. He just sits for hours with his head in the *Home Doctor*."

"Must be doing wonders for your sex life."

"Practically nonexistent. He's too frightened to come in case the strain of it gives him a heart attack, and then if he does manage it he takes off the condom afterwards, looks to see how much semen he has produced—in case he has a blockage somewhere—then examines it for traces of blood."

As a smooth method of changing the subject, Alison got up to go to the loo. Anna suspected she was going to chuck up her salad. When she returned, Anna sniffed for vomit, but only got L'Eau d'Issy. "Listen, Anna," Alison began the instant her bony bottom made contact with the hard Phillipe Starck chair. "I've had an idea for a story I think just might be up your street."


Dan bought the first round of drinks in the pub and then went to the can to feel his testicle. It was less than an hour before his appointment with the specialist. The pain was still there.

Almost passing out with anxiety, he sat on the lavatory, put his head between his knees and did what he always did when he thought he was terminally ill: he began to pray. Of course it wasn't real prayer, it was more like some kind of sacred trade-union negotiation in which the earthly official, Dan, set out his position—i.e., dying—and demanded that celestial management, God, put an acceptable offer on the table—

i.e., cure him. By way of compromise, Dan agreed that he would start going to synagogue again—or church, or Quaker meeting house, if God preferred—as soon as he had confirmation he wasn't dying anymore.

Mr. Andrew Goodall, the ruddy-complexioned former rugby fly-half testicle doctor, leaned back in his leather Harley Street swivel chair, plonked both feet on top of his desk and looked at Dan over half-moon specs.

"Perfectly healthy set of bollocks, old boy," he declared.

Kissed him? Dan could have tongue-wrestled the old bugger.

"But what about all this pain I've been getting?"

"You seemed perfectly all right when I examined you. I strongly suspect this is all psychosomatic, Mr. Bloomfield. I mean, I could chop the little blighter orf if you really want me to, but I suspect that if I did, in six months you'd be back in this office with phantom ball pain. My advice to you would be to have a break. Why not book a few days away in the sun with your good lady? Alternatively, I can prescribe you something to calm you down."

Dan had stopped listening round about "psychosomatic." The next thing he knew he was punching the air and skipping like an overgrown four-year-old down Harley Street toward Cavendish Square. He, Dan Bloomfield, was not dying. He, Dan Bloomfield, was going to live.

With thoughts of going to synagogue entirely forgotten, he went into John Lewis and bought Anna a new blender to celebrate. One can only imagine that God sighed and wondered why he had created a world full of such ungrateful bleeders.

# Apocalipstick

*a novel*

## SUE MARGOLIS

# APOCALIPSTICK
## On-Sale Now . . .

Rebecca was fiddling with the tuner button on the car radio. She'd been sitting in the monster traffic jam on Camden Road, engine off, for the best part of fifteen minutes. For the last two she'd been trying and failing to find some traffic news that might explain what was going on.

". . . still offering huge discounts on our exclusive range of *Lazee Dayze* recliners . . ."

Fiddle:

"Here's Brotherhood of Man, with *Save All Your Kisses for Me* . . ."

Jab this time:

". . . and my Alan was just lying there, completely limp—not even the faintest sign of life. So, I did what anybody would do. I got down on the floor and started giving him the kiss of life."

Rebecca found herself stopping to listen.

"And isn't that a cheery, feel-good story to brighten up this drizzly A.M. in the capital? Jacky from Borehamwood, there, talking about her house fire and how she successfully resuscitated Alan, her iguana."

Her nose wrinkled as she imagined puckering up to some slimy reptile. Not that she hadn't puckered up to one or two in the odd drunken moment. The only difference was, her reptiles had worn tight leather pants and called her "babe."

Fiddle:

". . . so best to avoid the Camden Road area if you can. More traffic news in the next hour. Caroline Feraday, 5 Live Travel . . ."

Rebecca Fine, newly appointed beauty columnist of the *Daily Vanguard* Saturday magazine, now let out a tiny yelp of frustration and switched off the radio. The monthly beauty, fashion and lifestyle meeting was due to start in half an hour, and unless the traffic freed up in the next few minutes, there was no way she was going to make it on time. It was her first meeting and she'd been so anxious to make a good impression. Her only hope was that other people would be driving in from north London and they would be late too. For now, all she could do was sit it out. She picked up her bag, which was lying on the passenger seat, and went rummaging for her lipstick and mascara.

She was staring into the driver's mirror, finishing her lashes, when the car behind her let out three long blasts of its horn. The first made her jump so violently that her mascara brush shot upward, leaving a gash of black from her eyebrow to her hairline, which made her look like some kind of unihorned devil. As the honking continued, she saw what had happened. A broken-down lorry, which had been causing the holdup, was now being towed away and the traffic was moving. Clearly the driver of the car behind her was more than a tad put out that she hadn't noticed. Her hand flew to the ignition, but the car refused to start. Honk. Honk. A twenty-yard gap had opened up in front of her.

"All right. All right." She was getting flustered now. Looking down, she saw the automatic gear lever was in drive. She shoved it into neutral. Honk. Honk. Honk.

As she turned the ignition key a second time, her eyes darted back to the rearview mirror. The honker was some guy in a flash sports car. No surprise there. Before she had a chance to move, he began pulling out to overtake her. He couldn't get up any speed because he was squeezing between her and the oncoming traffic. As he drew level with her, he leaned across the sports car's passenger seat and lowered the window. Rebecca lowered hers.

"My apologies for disturbing you," he smirked. Plummy voice, expensive suit, floppy Hugh Grant hair. Posh estate agent, probably. "It's just that some of us have jobs to go to."

"Look, I'm really sorry, but there was no need to blast me like that . . ."

Just then her mobile started ringing.

As she picked it up off the dashboard and pressed OK, the sports car roared off.

"And it's Mr. Subaru Turbo," she said in a singsong voice, "who wins the award for the smallest penis, this drizzly A.M."

"Hi, Becks. It's me," the voice on the end of the line giggled. "Listen, have I disturbed some kind of intimate moment? I mean I can always call back."

It was Jess.

"No, you're fine," Rebecca said, her tone brightening. She put the phone between her shoulder and chin and asked Jess to hang on while she pulled away. It was a difficult maneuver, since all the cars behind her had followed the Subaru and nobody was allowing her to rejoin the stream of traffic. Finally somebody let her in.

"God, he'd have thought twice about intimidating me like that," Jess said when Rebecca had finished telling her about the hooray honker.

"He would?"

"Too blinkin' right. You see I've got this brilliant new bumper sticker that says: 'I'm out of estrogen and I've got a gun.'"

Rebecca burst out laughing. "So," she said, "how's the baby?"

"Oh, you know," Jess said with a sigh, "fine, but knackering. In the two months we've had him I don't think either of us has had more than three hours' sleep on the trot." She paused. "Then there's my Bagpuss."

"Oh, sweet. Bought it for the baby?" Rebecca asked, assuming quite reasonably that her best friend had been to Toys 'R' Us and bought the furry TV character for the baby.

"No, you dope, Diggory hasn't got it."

Diggory. Jess adored the name. And since Rebecca adored Jess, she pretended to love the name, too, but secretly she worried that the poor child might grow up to become a bearded botanist in a cardigan.

"What, so you bought it for you? Getting in touch with your child within. Nice."

"Oh, God. Becks, listen. I haven't *bought* Bagpuss. I've *got* it. Let's put it this way, since giving birth, my pencil-gripping days are definitely a thing of the past."

"What? You could do that?"

"I don't know. I never tried. But if I could, I wouldn't be able to do it now. And I know Ed's noticed. Why else would we have only done it twice since the baby? The second time it took him ages to get a hard-on. He doesn't fancy me anymore. I just know it."

"Oh, come on," Rebecca soothed, "Ed's crazy about you.

Always has been. He's not going to go off you simply because you've gained a millimeter or two in the pussy department. You've got a new baby. He's exhausted like you are, that's all. Sex is hardly going to be what it was, not for a while anyway. You of all people should know that."

Jess was the agony aunt at *Femme* magazine. It always amazed Rebecca how she seemed able to get a handle on everybody else's problems except her own.

"Just keep doing the pelvic floor exercises," Rebecca went on, "and I'm sure everything'll spring back into shape."

"Yeah, you're right," Jess said, cheering up. "Look, you don't fancy popping round tonight, do you? Ed's got to work late on the news desk and I'll be all on my own with the Digsbury. I'm longing to hear how the new job's going."

"Great," Rebecca said. "I'll bring pizza."

The moment she hung up, her mobile went off a second time. She pressed OK, desperate for whomever it was on the other end to be one of her few friends who wasn't pregnant or recently delivered and with whom she could still have an above-the-waist conversation.

". . . still leaking when she sneezes . . . Hello? Rebecca?"

Rebecca's brow furrowed.

"Gran?"

"Sorry, darling, I've got Esther here. We're off to the sales. I was in the middle of telling her about my cousin Doreen's bladder operation. I didn't think you'd pick up so soon. So, did you see it?"

"What, cousin Doreen's bladder operation?"

"No, silly. The e-mail I sent you."

Grandma Rose was a Net head—a "silver surfer" who had forced herself to come to grips with new technology when she realized how much cheaper it was to e-mail her brothers and sisters in Miami and Sydney, not to mention her cousin Doreen in Montreal with the leaky bladder, than phone. With time on her hands, what had begun as a money saver had become a hobby verging on an obsession.

"No, sorry, I haven't had a chance to check my e-mail. I was out till quite late last night."

"Ooh, somewhere nice?"

"Just a bar in town with a few friends."

"And you ate?"

"I ate."

"So, what did you eat?"

"We all went out for sushi afterward."

"What? A few bits of raw fish? You'll fade away. You'll turn into your great-aunt Minnie. The woman ate like a sparrow. If it wasn't for her nose she'd have had no shape at all."

From the moment Rebecca's mother died ten years ago, her adoring, devoted Jewish Grandma Rose had taken it upon herself to worry, fuss and kvetch about every aspect of Rebecca's life. "Not that I want to meddle, but . . ." became her mantra. This of course was the surest sign that she was about to do precisely that, on a scale unsurpassed since Hitler meddled with the Sudetenland.

Top of Rose's causes for concern list was Rebecca's lack of a husband. This was closely followed by her granddaughter's health, which naturally included her eating habits. God forbid she should mention the gut pain she'd had last week after a dodgy prawn bhuna. Rose would have her off to a gastroenterologist before she could say barium enema.

"So," Rose continued, "did you, er, you know, meet anybody nice?"

"Gran, believe me, the only man I went to bed with last night was Jerry Seinfeld."

"Ooh, do I know him? You've never mentioned him. Well, I hope he took precautions."

Rebecca decided against teasing her grandmother further and explained that she'd been watching the TV show. (*Seinfeld* being her absolute, all-time favorite sitcom. Last night The Paramount Channel had been showing twelve episodes back-to-back. She'd managed to stay with it until just after one, before finally dropping off.)

"So, Gran—the e-mail."

"Oh, right," Rose said cheerily, clearly over her disappointment that Rebecca wasn't going out with Jerry Seinfeld. "Well, I was surfing yesterday afternoon and I came across this lonely hearts Web site. Listen, have I ever got a fella for you."

"Gawd."

"OK, get this: 'Orthopedic surgeon, Jewish. Midthirties. Looking for love.' Doesn't he sound just perfect?"

Rose was positively squealing with delight. " 'Dark. Six two. Lean, masculine guy. Not hairy chested.' Personally I like a man with a bit of chest hair, but never mind. Goes on to say he's got a mustache . . . You know, I think that Clark Gable look's definitely coming back . . . and that he's passive and very versatile. What more could you want? A man who doesn't argue and can turn his hand to anything. Then it says he likes to give O . . . I'm not sure what that last bit means. Maybe he donates to some orthopedic charity or something. My God, a philanthropist as well. So what do you reckon? There's an e-mail address."

"You sure that's all it says?" Rebecca said with faux casualness.

"Yes, except for some initials I don't understand at the beginning."

"What initials?" Rebecca asked. She knew precisely what was coming.

"G.W. M. Actually, thinking about it, I reckon that must mean good with money."

"Gran, it stands for gay white male."

Grandma Rose missed a beat.

"You sure?"

"Positive," Rebecca declared.

Another beat.

"Esther," Rose hissed, "Rebecca says he's gay."

Rebecca could hear her explaining about G.W. M. A few moments later she was back on the line.

"Esther reckons it might be worth contacting him anyway. She says perhaps he's not *very* gay. She could be right. It's possible he's just confused. So many young people are these days. You could help him sort himself out. What else have you got to do? After all, you haven't had a date for nine months. Why you had to finish with that Simon beats me. He sounded so nice. Two weeks you went out. How can you expect to get to know a person in two weeks?"

"Gran, you can't be a bit gay. It's like being a bit dead. And I've told you before, it just didn't work out between me and Simon. I know you worry, but I'm doing fine on my own, honest. And it's not like I don't have friends. Look, I gotta run, I've just pulled up outside the office and I'm running late. I'll speak to you later. Love you."

She was grateful for an excuse to get off the phone. There was no way she could ever tell her the real reason she ended it with Simon.

The truth was that Simon, an exceedingly cute stand-up comic and ventriloquist, had been just a tad off piste personality-wise. But not in a trendy, cool way—more in a weird, *Star Trek* convention kind of way. For a start, his hobby was wood turning and polishing. On their second date he presented her with an exquisitely finished mug tree. On the third, a newel!

What was more, he insisted the dummy—a pint-size football hooligan with a rictus grin, two earrings and a Tommy Hilfiger tracksuit—accompany them on all their dates. At first Rebecca thought this was a hoot, since Wayne (the dummy) would often pipe up with the odd witticism. The real problem—and the reason she finally ended it—began as soon as she and Simon started having sex. Whenever Simon came, the omnipresent Wayne would yell at the top of his voice: "Back of the net! Back of the fucking net!"

Apart from the occasional till-dawn-do-us-part relationship, there hadn't been anybody since.

"You know what you should do?" Grandma Rose had said soon after she finished with Simon. "Pack up and move somewhere where the men outnumber the women."

Rose immediately went on the Net to gather statistics. It turned out Rebecca's choices were the Shetland Isles, Qatar or Tower Hamlets.